Searching for a Silver Lining

Miranda Dickinson has always had a head full of stories. From an early age she dreamed of writing a book that would make the heady heights of Kingswinford Library and today she is a bestselling author. She began to write in earnest when a friend gave her The World's Slowest PC, and has subsequently written the bestselling novels *Fairytale of New York*, *Welcome to My World*, *It Started With a Kiss*, *When I Fall in Love*, *Take a Look at Me Now*, *I'll Take New York* and *A Parcel for Anna Browne*. Miranda lives with her husband Bob and daughter Flo in Dudley.

@wurdsmyth

MirandaDickinsonAuthor

www.mirandadickinson.com

Also by Miranda Dickinson

Fairytale of New York
Welcome to My World
It Started With a Kiss
When I Fall in Love
Take a Look at Me Now
I'll Take New York
A Parcel for Anna Browne

Searching for a Silver Lining

Miranda Dickinson

PAN BOOKS

First published 2016 by Pan Books
an imprint of Pan Macmillan
20 New Wharf Road, London N1 9RR
Associated companies throughout the world
www.panmacmillan.com

ISBN 978-1-4472-7607-4

1 3 5 7 9 8 6 4 2

A CIP catalogue record for this book is available from the British Library.

Typeset by Palimpsest Book Production Limited, Falkirk, Stirlingshire
Printed and bound by CPI Group (UK) Ltd, Croydon, CR0 4YY

Visit www.panmacmillan.com to read more about all our books
and to buy them. You will also find features, author interviews and
news of any author events, and you can sign up for e-newsletters
so that you're always first to hear about our new releases.

For Jo
So much more than just
a wonderful mum-in-law.
Thank you for being my friend.

Because you loved me
I can face today
Chase my blues away and smile
It's because of you
That happiness is mine

Because you loved me
All my crazy dreams
Find their feathered wings and fly
I am free, love
Because you loved me

'Because You Loved Me'
The Silver Five (1954)

Chapter One

'Ain't That a Shame'
Fats Domino

♪

The church was dark and cool, the chill seeping in through every brick and pew. Despite the warm day beyond its walls, inside it seemed as bleak as November. Why did funerals always feel cold, even when the sun was shining?

Matilda Bell stole a glance around as she pulled a too-thin black cardigan more tightly over her goose-pimpled arms. It was still early, but several members of her family had already gathered, their hushed conversations and solemn expressions a show of unity that somehow made her feel even more excluded. They hadn't noticed her yet; when they did she didn't know what their reactions would be. She had been his favourite, after all. Before the argument, that was. Before her stupid mistake . . .

She drew back further behind the tall, carved pillar that

partially obscured her from the view of the front pews. It was an old church, one filled with memories and inextricably linked to her family. It had been his favourite place of worship, more importantly. Which meant that the building's very fabric seemed carved with his name. It had always been such a warm, familiar place but today, with her grandfather's presence reduced to a whisper among the gathering mourners and a printed name on a service sheet, it felt colder than a grave. Bracing herself against a wash of sadness, Mattie let out a sigh, almost expecting to see her breath rising like mist.

I'll stay until the final hymn, she told herself. *Then I'll sneak out before any of them see me.*

She almost hadn't come at all. It was only because her sister had called her last week with the funeral details that she even knew about it. While nobody else in her family had said as much, she knew what most of them were thinking. That she had broken his heart and the pain of it had hastened his death. It was rubbish, of course: the post-mortem had revealed an aggressive tumour that had taken residence on his lower spine and spread with sickening speed to his liver. But deep down, Matilda knew the huge rift between her and Grandpa Joe couldn't have helped. She blamed herself; not only for the argument that had torn apart a relationship she'd always assumed to be unbreakable, but also for failing to realise her grandfather had been right all along. If only she'd laid aside her stubborn pride for one second, she might have seen it. But Matilda Bell had thought she knew best – just like she always did – and now she had lost everything she loved.

More people were filing in now – the great, the good and the mildly questionable of Kings Sunbury. Grandpa Joe had loved them all and they, in turn, adored him. Each new mourner seemed to assume a position in front of Mattie, making her feel shunted further down the queue away from him. *They* hadn't let him down, the accusing voice in her head insisted. *They* hadn't defied him . . .

But the time for 'if-onlys' was far in the past.

'Mattie? I thought it was you! What are you doing all the way back here? The rest of the family's up at the front.'

She stared blankly up at her cousin Jack, who was edging along the narrow gap between the pews towards her. 'Hi. I'm fine here.'

Ever the sunny optimist, her cousin was not likely to accept this. 'Nonsense! Your place is with us. No matter what's happened.' Seeing her expression, he sat down beside her.

'They blame me,' she stated, hot tears stinging her eyes.

'They don't.'

'*I* blame me.'

'Matilda, it's over. It's done. They aren't going to abandon you, whatever you think.'

'I broke his heart . . .'

'Cancer took him, not heartbreak. You're as bad as your mother for blaming the world's ills on your own failings. Let me let you into a secret: you're not that powerful, Matilda Bell.' His hand was warm on hers as he smiled. 'Come to the front with me. Today's not a day for this family to be divided. We've *all* lost him.'

She wanted to believe Jack, to think that something as

simple as shared family grief could heal the rift in the Bell family. But feelings ran deep and she knew what they were thinking: that in rejecting Grandpa Joe, she had dismissed all of them. Her friends had envied their close-knit family over the years, but now she was feeling the stab of the flipside – that when they were so close, arguments cut more deeply and were harder to heal.

'All the same, I'm happier here.'

'Then I'll sit with you.'

'No, Jack, you don't have to do that.'

'I know I don't. But you shouldn't be on your own today and I'll be damned if I let you be. So shut up and give me a hug, okay?'

Mattie loved Jack for his stubbornness. It reminded her of Grandpa Joe's – except that Jack had never doled out ultimatums over her love life. What hurt most was that she couldn't explain to her family the real reason her heart was breaking today . . .

'Don't cry, Mattie. You'll set me off.' Jack squeezed her hand and offered her a tissue from a small plastic pack.

'I'm sorry,' she sniffed, the chill of the church seeping further into her bones.

But she wasn't only crying for Grandpa Joe.

A signal from a churchwarden at the back of the church brought the grave-faced vicar to the lectern.

'Good morning. Would you all please stand?'

Mattie's knees buckled and Jack caught her arm as the opening bars of 'Because You Loved Me' echoed hollowly around the ancient stone walls. Grandpa Joe's favourite song, performed by The Silver Five – a once-famous singing group from the 1950s – as familiar to Mattie as the sound of her own voice. The music swept years of memories into the building as the funeral party processed slowly up the aisle. Mattie saw the loss etched in ugly lines across her father's forehead as he bore the coffin on one shoulder, flanked by her brother-in-law Fred and two paternal uncles, Reuben and Seth. Didn't they do this on special trolleys nowadays? Mattie was shocked by the physical bearing of Grandpa Joe's body into the sacred space by the men that had loved him most. Had things been different, would she have accompanied them?

She looked past the encroaching oak box to the front of the church, trying to get a glimpse of her mother, but she was obscured from view. Instead, she fixed on her older sister Joanna, who was holding the hands of her daughter and son as she watched her doting husband Fred carrying the coffin. Mattie could see the tension in Joanna's shoulders and knew her sister would be fighting back tears, just as she was. Not that Joanna would ever allow anyone to see that. She was the one everyone else turned to for support, her steady nerve and coolness famous in the Bell family. Mattie was fiercely proud of Joanna but today felt an emotional mess by comparison. As if sensing Mattie's gaze, Joanna half-turned her head, sending the briefest smile down the pews to her. Mattie nodded back. It was enough to know Joanna cared. They would talk later, but for now their mother needed Joanna's calming presence.

Reverend Philip Caudwell stepped forward to receive the funeral party, his expression ashen. Phil had been more than their local vicar, practically another member of the family for as long as Mattie could remember. The entire Bell clan had passed through the many traditions of St Lawrence's, from christenings to confirmations, Sunday-school anniversaries and countless Christmas and Easter celebrations. Joanna and Fred had been married here. Mattie had hoped one day the church would witness her own wedding. For her grandfather, it was a second home. He had been a stalwart of every fundraising effort there since his own childhood and counted Rev. Phil as a surrogate son.

The many solemn faces within St Lawrence's walls today had one thing in common: everybody had loved Grandpa Joe. Every person gathered in the cold church still mourned his passing. But Mattie was a prisoner amongst them. They could all publicly express their grief today: she couldn't.

Barely whispered hymns and grim-faced Bible readings seemed to float above her head and it was only when she felt the chapel's chill receding a little across her back that she realised her cousin had draped his suit jacket across her shoulders.

'You were shivering,' he whispered. 'Is that any better?'

Mattie nodded, emotion knotting in her throat.

Rev. Phil's eulogy was warmer than the garment surrounding Mattie, every word carefully chosen and delivered from the heart. It would have been clear to any stranger in the church that the vicar had not only known Grandpa Joe but also loved him dearly. Mattie could see the gentle undulation of her mother's shoulders, her head nodding as Rev. Phil relayed bittersweet anecdotes and spoke of a man whose love for his family and his friends knew no bounds.

Except with me, Mattie thought. *He found his boundaries with me, didn't he?*

She maintained her distance as the family moved outside to the far warmer church grounds to commit Grandpa Joe's body to the ground. Rev. Phil asked if any of the family wished to say a few words at the graveside, to which her father, Uncle Reuben and Uncle Seth responded; their words choked by sobs. Mattie wanted to push through her gathered family members and declare her love for her grandfather, to pour out her apology for defying him, even though it was too late and he would never hear her words. But nobody wanted to hear her say that today, did they? Whatever Jack said, she knew her mother and her uncles blamed her in part for Grandpa Joe's speedy demise. They had never said as much, but her mother's pointed remarks about how positivity could and should have helped her beloved father-in-law fight back were as damning as an actual accusation.

Finally, when the family moved away, followed hesitantly by Jack, Mattie moved to the open graveside, its edges bedecked with flowers, and stared down at the soil-strewn oak coffin in the dark earthen hole.

'I'm sorry,' she whispered, hurt and regret all but stealing the power of her voice as tears flooded down her cheeks. 'I'm sorry I didn't get to say goodbye. I know you were right now.' She took a breath, the scent of sun-warmed grass and damp earth filling her lungs. 'If I could make it up to you, I would. I'd do anything . . .'

The air around her seemed to still suddenly, even the birds in the cedar trees that edged St Lawrence's graveyard falling strangely silent. Kneeling slowly by the edge of the grave, Mattie gazed down at the brass plaque half-covered by scattered soil. This was the end of a season of her life, but was she prepared to carry this pain forever? She shook her head. 'No, I *will* find a way to make it up to you, Grandpa. I promise you that . . .'

Walking away from the graveside, she saw a familiar figure bounding across the vivid green lawn between the gravestones.

'Mattie! I hoped I'd catch you. How are you doing?' The vicar kept his smile steady despite clearly seeing the state she was in.

Mattie felt a rush of affection. 'Not good, Phil.'

Rev. Phil offered her his arm. 'I understand. He was a good man, loved by all. But he wasn't perfect. You and I both know that.' He raised a hand to silence Mattie's protest. 'And so does your family. They're hurt now and they might say or do things they'll later regret. But Joe loved you and he never stopped, despite being a stubborn ass.'

His decidedly un-vicar-like choice of words brought an involuntary smile to Mattie's face. 'Thanks, Phil.'

'Come back to the vicarage? Vanessa's laid on a great spread and the neutral territory might be beneficial.'

'I don't know . . .' The urge to disappear back to the safety of her home was strong.

'I'm not asking you, Mattie, I'm telling you. As a vicar. Bearing in mind who my boss is, best not to argue, eh?'

As she let herself be escorted to the vicarage, Mattie's

thoughts returned to the graveside promise she had just made. She didn't know how she would ever fulfil it, but a new determination burned, furnace-hot, within her. One way or another, she was going to make amends . . .

Chapter Two

'Memories Are Made of This' – Dean Martin

♪

'Blimey, I haven't seen one of these for forty years!'

The bearded man grinned as Mattie handed him the old Bakelite radio from the shelf behind the counter. Reuniting people with their past was one of the things she loved most about her business – every day at work new stories emerged of her customers' lives. She felt privileged to share them. And today's revelation was no exception.

Percy Walker had become a regular visitor to Bell Be-Bop – the small vintage goods shop Mattie had owned for two years. He had recently moved to the town after many years living abroad, and seemed to be furnishing his new house on the outskirts of Kings Sunbury almost exclusively from Mattie's shop. A suntanned seventy-one-year-old, he was enjoying reliving his youth through the items he purchased.

'I first heard Little Richard on this,' he beamed, his eyes focusing decades back. 'In my mother's front room, while she was round at my Auntie Elsa's. I managed to tune it to Radio Luxembourg and my rock 'n' roll love affair began. I was a Teddy Boy, you know, back in the day.' He patted his sunkissed bald pate. 'Quiff's long gone, mind, but I had quite the head of hair back then. How much for the radio?'

'Eighty,' Mattie replied, wondering if she should discount for her newly loyal customer. 'But if you want to help yourself to anything from the record box I'd be happy to throw those in for free.'

More than pleased with her suggestion, Percy hurried over to the chalk-painted tea crates containing stacks of 78 rpm records and began to eagerly leaf through the titles. Mattie felt her heart contract as she remembered doing the same as a young girl with Grandpa Joe's record collection. Through him she had discovered and fallen in love with 1950s and 1960s music, from Elvis Presley and Lonnie Donegan to Chuck Berry, Tommy Steele and Connie Francis. Indeed, much of his record collection had been her first stock in the shop, before Asher, before the argument and before the mistake . . . Shaking the pain away, she focused on her customer. Today was not the day to dwell on the past, even if the past was what was funding her future.

'I don't know why we don't just sell Percy the shop and be done with it,' she whispered to Laurie, her assistant, as she returned to the sales desk made from the front

11

section of a mint-green 1955 Ford Thunderbird. 'We could make a fortune and retire.'

Laurie grinned. 'And miss all the non-stop excitement of this place? Not on your nelly! Admit it, Mattie, you love running this shop. It's in your blood.'

Mattie couldn't argue with that. It had been a struggle to establish the shop in the provincial High Street of Kings Sunbury in the beginning. For what felt like months its only visitors came to peer curiously at the vintage stock, as if gazing at museum exhibits. Then Mattie started the online side of the business, and suddenly visitors began arriving not just from neighbouring towns but further afield, too. It was too early to deem the shop a roaring success, but sales in recent months had been promising and now, with a small but growing regular clientele like Percy, the future looked brighter. And today, with the sting of the funeral still raw, being here gave her hope for better times ahead.

'No world cruise for us yet, then.'

'Not yet, no. So,' Laurie leaned against the counter and Mattie knew what topic was approaching faster than an express train. 'How were your family yesterday?'

Feeling her stomach twist, Mattie shrugged. 'As you would expect. Dad's retreated into himself. Mum's still angry about everything. Grandpa Joe was more like a father to her than a father-in-law. She's devastated – I get that. But she's built a wall around herself that I can't breach. We didn't talk at the church, most of my family barely talked to me at the wake. No animosity or outright arguments, of course, that's not our style. But I was glad to leave, let's just say that.'

'And your sister?'

'Heartbroken, of course. Looking after Mum. But she called last night and we had the full post-mortem of events.' That had, at least, been one consolation in yesterday's painful progress. 'It was just a horrible day.'

Laurie pulled a comradely grimace and placed a hand on Mattie's arm. 'Well, it's over. The actual goodbye bit. Things'll get easier, I know they will. And how's the new place?'

'Still feels like I'm squatting in somebody else's house.'

'That'll get better too.' Laurie's smile was firm. 'Besides, nobody said it was a permanent solution.'

'I suppose so.'

Mattie remembered the sudden, unexpected move and the surprise on the estate agent's face when she'd agreed to rent her new home without even wanting to see it. It was impossible to think of that – and the reason she'd abandoned her former home so quickly – without thinking of Grandpa Joe. He'd been right all along, hadn't he? And she would never get the chance to tell him. Swallowing hard, she busied herself with a new till roll, keen for the well-meaning interrogation to end.

'It will. You couldn't have known . . .'

But I should have. Grandpa Joe knew.

'And I see you're wearing *it* again.' Laurie nodded at the gleaming silver tiepin tucked into the collar of Mattie's vintage dress. 'I'm glad.'

Grandpa Joe had given her the tiepin on the day she'd opened the shop. Made from a silver sixpence mounted on a candy-twist silver pin, it had been a twenty-first birthday

13

gift to him from a former school friend who was training as an apprentice jeweller in Birmingham's Jewellery Quarter in the 1950s. Mattie had seen Grandpa Joe wear it proudly at every occasion requiring smart dress, and remembered him polishing it religiously with a silver jeweller's cloth every Sunday morning before church. Since his death it had remained, wrapped in a black velvet pouch, at the bottom of the dancing ballerina jewellery box she'd kept from childhood. Until this morning. Laurie had asked her about it a week ago and challenged her to wear it again, 'To bring him back to you.' Why this morning she had felt differently, Mattie couldn't say; only that today she had run out of excuses not to wear it. Now, it gleamed as brightly as it ever had and brought with it the smallest glint of hope.

'It felt the right thing to do. You were right, Laurie.' Not wanting to engage further in a conversation that could quickly overwhelm her, Mattie changed tack. 'You can take your lunch if you like.'

If Laurie knew she was being dismissed she didn't let on. 'I will, if you don't mind? I have a couple of errands to run in the village.'

'No problem. I'm sure Percy and I will be fine.'

'You know,' Laurie lowered her voice, 'our Perce is a bit of a catch, if you fancied an older man for a change. He's a silver fox.'

Mattie loved Laurie for even mentioning it – even if Percy wasn't exactly her type. While her friends still hadn't broached the subject of Mattie's love life, Laurie Murdock was not a woman to keep her thoughts to herself. A divorcee in her late forties, she had long since abandoned concern for what others might think of her and was embracing her freedom of expression in more ways than one: most recently becoming a devotee of yoga and meditation. Truth, she always said, was the best gift anyone could give or receive; there was no point holding back if someone needed to hear it.

'I think I'll pass. But, you know, if you fancy your chances . . .'

'I might, you know. I've always been one for the older man. Oh, I almost forgot, a woman came in yesterday when you were at the –' she avoided saying the word *funeral*, her blush making Mattie feel a fresh wave of affection for her employee. 'Anyway, she left a message – *somewhere* . . .'

She rifled through the unkempt pile of leaflets, letters and sticky notes across the desk and Mattie made a mental note for the umpteenth time that week to have a clearout.

With a shout of triumph that made Percy turn in alarm, Laurie handed Mattie a yellow sticky note.

Gaynor Fairchild, centre manager from Beauvale Sheltered Housing.

Please call regarding an opportunity that may be of interest – 01562 . . .

'Did she say what the opportunity was?' Mattie asked, immediately wary.

'Nope. But she was crazily excited about the shop being here,' Laurie replied, heading towards the door as she struggled into her coat. 'Give her a call.'

15

Mattie glanced over at Percy, who seemed more than content settled on a folding metal chair by the box of records, and picked up the phone. Wasting time wondering what this stranger wanted wouldn't do her any good. Better to nip whatever it was in the bud right away.

A dour-voiced receptionist put her on hold for a full two minutes of dodgy lift-muzak before the sing-song voice of Gaynor Fairchild answered.

'Oh, I'm *so* glad you called! I was hoping you would. Look, we're in the middle of a crisis here at the mo – any chance you could pop by this evening after you close? I'll be here till eight o'clock tonight.'

Mattie barely had a chance to reply before the call was swiftly culled, leaving her staring bemused at the buzzing red Bakelite phone receiver in her hand.

'Interesting call?' Percy ventured, approaching with an armful of records.

Mattie wrinkled her nose. 'I'm not sure.'

Beauvale Sheltered Housing was situated on the far west of Kings Sunbury, its white-picket-fenced boundary marking the end of the houses and the beginning of the rolling Staffordshire countryside. Once a large farm, the main house and outbuildings had been converted to warden-assisted retirement dwellings in the late 1990s, the single-storey apartments nestled around a pretty courtyard with beautifully maintained communal gardens beyond. Parking her beloved red VW camper van on the wide gravel sweep of the visitors' car park, Mattie smiled as she considered what Grandpa Joe would make of her being here. Before their communication ceased it had long been a family joke that Grandpa Joe was the only person in England who *didn't* want to retire to Beauvale. *The Times* had listed it as one of the 'Top 10 Retirement Villages' in an article a few years ago; since then, the waiting list for one of its coveted converted stone croft apartments had become the stuff of local legend.

It turned out that the receptionist on duty was as grumpy in the flesh as her voice had suggested on the call earlier. She peered dismissively over reading glasses teetering on the end of her beak-like nose as Mattie explained she was there for a meeting with the centre manager. It felt a little like being judged by a disgruntled buzzard and Mattie had to bite her lip hard to keep her laughter at bay. She liked this place already and the urge to laugh was welcome after the pain of yesterday.

'Through the double doors,' Bird Woman snapped. 'First door on the left.'

Hurrying away from her avian-like disdain, Mattie ignored the nerves balled up in her chest as she knocked on a door bearing her caller's name.

'Come!' a bright voice chirped.

From a vulture to a blue tit, Mattie thought, opening the door.

Gaynor Fairchild was a woman entangled in a 1970s fashion love affair and Mattie liked her immediately. While the decade wasn't her speciality, she appreciated the passion of people who looked to the past for their inspiration. Gaynor had it all: brown and orange crocheted waistcoat over a flowing, gypsy-style blouse, low-slung bell-bottomed jeans, their flares made wider by hand-sewn triangles of darker denim, two rows of long wooden beads at her neck and the kind of perm Mattie had only seen in photographs of her mother at college in her teens. Gaynor's only concession to the current decade was a pair of bright orange Converse sneakers, which seemed deliciously at odds with the rest of her clothing.

'Miss Bell, I'm delighted you could come. Oh, and I see you're a lady after my own heart,' she gushed, practically skipping a circle around her as she took in Mattie's vintage Fifties rose-print dress. Today Mattie had styled her hair in an Audrey Hepburn-esque side ponytail and was wearing the bright red lipstick Laurie had bought her from a vintage fair last month. 'You're so *authentic*!'

Mattie smiled her thanks, omitting to tell Gaynor that this was what she wore for work, not her everyday clothing. Outside of shop hours she was more comfortable in jeans, but she'd discovered customers responded better when you were dressed in period clothes – it added to the vintage feeling when they stepped over the threshold of Bell Be-Bop.

'My brother calls me Barbara Good – you know, like Felicity Kendal's character from *The Good Life*? He thinks I'm stuck in a Seventies time warp. So I tell him, he should thank his lucky stars he doesn't have a Margot Leadbetter instead!' Gaynor chuckled at her own joke and seemed so pleased with herself for making it that Mattie wondered if she should have laughed, too. 'But anyway, where are my manners? I'm sorry, Miss Bell. Please take a seat. Would you like some coffee? Tea? I

18

have a lovely bit of Moroccan mint tea if you fancy it. I know, I know, I'm *such* a cliché!'

Mattie sank into a low, linen-covered armchair, already feeling exhausted by Gaynor's whirlwind welcome. 'Regular tea would be great, thanks. I can't stay long . . .'

'Of course, absolutely. You must be dead on your feet after working in your shop all day. I tell you, I thank heaven every day that most of my job entails me sitting down.' She picked up the receiver of her desk phone. 'Eileen, would you be a dear and bring us a regular tea and one of my Moroccan mints, please? Yes, the *one that smells funny . . .*' She pulled a face at Mattie as she ended the call. 'Our receptionist thinks I'm on some strange waccy baccy or something. She doesn't trust me. You know, I swear she goes through my desk drawers when I'm away from the office.'

Mattie suppressed a grin. Despite only just having met Bird Woman, she could already picture her prowling Gaynor's office after dark, her suspicions of the middle-aged hippy running riot. 'So, how can I help you?'

'As part of my remit here at Beauvale I bring in visitors to assist our residents in many ways – befriending, practical services like hairdressing, massage and chiropody, entertainment for our Wednesday afternoon social club, and so on. But I went on a training retreat at the start of the year and learned about an initiative some of my colleagues across the country are developing. It's called a "Memory Day". Have you heard of that?'

Mattie shook her head. 'No, sorry.'

'It's quite a new thing, by all accounts. But I'm very

19

keen to try it. Many of our residents, as you are probably aware, are coping with the onset of dementia, Alzheimer's, or post-traumatic stress following the loss of their partner. We do a lot of physical activities here at Beauvale but I also want to develop a programme that will help keep their minds active.' She paused as if expecting Mattie to comment.

Mattie smiled back, hoping it would encourage Gaynor to continue. An awkward stretch of silence followed. Keen to end it, Mattie spoke. 'Sounds – *interesting* . . .'

'Oh it *is*! Fascinating, I'd say. Memory Days bring residents back in touch with items from their lives, which can then help them to reconnect with the present. My colleagues at other retirement villages have used photographs, old cine film, music and clothing before, with some impressive results . . .'

She was interrupted by a thundering knock on the door and Eileen bustled into the office with tea, her disdain now an outright snarl. Mattie thanked Bird Woman when a steaming, Beauvale-branded mug was thrust a little too forcefully at her, but Eileen didn't smile back.

When she had gone, Gaynor grinned at Mattie. 'So, what do you think?'

'I think it's a lovely idea. But what would you want from me?'

'Well *you*, for a start. I was thinking you might bring some items from your shop – on loan, of course, and Beauvale will cover any breakages – and perhaps do a small talk for the residents? Maybe twenty minutes or so, with a chance for them to touch and discuss the objects

20

you bring afterwards? We would pay for your time and I daresay you might gain a wave of new customers from the event.'

While sharing vintage items from her shop was no problem, the thought of standing up in front of a room of pensioners to speak petrified Mattie. She had never been one to aim for the limelight, unlike her cousin Jack, who could command a room wherever he went. 'I'm happy to bring things, but I really don't think I could talk . . .'

'Nonsense, you'd be wonderful, Miss Bell!'

'Mattie, please.'

Gaynor reached across and grasped Mattie's hand, a motherly gesture more touching than inappropriate. 'Just tell them about your shop. And why you love the period so much. Remember that for many of the residents the 1950s were their teenage years. A special time. They won't be listening to you, not really. The moment they see your beautiful outfit and realise you run a vintage shop, their memories will come flooding back. So. What do you say?'

'So, what *did* you say?' Laurie asked between mouthfuls of what Mattie suspected was Friday-night Chinese take-away, given her assistant's love of routine. 'Rufus! *Down!* Forgive me, Mattie, I'm just wrestling a chocolate lab for the last of my spring rolls.'

Mattie smiled against her mobile phone in the darkness of the country lane where she had parked after her visit to Beauvale. She'd bought fish and chips from Captain Nemo's, Kings Sunbury's imaginatively named chip shop, and was watching the heat from her meal slowly steam

21

up the camper van windows. After she'd finished, she would reluctantly return to the bland rented semi on the far side of the village that still didn't feel like home. But not yet. For now, a takeaway meal in the familiar surroundings of Rusty the van was far preferable.

'I said I'd do it. You can come too, if you like.'

'But what about the shop?'

'It's on a Sunday, so it won't be a problem.'

'Hmm, I'm not sure I – *Rufus*! Ooh, I swear this dog'll be the *death* of me . . . Oh Mattie, I'm so sorry. I didn't mean . . .'

'It's okay, I know.'

Would people *ever* stop tiptoeing around the subject? Since Mattie had lost Grandpa Joe she had found the hesitancy and embarrassment of other people trying to avoid the 'D' word almost worse than the grief framing the edges of each day. People meant well – of course they did. But their carefulness only served to make her feel even more isolated than losing Grandpa Joe and the upheaval of recent weeks had done. She could almost hear the whispered conversations behind her back as she carried on with her life as best she could: *Did you hear she lost her grandfather? And after what happened with* that lad, *too. I hear Joe Bell wasn't even talking to her before he died . . .*

More than anything, Mattie longed for a return to normality. To be able to laugh at jokes with her friends in the pub, Kings Sunbury's coffee shops, or in the street; to talk about the weather, whatever was on TV last night or gossip about the latest news in the village – without this awful, ever-present seriousness hanging over everyone she met. They didn't know what to say. And Mattie couldn't blame them. If the roles were reversed, maybe she would be tongue-tied and overly respectful, too.

People in Kings Sunbury were kind and thoughtful, only too ready to offer words of comfort and 'I-baked-too-many' cakes and bread. In the first week following news of her loss, Mattie lost count of the number of casseroles brought to her temporary home – more than her small freezer could cope with and certainly more than she'd ever eat. She'd taken to keeping a pack of parcel labels and a Sharpie next to the door so she could make sure each newly delivered dish was returned to its rightful owner. But their gifts and platitudes, while kindly meant, reminded Mattie over and over again of what she had lost.

'When are you doing the Memory Day?'

Mattie rubbed a rogue tear from her cheek. 'A week on Sunday. We'll put together a selection of things from the shop and I'll take the British rock 'n' roll songs CD to play while the old people look at the stuff. Bit of Tommy Steele, Michael Holliday, Adam Faith and Alma Cogan will make a lovely atmosphere. I think it could be fun.'

'I love that CD. It's a wonder we haven't worn it out playing it so much at the shop. Do you have to make a speech?'

'I'm going to try my hardest to get out of it.'

'Why? I think this could be good for you,' Laurie blurted out, the sudden note of seriousness causing Mattie's heart to sink. 'Get out there. Talk about Grandpa Joe – his influence, I mean, not . . . you know.'

She was right, of course. It would be impossible to talk about Bell Be-Bop without mentioning the reason she'd fallen in love with the Fifties in the first place. Everything in the shop related to stories Grandpa Joe had told his granddaughter, long before the rift that tore them apart for good. One of Mattie's biggest regrets was that her grandfather couldn't see how well the business was doing now. At the time they'd stopped speaking, Mattie had been seriously considering giving up the premises and moving the business entirely online. But the fact was, everything about the little shop overlooking the village green in Kings Sunbury reminded her of Grandpa Joe. The first records she'd sold there had been from the huge box he'd given her when she was sixteen; the book titles she remembered from the dusty shelves in his study; the radios, telephones and crockery mirroring the ones he'd point out to her in the bric-a-brac shops of Bridgnorth, Ironbridge and Ludlow. *I had one of those in my first house . . . Oh, I remember that like it was yesterday . . .*

It wouldn't just be the residents entertaining dearly held memories when they touched Bell Be-Bop stock at the Beauvale Memory Day. It would be a chance for Mattie to be close to Grandpa Joe again – one step closer to fulfilling her graveside promise to him.

Chapter Three

'Getting to Know You'–
Bing Crosby & Victor Young
and His Orchestra

♪

Rusty groaned to a halt in the retirement village's car park on the day of the Memory Day and Mattie took a breath to steady her nerves.

'How are you feeling?' Laurie asked, ducking down to tidy the victory roll in her hair using the reflection in the wing mirror.

'Okay, I think.'

'Well you're doing better than me. My heart's going ten to the dozen and I don't even have to make a speech.'

Mattie grimaced. 'Thanks for reminding me.'

'Relax. It's just a few old biddies who'll share a nice cup of tea with you when it's all over.' She straightened back and looked at Mattie. 'How many people did Gaynor say she was expecting?'

25

'About thirty. Quite a few residents go to their families' homes for Sunday lunch so she said it wouldn't be the full contingent.' She shot a quick smile at her assistant. 'It's all going to be great, I'm sure.'

'That's the spirit.' Laurie hopped out of the camper van and joined Mattie at its side door, helping her to pull out a large box of vintage objects and an enormous wheeled suitcase. 'Blimey, have you packed Percy in this case? It weighs a ton!'

'Think of the money you'll save on gym fees,' Mattie laughed as they headed into the main building, hearing Laurie's puffs and groans as she wheeled the enormous suitcase behind her.

When they entered the room, both women stopped dead.

Beauvale's bright but overheated communal barn was packed with residents, its exposed oak beams reverberating with loud conversation from the gathered crowd.

'There are hundreds of them!' Laurie hissed. 'How do they fit them all in the buildings? Ten to a room?'

'Maybe they all have multiple bunk-beds,' Mattie grinned back. Laurie had a point. There seemed far too many people here for the number of converted outbuildings and cottages in the retirement village's plot. Her stomach somersaulted again at the prospect of addressing such a crowd. She should have coaxed Jack into helping. He would relish an audience like this.

'Where do we put the stuff?' Laurie asked, still whispering, casting her eyes warily around the room at the already seated, loudly impatient crowd.

'Gaynor will tell us. There she is – follow me.'

Mattie headed quickly to the far side of the oak-gabled room where Gaynor – resplendent in a yellow daisy-covered maxi-dress and sparkly orange scarf – was fussing over the refreshment table. 'Gaynor, hi.'

'Mattie! You're here! Excellent! And you must be Laura?'

Laurie's smile was more gritted teeth than grin. '*Laurie*.'

'Excellent! What about the turnout, eh? Unbelievable! My colleague Nancy from Springhill Retirement in Stone Yardley has bussed over a bunch of her residents because she loved the idea of the Memory Day so much. So, we have something of a full house. Now, I've put out two trestles at the front with white tablecloths – see them? Pop all the things on there and we'll get cracking in about ten minutes, yes?'

Mattie realised her hands were shaking as she and Laurie filled the display tables with books, items of clothing, magazines, records, old telephones, coffee pots, cups and saucers, radios and vintage scent bottles. Loud *oohs* went up from some of the elderly ladies nearest the front as they began to spot familiar objects and the noise level of chatter rose several notches in the room.

'I'm so nervous,' Mattie confessed to her colleague.

'Me too. But if I was you right now I'd be *petrified*.' Laurie handed her a CD player disguised as a Fifties-style record player, and hurried off to find an extension lead to plug it into the wall.

The tables laid, Mattie hid the boxes behind the long white tablecloths reaching almost to the floor and stood up to smooth the front of her Dior-inspired black and white circle-skirt. The coolness of the satin fabric calmed her as she took in a deep breath.

'*I* had one of them.'

Mattie started and looked round to see a small, bright-eyed old lady leaning on an opulent-looking carved mahogany cane. 'Sorry?'

'One of them skirts like you've got on. Dior New Look – back when clothes made women look like proper women. Bought for me from Paris itself. Only mine had a daft poodle on it.' The lady's broad Liverpudlian accent stood out a mile in a roomful of Staffordshire locals. But then, so did its owner. She was dressed not in the greys, beiges and muted pastels of her fellow residents, but in scarlet – a matching sweater and skirt with red kitten heels, a startling choice for a woman of her years. Her hair was immaculate, the only concession to her age the silver grey of her curls, tinted with a faint lilac wash. Two strings of large pearls lay around her neck, huge gold hoop earrings competed with the necklace for attention, and on her wrist an expensive-looking gold watch glinted in the light from the halogen spotlights high in the barn roof.

Mattie liked her immediately.

'This is a replica, I'm afraid,' she admitted, lowering her voice a little. 'I couldn't afford an original Dior.'

'Secret's safe with me, kid,' the lady grinned, tapping the side of her nose with a scarlet-painted fingernail. 'We're not all millionaires, are we?'

'Thanks, I owe you.' Remembering her manners, Mattie offered her hand. 'Mattie Bell – pleased to meet you.'

The old woman's eyes twinkled like a naughty two-year-old's. 'Reenie Silver. And the pleasure's all mine.'

'Cooo-eeee! If we can all just have a bit of *hush*, please?'

Gaynor's voice chirped loudly across the room, calling the nattering residents to order as she headed towards Mattie. Reenie Silver rolled her eyes and positively sashayed over to claim her seat in the front row. Mattie noticed with amusement that several of the male residents sitting near her were casting winks in the old lady's direction.

'Lovely. Smashing. *Well*, everybody, have we got a treat for you today? Yes indeed! It is my very great pleasure to welcome Matilda Bell from Bell Be-Bop vintage shop in the village. She's come today to talk a little about what she does. And I know that many of you have already spotted the things Miss Bell has kindly brought with her from her shop. So after she's chatted to us, there will be lots of time to come up and see the items while we serve tea and coffee. And, as an extra treat, our very own Winnie has been busy in the kitchen making her famous butterfly buns.'

This announcement was met with louder rumbles of approval than the rest of Gaynor's speech, but it helped Mattie to relax a little. In a popularity contest between her and cake, she was more than happy to come second. Gaynor finally stepped aside to give Mattie the floor . . .

The speech passed in a blur, Mattie finding her feet as her enthusiasm for her business overtook her nerves. Gaynor had judged the audience correctly: once into her talk Mattie noticed their eyes straying past her to the goodies laid out on the tables behind, and the not-so-whispered conversations

29

about objects they recognised. At the end, following polite applause, Beauvale's director, Dr William Lancaster, stepped forward to thank her, and relief flooded her frame as the residents and guests hurried from their seats towards the tables.

Reenie Silver headed straight for Mattie. 'You were bleedin' good, you were.'

'Do you think so?'

'I know so. Takes guts to face a crowd on yer own. I should know. The room *loves* you. Haven't seen this lot so excited over anything for months. It's like God's waiting room in here most of the time. Depressing, when you've lived life as much as me.'

It was impossible not to smile when talking to the vibrant old lady, Mattie thought. Throughout her talk her eyes had kept being drawn to the lady in red, who appeared to be sitting in regal splendour, even though her chair was identical to all the others in the converted barn space.

'Right, well, I'll let you go and get a cuppa. I expect you're gaspin'. Nice to meet you, Mattie Bell.'

Mattie watched the crowd of residents part like the Red Sea as Reenie sailed between them to the Bell Be-Bop tables.

I hope I'm that confident when I'm her age, she thought.

'Excellent presentation, Miss Bell,' William Lancaster smiled as he approached, carrying two cups and saucers. 'I took the liberty of bringing you a cup of tea.'

'That's kind, thank you.'

'And I see you've met our resident celebrity.' He nodded in the direction of the old lady in red.

'She's quite a character,' Mattie replied.

'Reenie's much more than that. Quite famous in her day, by all accounts. She was a singer with The Silver Five in the 1950s – have you heard of them?'

Mattie's world seemed to screech to a halt. 'The Silver Five?'

Mistaking her shock for confusion, Dr Lancaster continued. 'They aren't as well remembered now as some of their contemporaries, although their songs have been revived over the years. I think Tom Jones covered 'Because You Loved Me' once. That's the song they're remembered for. Well, our Reenie was a rising star of British rock 'n' roll in the fifties. I think she did some TV work in the seventies on variety shows with Cilla Black and Lulu, too.'

Mattie had heard the story of The Silver Five so many times she could have recited it by heart. Grandpa Joe had fallen in love with them as a young man in his twenties, and for many years seemed to be one of the few who truly appreciated their music. His vinyl records of their songs were his most prized possessions. Had he not broken all ties with Mattie before his death, she was certain she would now own them. *I was their biggest fan*, she remembered him saying, her heart breaking as the sound of his voice flooded her mind. *Only had the chance to see them perform once. But I missed the concert and it turned out to be their last.* He'd always looked so sad when he'd said it, a glimpse of the young man he once was flickering across his pale blue eyes. Then he would rally, putting one of the records onto the creaking turntable of his beloved record player and grabbing Mattie's hand to twirl her to the sweet-sounding close harmonies and cheery skiffle rhythms of their songs.

Mattie looked over to the front of the room, where a group of elderly residents were picking up items from her shop. Reenie stood out a mile, but it was more than just her chosen colour of clothing. It was as if she was surrounded by light, her every move watched by those around her. Grandpa Joe called that kind of presence a 'Ready-Brek glow'. The memory of her grandfather caused a stab in her heart, and she looked quickly down into her half-empty teacup.

'Ah, let me get you another. You must be thirsty after your wonderful talk,' Dr Lancaster offered, mistaking her demeanour for thirst. He took the teacup from Mattie's hands and hurried away through the crowd of residents. Mattie let out a sigh and kicked an invisible pebble with her flowered kitten heels. Would Grandpa Joe's memory ambush her forever?

'Penny for 'em?'

The enigmatic old lady had traversed the room with impressive speed and was practically face to face with Mattie when she looked up. 'Sorry?'

'Pardon me for noticing. Only you look like someone wazzed on your chips, love.'

Mattie suppressed a laugh. 'I'm fine. Sorry.'

Reenie shrugged. 'No need to apologise. We all have our moments.'

'Dr Lancaster was telling me that you're a famous singer?'

The old lady clicked her false teeth behind pursed ruby lips. 'Should have been more'n I was, truth be told. But that's a story for me memoirs.' A wicked twinkle flashed in her pale grey eyes. 'Singer with The Silver Five – named after myself, of course – 1951 to '56. Then solo until 1980. Almost had my own TV show, I did. Headlined five weeks at The Sands in Vegas, '71. Bloody tedious cruise-ship tours after that. But back in the day, they said I was the British Connie Francis. And now here I am: doyenne of Beauvale Retirement Village. Piggin' Lulu can't say *that*, now can she?'

Mattie almost told Reenie about Grandpa Joe. But it didn't seem right, somehow. Besides, the sting of loss was so keen today that she doubted she could find the words. Instead, she observed Reenie Silver with interest, trying to imagine her as the beautiful, raven-haired songstress who had led a group so seemingly destined for greatness – and had stolen her grandfather's heart many years ago.

One thing was certain: Reenie had lost none of her ability to command a room. She seemed so at odds with the other old folks, her brassiness unexpected in a lady of her age. When a gentleman who must have been in his late eighties tottered up and offered to accompany her to the refreshment table, Reenie shot him down in flames.

'Away with yer, Stan Massey. Last time I took your arm you were after goosing me – and don't you deny it. Three husbands I've had and the last one that tried your trick ended up with a bloody nose!'

As the pensioner slunk away, a titter broke out from a timid group of ladies standing nearby. Mattie had noticed them earlier, following Reenie around as she prowled the room, always maintaining a respectful distance, yet clearly hanging on her every word.

'Please don't let me keep you from your friends,' Mattie said, suddenly concerned that she might be hogging Beauvale's resident celebrity.

'Who? That lot? They're not my friends, girl!' Reenie scoffed, leaning a little closer to Mattie but maintaining a speaking volume loud enough for her hangers-on to hear. 'I call them the Three Furies. On account of how the sight of them makes me bleedin' furious.'

'Do you like it here?' Mattie asked, the question leaving her lips before she thought better of it. Reenie seemed out of place in the retirement village, even if she clearly ruled the roost. Grandpa Joe's words about places like this had been playing on her mind: *It's just a pretty-pretty holding cell for old fuddy-duddies until they pop off. You'd never get me in one of those places* . . .

'Can't complain. Staff are okay, food doesn't kill yer.' She cast a sideways glance at Mattie and let out a deliberately heavy sigh. 'Just wish I had family to visit, you know.'

'You don't have any family?'

'That's not to say I haven't lived, of course. I've lived more than most people get a chance to. Three marriages and more money than I know what to do with. But it's not the same when nobody comes to see you.'

'You don't have any living relatives at all?'

'A few, but they're distant in every sense of the word.'

'And no friends?'

'Plenty of them – in here. But none from me life. Just the way it is, Mattie. I don't make the rules. Still, it's a

34

shame. I mean, I watch all these other sad beggars jumped on by family every weekend and I'm a bit jealous of them, you know, being on me tod and that. You get used to it, 'course. That's what a lifetime on the road teaches you.' Reenie turned to gaze up at Mattie, a beatific smile on her face, and to her horror Mattie saw a single burgeoning tear in the corner of the old lady's left eye.

It was just so sad. For all her illustrious past and considerable material means, Reenie Silver was lonely – a fact that made Mattie want to cry with her. Grandpa Joe might have cut her out of his life, but he was never alone. When Grandma Bell had passed away seven years ago, the whole family had rallied round, determined that their beloved patriarch be loved and cared for. The thought of him ever being alone or lonely was abhorrent to them: he had founded the family and his place was right at the beating heart of it. How could anyone allow an elderly relative to exist without visiting them? In the final months of Grandpa Joe's life, Mattie's one consoling thought had been that he was surrounded by so much love from the rest of her relatives. She might have been denied the chance to spend time with him, but everyone else in the Bell clan was taking up the slack.

The idea came about as easily as breathing; later, Mattie would marvel at how spontaneous it had been, especially given her recent reticence about every other aspect of her life.

'I'd visit you. If you'd like?'

Reenie Silver stared up at her and for a moment Mattie worried she might have taken offence at the offer. 'You'd do that – for me?'

'I'd love to. I—' Mattie gulped back the tug of emotion in her throat. 'I lost my grandpa last month and I still miss him. His stories about the Fifties made me want to start my business. I would be honoured to hear yours – if you'd care to share them?'

Maybe learning about his favourite band will bring me closer to him . . .

Reenie folded her arms. 'So a trade-off, eh? I get a visitor and you get someone to fill the gap left by your grandpa?'

Mattie wouldn't have exactly phrased it like that, but it seemed a decent enough idea. 'I suppose so.'

'You might be on to something there.' The twinkle returned as Reenie dabbed the lone tear from her eye with a lace handkerchief produced from a sleeve of her sweater. 'But I have one condition.'

'Name it.'

Reenie tugged at Mattie's elbow to move them a little distance away from the Three Furies, who were watching like over-anxious prairie dogs. 'Bring us some of them posh violet crèmes from the chocolate shop in the village when you come, okay? Nurses won't let me have them, see. Cholesterol, apparently. I'm eighty-four years old: why do I have to worry about cholesterol at my age? More likely to be bumped off by the wine in me coat cupboard I'm not supposed to be drinking.'

All things considered, a bag of artisan chocolates was a small price to pay if it meant Mattie could feel close to Grandpa Joe again. All her life she had heard of his love of Reenie's old group, yet she knew so little about any of the members. Talking about a period of time he'd had in common with Reenie would bring Mattie back to her life before the ultimatum, long before the rift was made, when she would sit for hours indulging in deliciously evocative details of her grandfather's stories. The former singing star fascinated her, and the chance to learn more about her illustrious past was too enticing to miss.

'Deal,' Mattie said, feeling the strength in the old lady's handshake as they traded smiles. 'When shall we start?'

'Next Sunday,' Reenie replied, not missing a beat. 'And don't forget the contraband.'

Chapter Four

'These Foolish Things (Remind Me of You)' – Etta James

♪

Kings Sunbury was quiet and still beneath a pink-gold dawn sky when Mattie headed out to work on Monday morning. She hadn't slept well, but that was nothing new. Since moving into her rented home sleep had eluded her regularly. It was as if the moment her head touched the newly purchased pillow on her temporary bed it began to fizz with questions she'd kept at bay during the day.

Maybe that was the problem, she thought, as she coaxed Rusty into reluctant action along the winding lanes between darkened houses. There were so few comforting things around her to lull her to sleep. Everything in her house was new, bought in a hurry. She had left so much behind in the house she *should* have been living in – but all of it ceased to have meaning the moment she found out Grandpa

Joe had been right all along. Strange how furniture, pictures and ornaments just became *things* when life took a turn. She'd grabbed only what she could carry, throwing it into black bin bags as her possessions merged together through her tears. Most of her furniture was still in storage, the little she had managed to take to the house before the split reluctantly returned to the unit by Asher.

Her skin went cold. *Asher*. She didn't want to think of him again.

The little that had made it into her new home were sparse essentials: her jewellery box, files for work, her laptop and a box of books that had seemed important when she was moving out but she was pretty convinced she'd never read again. She didn't even have a bookcase yet. Instead, the books formed a makeshift bedside table, the sight of their comfortingly broken spines and thumbed pages strangely reassuring. She would get around to sorting everything, of course. Just – just *not yet*.

No matter what else was happening around her, Mattie loved this part of the day. The thrill of opening the door of her own shop was the same today as it had been on her very first day of trading and she never wanted to lose that sense of wonder and pride. Inside, the shop smelled of beeswax polish, chalk paint and roses, old leather and wood – a heady mix unique to Bell Be-Bop. When the day was done and she returned home, this fragrance would always linger on her clothes, a constant reminder of how lucky she was to be doing what she loved, day in, day out.

Today, the shop was quiet – not unusual for the beginning of the week – but Mattie wished for customers to take away the silence. It was Laurie's day off and Jack was unlikely to appear. Even Joanna had a prior engagement, so their usual lunch was postponed. Mattie looked around the shop, her to-do list frustratingly complete. Right now, she didn't need thinking space. Her brain ached enough from going over things she would never solve.

When the small brass bell over Bell Be-Bop's door heralded a customer's arrival just after midday, it was all Mattie could do not to run over and hug the incoming person. When the amused smile of the family vicar appeared, she didn't hesitate in welcoming him.

'Blimey, slow day, is it?' he chuckled, almost knocked off his feet by the force of Mattie's hug.

'Sorry,' she laughed, stepping back. 'It's lovely to see you.'

'If only all my parishioners were so happy to greet me,' he smiled. 'Most of them think I'm after something.'

'And are you?'

'Well, that depends. Has your kettle recently boiled?'

'Milk, one sugar?'

'Perfect. Just don't tell Vanessa. I'm supposed to be cutting out sugar.'

'Tsk, Phil, I'm not sure I should enable your dishonesty. And you a man of the cloth.'

'I know. Thankfully God knows me better than anyone.' He glanced heavenwards. 'And he knows I'm weak.'

As Mattie made tea she could see Phil inspecting a display of her latest stock.

'I love how you do this,' he said, accepting a mug from Mattie.

'Thanks, Phil.'

'I mean it. You have such a skill for making a random group of objects evoke a period of time. Vanessa always comes back from your shop raving about your collections. It's a good job we have a finite supply of money or I reckon she'd buy you out of stock.'

Mattie offered the minister a seat in a 1940s display by the window. The armchairs she'd found in a flea market three years ago had finally found a home – not in the living room of what would now never be her marital home, but in prime position in her shop. She was glad that at least some of her beloved furniture was out of storage. Her heart sank again as she pictured the rest of her possessions in cardboard boxes languishing in the grey steel confines of a faceless storage unit on the outskirts of Telford. When she'd put them there she'd imagined herself and Asher unpacking them in their newly refurbished home. Now they were just gathering dust. She must make time to fit them into her new house, she resolved. Just as soon as she felt ready . . .

'So, I have something for you.' Phil's smile had become earnest concern, immediately alerting Mattie's defences. 'I wasn't sure when was a good time.' He paused, waiting for a response. When Mattie said nothing, he stood and picked up a cardboard box he'd left on the shop counter. 'Here.'

'What is it?'

'It's a *box*, Mattie.'

She shook her head. 'You're an idiot.'

'Fair point. Okay, here's the thing. You know I visited Joe in the hospice – at the end?'

Mattie nodded, the sudden mention of her grandfather stealing the air from her lungs.

'In the last two weeks of his life I visited every day. He had a lot he wanted to talk about and I was only too happy to listen. And I confess, I had an ulterior motive. I wanted to get him to talk to *you*.'

'Really? I had no idea . . .'

'I know. That's why I'm telling you now. I'm sorry I couldn't change his mind.'

'Phil, don't beat yourself up about it. He was never going to back down.' Saying it aloud took none of the sting from the confession. *And neither was I . . .* Mattie kept her eyes trained on the box in Phil's hands, not trusting her tears to stay back if she raised her gaze. 'But thanks for trying.'

'He loved you, you know. Despite everything that happened.'

'He had a funny way of showing it.' Mattie stopped herself, horrified by the bitterness her voice held. 'I'm sorry. I know he did, deep down. He'd just made his stance and I guess any effort to change it would have looked like defeat. He hated admitting he was wrong. We were always too alike in that respect.'

'I told him he was running out of time. It's the one thing we're trained *not* to say, but I think Joe needed to hear it. I told him he would regret not saying goodbye. I think he understood. On the last day I saw him, he told me to give you this.' He patted the brown cardboard box. 'I waited until now because – well, I thought maybe you'd had some time after the funeral and you might be ready.'

'Ready for what?' She peered at the box. 'What's in it?'

'I don't know. But he was very specific about where I would find it and that only you were to know he'd given it to you. I had to go to the house while your mum was at the hospice and find it. You see, even right at the end he was still calling the shots.'

'Why did he want me to have this?'

'He said you would find answers in there. About why he acted as he did. And why it mattered.' He handed the box to Mattie. 'He said, "This is who I was. Mattie will understand." I don't know if that means anything to you?'

Shaking her head, Mattie pulled back the parcel tape sealing the box lid. It had been in place for a considerable time, judging by the way it shredded into pieces. When it was finally removed, she opened the flaps. Inside, stacked neatly like leather-bound soldiers ready for an inspection, were thirteen A6 diaries, from 1944 to 1956. Each cover was a different shade, creating a muted rainbow of dusty leather. The smell instantly took her back to Grandpa Joe's study where she'd spent so many Sunday afternoons looking at his collection of books.

'I didn't know he kept diaries,' she said, picking one up and feeling the weight of it in her hands. When she opened the pages her heart contracted as she saw the familiar tiny handwriting. The family joke was that Grandpa Joe's writing was always best viewed under a microscope. In these small diaries each entry was an essay, the words meticulously crammed onto each page. It reminded Mattie of the book-shelves in the farmhouse, with every available inch of space claimed by well-stacked books. She thought of her sister and mother now having to unpick years of Grandpa Joe's careful constructions and didn't envy them the task. 'What did he tell you about them?'

Phil shrugged. 'I didn't know the box contained diaries. All he said was that the contents of it represented the man he was and that you would find answers there. He wouldn't be more specific. I'm sorry. I know this isn't the reconciliation you deserved. But maybe you'll find some comfort in the diaries. Maybe that will be some consolation.'

When Phil had gone, Mattie opened the box and spread the diaries out across the Thunderbird countertop. Before her lay thirteen years of Grandpa Joe's life represented by the faded, cracked leather books. Thirteen years of his life she knew hardly anything about.

She had heard the stories he'd rolled out at every family lunch and gathering – idyllic, sun-soaked reminiscences of a country childhood, even wartime tales warmed by the rose-hued filter of time. In Kings Sunbury evacuees from the big cities found refuge, billeted at farms in the safe haven of the Shropshire countryside. Grandpa Joe often talked of summer fairs and boxcar races, WI jam drives and surprising plenty on farms where livestock and produce escaped rationing. But the years after the war leading to the twelve months of his apprenticeship in London in 1956 were a noticeable gap. All he had said about his teenage years was that he had been 'content', always returning to his childhood tales when pressed for more. Mattie couldn't remember having asked him much about the missing years and now, as she surveyed his diaries, she wondered what secrets they might contain.

It was strange to think of Grandpa Joe as anything other than an older man, but something Rev. Phil's wife Vanessa had said after the funeral had stayed with Mattie: 'Just think, your grandfather lived almost an entire lifetime before you and Joanna were born. His life was like an iceberg: two-thirds of it were lived before you came to be.'

Mattie ran her hand across the diaries. 'So who were you really, Joe Bell? And why do you want me to read these?'

The first two – 1944 and 1945 – were not completed every day, the large handwriting often spilling over onto two or three pages, with childlike drawings sometimes taking the place of words. Finding stories she'd heard Grandpa Joe tell, she skipped through the entries in just over an hour, thankful that Bell Be-Bop remained quiet for the rest of the afternoon.

Not long before closing time, she picked up the 1946 diary – a dusky red leather cover with the ghost of gold marking the year. Opening at a page halfway through, she began to read.

The handwriting was noticeably older than in the previous two books, but concentration was marked in every stroke. Eleven-year-old Joseph Nathaniel Bell seemed mostly interested in beating his best friend Clive Adams at tiddly-winks and conkers. Reading on, there were tales of village gatherings for Bonfire Night, Advent and Christmas; Joe's pride-and-joy present from Father Christmas being a hand-made wooden Spitfire he was certain the man in the red suit had bought from his own father; and protracted

45

disputes with his younger brother Eric, eleven months his junior and seemingly hell-bent on getting Joe into trouble.

December 1946

Mother is angry. Eric bent her best pie tin when he used it as a sledge on Primrose Bank. She sent him to bed with no supper but when he went up he said it had been my idea. Now I am hungry in my bed, too. Eric looks like the cat that got the cream. Mother is banging pots on the stove in the kitchen and I am planning my revenge. Eric should watch his back. I won't forget this!

Mattie found the thought of Joe Bell smarting at such injustice oddly comforting. *At least he knew how it felt once.* Suddenly, she wanted to share the revelation. The arrival of the diaries was too significant to keep to herself. Grandpa Joe might have insisted they remain secret, but he wasn't here now and this was the first good thing to happen to Mattie in a long time. So, her decision was easy. As soon as she'd closed the shop, she called her sister.

'Mattie! I can't tell you how good it is to hear you! How's everything?'

'I have something I think you'd like to see, J-J. When are you free this week?'

'Come for dinner this evening? Fred's at a conference in Manchester and won't be back till tomorrow. The kids would be over the moon to see you.'

Mattie was only too happy to forgo another dinner-

46

for-one to visit her sister's picture-perfect cottage in nearby Ironbridge. She had missed seeing her nephew and niece, who clearly felt the same, as she was almost wrestled to the doorstep by two delighted bundles of laughter.

'Ethan! Ava! Let your auntie breathe,' Joanna called down the Minton-tiled hallway, drying her hands on a tea towel as she strode to Mattie's aid. 'Sorry, darling, Fred's mother gave them Haribo when she popped over this morning. Anything other than Percy Pigs sends them doo-lally. Help Auntie Mattie up, please, kids!'

Finally released from the children's hugs, Mattie followed the family into the large kitchen. Ethan and Ava hurried off to gather armfuls of their latest toy acquisitions to show their aunt as Joanna made tea in a kettle that looked like it had cost more than most of Mattie's belongings combined.

'It's good to see you,' Joanna smiled. 'We've missed your visits. The kids have been like shaken-up pop bottles since they heard you were coming. How are you?'

'Good. Better than I've been for a while, actually.'

'So, tell me about this famous old lady you're going to visit?' She grinned as she filled an Emma Bridgewater teapot printed with pink and red hearts. 'I bet she's formidable.'

'She is. You'll have to meet her, J-J. I think her stories are going to be amazing.'

'Grandpa would be over the moon.'

'He would. That's another reason I want to visit,' Mattie admitted, blushing a little.

'Because it might bring you closer to him?'

'Something like that. Do you think that's selfish?'

'Not at all. It sounds like you and this lady might be good for each other. I expect she'll love sharing her memories with you. Besides, it's good to see you smiling,' Joanna said, reaching out to touch her sister's shoulder. 'Heaven knows we both could do with more of that.'

'*Mu-uuum!* Ava won't give Glitter Sunset Barbie back!' Ethan's plaintive cry reverberated into the kitchen.

Joanna gave a wry smile. 'My son's decided he loves Barbie dolls,' she shrugged. 'It's like London Fashion Week in our lounge at the moment. I swear he's going to be the next Marc Jacobs. *Ava!* Give your brother back his Barbie, please.'

Ava appeared in the doorway, the garishly dressed doll clutched possessively in one hand. 'But *Mum*, I need her to play Killer Pirate Queen and Ethan only wants to do stupid "Milan Catwalk".'

'Ava Bell-Jones, you have plenty of other strange creatures in your toy box that will make perfectly good Killer Pirate Queens. Give Barbie back to Ethan and *play nicely*.'

With a loud tut and a bottom lip pushed so far out it practically touched the tip of her nose, the little girl stomped back into the lounge. One thing was certain, in this household Joanna most definitely ruled the roost. Mattie often marvelled at the way her sister breezed through every challenge her life presented. It was such a different life from what she'd always talked of having: travelling the world, moving to the States, not really bothered if she became a mother at all. And yet, from the moment Ethan was born, it had been as if Joanna had been made for motherhood. Fred didn't like the idea of her working, so

48

she'd stayed at home instead, starting a lifestyle blogging business in the evenings that was beginning to bring in money. She was an awesome mum, the kind Mattie hoped to emulate if she ever had children. Always calm, taking everything in her stride, yet never seeming to lose her identity in the endless demands of family life.

'Who knew I would end up with poster kids for the Let Toys Be Toys campaign, eh?' Joanna smiled. 'I've made a lamb tagine for tea – hope that's okay?'

'Sounds wonderful. I seem to have had a lot of beef casseroles lately.'

'Neighbours still bearing gifts?'

'Yep. It's a lovely thought to bring food but I'm starting to hide when the doorbell rings.'

'That's the village for you. Generous to the point of distraction. Help me set the table, would you? We'd better act fast to prevent Barbie-geddon from escalating.'

When the children had been bathed, read a bedtime story and tucked into bed, the Bell sisters retreated to the calm sanctuary of Joanna's front room.

'How do you do this every day?' Mattie asked, her head beginning to throb at the temples. 'They're wonderful but they're exhausting.'

'You get used to it. I'm just glad they have each other – regardless of the feuds, they're close. That's important to me.'

Mattie studied her sister. It seemed an odd thing for her to say. 'Is everything okay?'

'Of course. So, what did you want to show me?'

'Phil gave me a box from Grandpa Joe. These were

inside.' She pulled the stack of small diaries from her bag and spread them out across the coffee table.

'His diaries?'

'I didn't know he kept them. I certainly wasn't expecting to ever read them.'

'And he left them for you?'

Mattie nodded, watching Joanna's expression closely. The last thing she wanted was to alienate her sister. 'He said they would help me to understand him better.'

'Do Mum and Dad know?'

'Not yet. I wasn't sure how they'd cope with that at the moment.'

'I think that's wise. Oh M . . .'

'Are you all right? About this?'

'It's a bit of a shock – to see his handwriting . . .'

'I know.'

'But I wouldn't ever begrudge you these. I had him to speak to in the last months. I asked him everything I wanted to know; I had time to say goodbye. You weren't given that. I think this is – *lovely*. A real chance to get back something that stupid row stole from both of you. Have you read any of them yet?'

Mattie nodded. '1944 and 1945. I thought you might like to read them. They're all about the war and Bill Godfrey coming to stay at the farm as an evacuee – you remember Grandpa used to tell us stories about him?'

'Remember? They were his favourite tales. Especially at Christmas. "We hadn't warned Bill about where Mother smoked the ham – and when Father pulled it down from inside the chimney . . ."'

'". . . *the poor lad thought we'd cooked Father Christmas!*"' Mattie finished the sentence, remembering the booming laugh that always accompanied their grandfather's punchline. 'It's strange to read them from the time they happened – without all the years of embellishment.'

Joanna looked at Mattie, her hazel eyes apparently seeing through to her bones. She'd always been able to do this, and Mattie braced herself against the familiar unease that came with it. 'But how do *you* feel about it?'

'I honestly can't say yet. It's a connection to him that I never had before, so that feels like something new. But it can't take the place of a hug, or a smile, or a goodbye kiss.' Loss, like a blunt knife, bit into her heart.

'No, it can't. But it's still a gift. And maybe, when all's said and done, that's what matters.' Joanna carefully placed the diaries back on the table and wrapped her arms around her knees. 'Mattie, I need to ask a favour and I'm not sure how to do it.'

'Just ask me.'

'Things aren't good – with Fred and me.'

Her confession shook Mattie to the core. 'Oh J-J, no!'

'I haven't said anything before because – I didn't know what to say. How to even approach it. Mum's in no state to even hear about it; you've had this awful situation to deal with.' Tears filled her eyes. 'I was supposed to be the one looking after all of you. The one that held it all together.'

Her heart breaking, Mattie rushed to her sister's side, gathering her up in her arms. 'That was never your job. Oh Jo, I'm so sorry.'

51

They held each other as the weight of months shifted, Joanna keeping her sobs below a whisper in case the children heard. Mattie wondered how many silent tears her sister had shed, and hated that she'd been so wrapped up in Asher and the row with Grandpa Joe to see what was really going on. Joanna and Fred gave the outward appearance of a happy, settled marriage: comfortable home, a lovely family and a peaceful life. Was any of that real?

'How long?' she asked, finally.

'Years. But the last six months have been hell.' Joanna pulled away and for the first time Mattie saw truth staring back at her. 'I decided today that I'm not prepared for the kids to live in the middle of this anymore. Or me. We all deserve better. We need to get away. The money from the blog will tide us over for a while, but I need something else to supplement it. I feel awful asking, Mattie, but do you have any work at the shop? I could do anything – for however many hours you have.'

'Yes, of course.' She answered before she'd had time to consider the implications. She would find the money from somewhere, no matter what. 'I can work out a rota with Laurie. Where will you go?'

'We'll rent somewhere. That's our best option, I think. I'd ask Mum but she just wouldn't be able to manage with me and the kids under her feet. She's still coming to terms with her loss – she needs time and space.'

Immediately, Mattie thought of her own rented house, with its two spare rooms and an emptiness that made it hard to ever think she'd call it home. 'Why don't you move in with me?'

Joanna's eyes grew wide. 'M, I couldn't ask you to have the kids . . .'

'You haven't. I'm offering. I'd love to spend more time with Ava and Ethan. My new place is too big for just me. I wasn't exactly thinking of a perfect home when I rented it. There's plenty of room for all of us.'

Later, tucked beneath a blanket in her living room, Mattie knew she'd made the right decision. The house would feel brighter and more alive once it was filled with Joanna, Ethan and Ava's fun, energy and laughter. And maybe then it would start to feel like a home.

Chapter Five

'What a Difference a Day Makes'
– Sarah Vaughan

♪

'Matilda! I must say I was thrilled when I saw your name on the visitor sheet!' Gaynor's sunny beam seemed to illuminate the all-white space of Beauvale's reception area. 'And you're here to visit Reenie? How lovely.'

Mattie smiled as Gaynor – positively glowing today in a bright orange daisy-printed smock and mint-green bell-bottoms – bustled her through the doors past the grey thundercloud otherwise known as Eileen. In her off-duty clothes, she felt a little underdressed next to the centre's operations manager. 'We got on so well at the Memory Day. I'm looking forward to hearing more of her stories.'

'Reenie has more than a few of those to tell,' Gaynor chuckled. 'She's led quite a life.'

They walked through the communal barn to a large conservatory looking out across the Shropshire hills. The space hummed with conversation and activity as visitors mingled with residents. Children dashed between the high-backed leather armchairs and out through the open conservatory doors to the courtyard garden beyond, while proud great-grandparents looked on. As the Sunday morning sunshine streamed in, mirroring the warm and happy atmosphere that filled the barn, Mattie was reminded of Sunday lunches at her grandparents' redbrick farmhouse at the opposite end of the village – always so filled with laughter and life. Her family would be clearing the house out this weekend, its former occupants no longer needing the things with which they'd surrounded themselves in life. The thought of the once-bright home lying dimmed and empty made her sad.

Sitting in splendid isolation from the other residents, Reenie Silver occupied the best position near the open doors, her eyes trained on the blue hills rolling beyond the complex. Today she was a woman in black and gold – dressed more for afternoon tea at the Ritz than a Sunday morning in a Shropshire retirement village. If she felt alone in the hubbub she didn't show it, her chin held high and proud.

Gaynor tiptoed respectfully to her side, gently patting the old lady's shoulder. 'Reenie, dear, Matilda Bell is here to see you.'

Reenie turned with a beatific smile. 'Mattie Bell, you're here!'

'I am. Hi, Miss Silver.'

Reenie was rising to her feet and Mattie noticed the preposterously pink fluffy boudoir slippers at odds with her elegant black-and-gold-striped dress. 'Call me Reenie, kid. Excuse me being in my civvies. Sunday slippers are one thing I've retained from me days in LA.' She extended her hand, which Mattie shook. 'How about this one, eh Gaynor? She's a good girl, coming to visit this little old lonely muggins on her day off.'

'She is indeed.' Gaynor smiled proudly at Mattie, as if bestowing a surrogate mother's blessing.

'It's my pleasure,' Mattie replied. 'Can't have you on your own on visiting day.'

'Quite.' Reenie's smile was a little thin, and Mattie wondered if she'd embarrassed her in front of Gaynor. 'Well, we'd better let you get back to it, Gaynor, love.'

'But you—' Gaynor was silenced by a glare from Reenie that could have frozen sunbeams. 'Ah. Yes. Actually, I do have rather a lot to be getting on with. *Accounts*. You know the thrill, I'll bet?' And with that, she turned on her hessian platform heels and hurried away.

Odd, thought Mattie. But then, she was quickly learning that Gaynor Fairchild was a woman of surprises.

Reenie was still smiling. 'So. You brought 'em?'

Remembering the pink-and-white-striped box she had brought from the chocolatiers in the village, Mattie reached into her handbag, stopped suddenly by Reenie's vice-like grip on her wrist. '*Not here*,' she hissed with a furtive glance over her shoulder, as if expecting to see a concealed spy by the potted begonias. 'Come with me.'

'Er – okay . . .' Mattie managed, taken aback by the sudden pull on her arm.

Retaining her grip on Mattie's hand, Reenie marched out into the courtyard garden, greeting residents as she sailed past. 'Mornin', George . . . All right, Vera? . . . Hangin' baskets look grand, Howard . . . Shirley, your great-grandkids get bigger every week. What you feeding them, eh?'

They walked to the edge of the garden, where an elegant beech bench with scrolled arms surrounded by blue pots of English lavender faced out past the drystone wall, looking over the fields and hills. She released her hold on Mattie, and sat down with all the practised elegance of a head of state. 'That's better. Now, hand 'em over.'

Mattie did as she was told, watching as the old lady tore into the box and stuffed two chocolates into her mouth, closing her eyes and letting out a moan of satisfaction. She couldn't help feeling like a dealer of some illicit substance, seeing the effect the artisan confectionery had on her companion. Reenie hadn't been kidding when she'd called the chocolate shop *fancy*. If 'fancy' meant ridiculously overpriced, she'd have to be careful what else she agreed to buy for these visits. Reenie Silver had expensive tastes. Even her froufrou slippers looked as if they'd once carried an exclusive price tag. Grandpa Joe might have laughed at Mattie's expense – in more ways than one. She shook off the thought.

'Nice?' she asked.

'*Heaven*,' Reenie mumbled back, patting the box as if it were an old friend. 'Keep bringing me these, kid, and I'll be your friend for life.'

If I keep bringing you these I'll be bankrupt in a month, Mattie grimaced to herself. 'Glad you like them. So – um

57

– how's your week been?' What else were you supposed to ask a woman you hardly knew at all?

'Come on, you can do better than that.' Seeing Mattie's expression, Reenie gave her a playful jab in the ribs with a bony elbow. 'I'm just joshin' with you. I appreciate you coming over to see me. Truly. But we don't have to do small-talk pleasantries, Mattie Bell. We can be more exciting than that. So, why did you want to visit me, hmm? And please don't tell me it's because you felt sorry for an old bird. Charity like that I don't need.'

Mattie could feel a hot blush spreading from the nape of her neck. 'I did have an ulterior motive,' she admitted. 'My grandpa was a big fan of your group.'

Reenie raised a wobbly-painted eyebrow. 'The Silver Five?'

'Yes. He loved your music. It's one of the things I remember most about him.'

'Well, blow me over the white cliffs of Dover! I thought the only person who remembered us lot was the taxman when it came to royalty time. A big fan, you say?'

'He considered himself your greatest fan. Had all your singles, and the album you released in 1955.'

'Bloody hell, I thought those had long since been melted down. So, out of interest, which of us was his favourite?'

Mattie was tempted to lie, not wanting to say anything that might prevent Reenie from talking about her past fame. If she thought Grandpa Joe had lusted after her in his youth, she might say more to Mattie. But the truth was, she didn't know. Grandpa Joe always referred to the group by their collective name only, which is why she hadn't realised who

Reenie Silver was when they first met. 'He never said,' she admitted. 'I think he loved you all equally.'

'Oh, right.' Reenie sucked air in through her dentures. 'Well, it was a long time ago. A lot's happened to this old hoofer since.'

Fearing she might be defeated before she'd even begun, Mattie changed tack. 'And that's what I really want to hear about. You must have led such an interesting life, Reenie. I'd love to listen to your story.'

A pair of chattering blackbirds danced across the sky above them, skipping out to the open fields. Reenie's pale grey eyes watched their arcing flight and the smallest hint of wistfulness flickered there for a moment. 'You miss your grandad?'

'Terribly. He was such a larger-than-life character. Life without him in it seems too sparse.' Mattie swallowed hard. 'You'd have liked him.'

'You got a picture?'

Mattie hesitated. Nobody knew she still carried a small, black and white photo of Grandpa Joe in her wallet that had been taken in the early sixties. She had found it in the bottom of a box of records he'd given her when she was about to open her shop, and it made her smile. Despite everything that had happened to destroy the relationship they'd shared, his smiling, youthful face still gave her hope. Should she share the treasure with Reenie?

'I bet he was good-looking,' Reenie continued, her eyes narrowing as if she'd spotted Mattie's dilemma. 'I mean, you're pretty. You don't get that if your family's been whacked with the ugly stick. What was his name?'

'Joseph Bell.'

'Joe, eh? Had a piano player in Vegas called Joe. I used to sing that old Frank Sinatra line, "*So set 'em up, Joe, I got a little story I think you oughtta know*" to him every night before we went on stage.' Her voice cracked a little as she sang, but Mattie could hear power there that could only come from years of experience. 'Handsome, he was. I think we might have had a bit of a fling once, you know.' Lilac-rinsed curls danced as she let out a decidedly naughty chuckle. 'Piano players. My Achilles heel. Couldn't walk past one without hopping into bed with him. You take my advice, Mattie Bell: avoid the piano players. Won't just be the keys they'll fiddle with, if you get my meaning.'

It was slightly disconcerting to hear such frank advice coming from an octogenarian, but the glimpse into Reenie's colourful past was enough to convince Mattie. She had to hear more. Reaching for her wallet, she pulled the photograph out from its hiding place behind her driving licence. 'He was handsome. Here.'

Reenie accepted the photograph with a low whistle. 'You aren't kidding. Are you sure we never met? He looks familiar . . . Not that it means anything, mind. I met a lot of cute fellas in my life. Shame if I didn't meet this one, though. Hello, Joseph Bell.'

Mattie winced as her heart contracted. *I hope you can see this, Grandpa.* 'It would have made his day to hear that.'

'Oh, I'm sure he heard it. They're all up there, I reckon, watching us from the cheap seats. I 'spect I'll find out myself, soon enough. I'll have a fair bit of explaining to do if they're *all* there, of course . . . But then, what's a life if you haven't got a few things wrong, eh?'

'I like your attitude.'

'Why, thank you. I'm proud of it myself. So,' she folded her hands in her lap and squinted up at Mattie. 'What d'ya want to know?'

The sun dipped behind cotton-wool clouds, but Mattie could feel a glow spreading within her. It was the same anticipatory thrill she'd experienced as a child faced with shelf upon shelf of books at the Severnside Book Emporium, Grandpa Joe's favourite bookshop. 'Everything,' she breathed. 'Tell me everything.'

'Everything might take a while, Mattie Bell. I've been round the block more times than you realise.' Reenie settled herself in her chair and selected another violet crème. 'Righty-ho. Buckle up, kid, 'cos this ride could get bumpy.'

Mattie smiled. 'I'm not scared.'

'Glad to hear it. Well, it started when me ma went into labour on the scullery floor . . .'

Chapter Six

'The Story of My Life'
– Michael Holliday

♪

'And then all the neighbours came round, fussing over her poor mum as she was giving birth. She said everyone did that where she grew up – your house was as much theirs as it was yours and nobody ever locked their front doors . . .'

'Old people always say that,' Jack grinned, offering Mattie a chip from the steaming paper nest holding his lunch. How he ate so badly and wasn't the size of sub-Saharan Africa was a marvel. 'I bet they did. Gramps' front door was like Fort Knox, remember? All those sliding bolts and chains. You'd think he had gold bullion in his front room or something.'

'Reenie said they didn't. Terraces in Liverpool might have been different to Shropshire farmhouses.'

Jack grinned. 'Sorry. I interrupted you. So her mother didn't even know she was expecting?'

Mattie blew steam from the chip she'd taken. 'Apparently not. Reenie was a late baby – her mum had already given birth to eight children and was well into her forties so she assumed her baby-bearing days were over. She called Reenie her "little surprise package" – although her father was less lyrical about it. He called her "the postman's delivery".'

'Ouch. That must have hurt.'

Mattie considered how breezily Reenie had told her this fact of her life. She didn't appear hurt by it, but Mattie couldn't be sure that wasn't years of mask-wearing. 'She said he was proud of her when she started doing well in her teens, so I guess he grew to love her.'

'You like her, don't you?'

'I do. The thing is, Jack, she's nothing like Grandpa Joe was. She talks about her past like she's proud of every bit of it. Even the bad stuff. I don't think I'd admit to a relative stranger that my father suspected I was illegitimate, but to Reenie it's part of her story. I've never met anyone like her. She's a character, but there's a brassiness about her that you don't expect to find in an elderly lady.'

'Did you ever feel that sometimes Grandpa wasn't telling you the whole story?' Jack asked, throwing a crumb of crispy fish batter at a hopeful-looking pigeon.

Mattie stared at him, momentarily taken aback by his sharpness. As a writer he'd always been able to cut to the heart of a situation, but he'd never shared this observation with her before. It felt strange to be discovering new things about their relationship with Grandpa Joe. 'I did – often. I think he was quite a private man. More so after Grandma died.'

Jack smiled, but Mattie noticed his eyes didn't. 'I wonder if he did meet Reenie Silver. And they had a torrid affair. Can you imagine your mum's face if she found that out about him?'

'Somehow I don't think he led quite as colourful a life as Reenie seems to have. I'm still not sure how much of what she tells me is gospel truth, but she makes me laugh.'

'I'm glad someone does.'

'What's that supposed to mean?'

'Nothing.' Jack screwed up the remainder of his lunch in the chip paper and lay back on the picnic blanket. 'It's good to see you smiling again. I was beginning to think it would never happen.'

Mattie observed her cousin. Had she been so noticeably down? She'd done her best to keep the hurt buried, believing that she could fool everyone else into thinking that she was happy. Obviously, she'd failed. 'So much for my acting skills. I thought I was doing well.'

'You were. You *are*. Don't forget that I know you too well. Everyone else thinks you're coping.'

'Well, that's a comfort.' She picked at the grass as a bee hummed past her ear. 'It's nice to hear about someone else's stories from when Grandpa was young. Like all the other stuff was years away from happening. Like a fresh start. I always loved to hear him reminiscing about the Fifties – but that ended when we fell out. I think talking to Reenie will bring that part of him back a little.' She shrugged away the building pain. 'Her life sounds exciting, anyway. You should meet her. She'd love you.'

'She'd terrify me, if what you've told me about her is anything to go by. She'd eat me alive.'

'Probably.'

Mattie grinned at the thought. Reenie would take one look at Jack and think she'd won the lottery. With his blond hair, Adriatic-blue eyes and tall, athletic frame, he was a catch in anyone's book – as half the female residents of Kings Sunbury their age could attest to. Mattie loved her cousin, not least because he appeared to be so unaware of the effect he had on the opposite sex. She imagined their grandfather had been the same in his youth. Certainly he'd had no idea that Grandma liked him, causing her to eventually corner him in the Green Man pub at the centre of the village and yell in full earshot of all the regulars, 'I love you, you stupid man!' Her unconventional declaration passed into the folklore of the village, with Grandpa Joe still being ribbed about it up until his death.

'So are you going back?'

'Yes, definitely. I think Reenie and I are going to become the best of friends.'

Mattie took a deep breath of fresh, country air as she began to walk along the narrow footpath at the edge of the fallow field. The sun shimmered in dappled patches through the verdant branches of ancient oaks growing in the woodland where she had once played with Joanna, Jack and their other cousins as children. It was a route so familiar, so etched into her mind, that she knew each step by heart, catching herself closing her eyes as the sounds and smells of the sun-warmed fields mingled with her memories.

In the next field down, she'd first seen Nick Currie, the first true object of her affections, at the tender age of fifteen. He'd been playing football with a group of boys from school in the thick grass criss-crossed with tractor tracks, and Mattie had been walking with Joanna. She'd stopped dead, seeing him – something her sister had never let her forget – and thought she might never breathe again. Of course, the boy with golden hair and eyes so blue had never even noticed Mattie's existence, but the memory of her first experience of all-consuming attraction burned strong in her mind. Instantly, she thought of Asher. She had never really learned from that first foray, had she? When she met Asher for the first time at a birthday party in a Shrewsbury brasserie, she was as pole-axed by lust as she had been in these fields fifteen years before. Had she been blinded by their obvious chemistry? Was that why she hadn't seen him for the rat he really was?

She pressed on, her footsteps noticeably quicker as she kicked out her anger in the red dust of the sandstone path. The smell of disturbed sand mingled with the cool dankness of the woodland as the path momentarily crossed the boundary via a green oak gate, reminding Mattie of many hundreds of hide-and-seek games played here during Bell family picnics in the top field. So much had happened during the last few weeks that she needed the space provided by this solo excursion to try to unravel the mess of it all.

I don't have answers, she told herself. *Perhaps I never will.*

But one thing shone brightly in the fug of questions, memories and regrets: her emerging friendship with a certain once-famous octogenarian. Reenie had only begun to tell her story, but already Mattie was hooked. The old lady was unmistakably a performer, each new twist in her tale carefully structured to draw her audience in. Mattie tried to imagine her in her heyday, breaking hearts across Great Britain and further afield with her raven curls and devil-may-care attitude. On her most recent visit to Beauvale, Reenie had shown Mattie a handful of black and white photos including her very first publicity shot, taken not long after she joined the Ted Farnsworth Orchestra. Obviously young, and painfully thin from a childhood spent in poverty, she had a knowing expression beyond her years – and even in the stilted pose for the camera, her face exuded life and mischief. From what Mattie could remember of her voice, the combination would have been a killer package. No wonder Grandpa Joe had described his first hearing of a Silver Five record as 'like waking up from a long, grey dream and finding myself in a rainbow'.

If anyone needed to find themselves surrounded by colour right now, it was Mattie. She'd had enough dark soul-searching lately. It was time for a different focus.

As she climbed the stile that crossed the stone wall behind Kings Sunbury's post office and headed into the village, Mattie caught sight of the peppermint-green-and-yellow-striped awning above Bell Be-Bop across the village green. It made her smile – as it always did – and instantly she was reminded of the day she'd first thought of owning a vintage shop. Right from the beginning she'd pictured her shop exactly as it looked now. It would be filled with the kind of Fifties ephemera she'd loved to hunt for in vintage markets and antique shops, objects that seemed to embody the innocent optimism of the decade. War was over, the dark days of austerity and rationing were slowly receding and people were daring to dream of a brighter future. When Grandpa Joe talked about the 1950s his eyes would come alive. He said it was the 'greatest time to be young', with all the emerging music, films, technologies and innovations. The influence of the USA, with its extravagance and ultimate belief in the American Dream, must have seemed so glamorous, so exotic to a young generation searching for its own identity. Even now, as Mattie looked at a time long gone, she was inspired by the colour, hope and zest for life that the items she sold in her shop represented.

Reenie Silver had lived the dream in the 1950s – Mattie knew that already, from the little she had already learned. *Maybe*, she thought, passing the ludicrously expensive artisan confectioners and smiling at the thought of Reenie's contraband, *if I can experience Reenie's world through her memories, I can find that hope in my own life.*

'I didn't do too well in school,' Reenie admitted as she and Mattie sat on a bench overlooking Beauvale's small duck pond. They were throwing scraps of still-warm croissant to the resident ducks, who clearly appreciated the finer things in life. 'Never been good at taking orders from other people. I learned to read, mind, add up a bit and write my name. Those things stood me in good stead, but trigonometry, not so much. Always got picked for the lead in the Christmas play, though. I think my headmaster was a bit of an early fan. That, and me mam threatened to tell the neighbours about him and Mrs Ollerenshaw from the corner shop. You see, kid? Having friends in the right places always helps.'

'Did you get a job when you left school?'

'My dad wanted me to – he wasn't keen on me finding a chap and getting up the duff like me school friends. His mam was in service when she was twelve years old, and he thought it had made her the woman she was. Well, I didn't want to be a domineering *nutter* like Nan, so I made other plans.'

'What did you do?'

Reenie's eyes twinkled behind the darkened varifocal lenses of her glasses. 'Hopped on the first wagon outta there. Lied about my age and blagged a lift as far as Birmingham with a flour lorry, then persuaded a typewriter salesman to take me to London. I met a girl from Skeggy at King's Cross station who was visiting her wannabe-actress cousin in Shoreditch, and she offered me a bit of space on her floor. I stayed for three days, then when the girl went home, her cousin offered me the spare room in return for a bit of cleaning. Well, being the youngest of nine kids I knew about cleaning. My ma had me scrubbing our front step from five years old; I was black-leading the grate by the time I was eight and doing laundry from nine.'

'Wow.'

Reenie gave a shrug, the brass buttons on her jade-green wool jacket sparkling in the sunlight as she did so. 'Where I came from, you did what you had to do to get by. Never been afraid of a bit of graft, me – and it's helped me fall on my feet every time. So I kept my head down, got on with it and when I had a few spare hours I'd go over the ads in *The Stage*, looking for auditions. Four months in, I got lucky.'

Keen for more of Reenie's breakfast, one of the ducks waddled out of the water and stood expectantly at the old lady's jade-slingbacked feet. Reenie gave a loud tut, but threw another chunk of patisserie to her avid audience.

'Was it your first audition?' Mattie asked.

'First and only, as it turned out. Until the bleedin' BBC wanted me to screen-test for a TV special in 1975. But that's another story. Anyway, I was late getting out of the actress's flat and missed the bus. Had to leg it to get to the theatre in Covent Garden where the auditions were taking place. Ted Farnsworth and his Orchestra – I'd heard them on the wireless back in Liverpool, listening with me ma and sisters on a Friday night. They were proper famous and sounded like the bands in the Hollywood pictures I used to sneak into the cinema with my brothers to see. I knew nothing about singing with a band, but I knew I had a crackin' voice and I knew nobody wanted that job more than me. Turns out that's pretty much all you need to know to make your dream happen. Self-belief, Mattie Bell, that's what's required. And brazen *balls* the size of the Mersey Birds.'

Mattie burst into giggles. 'I can't believe I've just heard that phrase coming from a sweet old lady!'

'Sweet? There's nothing sweet about *this* old bird, love. Glad I'm entertaining you.'

'You are.' Mattie smiled. 'I love hearing your stories. They're amazing.'

'Amazing, is it? Already? We've five more *decades* of this stuff to come – I'd better up my game . . . Now, where was I?'

'On your way to the audition.' She could picture Reenie as a bright-eyed young girl, full of determination to make something of her life. Mattie wasn't sure she would have had the presence of mind in her teens to do anything other than dream. It took a special kind of spirit to take the risks Reenie Silver had done in her life – and Mattie couldn't help but be inspired by it.

'Ah, right you are.' Reenie rubbed her hands together, the collection of gold rings she wore nestled beneath wrinkled knuckles clinking together. 'So, there I was, fifteen years old pretending to be seventeen, with nothin' but bloody-minded ambition and holes in me jacket. When I reached the theatre the stage manager said they'd seen all they wanted for the day. Tried to stop me at the stage door, he did, but I wasn't having that. I hadn't come all that way and cleaned some jobbing actress's unmentionables for months just to be fobbed off. I pushed past him and marched right up on that stage like I owned it. Ted Farnsworth was walking out, but he sat right back down like his mother had just told him to. I sang "Here Comes the Night" from a sheet of music one of the guys before me had chucked in a bin in the wings. All in the wrong key, mind, but I made it work. Ted nearly had heart failure when he heard me sing – and he signed me on the spot. Two shillings and sixpence for every gig, nine songs a set. I thought I'd died and gone to heaven.'

'Wow. I bet your parents were proud.'

'They were when they saw the money I was sending home,' Reenie grimaced. 'Money always spoke louder than actions in our house. I didn't care. I was doing what I wanted, not stuck in some dead-end existence back at home. It was hard work, but not as hard as living a life you never chose for yourself.'

'That's inspirational. Really.'

'No, it's not. Bleedin' 'eck, Mattie, if you think getting off your backside to get what you want out of life is inspirational, you obviously haven't done much with yours. No offence,' she added quickly, flashing a mischievous smile at her companion. 'What do you want for *your* life, Mattie Bell?'

Mattie stared at her. She had been so caught up in Reenie's story that she hadn't even considered her own life. 'I want to be happy.' The answer seemed to sneak out from a place deep inside her. Faced with a sudden rush of emotion, she added, 'I mean, I want the shop to be a success. I want to be secure, find a home I'm happy with . . .'

'*NNNUURR*, wrong answer,' Reenie said, her buzzer impression so shrill it made Mattie jump. 'What you said first was far more interesting. I think we should talk about *your* story for a while.'

The hopeful duck at Reenie's feet, seeing the croissant gone, lifted its beak in disgust and splashed back into the pond, complaining loudly.

'I don't think so. Your life is much more interesting.'

The old woman surveyed her visitor with a stare that saw more than she said. 'Maybe. I'll ask you again, mind. So you'd better be thinking of a better answer than your last one for when I do. Cuts both ways, this arrangement. I'll tell you my stories if you tell me yours. There's a lot more to you than you're letting on, Matilda. Now, did you bring the chocolates?'

Unnerved by Reenie's sudden perceptiveness, Mattie felt herself shrinking back against the weathered oak of the bench as she handed over the pink-and-white-striped box.

Chapter Seven
'Who's Sorry Now?' –
Connie Francis

♪

14 March 1949

I am 14 today!

Mother made a cake and Father gave me a bicycle given to him by Silas Wright. His repairs have made it almost good as new. I cycled from the very top of Goldsforge Hill and it felt as if I was flying.

Bill Godfrey sent a card and a long letter. I am glad we stayed pen pals after the war. His tales of London are wonderful, even though where he lived before the Germans bombed no longer stands. He writes that it is dirty and much rebuilding is still to be done, but the stories of his friends and the japes they have make me long to see it. There is an entire railway system that runs under the ground. Just imagine! Shrewsbury doesn't have that, nor Bridgnorth.

I've told no one, but I have decided that I want to visit London. Perhaps even live there one day! It is my secret, marked here and nowhere else. I will make it happen, I swear it . . .

Mattie sat back and stared at the diary entry. It was the first mention of London in the memoirs and already it changed what she knew about Grandpa Joe's association with the city. She had always assumed that the year he'd spent there had been a necessity first and foremost, serving an apprenticeship to his uncle. But now she saw that a starry-eyed, fourteen-year-old Joe Bell had begun to dream about London seven years earlier. Was this what Grandpa Joe had promised Rev. Phil she would find here?

She rubbed her eyes and pushed back her dining chair. Her living room was a sea of boxes containing half of Joanna, Ethan and Ava's belongings. Already the characterless house felt a little more animated, as if bright echoes of her sister, nephew and niece were escaping out through the brown cardboard. Joanna was bringing the remainder in the morning, and in two days' time Mattie's new housemates would officially move in. She couldn't wait. Joanna was already working on a revamp of Bell Be-Bop's website: when she moved in fully she would do more shifts in the shop. Laurie loved her and Mattie was excited about what her sister could bring to the business.

She would share her latest discovery from the 1949 diary when Joanna arrived tomorrow. For now, she added it to the picture of Joe Bell forming in her mind. It was good to be learning new things about him; it took some of the sting from the last memories she had of her grandfather. Trading old for new, soothing the pain of loss with the promise of the past. It felt like her healing was beginning.

During Mattie's fourth Sunday visit to Beauvale, Reenie Silver finally asked the question she'd been dreading. Even though it was inevitable, given the amount of time Mattie had spent talking about her grandfather, she still found herself completely floored.

'So, what happened?' Reenie's question was sharper than a meat cleaver, severing their previous conversation topic with a single, swift blow.

'With what?'

'Something wasn't right when you lost your grandad. It's written all over your mush, love.'

Could Reenie Silver see so much when she hardly knew her? Mattie fought to keep her expression steady, but knew the old lady had her number. She sighed. 'There was a guy . . .'

Reenie clicked her dentures. 'Oh, Mattie, there always is. Married, was he?'

'What? No, he—'

'I mean, you'll get no judgement from me on that score, kid. "Let her that is without sin chuck the first stone," and all that. Sometimes you meet someone right at the wrong time and you just have to go with it . . .'

'Reenie, he wasn't married.'

'Gay, then?' She nodded sagely. 'Been there, got the rainbow T-shirt. Don't look so shocked, love, we did *have*

76

them in my day, you know. Just wasn't always that easy to tell, not if you were a girl from the Mersey like me. I broke my heart over two fellas who turned out to be the love of each other's lives once. Just look at poor Rock Hudson. Half the world thought he was shagging Doris Day, and look how wrong they all were!'

'Asher wasn't gay, either.'

'*Asher*?' This seemed to disappoint Reenie. 'Was his father bleedin' Methuselah? I swear parents are going backwards in naming their kids these days. Biblical names were all the rage when *my* folks were breeding. So what did this *Asher* have to do with your grandad, then?'

Mattie ignored Reenie's dismissal of her former fiancé's name, and began to explain. 'I met Asher when I was temping, trying to make enough money to set up my business. He pursued me like a terrier for six months before I agreed to go on a date with him – and we never looked back. I thought he was my soul mate, lame as that sounds. But Grandpa Joe hated Asher from the first time they met.'

'That's a grandparent's prerogative, Mattie. Not that I'd know, but I imagine I'd be *vicious*.'

'The thing is, he was never like that. Out of all of us, Grandpa Joe was the one to reserve judgement, to dole out second and third chances long after everyone else had given up on people. I couldn't understand why he disliked my boyfriend so much. I mean, even my mother loved him, and she's the least easily impressed person I know. I tried everything to get the two of them together – we'd "just happen" to meet up with Grandpa Joe and my sister

Joanna on Saturday mornings and suggest having lunch together; my dad conspired to invite Grandpa Joe and Asher out to play golf for the day on more than one occasion; my uncle Seth even pretended his car had broken down so that the two of them could come to his rescue. Nothing worked.'

The memory of her family's doomed attempts to reconcile Grandpa Joe with Asher chimed like a church bell in Mattie's mind. She'd hated the look of disgust on her grandfather's face whenever he saw her with Asher, as if he was ashamed of her. She'd never seen him like that: the alien, ugly frown, laying siege to a face usually so creased with laughter.

'Did you love the lad?'

'Yes.'

'Did you tell your grandfather that?'

Mattie had, over and over again, until the words themselves seemed to become meaningless, stripped of their power by her grandfather's stony silence. 'And then Asher proposed – and when I told Grandpa Joe, he gave me an ultimatum.'

Even now, after his death and six months since that awful conversation, Mattie could hardly believe it.

'You're kidding me.'

'I wish I was. Grandpa Joe said I had to choose. He wouldn't listen to me when I begged him not to make me.' His words still haunted her: *I won't have it, Mattie. I won't have you marry that man. It's your choice: him or me. It's up to you.*

'Bleedin' Nora. That's harsh.'

Emotion gripped Mattie's throat like a vice as she fought tears. 'What was I meant to do? I loved both of them – but Asher wanted to spend the rest of his life with me and I felt sure that if Grandpa Joe saw that in action, he'd come round eventually. So I chose Asher. And I walked away from my grandfather.'

Reenie's eyes were wide as she bit into another violet crème. 'And then he died?'

Mattie nodded, her voice little more than a whisper. 'He was diagnosed with late-stage cancer and given six months. He died after five and a half. And he refused to speak to me, even when he knew he wasn't going to survive.'

'Stubborn old beggar! I bet your ma was livid.'

Oh, if only . . . 'She thought we should have sorted everything out. I think she blamed me for how quickly the cancer spread. Which is crazy.'

'And your pa? Did he agree?'

Mattie sighed. 'Dad's a man of few words. I think he just wanted to grieve for his father privately. He knew how devastated Mum was – I think it was easier not to intervene. I couldn't reach either of them: what more could I have done?'

'Not a fat lot, judging by what you've told me. So where was your chap while all this was goin' on?'

Asher should have been by Mattie's side, supporting her even if her grandfather didn't. If he'd done that, it would have been easier. Instead, he'd said he wanted to renovate the house they'd recently bought together so that it would be ready in time for their wedding. He'd been so committed to making everything perfect, and Mattie had loved him for his practicality when everything else around them seemed to be descending into chaos.

Which is why she'd thought nothing of the unfamiliar car parked in the driveway of their soon-to-be home, knowing that Asher had called in the services of a small army of tradespeople to help him finish the job in time. And why she hadn't been surprised when she heard noises coming from the newly installed bathroom, where she presumed Asher – ever the perfectionist – was making last-minute alterations to the slate tiling he'd insisted they buy.

It had all been so *unimaginative*.

The cries of her fiancé and a vaguely familiar blonde quickly turning to shouts of indignation as Mattie had flung open the brand new shower door, sending their soap-covered, naked bodies sprawling across the expensive slate floor. The gut-twisting nausea when his blonde partner was revealed as the checkout woman from the DIY store where they'd spent a small fortune over the previous six months . . .

And worse than all of it – the realisation that Grandpa Joe had been right. Two days after his death. When nothing could ever be put right again.

'The little *knob*.' There was something to be said for Reenie's bluntness, given the evidence she'd heard. 'I hope you cut off his necessaries.'

Mattie laughed, despite the still-raw pain of her discovery. 'Maybe I should have done.'

'Probably couldn't have found them if you'd looked for 'em,' Reenie winked. 'Men like that are generally lacking in the balls department.' She patted Mattie's hand with red-painted fingernails. 'But now I know why you miss your grandpa so much. It's like unrequited love, isn't it?'

Mattie had never thought of it that way, but Reenie had nailed the aching, tearing sensation she'd been accosted by ever since. She was feeling the kind of pain usually reserved for a heart broken by love – only it wasn't the loss of Asher that was causing it. 'That's exactly how it feels. I miss him, Reenie. And I wish with all my heart that I'd chosen him over Asher. I wish I could put it right.'

'Ah, but the world would be built of stardust if wishes were bricks. Line from one of my songs from way back when, that. Load of old toss, most of it, but you know what I'm saying.'

Mattie nodded, feeling surprisingly lighter for her confession. 'Thank you.'

'What for?'

'For listening.'

'Love, I'm eighty-four years old. Listening is pretty much all I'm good for nowadays.' She folded her hands in her lap and watched one of the Beauvale residents struggling with a tray of teacups. 'Tsk. I see Trevor's doin' his Iron Man impression again. Trev! Love! You know what the doc said about carrying too much.'

The old man nearly dropped the tray in surprise, his face flushing when he turned towards Reenie. 'I'm just fine, thank you,' he called back in a voice so wobbly it was clear he wasn't at all.

Reenie shook her head. 'He's doing it to impress me.

Thinks if he can strain his poor old back carrying a tray of tea, I'll think he's Clark bleedin' Gable. Trev! Put them down, kid! Gaynor'll have your guts for garters if she sees you. Oi, *Chardonnay*,' she yelled in the direction of a sullen-looking young orderly. 'Stop pickin' your nail varnish and help our Trev, will you? If he puts his back out, it'll be your job on the block.'

Mattie watched this spectacle unfolding: the orderly slouching across to the teetering old man and catching the edge of the tray just as it started to droop at a dangerous angle; Trevor protesting at her intervention, while over in one corner Reenie's Three Furies made encouraging noises in support of their idol's actions. In the month that Mattie had been visiting Beauvale she had become accustomed to the unique soap opera playing out beneath the exposed barn beams – most of which, it had to be said, revolved around her elderly friend. From the comfort of her armchair, Reenie Silver was in the thick of it all, calling the shots when necessary, keeping a close eye on proceedings and controlling her comfortable, overheated kingdom often with no more than a raised eyebrow. It was impressive to watch, and made Mattie like her even more.

Chapter Eight

'Miss Otis Regrets (She's Unable to Lunch Today)' – Ella Fitzgerald – 1956 version

♪

'No, Jack, not like that. Tissue first, Bell Be-Bop stickers next and the card tucked into one of the flaps on top . . .' Mattie reached across the pile of vintage items to rescue a badly wrapped package from her cousin's hands. After a sudden rush of international orders on her shop's eBay store she was glad of help – and the timing of Jack's latest break between freelance copywriting jobs was fortuitous. But his self-professed expert packaging skills were proving to be less than impressive.

Sitting on the floor of the shop surrounded by mint-green tissue paper and bubble wrap, her cousin groaned. 'Three months visiting Reenie Silver has turned you into a diva. Next thing we know, you'll be demanding a star on the shop door.'

Mattie threw a roll of parcel tape at him, but didn't really mind his jibe. Visiting her new friend at Beauvale had become the highlight of her week, and behind it other areas of her life were quietly settling. Joanna and the children were fully moved in, their laughter and joyful noise filling the house with light and warmth, making going home a pleasure, not a battle. Slowly but surely Mattie was rebuilding the relationship with her mum, which felt like a significant step. Above all else, she felt happier than she had for a long time – as if a fair wind was steering her life.

'Maybe I should have one,' she replied. 'Reenie has one on her bathroom door, you know.'

'You're kidding?'

'Nope. A genuine gold glitter star that she says she took from her dressing room when she was performing in Los Angeles. She also has a mirror with lights around it, like you see in old movies. I think it's fabulous.'

Jack gave up trying to find the end of the tape on the roll. 'I like it when you talk about Reenie. You light up. It's almost as if you've fallen in love.'

It was a strange observation, but as Mattie considered it, she realised Jack was right. In a way, she *had* fallen for Reenie – for her vitality and the vivid pictures of the glamorous Fifties her memories drew. Befriending her had become so much more than just a link to Grandpa Joe: it was as if she welcomed Mattie into a bright, hopeful world.

The experience had certainly inspired Mattie in her shop. She had spent the past week building a new display, filled with objects from 1956: concert programmes from

London, Birmingham and Glasgow from that year; vinyl records by Bill Haley & His Comets, The Dream Weavers, Pat Boone and Frankie Laine; a curvy maroon Bakelite Tesla 'Talisman' transistor radio; an original film poster for *High Society* and a Monte-Sano & Pruzan semi-fitted empire-line coat from New York, amongst other things. Grandpa Joe had talked about 1956 as his 'London bachelor year', and while he'd given few details of what he'd done during his year in the capital, it had retained an air of intrigue for Mattie since she was a teenager. She had been tempted to skip straight to his diary from this year, but had decided to read the diaries chronologically, for fear of missing an important detail in her search for the real Joe Bell. Certainly she'd learned much about him already: far from being the cautious, well-behaved man she had always known, in his childhood and teens he had been a dreamer and sometimes a rebel.

18 September 1951

Harvest is full upon us and the work is so hard.
Somehow it feels worse this year than any other.
Father is in his element, his eyes bright and his face
red as he works, and I can see Mother casting
admiring glances in his direction. It's as though she
only sees the man she married at this time of year.
He laughs and jokes with the hired hands, charms the
grain merchants and holds his own in debates around
the bar at The Crescent and Owl.
*   I will never be like him.*

I hate the early rising, the work that breaks my back from before sunup to after sunset. Each day it is harder to pull my body from my bed. I feel an old man, yet I am barely 16. How can I stand another fifty years of this?

I am not a farmer. I never will be. I want more. I want London.

The dream is still alive from my ninth year. I am good with numbers and calculations, not scythes and seed drills. Uncle Charles has an accountancy practice in London and I have often heard Father dismissing his younger brother's profession. He thinks my uncle abandoned the Bell tradition when he chose it. But he doesn't know I am more like his brother than like him.

I long to tell Father. But would it break his heart?

Working alone in the shop the next day, Mattie mulled over the diary entry she had read the previous night. All she knew of her great-grandfather was that he had been born with the countryside in his blood. A fifth-generation farmer, running White Tudor Farm had been all Joseph George Bell senior had known from the age of sixteen, when his father had died during the harvest at just forty-nine years of age. In his diaries, Grandpa Joe had made no attempt to hide his fear of his own father. Was this what he had meant about the diaries revealing the man he really was?

Mattie looked up from the time-yellowed pages, a stab of irritation hitting home. If he knew what it was like to want something so badly, why had he made *her* choose?

'So, this is where you hide all day?' The perfect

red-lipped smile of Reenie Silver greeted her from the shop doorway, the brass bell above the door jingling a welcome fanfare.

Mattie stashed the 1951 diary beneath a stack of invoices. 'How lovely to see you! What brings you here?'

'I had a free morning so I thought I'd pop out to see this shop of yours.' Reenie's bright eyes surveyed the interior. 'Blimey, this is a blast from the past. It's a bit disconcerting to find out you're *vintage*. Maybe you should stick me in a corner with a price tag round my neck.'

Mattie smiled. 'Nobody could afford you.'

'Smooth, Mattie Bell, very smooth. Keep talkin' like that and we'll be the best of chums. So, are you going to give me the guided tour?'

'Certainly.' Mattie moved from behind the Thunderbird counter and offered Reenie her arm. 'Step this way.'

As she escorted her friend around the carefully curated displays, Mattie couldn't help stealing glances to see her reaction. Reenie wore an odd smile, a faraway wistfulness that hinted at a whole world beyond the objects she was seeing.

Finally, they arrived at the 1956 display and Reenie stopped as if a hand had been pressed to her chest.

'1956. The year that changed everything.' She chuckled, but her eyes didn't smile. 'Hark at me, eh? I sound like a Channel Five documentary.' She shook her head, pristine lilac curls swaying gently. 'The year that made me and nearly broke me. I made my biggest leap and my biggest mistake in '56.'

'You did?'

'Year I left the group, wasn't it? Set out on my own, Miss Reenie Silver off to conquer the world. Ma used to say to watch out for holes when you walked on clouds. She was right. '56 was the year I got everything I ever wanted, but it cost me more than I could afford to pay. Still, you live and learn, eh?'

'So, did she say what her biggest mistake was?' Joanna had been listening to Mattie's account of Reenie's visit with ever-increasing wonder as they sat at her dining table that evening.

'Only that she regretted how it ended with The Silver Five. I suppose it's normal to regret a break-up in some way.'

'Like you and Asher?'

Mattie glared at her sister. 'No. I don't regret that at all. I only wish I'd never got involved with him in the first place.'

'No second thoughts? Not even now the dust has settled?'

'Absolutely not. I lost more than I ever found with Asher Jenkins.' She pushed the stab of hurt away and gazed out of the open French doors to where Ethan and Ava were playing a giggling game of tag in the back garden. 'I'm going to find out what Reenie's regret is, though. I think she wanted to tell me today.'

'Double helpings of violet crèmes this Sunday morning, then?' Joanna's eyes sparkled with mischief.

'I think it might take more than that . . .' Mattie's mind whirred with possibility. If 1956 was a year that had altered Reenie's life, as it had Grandpa Joe's, surely that wasn't a coincidence? Maybe Mattie could solve both mysteries and find – what, exactly? Redemption? Closure? Whatever it was, she felt a strong compulsion to uncover the truth Reenie had so deliciously dangled in Bell Be-Bop.

7 January 1955

My secret is out.

I have never seen Father so downcast. I fear I may have broken him. But when he talked this evening of my taking the farm when he retires, I couldn't hold my silence any longer. He said he knows what's best for me. I said he was wrong.

Mother has said nothing since my revelation. She is knitting in her chair by the hearth, her eyes set firm on me. But I did the right thing.

I will say it again, I DID THE RIGHT THING. I will die if I stay here. There is a world beyond the farm boundary, and Joe Bell is destined to explore it. I am not a farmer. I don't have the love of the land coursing through my veins like Father does. I have tried so hard to please everyone, to make it happen. But I am almost twenty years old and if I don't break free now, I may as well be buried alive to rot here.

I'm scared, though. There was no resolution tonight and I can't tell what my father is thinking. I will lay low until he talks to me again . . .

8 February 1955

A month! It has been an entire month since I told Father I didn't want the farm and still nothing! Every day I think, This will be the day! – but it's as though he has forgotten I ever said it.

Today I asked Mother and she didn't answer. She thinks me selfish, and maybe I am. What if I have lost their respect but am still to remain here? I can't stand not knowing what my fate will be.

I have thought of little else since that night. Without my parents' blessing I must take matters into my own hands. I am going to leave. There's no other solution. It breaks my heart, but what choice do I have?

I've been collecting essential supplies, have a little money saved and am ready to go. If the moon is full tonight, I will leave the farm forever.

9 February 1955

My plan failed.

Amos Miller caught me crossing his land at midnight and told me to go home. He said I owed Father more than a midnight disappearance. Why did I choose the shortcut when the open lane would have kept me hidden from the neighbours?

I'm back in my room again and the look on Mother's face when she heard what I'd been trying to do is enough to make me remain here. Until Father is

*ready to talk to me, I'm trapped again. And I don't
know what will happen . . .*

Mattie was still thinking about the diary entry when
she took Reenie out to the beautiful riverside town of
Bewdley for the afternoon. Reading her grandfather's plan
– and the desperation its failure caused him – was like
reading the words of a stranger.

This is who I was . . .

Was it? Why, then, did he make her choose between
him and Asher?

Pushing the thought away, she smiled at Reenie. They
had found a bench on the footpath overlooking the River
Severn, and Reenie had fallen quiet for a while. Mattie
was reminded of the easy silences that would settle between
her and Grandpa Joe when they sat together on Goldsforge
Hill above the village on heady summer afternoons. Mattie
felt a soothing sense of her grandfather pass by. *Those*
were the memories she should hang on to, not how it had
all ended.

'Can I ask you something?' she said, when enough time
had passed.

'Sure.'

'You said in the shop that 1956 was your biggest regret.
What happened?'

Reenie flicked a stone with the end of her walking cane.
'My group, The Silver Five. It was my fault it ended.'

Mattie turned to her, taking in the news. In every conversation she'd had with Grandpa Joe about his favourite
group, he had always insisted that the pressures of show

business had been responsible for their decision to disband. He had never blamed anyone other than the industry that processed bright young starlets at an alarming rate, spitting them out as soon as trends moved on. What would he have made of this?

'How was it your fault?'

Reenie let out a sigh, and fiddled with the gold charms on her bracelet. 'Our biggest gig – the one we'd waited to happen – I scuppered it. Me, the one who'd had enough ambition for all of us. Saturday, 29 September 1956 at the Palm Grove, Soho. Even with our manager's grand schemes we hadn't been considered to appear there for the best part of four years. It was the kind of place you dreamed of headlining. Chandeliers, crystal and gold everywhere and a dance floor so polished it shone like glass. It looked like an expensive set from a Fred and Ginger movie. Oh, and lovely Jacob Kendrick, the owner – now he was mighty pretty to look at, too. The *crème de la crème* played the Palm Grove: Sinatra, Ted Heath's band – he was the British answer to Glenn Miller, you know – Ella Fitzgerald, Vera Lynn. Not a ragtag band of kids like us, all skinny limbs and hopeful faces. But we had our break when a scout from the club snuck into one of our concerts in Hackney and invited us over.

'There's not much I regret, kid, but that's the one that sticks in me throat when I think of my life. We never spoke again. Some of them tried, but – water under the bridge and that. All over, just like that, on the night of our biggest gig. Amazing how you can go from living in each other's pockets every day for four years, to five total strangers overnight. They say the business does that – she's a cruel mistress. She'll snap your neck when you're riding high. I've seen it in my own life enough times.'

'What happened?'

'It was a long time ago, love. No use going into it all now.'

'But you said it was your fault . . .'

'And none of the band would disagree. But *sixty years*, Mattie! Grudges held that long leave grooves in your hands and twists in your spine. You can't change something that big. I just have to resign myself to it.'

'You okay, Mattie?' Percy's question jolted Mattie from her thoughts.

'Oh, I'm sorry, Percy, I didn't hear you come in.'

'Wherever you were just now looked like a place worth visiting,' her customer grinned.

'She's been like it all week,' Laurie said, bustling in from the stockroom. 'Away with the fairies. Or should I say, the *Reenies*?'

Mattie ignored her assistant. So what if she'd been preoccupied since her last visit to Beauvale? It made a pleasant change to be thinking about something other than Grandpa Joe and Asher. It was a mystery that had her hooked.

'Reenies?'

'She's being rude about a friend I've made recently. Don't encourage her.'

'Ah, I see.' He leant across the counter and added, with a wink: 'Jealous, probably.'

'I heard that!' Laurie marched over to them. 'And for your information, Percy Walker, I don't need to be jealous of a troublesome OAP.'

'Reenie is far from your average OAP,' Mattie returned. 'She's famous. Or used to be. Do you remember The Silver Five?'

Percy's smile was warm and wistful. 'Of course I do! I bought my mother their record – what was it now? Oh yes – "*Because you loved me, I can face today, chase my blues away and smile . . .*"' Laughing, he grabbed a very surprised Laurie and waltzed her round the shop floor, singing Reenie's biggest hit.

'Ooh! No! Put me *down*, Percy!' Laurie protested, blushing profusely and trying her best not to look like she was enjoying the experience.

Mattie watched the pair dancing across the oak floor-boards and imagined herself as a young girl of nine or ten, spinning across the quarry-tiled floor of her grand-parents' farmhouse kitchen as Grandpa Joe twirled her around, the old familiar boom of his voice warming every surface it reverberated off. Those times where she had been swept up in the memories he held dearest had been the happiest of her life so far, and she longed to reclaim that feeling of complete safety and utter freedom.

Reenie should see this, she thought. *She should see what her music means to so many people . . .*

That was it!

If Reenie could understand how loved she was – and how much The Silver Five were still missed today – perhaps she would change her mind and put things right now.

She'd said one member, Tommy Mullins, was still in contact with all the original members. He knew where they lived now, and even arranged a yearly get-together (which, of course, Reenie had declined to attend every year). It was remarkable that they were all alive – but how long would that be the case? Very soon, it would be sixty years since the fateful booking at the Palm Grove.

It was all Mattie could do not to squeal out loud as the idea grew. Sixty years – a significant anniversary: what better way to honour the memory of what The Silver Five had been and finally reconcile its members, than to bring all of them together by this date?

But would it even be possible to bring all five original members of the singing group back together in the same room? She doubted they lived close to one another. Reenie had been firm about her former colleagues not seeing her living in sheltered accommodation, however grand Beauvale was. Could Mattie bring them all to another venue for a tearful reunion? Without knowing exactly what it was that had caused their split in 1956, it was difficult to know whether this would work. If Reenie had chosen to ignore them for all these years, why would any of them – excepting Tommy, perhaps – be willing to make such a journey at all?

Mattie's need to know what Reenie had done on the night of their final appearance was stronger than ever. If it was something unforgiveable, her clever idea would be over before it had even begun. She *had* to persuade Reenie to talk about it.

'If only they still had clubs now like they did in the

Fifties,' Percy sighed, returning a flushed Laurie to the sales desk. 'Girls, you would have loved them. The lights, the live bands, the glamorous surroundings – I went to Soho once, and the clubs there were beyond belief.'

Mattie recalled Reenie's words about the best club venues, and wished she could have seen them. Her love of vintage things often led to her think she'd been born in the wrong era. Everything she'd heard and read about the optimism and hope of the 1950s made it alluring. 'Perce, did you ever visit the Palm Grove?'

'Sadly not. But some of my friends from London went often. Why?'

'No reason. I just wondered if you knew what happened to it.'

Percy mopped his brow with a handkerchief. 'Most of the famous places closed in the seventies and eighties. Bulldozed, most likely. Prime real estate like that in the centre of London? I imagine the developers were all over it like a rash. You could check online – there are some good archive sites dedicated to the Soho clubs.'

Mattie didn't hesitate. As Laurie and Percy talked about the music he'd loved from the Fifties, she grabbed her laptop and slipped into the storeroom at the back of the shop. The initial spark of an idea fizzed and grew in her mind as she typed '*former palm grove nightclub soho*' into the search engine. Would it still be there after all these years?

Scrolling through the first page of results, she found nothing, bar mentions on a few websites dedicated to 1950s music history. But when she clicked the next page, the third entry from the top made her breath catch. Heart thumping, she opened the link – and suddenly it was as if the small storeroom was invaded by a burst of light and colour and sound.

It was still there. Not as the Palm Grove, but as a comedy club. The website carried two photographs of the interior, side by side: one taken in 1952, the other in 2015. While the décor was different, it appeared that the auditorium at least was virtually unchanged. This was it! The perfect venue for a reunion – for the past to be put right, in the exact place where it had fallen apart . . .

But would it be possible to get into the club, let alone stage an event there? Would Reenie want to go back to the place where her biggest mistake had taken place? And what about the others? Would they want such a physical reminder of how their group disintegrated? Mattie thought about the house she'd bought with Asher – the house currently on the market, awaiting another starry-eyed buyer. She couldn't even bring herself to drive down the road on which it stood anymore. She certainly couldn't imagine being taken back into the bathroom to revisit the place where her life had fallen apart. What if Reenie's former friends felt the same?

Maybe she should think of something else. Sixty-year grudges were unlikely to be solved by a publicity stunt and a lot of wishful thinking.

Scrolling back through the history of the Palm Grove, the tussle continued in Mattie's mind. She couldn't shake the spark of excitement that fizzed within. It was *still* there. Perhaps she was meant to discover that today – just like she was meant to meet Reenie Silver at Beauvale's Memory Day. After Asher, Mattie had dropped her long-held belief that everything happened for a reason – but now she thought of how much happier she would be if she could believe that again.

If finding the former Palm Grove was a sign, shouldn't she act upon it? This was a chance to follow her heart. Reenie had said she regretted what happened at the Palm Grove – the events that led to The Silver Five's sudden, devastating end. It was the only regret she'd admitted to in the months Mattie had been visiting her. That *had* to mean something. Maybe it wasn't just Mattie who needed a shot at redemption: maybe Reenie Silver needed this, to end her days happily. And maybe she had been waiting all these years for someone like Mattie Bell to make it possible.

Chapter Nine

'Hit and Miss' –
The John Barry Seven

♪

'Reenie shouldn't be long,' smiled a young nurse as Mattie took a seat in the day room. She was one of the youngest members of staff at Beauvale, but seemed to have an easy rapport with the residents. Reenie called her 'Chatty Charlene' and meant it as the highest praise: *Always sunny, that one. Remembers every conversation you've had and knows how to natter like the best of them* . . . 'Are you off out anywhere nice?'

'We're popping over to Bridgnorth,' Mattie replied, the first stage of her plan being revealed. 'Reenie was telling me about a tea room there she particularly likes, so I thought I'd treat her.'

'That's lovely. You know, she's been a lot brighter since she met you,' Charlene confided, ducking her head slightly in case any of the other residents heard. 'I'd been worried

99

about her before, what with her hip operation and everything.'

'Oi, missy, should my ears be burning?' Reenie chuckled as the nurse jumped to attention. 'Relax, love, you know I'm hoping you're both talking about me. Occupational hazard in my business. The time to worry is when people *aren't*.'

'I'll leave you to it,' Charlene blushed. 'Have a nice day out.'

'Day out?' Reenie settled into a chair. 'You busting me out of this joint, Mattie Bell?'

'For a couple of hours, if you'd like?'

'Would I like? That's more than enough time for mischief and a decent cuppa tea. Let's go!'

Bridgnorth was a picture in the warm sunshine, and as Mattie escorted Reenie along High Street in High Town, she congratulated herself for choosing today to visit. It couldn't have been a more perfect setting for the proposal she was about to make to Reenie. The town looked beautiful, decked out in red, white and blue bunting for the annual summer festival and with swaying baskets dripping with gorgeous flowers swaying from every lamppost for Britain in Bloom. It was already buzzing with visitors both local and global, drawn to the pretty market town with its deep river, romantic castle walls and steam railway.

'I've always loved it here,' she said as they walked, ghosts of a thousand memories of similar strolls with Grandpa Joe, her parents and Joanna and Jack overlaying the scene she saw today.

'It's a special place all right. First time I visited Beauvale

I came here for coffee afterwards to mull it all over. It was the walk along this street that swung it for me.'

'I can see why.' Mattie stopped outside a gorgeously decorated shop front stuffed with vintage-looking items and chalk-painted furniture, stands of fresh-cut flowers and potted roses adding a bouquet of scent outside the door. 'Shall we?'

At the back of the fancy goods shop nestled a small café decorated with pages from vintage comic books. Mattie saw the broad smile of her friend as they found a table. It was *perfect*.

She waited until their order of afternoon tea arrived and made herself drink a cup of tea before she spoke, but it was all she could do to contain her excitement. All night she'd thought of her idea, how wonderful it would be and how it could help Reenie come to terms with her past. It made a change to spend the night awake from excitement, instead of the constant rollover of regret.

'You remember what you told me about the Palm Grove last week?'

Reenie's eyes narrowed over the rim of her violet-covered teacup. 'Here it comes.'

'Sorry?'

'You've been like a coiled spring all morning. The last time I was with someone that jumpy, it was my third husband on the day he proposed. You're not thinking of popping the question, now, are you?'

'Ha – nothing like that. But it is a kind of proposal.'

'Spit it out, girl!'

'Okay.' Mattie took a breath, acutely aware of so much

more riding on this than she'd anticipated. 'I know you said you couldn't have the rest of The Silver Five come to visit you at Beauvale . . .'

'Absolutely *not*.'

'What if you were all to meet at the Palm Grove instead?'

Reenie snorted into her tea. 'Give over, Mattie! That place closed years ago.'

'What if it still existed?'

'It doesn't. It's probably been bulldozed and one of them swanky million-pound bedsit complexes built on its ashes. All of the great Soho clubs went that way.'

'The Palm Grove didn't.'

'I told you: it closed years back.'

'The nightclub did, but the building is still there. It's a comedy club now – and you'll never guess who owns it.'

'Richard Branson? That smug bloke off the easyJet adverts? I don't know.'

'It's called Kendrick's.'

The name hung in the pastel-hued air between them. Reenie's intake of breath was a little shaky; when she spoke, it was as if the wind had been snatched from her sails. 'Kendrick's?'

Mattie nodded, thrilled by her response. 'Jacob Kendrick's grandsons own the club.'

'He had *boys*? He'd have loved that . . .'

'Listen, I know you don't want the others seeing you in a retirement village. But what if they didn't? What if you brought them back together at the Palm Grove – putting things right at the very place where everything was broken?' As Mattie spoke, she could picture every detail of the event: five former friends reunited, with members of the press invited to document the scene. It would be a celebration of one of British rock 'n' roll's golden groups, a coup for both the artistes and the venue that almost hosted them sixty years before. 'We could organise a celebration dinner there, with a photocall for the press – make it a celebration of everything you all achieved.'

'I don't think so . . .'

'Don't say no yet, Reenie, just think about it. You could show them how sorry you are by giving them the limelight they all deserved back then. By reminding the world how great The Silver Five were – what a legacy you've created for British pop music. Before Cilla, before Cliff, before Lulu – the five singers who electrified British teenagers after the dark days of the war, who brought the new optimism and hope for the future before the American music invasion . . .'

'I said, *no*. It's a sweet thought, kid, but it's too late. What's done is done.'

'But if you had a chance to put things right – to change how it ends . . .' She hated the whine of desperation in her voice.

'Is this *you* talking now? I *get it*, Mattie. I'm sorry for your loss. But I'm not the magic bullet that makes it all go away.'

Totally wrong-footed, Mattie tumbled over her words. 'I – I didn't mean . . . That's not why I said . . . I'm not asking you to make things right for me. All I know is that I wouldn't wish the hurt and anger and loss I've felt since my grandpa died on anyone. I've carried it for just over six months. I can't imagine bearing that for sixty years.'

Reenie set her jaw firm and pulled her handbag onto her lap. 'I'm ready to go home now. Thanks for the tea.'

Chapter Ten

'Softly, Softly' –
Ruby Murray

♪

Mattie was still kicking herself the following day. By six p.m. she realised she'd spent all day thinking of alternative ways she could have asked Reenie. Knowing Joanna and the children were having tea with her mum, Mattie decided to sort stock for a couple of hours instead of heading straight home. Since Grandpa Joe's death, Mattie had cherished spending time in her shop. She could keep busy, play music she remembered sharing with her grandfather and escape to a time filled with glamour and optimism.

Spending time with Reenie had challenged her rose-tinted view somewhat, but the wistfulness with which her friend spoke of the 1950s fired Mattie's imagination.

'Tell me about the glamour,' she'd asked Reenie once. 'I imagine it to be a really glamorous time.'

'Not always. Not for most of the time. But we *dreamed*

of glamour and that kind of made it seem possible, if you see what I mean. Me and the girls in The Silver Five spent most of our time in hired dresses we were forever having to mend in dingy dressing rooms with only one working light bulb. But when we were on stage, we *were* the glamour. Some of the music halls we played in Europe hadn't long been open after the war. Some of them were little more than a shell. But the people wanted music, you see. Music heals the heart the way nothing else can. Berlin was the best for that. We were doing our set, and beneath the spotlights I could see men and women on the front row in tears. That's when you realise what you're doing isn't just "entertaining". You're helping people escape – and the Good Lord knows, after that war there were plenty that needed rescuing.'

'What about after you went solo?' Mattie had asked, careful to avoid the subject that Reenie had so far resisted broaching.

'Oh-ho, that's when the glamour *really* started!' Reenie's smile had been pure pride. 'Talk about wining and dining! Rico took me to all the parties – bought me dresses straight from Paris, had me going to the best hairstylists in London, the works. He said he was investing in me. He wanted me to look like a star already.'

Since that conversation, Mattie had searched the web for details of the enigmatic impresario 'Rico'. Ten years before Brian Epstein began to mastermind the careers of the Beatles and Cilla Black, Rico was one of a clutch of up-and-coming music moguls, determined to find the brightest stars in the British music scene. While his trademark silver silk suits, diamond cufflinks and sweep of perfectly waved black hair hinted at Latin roots, in reality Rico had begun life in the far less exotic surrounds of Castle Bromwich, Birmingham, as plain old Harry Slack. Reinventing himself following his relocation to London in the early 1950s, Slack spent a year blagging entry to the best parties, schmoozing the influential executives from fledgling music labels and, by all accounts, outright lying his way into their good books. The Silver Five had been his first real success, formed by a combination of covert talent-scouting missions among the music clubs of Soho and Chelsea and adverts placed in *The Stage* newspaper, seeking 'young, good-looking male and female singers for a standalone group'. He had discovered Reenie when she was singing for Ted Farnsworth's Orchestra and had been so taken by her voice and presence that his idea to form the group had been birthed.

Reenie talked about Rico with fondness, but Mattie always felt that there was something else in the practised lightness of her voice whenever he was mentioned. It was more than flippant, the kind of response she had heard her mum give when talking about people at her Women's Institute meetings that she didn't really like. One thing was certain: Rico had definitely gone all out to charm young Irene Silverman.

'Oh kid, the *parties* he took us to – honestly, you'd've *died*! Champagne towers, diamonds everywhere, the best in the business schmoozin' and carousing, and there's little old me from Woodbine Street, Liverpool, slap bang in the middle of it all! They said I was going to be the British

Brenda Lee – the female Elvis Presley. Bigger than Alma Cogan, they said, bigger than Connie Francis . . . I once had a turn around the dance floor with Tommy Steele, you know, who back then was the handsome, snarlin' boy of the moment. He blanked Petula Clark for me! I think we might have had a thing for a bit. Or maybe just a snog and a fumble in a back room . . . good days, Mattie. Good old days . . .'

Mattie hung the last garment on the rail and broke up the cardboard storage box, adding it to the pile beside her. Stretching the stiffness from her legs, she chided herself again for not persuading Reenie to reunite with her former group. She shouldn't have mentioned it. Or at least, she should have thought more carefully about how to present the idea. How was she ever going to fulfil her promise to Grandpa Joe now? If only Reenie had agreed to the plan . . .

She stopped herself. Reenie had every right to refuse Mattie's meddling in her private affairs. It was selfish of her to expect otherwise. Laurie and Jack had been right: she was banking on the old lady to be the solution to her problems. It didn't matter if The Silver Five were never reconciled. That was Reenie's decision, and if Mattie considered herself a friend to her, she had to respect it.

'It's just that it would have made him so happy,' she said aloud to the vintage items. 'But I'm an idiot for thinking it could work.'

The Blue Lady portrait on the wall opposite gave her a wistfully sympathetic look. Over in the corner, the tea chest stacked with old 78 rpm vinyl seemed to glow through the dust that lined its sides. Grandpa Joe's old tawny-brown Bakelite radio on the shelf above the till had its soothing half-smile still, as if to say that nothing had really changed. *I'll find a way through this*, she promised herself. *I will be happy again.*

The sound of The Platters' 'Only You' from her mobile sent Mattie scrambling to her feet to fetch it from the counter. She had chosen the ringtone when planning her new future with Asher, but hadn't changed it because she remembered being twirled around the farmhouse kitchen by Grandpa Joe to the song.

'Hello?'

'Hi, Mattie. It's me.'

Suddenly Mattie felt sick. Sinking heavily onto the chair beside the counter, she closed her eyes. She had been dreading this moment for weeks. 'I don't have anything to say to you.'

She heard Asher cough on the other end of the call, something he always did when he was nervous. Too right he should be nervous! This was the first time he'd attempted to talk to her after she'd discovered him with Debs the DIY cashier. 'We have to talk. It's about the house. And – things . . .'

Things? By 'things' did he mean trifling details such as breaking her heart, betraying her trust and not even pretending to be sorry when he was found out?

'I'm busy. You'll have to talk to my solicitor.'

'And what if I want to talk to you? Come on, Mattie – whatever's happened between us, we can still be friends.'

The suggestion jarred her heart. 'No. No we can't, Asher.'

'You say that now. But we still need to talk. I owe you an explanation . . .'

'I'm not interested in your excuses. Goodbye.'

Ending the call, she took a deep breath that shuddered out into the quietness of the shop. She hadn't been ready to talk to him, and wished she'd checked the number before answering. The sudden re-emergence of his voice served only to remind her of how much she had lost because of him.

Just then, her phone rang again. Was Asher really so thick-skinned? Snatching up her phone, she growled into it, 'What is it now?'

'Bleedin' hell, Mattie, who rocked your cage?'

Mattie quickly stood, like a naughty child found out. 'Hi, Reenie. I'm sorry. Are you all right? It's past ten o'clock.'

'The night is young, Matilda! Matter of fact, it's Rave Night here at Beauvale. Our Trev's just spiked the punch with Advocaat . . . No, I'm kidding. I wanted to talk to you and it couldn't wait. Thing is, I'm *in*.'

What was that supposed to mean? 'In Beauvale?'

'Well yes, *obviously* I'm in Beauvale. I mean, I'm *in*. For the trip. For the gig.'

Mattie couldn't breathe. She began to walk across the shop floor to the bay window, which was speckled with streetlamp-illuminated raindrops.

'Mattie? Kid? You still there?'

'Yes – I'm here. I don't know what to say. What made you change your mind?'

'I talked it over with – well, a few people, actually. And you're right. I owe that lot an apology. While I'm still

110

breathing, not after I'm gone. And I might not get another chance. I –' the smallest crack sounded in her voice, and the suddenness of it made Mattie's skin prickle. 'I had a bit of a turn this afternoon. Nothin' to worry yourself about, mind; it'll take a lot more than a bit of a wobbly old head to bump me off . . . But it got me thinking. Turns out I'm not as invincible as I thought I was.' There was a pause, and Mattie could hear Reenie's breath coming in short, sharp bursts. 'You've gone very quiet, love. Am I too late to be asking now?'

Mattie fought back tears as she shook her head. 'No, you're not too late. This is the best news I've had in a really long time.'

'Okay, good. *Excellent*, Mattie. We're going to have the *best* time!'

Ending the call and bursting into long-held-back tears of relief, Mattie suspected Reenie was right . . .

Chapter Eleven

'The Things That I Used to Do' – Guitar Slim and his Band

♪

Mattie arranged to take Reenie to visit Kendrick's the following week. The first part of their plan was straightforward: they would have lunch at the club and ask to see the owner. Reenie would explain who she was, and try to blag a tour of the venue for her to reminisce. *Then* the tricky part would come.

'Butter him up, then *wham*! Hit him with our dastardly scheme!' Reenie exclaimed as they sat opposite each other on the train heading to London. 'It can't fail.'

Mattie crossed her fingers beneath the table in first class that Reenie had insisted on booking for their journey. 'Let's hope not.'

An hour later she helped Reenie out of a black cab, and the pair faced the club. It was a brick building at one corner of a small square – unremarkable from the outside, except for a row of lights around a curved porch entrance and three sets of brass-edged double doors.

'This is odd.' Reenie was staring up at the building as if seeing a world around it that no longer existed.

'Are you okay?' Mattie had spent so long being excited about her idea that she hadn't fully considered she was playing with someone else's memories.

'Long time ago, kid. Lots happened since. Let's get inside, eh?'

A young man dressed in a white shirt, black waistcoat and jeans met them as they entered the former nightclub.

'How can I help, ladies?' he asked in a strong Northern Irish brogue.

'We have a reservation for lunch, under Bell,' Mattie said. 'I'm afraid we're a little early.'

'Not a problem,' he beamed, shaking both their hands. 'We have plenty of tables. Come in and I'll get you both settled.' He pushed open a set of black doors and held them open for Mattie and Reenie to pass into the heart of the club.

Mattie heard a sharp intake of breath beside her. She kept her eyes ahead, but gave Reenie's hand a firm squeeze.

The interior of the club was painted almost completely black, with the exception of a pair of dusky red stage curtains that appeared to have hung there for many years. In the former circle near the entrance, round wooden tables and black leather curved benches formed little bays where a few people were eating. Soft jazz played from concealed speakers, and behind the long black bar a barman was polishing glasses and gazing into space. Mattie tried to mentally

113

superimpose the image of the Palm Grove in its heyday over this mostly monochrome venue. It seemed a little sad, as if draped in mourning garments for its former life.

Reenie was very quiet as they walked to their table, and Mattie didn't want to intrude on her thoughts. But what must it be like to see a place from your past looking so different? She remembered once going back to Cheltenham, where she had been a student, and the numb shock she'd felt on discovering her former digs were now boarded up and abandoned. It had felt like losing a friend.

'I'm Derry, bar manager here. Pleased to meet you both,' the man said, offering his arm to steady Reenie as she sat down. 'I'll get your menus. Make yourselves comfy and if you'd like drinks, you can order them from the bar.'

Reenie's knuckles were white as she clutched her handbag on her lap, her eyes haunted by a thousand ghosts Mattie couldn't see. She waited a few minutes to give her friend space, but soon her concern was growing.

'Do you still want to be here, Reenie? Because we can leave if you want.'

'Don't be daft. I'm just – taking it all in.' She gave a weak smile. 'Gaynor said a shock might be bad for my heart. Just give me a minute.'

It was suddenly horribly clear to Mattie what her idea actually meant for Reenie. This wasn't just a rose-tinted trip down Memory Lane – it was revisiting the place where she'd inflicted a wound that hadn't healed in sixty years. 'Why don't I get us a drink?' she offered, glad that they had come by train and taxi today. Alcohol was definitely in order to combat her nerves.

'Brandy and pep. *Double*.'

As she hurried to the empty bar, Mattie weighed up the wisdom of Reenie drinking, considering all the medication she was taking. But when the alternative was a shock-induced coronary, perhaps a glass of stabilising alcohol was allowed.

The barman looked up from the crate of bottles he was unpacking and stood quickly. 'Sorry. Didn't see you there.'

'White wine, and a brandy and peppermint, please.'

He nodded and pulled glasses from above the bar. 'Are you here for lunch?'

'Yes.'

'I can recommend the salmon.' His eyes were sharp against the open friendliness of his face. Since arriving in London Mattie had already become acclimatised to being ignored by strangers, and the contrast here was a shock.

'Oh. Thanks.' She dug in her purse to escape the pressure of finding another conversation topic. Back in Kings Sunbury most of the barmen didn't even know what was on the pub's menu without looking, let alone be able to offer a personal recommendation.

She wondered how Joe Bell had found his first visit here in 1956. He had talked of seeing some famous acts at the club – one of the few details from that year he would share. Standing at the bar, Mattie could almost feel the footprints of her grandfather worn into the wooden floor beneath her own feet.

'Miss?'

The past dissipated like smoke as Mattie realised the barman was talking to her. 'Sorry – I was miles away.'

He smiled. 'Wherever it was, it looked nice. Is there anything else?'

'No thanks – oh, wait a minute, I don't suppose you have one of those old-fashioned paper cocktail umbrellas, do you?'

The barman rubbed a hand to his chin, pin-sharp green eyes filled with amusement. 'Do you know, I think we might. Hang on . . .' He ducked through a velvet-curtained doorway and Mattie could hear the clack-clack of his shoes on old parquet flooring. Grandpa Joe's farmhouse had a small snug with a very old parquet floor, the wooden tiles of which had been lifted and bent by time. As children Mattie, Joanna and Jack had spent hours on Sunday afternoons dancing across it pretending to be Gene Kelly and Fred Astaire, the loose wooden pieces turning their steps into tap-shoe beats.

The wooden taps sounded again as the barman returned, holding aloft a pale pink paper cocktail umbrella as if it was a sporting trophy. 'There you go,' he grinned. 'I don't think the box it was in has been opened since 1986, so it's definitely retro.'

Mattie's smile rested comfortably on her lips all the way back to Reenie.

'What's up?'

'I got you a present.' Mattie gave Reenie her glass, and popped the umbrella in with a flourish.

Her friend's porcelain cheeks flushed. 'Nice touch, kid. Although when I used to come here, I never got one of these. It was more a cheeky swig from a smuggled-in whisky bottle.'

116

Mattie lifted her glass. 'Well, here's to making *different* memories in this club.'

'Too right.'

'You never said you'd been here before – apart from the night of the concert. Did you know it well?' Had Reenie been at the club at the same time as Grandpa Joe?

'My mate Marcie used to be one of the dancers for the crooners, and we'd sneak back to the dressing rooms for a quick ciggie and a slug of booze before she finished her shift. Sometimes we'd sneak into the club when the door manager wasn't looking. Marcie had her admirers, you see. That's why it was a shock – seeing it today. Thing is, I'd wanted to play on that stage for years before The Silver Five. So, how are we going to do this? You seemed chummy with the barman.'

'I think he was amused by me asking for this,' Mattie replied, twirling the cocktail umbrella. 'I think we wait for the other guy to come back, and then ask if the owner is in.'

'And if he isn't?'

'Let's just hope he is.' Should she have asked when she called to book the table? Mattie had been so caught up in bringing Reenie to the former Palm Grove that she hadn't even considered the owner might not be there during lunch service. It was an age until the friendly bar manager returned, by which time the corner of Mattie's menu bore apprehensive creases.

'Now, what can I get you ladies?'

'One salmon mornay and one rack of lamb, please,' Mattie replied, hearing the slight wobble of nerves as she

117

spoke. 'Actually . . . the reason we came was because Ms Silver was one of the acts booked to play at the club when it was the Palm Grove.'

Derry gave Reenie a surprised smile. 'Is that so? When was this?'

'1956,' Reenie beamed. 'I was lead singer with The Silver Five.'

'Well, how good is that? I had no idea we were entertaining VIPs this afternoon! Hey, my boss would be over the moon to meet you. Shall I call him over?'

With a surreptitious wink at Mattie, Reenie clasped a hand to her heart. 'Would you? That would be wonderful.'

Derry nodded and looked out over the club. 'He'll be made up, honestly. His grandfather used to run the place, and . . . Ah, here's your man now. Gil! Over here!'

Reenie's eyes were as wide as saucers as the club's owner approached. 'Oh, he's just the spit of Jake . . . *Look*, Mattie.'

Derry was relaying the details about them to his employer as Mattie turned – and saw the tall, sandy-haired barman strolling towards them. Reenie was right, she realised now – he was the image of the photo of Jake Kendrick she had seen on the website. He wore his hair a little longer, but there was an obvious curl to it, reminding Mattie of the styled quiff his grandfather had worn. How hadn't she spotted it at the bar?

'That explains the cocktail umbrella,' he grinned, reaching out to shake Reenie's hand. 'The Silver Five, eh? My grandfather used to talk about you, Ms Silver.'

'I hope it was all good stuff?'

'It was.' He turned to Mattie. 'I owe you an introduction. I'm Gil Kendrick. I co-own the club with my brother Colm. Unfortunately he isn't in today – he'll be sorry he missed you.'

'We did arrive unannounced. I wonder, could we be cheeky and ask for a tour of the club?'

'Sure – it would be my pleasure. Would you like to go now?'

'Now's as good a time as any, Mr Kendrick,' Reenie said, rising slowly and accepting the offer of his arm to help her.

'Please – call me Gil. It's great to meet a friend of Grandad's.'

'Call me Reenie,' the old lady purred, patting his arm coyly. 'Lead on, Macduff!'

They began to walk slowly from the table towards the large space beyond, which had once housed Soho's most glittering dance floor. Gil pointed out the different areas, most of which were still visible even under the uniform black paint.

'So, diners sat here and sometimes surrounding the first part of the floor, depending on the acts Grandad had performing. Originally there was an orchestra pit just in front of the stage, but after the war, when big bands tended to be the main draw, Jake moved them onto the stage. I believe he extended the stage back in around 1951, building new dressing rooms and adding about twenty feet to the performance area.'

'I first met him not long after that work had happened,' Reenie nodded. 'He was so excited about it, as I recall.

You know, this place still has the magic it had sixty years ago.'

'Does it?'

'Oh, yes. I met my manager Rico here. Snuck in with my mate who was waitressin' because Matt Munro was doing a set – and there he was. Harry Slack, leanin' on the bar, looking for all the world like he'd stepped off the plane from St Tropez. He bought me cherry brandies all night and I thought all my birthdays had come at once.' She let out a sigh as she they moved down towards the stage. 'The Palm Grove was like Hollywood in Soho. Not dark and dingy like it is today – no offence, Gil.'

He smiled. 'None taken. What was it like back then?'

'Gorgeous. Chandeliers everywhere, candelabras on every table, gold chairs and pink linen tablecloths so thick and luxurious you could've worn 'em as an evening gown.'

Looking around the modern club, with its careful mix of black and chrome, it was difficult to imagine the opulence it had become renowned for during the late 1940s and early 1950s. Only the pair of rich red velvet curtains that encircled the stage gave a clue to the club's former glory.

'In my day,' Reenie continued, her gold rings clicking together as she pointed to a slightly sunken area just in front of the stage, 'the best dancers in town used to head here after their West End shows. Your grandad was a peach like that. All very hush-hush, mind, but I know a fair few girls who kept roofs over their heads in the early days because of the cash he'd bung 'em for dancing. He said it made his club look good. It did, as well. You walked

120

into this place and it drew you into a fantasy world. You might be the least interested of a party, but I'd guarantee by the end of the night you'd be willing to do anythin' to grab a piece of it.'

Mattie followed behind Reenie and Gil, surprised to hear her friend's stories of the former owner. Why hadn't Reenie mentioned this before? All she had said of her link with the Palm Grove prior to their visit was that a talent scout from the club had seen The Silver Five performing, and invited them to appear. That scout couldn't have been Jake Kendrick, could it?

'Bringing back memories?' Gil asked.

'More than a few, kid. Answer me one question, though: when you must've spent so much making this place modern, why on earth did you hang on to those moth-eaten stage curtains?'

Gil stared at the old lady, then broke into the warmest smile Mattie had seen him wear since their arrival. 'Well spotted, Miss Silver.'

'Those are the original curtains?' Mattie asked, her interest immediately piqued. One of the things she loved most about working with vintage goods was the sheer variety of fabrics. Such a tactile representation of the past never failed to make her think of the item's previous owners, her fingers tracing the same paths as those of unseen individuals, generations before. 'Sorry, do you mind if I . . . ?'

'Sure. Be my guest.'

Gil was clearly amused by her sudden enthusiasm, but Mattie didn't care. While Grandpa Joe hadn't seen Reenie perform at the Palm Grove, she knew from the conversations they'd shared that he'd spent many a Friday and Saturday evening in the sumptuous surroundings of the club. He might never have appeared on its stage, but this solitary remnant of the club's original fabric was the closest link in the place to the grandfather she missed. She took the three steps at the side of the stage and ran a hand down one of the folds of red velvet. On close inspection she could see patches where the material had been worn thin, the brown threads of the backing fabric along the hem clearly visible in a few places. The curtains had the scent of old fabric: modern velvets just didn't smell the same. It reminded Mattie of the scent that lingered on her clothes the day after she'd baked bread and scones with Grandma in the farmhouse kitchen: toast-like, with hints of sun-roasted dust.

'My brother wanted to bin them.' Gil's voice was soft when it sounded by Mattie's side. Surprised, she turned her head to see he had joined her on the stage.

'You did the right thing ignoring him,' she smiled back. 'This kind of quality just doesn't exist anymore. How old are they?'

'Grandad commissioned them when he opened the club in 1931. They once had the initials P. G. and a palm tree logo embossed on them in gold.' He lifted one edge of velvet curtain and held it up to her. In the light from the overhead spots, Mattie could just make out tiny flecks of gold paint and a faint outline where the velvet was darker in colour. 'I take it you're interested in this sort of thing?'

'I am. I own a vintage goods store. Old fabrics are a

particular favourite of mine.' Suddenly realising how odd it was to be discussing the merits of eighty-five-year-old velvet with a relative stranger, Mattie smiled. 'It keeps me happy.'

Gil laughed. 'I'm the last person to mock someone's personal obsessions. Here's a tip: don't ever get me started on Tommy Cooper. I could recite his routines to you for *hours . . .*'

It was an innocent comment that felt like an invitation. Mattie felt her smile broaden to mirror Gil's. Velvet and vintage comedians, it transpired, were a potent mix when discussed on this stage. Aware of Reenie, who was watching them both with sly interest, Mattie hurried back to the former dance floor.

'And there was me thinking *I'd* be the oldest thing in the place today,' she said, raising an eyebrow. 'Usurped by a pair of curtains – charming!'

'Sorry, Reenie. Occupational hazard.'

'You and your business. I don't know. Next thing I know you'll be flogging me to the highest bidder.' Reenie's eyes sparked with mischief as she patted Gil's arm. 'Pay no attention to me, I'm just having a bit of fun. I do appreciate being here. Sincerely. It's bringing back a lot of memories.'

As Gil escorted them around the three rooms of the club and the bank of dressing rooms beyond the stage, Mattie silently rehearsed her proposition. It had been all she could think of for two weeks and, until this morning, she had been confident of her request. Now she was here, it occurred to her that it might put Gil in an impossible position. They weren't offering to pay for the event, only to provide the group – and Mattie had no guarantee that any of the remaining four Silver Five singers would agree to attend.

And yet, being here made her believe that it *could* be possible.

She could be swept up in the romanticism of what this place had once been, but it was almost as if the club was spinning its magic around her head, as if the crystal chandeliers and hundreds of blazing candles were still alight. *I can't go back now*, she thought. *I've come too far*.

Grandpa Joe would call this 'an unexpected door'. He'd mentioned it often when reminiscing about the opportunities his own life had afforded him. 'You take my advice: if you stumble upon an unexpected door, don't hesitate. We can wait a lifetime for opportunity to call on us; unexpected doors don't announce themselves, but wait to be found. They're easy to miss or dismiss – trust me, love, I know only too well. If you find one, open it. You won't regret it . . .'

'I remember this room,' Reenie exclaimed, as they stepped into a long, narrow dressing room. She clapped her hands together and shuffled over to one of the mirrors that still had its bare light-bulb surround. 'I stood in for one of the dancers one night, you know, Mattie, long before I was in The Silver Five. One of the girls twisted her ankle tripping down the stage steps, and couldn't go on. Well, I'd watched the routine enough times to know the moves, and her costume fit me. So me and me mate Marcie giggled our way through the performance on the back row.' She grinned at Gil. 'Your grandad thought it was hilarious when he found out.'

'Did he? He never told me that.'

'I'll bet he never did. This one here,' she pointed at Mattie, 'thinks she knows everything about me, but we've barely scratched the surface. You only know what we choose to tell you.'

This was true in more ways than one, Mattie thought. Gil had no idea what she and Reenie planned to ask. Was now the right time? Taking a breath and willing whatever magic still clung to the fixtures of the club to come to her aid, Mattie seized the opportunity.

'Talking of which, there's another reason we wanted to visit today,' she said, every nerve ending on her skin prickling. 'We don't just want to help Reenie reminisce.'

'You don't?'

'The thing is – Reenie's group never played the gig they were booked for. They broke up that night. We'd like to try to reunite them for a final time, sixty years later. Bring them all back together here, where the split happened.'

'For what?'

'To see the place – like Reenie's done today. Have lunch here, invite the press, make it into a celebration of one of British rock 'n' roll's founding acts and this club's place in music history.'

'Okay.' Gil's eyes narrowed. 'So, what's in it for me?'

'Um . . .' Suddenly, Mattie was stumped. She'd assumed the publicity from the story would be enough. 'Publicity?'

'Free publicity. That I pay for.' His brow softened. 'I'm sorry to sound mercenary, but I'm running a business. The link with my grandfather is a great one, but are you proposing I forgo a day's worth of business for a PR stunt that – forgive me – might only generate a little local interest?'

'Of course not.'

Mattie turned to look at Reenie, who was leaning on her walking stick now, eyes alive. 'Reenie?'

'We'll do the gig. For real, this time. You turn this place back into the Palm Grove for one night, sell the tickets, and Mattie and me will do the rest.'

Mattie felt as if the room was slowly slipping away from her. 'What do you mean? Reenie?'

'What are you suggesting?' He was interested now, and Mattie watched in mounting horror as the old lady and the club owner began to mirror one another's body language, blocking her out.

'We'll get you *all five* Silver Five members. One last gig, before we all pop off to eternity. Picture it, Gil: "The Most Anticipated Reunion in Pop Music History". The originators of the world-famous song "Because You Loved Me" brought back together after a sixty-year rift. The gig that never happened, finally taking place on the sixtieth anniversary of the original date. Tickets would *vanish* in no time. You could charge whatever you liked. Money for the club, a huge coup for Kendrick's, a perfect publicity storm.'

'*Reenie* – can we talk about this?' hissed Mattie, panic making her whisper seem strained.

'No need, kiddo. You were right. I can't meet my maker knowing I could have made this better before I died. A nice afternoon jolly in London won't cut it. Being here has made up my mind. The only way I will put things right is to do the gig I skipped out on. So, what do you say, Gil Kendrick?'

He was rubbing a hand slowly across his chin, and Mattie couldn't believe he was even considering Reenie's proposal. 'I don't know. It's a lot of money to invest. And how do you know anyone still remembers you?'

'They remember, don't you worry. We were stars while Elvis Presley was still scribblin' songs at his mother's knee. "Because You Loved Me" is one of the most covered songs in recent history. Five of us share credits with the song-writer's family, and we've all made a living out of it. People still remember. Trust me, they'll come.'

'Now, just wait a minute!' Mattie interjected, bringing her hand a little too forcefully down on the dressing-room table. 'I'm sorry, Reenie, but how on earth will you get all of the band members to come? Most of them haven't spoken to you for sixty years.'

Reenie gave a girlish giggle. 'That's the best bit. We visit them. In person. You and me. Persuade them to come. I'll make my apologies and get them on board. I know them. They may have spent most of their lives hating me, but none of them will turn down the chance for one last gig.'

It was good to see her friend so animated, but Mattie feared Reenie was finally losing her marbles. She lowered her voice, turning a little away from Gil Kendrick, who was scribbling calculations on a scrap of paper. 'Reenie, this is a lovely idea, but how are we going to visit everyone and arrange this gig in time? The date is only four weeks away. And we don't even know if they would see you, let alone agree to a concert.'

'So, we surprise them. Just turn up. What can they do, eh?'

'Call the police? Slam the door in our faces?'

'Not if you had a promoter with you, bringing a cast-iron contract,' Gil said, causing them both to turn.

'Trust me, Gil, my word will be enough.'

'All the same, Miss Silver, I should be there. If I'm going to commit money to this, I want to protect my investment.'

'So, you don't mind taking Reenie all over the country?' Mattie asked, suddenly impressed.

Gil's mouth opened to speak, but Reenie got there first. 'Not likely! *You're* driving, Mattie Bell.'

'*What?*'

'This was *your* idea. The whole "If I'd had a chance to apologise I'd have done it" speech. Well, this is your chance.' She dropped her tone to a hoarse whisper. 'To do it for You-Know-Who.'

'I have a business, Reenie! I can't just leave it for a week . . .'

'Nearer two weeks I'd say, kid,' Reenie sniffed. 'That van of yours will need it. I reckon a week and a half would give us time to get round to everybody. The rest of the group are all a little – *spread out*, see? Moved as far away from each other as we could.'

Mattie was horrified by the suggestion. How could Reenie be volunteering her services with no regard to her business – or what she might want? But the mention of

Grandpa Joe and her graveside promise pulled her up short. What if this was a way to make amends for the past? Joe Bell had loved The Silver Five. What if she really could reunite them, and make the gig he missed finally happen? Her fingers found the silver tiepin on her collar, and in a heartbeat she knew what she should do.

'*If* Joanna and Laurie are willing to cover the shop,' she began slowly, already seeing triumph glowing from Reenie's smile, 'and *if* we can persuade Beauvale to sanction the trip . . .'

'*Pffft*, you leave Beauvale to me. And I've met your sister and Laurie. I reckon they'd run the place like a dream for you. Do we have a deal?' Reenie held out her hands, one to Mattie, one to Gil. The two of them exchanged glances, each weighing up the other, before their hands met in the centre of the table.

'What was *that*?' Mattie demanded, as soon as their taxi had driven clear of the street.

'That, Mattie Bell, was ingenuity in action!'

'I thought you said you couldn't be in the same room as them?'

'I changed my mind.'

'That's one heck of a U-turn, Reenie! And what if they don't agree?'

'They will. They'll see Gil's contract, and that'll be all they'll need.' She grimaced. 'Not that I'm happy about him tagging along. Blimmin' cheek! Just like his grandfather . . .'

As the taxi took a sharp right turn, Mattie felt her

stomach lurch, the full realisation of what she had agreed to in the club now dawning. A week and a half on the road with a frail and unpredictable OAP and a materialistic club owner, abandoning her common sense along with her reason? What was she *thinking*? How could it end in anything other than disaster? Would five people, as good as strangers now, really put aside a sixty-year rift for the sake of one gig? And what about the shop? What would Laurie and Joanna say? She'd made them complicit in this scheme without ever asking their opinion. How would she feel in their position?

Wait . . . she *knew* how she'd feel. Like someone else was dictating her actions. Like Grandpa Joe had done to her.

But the prospect was too enticing to ignore. Perhaps they would understand. Perhaps time away from home would be good for her. She had been so consumed with losing Asher and Joe – and keeping all the plates spinning at work – that she hadn't allowed herself time to absorb what had happened to her. She hadn't spent any time away from Bell Be-Bop since opening the shop. And now it occurred to her that she hadn't really done anything for herself for several years. A crazy road trip criss-crossing the country, on a completely uncertain premise and with companions she hardly knew, might be just what she needed.

'What about Beauvale? You know your health isn't good. *They* know it, too.'

'Beauvale won't stand in our way. I pay them enough to be able to do what the heck I want, once in a while.

We can *do* this, Mattie. And if we can't, we'll have the time of our lives trying . . .'

There were a million and one reasons not to embark on Reenie's crazy scheme. But one reason in its favour superseded them all: Mattie *wanted* to go.

Chapter Twelve

'At the Hop' –
Danny & the Juniors

♪

On Sunday morning, Mattie arrived at Beauvale as usual with the requisite pink-and-white-striped chocolatiers' box in one hand and an unassuming-looking shopping bag in the other containing a wealth of secret things. She exchanged a breezy greeting with Gaynor in the covered walkway from reception to the communal barn, all the time feeling like a spy carrying top-secret intelligence for a clandestine meet.

'Reenie's on top form today,' Gaynor said. 'Anyone would think she knew something we didn't.'

Gritting her teeth into a smile, Mattie nodded and hurried through the old oak barn doors.

Reenie grabbed her elbow the moment Mattie reached her side. 'Have you got it?' she hissed, eyeballing two of the Three Furies who had dared to stand too close as they scurried into the shadows of the barn.

Mattie nodded. 'Where do you want to do this?'

The old lady took the box of violet crèmes from Mattie and made a great show of opening it, selecting a chocolate and taking a bite. 'Kitchen,' she replied, mid-chomp. 'I've cleared it with Sandra the catering manager.'

'Really? Couldn't we just go to your room?' Mattie asked, wondering if such extreme lengths were necessary.

'And have *that lot* with glasses pressed to the wall next door? Not flippin' likely! It's like a blue-rinse MI6 in here, kid. The walls have ears *and* twinsets.'

Together, they strolled as casually as anyone can into an industrial catering kitchen. Sandra, who it transpired was a middle-aged lady of Amazonian proportions, momentarily blocked their path, Mattie coming within inches of a potentially embarrassing nose-to-expansive-breast collision.

'Go right ahead,' she boomed, with a sly wink that would have terrified even the bravest visitor to her establishment.

'How did you persuade that woman to let us in?' Mattie asked, as they rounded a large double-freezer unit where a stainless-steel table had been cleared for them.

'Turns out she's a massive Elvis fan. I had a few of his signed postcards he gave me during my Vegas stint in '73, so . . .' Reenie rotated a red-painted fingernail inviting Mattie to draw her own conclusions.

'Really? But those would be worth – a *lot* of money. Should you really be giving them away?'

'Nah. I've a box full of the things. Gathering dust in me wardrobe, to be honest. And I don't need little scribbled-on scraps of card to remind me of the beautiful thing we had . . .' For a moment, Reenie was lost to the world, her thoughts far away from the disinfectant-heavy air of Beauvale's catering kitchen.

Torn between wanting to press Reenie further and redirecting her attention to the job they had come to do, Mattie opted for the latter. If today's plan came to fruition, there would be plenty of time to hear her possibly apocryphal showbiz stories during their road trip. '*Anyway*, we should probably get on with this?'

'Oh yes, yes. Right you are. So, you've got it?'

Mattie nodded and held up the carrier bag. 'All here. Do you have the most recent list of addresses?'

'I certainly do. Still had it in the card Tommy sent me last Christmas.' With a surreptitious glance over her shoulder, Reenie slowly reached into the neckline of her peacock-blue kaftan and, to Mattie's alarm, produced a folded sheet of paper from the generous depths of her cleavage. 'Old trick I learned in the trade, kid: your bra is the high-security safe the Good Lord gave you. Besides, if anyone's brave enough to try rummaging around in there, at least it'll put a smile on your face!'

Trying to push the unwanted mental image of Reenie's high-security bra from her mind, Mattie pulled a large road atlas from her carrier bag and laid it face down on the table. On its back cover was a map of the British Isles, with the major cities and towns marked across it. A spiral-bound notebook followed, together with a biro and a sheet of silver star-shaped stickers. Reenie unfolded the sheet of paper, upon which were written five short paragraphs in an economic, tidy hand.

'Right. So, where is everybody on the map?'

Through cat-eye-shaped glasses on the end of her nose, Reenie consulted the list. 'Darling Tommy is in Alnwick. That's *Northumberland*, love.' She stabbed at the north-east side of England with a red-painted false nail.

'Northumberland. There.' Mattie marked the first location with a silver star.

'Nice touch.' Reenie gave an appreciative nod. 'Next, young Alys lives near Crickhowell, Wales.'

A second star was placed on the opposite end of the map, Mattie covering her smile at an eighty-one-year-old woman being referred to as a juvenile. 'And the other two?'

'Chuck's in Bath. Sorry, kid, I mean Johnny Powell. We all called him Chuck, but I'm beggared if I can remember why now. And June lives in Cambridge.' Two more stars were added at opposite sides of the country.

'And Kendrick's is here,' Mattie said, placing the last star in central London. Her heart sank as she stared at the map. Four people, living at almost the four corners of the UK: how many miles separated them?

'So. What do you think?' Reenie Silver was gazing intently up at her, something resembling hope shining in her eyes. 'Could we do it?'

'I really don't know.' Mattie's mind was a-whirr with possibilities, logistical questions and practical concerns. *Could* they do this? A thirty-two-year-old and an eighty-four-year-old, travelling the length and breadth of the British Isles in a camper van that hadn't attempted much more than forty miles in one day before? Reenie laying her biggest regret to rest. The Silver Five finally reunited. And Grandpa Joe's favourite group finally able to perform the most important gig of their lives . . .

Mattie Bell was never one to retreat from a challenge, just because it seemed too difficult to meet. There *had* to be a way to make this happen. 'It won't be easy,' she admitted, seeing a smile already broadening across Reenie's downy face, 'but I think we can.'

'Woo-*hoo*!' Reenie grabbed Mattie and hugged her so hard, she feared the old lady's reading glasses might become permanently welded to her shoulder. 'I *knew* you'd come up trumps! Righty-ho, then, let's get *planning*!'

6 December 1955

All is set!

Uncle Charles has confirmed by letter that I will work for him as his apprentice from 8 January. Father is delighted, Mother less so, but she knows I must fly the nest sooner or later. It's all I can think of now. I dream of London, of the lights and noise and possibility for adventure. Kings Sunbury seems too small all of a sudden. It is time for me to make my mark.

I'm to live with Uncle Charles in his house. I am passing the time before I leave by compiling lists of sights I want to see: Buckingham Palace, the changing of the guard at Horse Guards Parade, the British Museum, dinosaurs at the Natural History Museum, maybe even ballet at Covent Garden. I suppose not

all of them will be possible but right now I am
inclined to believe all of it is within my grasp.
   I cannot wait to leave . . .

The plan was simple: take ten days and travel across the UK to visit the four other Silver Five members. The road trip would begin in Alnwick, Northumberland, with Tommy, then move to Cambridge with June Knight, across the country to Bath to see Johnny 'Chuck' Powell, and over the border to Wales to a village nestled on the edge of the Brecon Beacons National Park to see Alys Davis. From there, Mattie and Reenie would head to London, where – if the plan worked – the gig would finally take place at the Palm Grove.

The plan itself was easy, but overcoming differences, forgiving past injustices and reuniting five OAPs who had mostly avoided discussing the event that tore them apart was anything but.

Reenie remained resolutely sure that all of her former bandmates would agree, but Mattie saw her gritting her teeth several times when she thought nobody was watching. Was there more to The Silver Five's end than she'd let on?

'Well, I'll say one thing for her, Reenie Silver is a woman who knows what she wants,' Joanna said, lifting two bowls of pasta above her head as Ethan and Ava raced to the table. 'But are you certain this is what *you* want?'

Mattie took her seat, loving the warmth of a family mealtime. 'Actually, crazy as it seems, I think it is. I feel awful putting it on you and Laurie to manage the shop, though.'

Joanna waved her concern away with a pasta fork. 'Oh, don't worry about that. We'll walk it. I'm just checking that you haven't been bludgeoned into doing this because you're too nice to say no.'

It was time to put her cards on the table. 'I *have* to do this, J-J. I made a promise to Grandpa at the funeral: I want to make it up to him.'

'Oh, Mattie, you have nothing to make amends for. Grandpa Joe asked you to do an impossible thing. He had no right to sling ultimatums at you. Listen, the best way you can make it up to him is to prove how amazing you really are. Look at what you've achieved! And now with that idiot Asher gone, you can get on with being even more successful.'

'That's kind of you to say, but I need to do this.'

'I wish the old bloke could see what pain he caused,' Joanna said, suddenly. 'I'm sorry, but he threw away his last chance to spend time with you. I love him and I miss him too, but he was far from perfect, M. You don't have to do some epic task to posthumously win back his approval.'

'I want to do it, though. Not just for me, but for Reenie too. Her health isn't the best; Gaynor at Beauvale told me privately it's worse than Reenie says. The group missing the gig sixty years ago is her biggest regret. If I can help five old people settle a score to make the remainder of their lives happy, how wonderful will that be?'

'The ultimate vintage collection for you to curate,'

138

Joanna said, her face instantly relaxing into a smile. 'Oh, Matilda Bell, I do love you. Just go and have a good time. Well, as good a time as you can have in a camper van with a crotchety old pensioner . . .'

And a club owner I hardly know. Who I'm not entirely certain of, Mattie added in her thoughts. Put like this, the road trip wasn't exactly inviting. But the end result she and Reenie hoped for *was*. And that was what mattered.

Chapter Thirteen

'Just Between You and Me' – The Chordettes

♪

A week after she had begun planning the trip – and the evening before she and Reenie were due to embark on it, Mattie sat at her dining-room table, maps and schedules forming a multi-coloured tablecloth across it. With Gaynor now reluctantly on board, Mattie wanted to make sure everything else was ready for the journey. Over a thousand miles of unknowns stretched into the distance before her, and she couldn't help but be awed by the task she faced.

'Kids are in bed. Here,' Joanna handed Mattie a mug of tea as she entered the room.

'Thanks. Are they okay? Ava seemed a little subdued this evening.'

Her sister gave a shrug of resignation, her smile edged with sadness. 'She was. They're both very up and down at the moment. I expected it, to be honest. Fred called to speak to them after school and he's making noises about taking them on holiday in October half-term. It's just another familiar thing that's changed for them.'

'Will you let them go on holiday? That won't be easy for you.'

'I'm dreading it, but I won't stand in their way if they want to go. It'll get easier the more they settle into the new arrangements. They both love being here, though. Being with you is a constant they're comfortable with.'

'And tomorrow I'm going away for ten days,' Mattie said, feeling immediately guilty that she hadn't considered her nephew and niece's feelings while she'd been planning with Reenie.

'Oh, don't worry about that. They're excited for you.' Joanna looked across the dining table. 'These plans look incredible, M.'

'Thanks. I'm just trying to get everything clear in my head before tomorrow.'

Joanna laughed. 'You do realise you're nuts to even be contemplating this?'

'Ha. Maybe. Okay, yes, I know it's a little out there.'

'Understated as ever. I envy you a little, you know.'

'Do you?'

'Yes, I do. This is a completely barmy idea and yet you're throwing yourself into it wholeheartedly. You always have. I remember you as a toddler, just marching straight into everything. Mum used to say you didn't go around things, you went *through* them. Little determined face, fists clenched, stomping forwards.' She smiled. 'And now I sound like Mum.'

'Except Mum hasn't said that sort of thing to me for

a while now.' The admission made her heart heavy. Things were getting easier between them, but it was a slow process.

'Well, *I'm* saying it. You're doing an incredible thing for these old people. You're giving them the chance you never got: to change their minds. I think that's a noble act.'

Mattie smiled. 'I'm not sure any of them will forgive Reenie. Apart from Tommy – the guy who's tried to keep them all in touch over the years. He sounds lovely, a real character. I'm looking forward to meeting him.'

'You're going there first?'

'Yes.'

Joanna picked up the printed tour itinerary Mattie had put together, which would soon become their bible. 'Alnwick, Cambridge, Bath, Llan – *Llan* . . . I can't even begin to pronounce that . . . and London. That's some schedule. Are you sure you can fit it all in?'

'I'm going to give it my best shot. And the fourth stop is Llangynidr – it's where Alys Davis lives now. On the edge of the Brecon Beacons. It's meant to be gorgeous there.'

Joanna looked up, eyes wide. 'Hang on – you mean *the* Alys Davis? The Gloria Hunniford of Wales?'

'The very same.'

'Oh *wow*, Mattie! She's a national treasure! Remember that show she used to do on Saturday nights way back when we were kids – ooh, now, what was it called?'

'*Sing Me a Saturday*. Grandpa Joe adored it. Grandma too, as I recall.'

'That's it! I can't believe you're going to meet her!'

x

142

'I think I might be a bit starstruck. I'll have to hide it from Reenie, though. I get the feeling she isn't too impressed by the career Alys has had.'

What little Reenie had said about the youngest member of The Silver Five had left Mattie in no doubt of her true feelings. It seemed that as Reenie's star was fading, Alys's was very much in ascension; she had reinvented herself as a doyenne of light entertainment television at the time when Reenie found herself playing cruise ships in the 1980s.

'Talk about captive audiences,' she'd joked to Mattie, but the resentment painted in firm strokes across her brow told a different story. 'I'd have been better off playing to inmates in prison, though. At least they wouldn't have been so drunk and you could leave the premises without a life raft . . .'

'I'm so proud of you.' Joanna pulled Mattie into a huge hug. 'You just take care of yourself, okay? Have an amazing time. Don't worry about us. The kids are excited for you. And don't worry about the shop. Laurie and me will be fine.'

'I know you will. Thanks so much – I couldn't do this without you.'

'My pleasure. I'll probably be asleep when you leave in the morning, but call me when you get to Alnwick, okay?' Joanna pulled back and gently stroked Mattie's face. 'I love you, little sis. This trip's going to be amazing.'

That night, too excited to sleep, Mattie picked up Joe's small, moss-green diary from her bedside table and ran a finger over the faded gold date printed on the cover. 1956: the year she had heard him talk about so much. He was still a young man then; almost an entire lifetime to live before Mattie ever knew him. He'd mentioned his year in London as his 'wild bachelor year'. While in London, he'd first heard about The Silver Five and had become a fan. He said their music captured how he'd felt, just turned twenty-one, discovering the delights of the capital and being independent for the first time in his life. His stories of a London rediscovering itself as the long shadow of the Second World War finally retreated were as vivid and bright as the city he described: new music, new art, new fashions all embodying the irrepressible optimism of the early Fifties.

Mattie found the first entry in the diary and read:

Saturday, 7 January 1956

Am on a train heading to London. Can't remember ever being this excited about anything before, even Christmas. Father very proud when he waved me off at the station. 'You'll come back a man,' he said. Here's hoping.

Have written to Bill Godfrey with new address, asking the old hand at London living to take pity on this poor country lad. Hopeful he'll respond – we always got on so well when we were younger. I will make friends. I always do. Captain Chummy strikes the Capital!

Can't wait to get started. Watch out, London – Joe
   Bell is on his way!

Mattie traced her finger over the confident pencil strokes, feeling a rush of love for the young man about to embark on his dream.

'Hello, Joe Bell of 1956,' she said, her throat tight with approaching tears. 'You and I are going on a journey together.'

Chapter Fourteen

'It's Just a Matter of Time' – Brook Benton

♪

An alarm call at four a.m. brought Mattie from the little sleep she'd managed to steal during the night. But she felt alive – buzzing with what lay ahead. Pulling on a hoodie to ward off the early chill, she scrambled her remaining things together and headed outside to where Rusty had been languishing under an old blue-and-white-checked travel rug to ward off the worst of the early autumnal frost.

Climbing inside, she inhaled Rusty's unique aroma – old leather, Flash liquid and biscuit crumbs. She could see her breath illuminated by the light from the porch of her house, the windows beginning to fog from her body heat. Pulling a torch from under the pack-away sink, she consulted her checklist, methodically marking off each item. There would be opportunities to buy anything she missed on the journey, but she wanted to check everything now, before the demands of the schedule took over.

Stowing her boots, extra layers and jacket behind the back seat, she took Grandpa Joe's 1956 diary from a side pocket in her well-packed holdall and moved it to her handbag. He could ride metaphorically in the front seat with her and Reenie. Grandpa Joe had considered himself one of life's front-seat passengers – always at the sharp end of everything, wanting to lead rather than be led. On the few occasions he'd travelled in Rusty for family holidays, the front seat had been his natural choice. He admired the raised view from the front of the van, falling into comfortable quietness as Mattie drove him through Shropshire and over the border to Wales. She thought now about the border-crossing the Silver Five road trip would make soon – her first foray into Wales since she and Grandpa Joe had stopped talking. She'd always had such happy memories of Bell clan gatherings in Barmouth, Criccieth and Harlech over the years, but the prospect of being in Wales without any of her family made her sad. She shook the thought away. This was going to be amazing.

Confident everything was in order, she clambered back out of Rusty and tiptoed back into the house. The brief return of heat flushed her cheeks and she caught sight of her reflection in the hall mirror. What she noticed was a bright sheen of hope in her brown eyes, something she hadn't seen for many months. Maybe the future beyond the road trip and resulting reunion would see her hope fixed permanently. Even now, with all the excitement and challenge lying in wait, Mattie found herself looking forward to discovering what her world would look like at the end. She remembered one last thing: going upstairs to her bedroom, she took Grandpa Joe's silver sixpence tiepin from its home on her bedside table and pinned it to her hoodie as she returned downstairs to the hall. Taking a deep breath, she smiled at her reflection a final time, then turned off the lights and locked the front door.

The morning had still to begin, a ghosting of dawn mist guarding the surrounding fields as Mattie escorted Reenie across Beauvale's gravel drive to the waiting vehicle.

'That's it?' Reenie said, pausing to stare at Rusty. '*That's* our tour bus?'

'Not exactly a tour bus,' Mattie smiled. 'But an excellent travelling companion.'

'No wonder you've insisted on booking taxis when you've taken me out before. I hope that thing's got a heated rear windscreen to keep our hands warm while we're pushing it.' Reenie clicked her dentures as she climbed shakily into the passenger seat. 'Good job I took care of the accommodation. You'd have me kipping in a yurt, judging by this hippymobile.'

'Trust me, it's very comfortable.' Mattie closed the door, wishing she wasn't quite so skilled at lip-reading as Reenie flipped her pashmina over her shoulder and said exactly what she thought.

'I do hope you know what you're doing.' Gaynor arrived by Mattie's side. 'Miss Silver isn't an ideal passenger.'

Mattie was getting that sense already. Could she really endure Reenie's sharp opinions for ten days? 'It'll be fine,' she said, the firmness of her resolve more forced than instinctive. *It has to be fine. We've come this far . . .* 'Honestly,

Gaynor, don't worry. Reenie wants to make this trip as much as I do.'

Gaynor didn't smile. 'You have her medication? And the schedule for it all?'

'Yes.'

'And you understand that a lady of her age and medical challenges will require more comfort breaks than you will? Don't smile, Mattie, this is a major consideration.'

'It's all worked into our itinerary. And we can accommodate any unexpected issues, too.'

Gaynor sighed. 'I shouldn't be letting you go. It's highly irresponsible of me. I lied to my boss, for heaven's sake! He thinks she's visiting her niece in Weston-super-Mare for a fortnight, taking it easy. If Dr Lancaster finds out where she's really gone, I can kiss my career goodbye.'

'Gaynor, this is really important. It isn't a daft whim.' Seeing her charge impatiently tapping her wrist through the passenger-door window, she pressed on. 'I realise she isn't easy. Please believe me, I know what I'm letting myself in for. But I believe in this trip and what it's trying to achieve.'

'You're making it sound romantic.'

'It *is* romantic, isn't it?'

Kicking the gravel with a platform toe, Gaynor nodded. 'So go. Before I think better of it.'

They had arranged to meet Gil at Shrewsbury station, half an hour's drive away from Kings Sunbury through the most glorious Shropshire countryside. The first pinking of dawn was illuminating the horizon beyond rolling fields, throwing the trees lining the tops of gentle hills into dark silhouette. Mattie loved this time of day, but this morning her mind was too packed with considerations and plans for what lay ahead to fully appreciate the beauty surrounding them.

'I still say he didn't need to come,' Reenie said, as the camper van pulled into the station car park.

'He's right, Reenie. Our case will be a lot stronger if we have the promoter with us. Don't worry. I'm sure it's going to be fun.'

'It'd be more fun if he left us to it,' Reenie muttered, staring out of the window.

In only thirty minutes Reenie had proved just how difficult she could be, and Mattie was relieved to leave her in Rusty as she walked over to the station. *It's early days*, she assured herself, *we're both still getting used to each other*. She could imagine Jack's face, though. He'd have jumped out of the van mid-journey like something out of a Bond film by now, if he'd had to put up with Reenie's constant complaints.

I have to keep focused on the end goal, she told herself as she waited on the platform. Ten days wasn't a long time, in the grand scheme of things. She could survive ten days if it meant her heart was finally at peace. Anything was better than living life with regret.

Eight minutes late, the train slowly pulled into the station, and Mattie scanned the faces of the alighting passengers to find Gil. He wasn't hard to spot, standing a good half a foot taller than his fellow travellers. He carried a large leather weekend bag on one shoulder with a folded grey jacket tucked between the handles and was casually dressed in an olive-green jumper over a white T-shirt, dark blue jeans and grey trainers. His blond hair was wavier than she remembered, but the knotted seriousness of his expression was the same. Even as he approached he appeared to be thinking better of it, a slight shake of his head revealing more of his thoughts than he intended.

When he raised his head, Mattie waved back, rewarded by the lightest of smiles.

'Here I am,' he said, and for a moment Mattie thought he was going to kiss her cheek. He didn't, the lack of any action making their greeting awkward.

'Here you are. Ready for a road trip?'

'I guess I am. Are you?'

It was a relief to see him as uncertain as she felt. 'I think so. It's really special, what we're doing, you know.'

'You sound like you're trying to convince yourself.'

They had started to walk towards the car park, Gil bumbling a little in letting Mattie go through the door first. She considered attempting a joke, but very quickly dismissed the idea. She didn't know him well enough to know what might be appropriate. Why did she suddenly feel so awkward around him?

'So – there's my van.'

'Really? That's our ride?'

Excellent. Trust the only thing to bring a smile to Gil's face to be mockery of Mattie's vehicle. She'd endured enough moaning from Reenie already.

'Yes, really. Problem?'

151

'Won't be a problem for me, but I expect it is for you. How *old* is that thing?'

'Fifty-two years.' If Mattie could have hugged Rusty at that moment, she would have. 'He's served me well for ten of them. And he has a clean bill of health from my mechanic, as a matter of fact.'

Gil chuckled. '*He?*'

'She talks to this rust-bucket.' Reenie had wound down the passenger window and was leaning out like a super-glamorous trucker. 'It even has a name.'

'Wow. Do people *do* that?'

'Some people do. I do. Rusty is my faithful friend.'

'*Rusty?* Oh, this is too good . . .'

'Rusty is the word,' Reenie grinned. 'Nice to see you, Gil.'

'You too, Miss Silver.'

Still smarting from her passengers' bonding over their dislike of her camper van, Mattie stared at them both. 'Rusty and I have been through a lot together.'

'Roadside rescues, towing, mechanical failure . . .' They were laughing now as Gil slid open the side door, threw his bag onto the back seat and climbed in.

Mattie walked around the front of the van and gave its headlamp a surreptitious pat. She loved Rusty, regardless of what anyone else thought. She'd bought him after finishing university, fulfilling an ambition from her early teens to own a classic VW camper van. In truth, he'd seen better days and, she suspected, worse owners, but Mattie loved him as much as anyone can love a cantankerous vintage automobile that costs a fortune to run.

'Right. Is everyone ready?' she asked, settling into the driver's seat and adjusting the satnav she'd bought under duress after Jack insisted it was safer than printing off reams of internet route-planner directions for the epic journey ahead.

'As we'll ever be.' Reenie winked at Gil in the sun-visor mirror as she reapplied her lipstick. 'Let's go!'

Chapter Fifteen

'My Feet Hit the Ground' – Cliff Richard

♪

One thing very quickly became clear about Mattie's passengers: they were as different as it was possible to be. Reenie filled every available moment with chatter, her stories and anecdotes peppered with judgements on just about everything she saw, from place names on motorway signs to the dress of other road users in the surrounding lanes as they made steady progress up the M1 towards Northumberland. Gil, meanwhile, sat in silence behind them, an amiable statue that occasionally broke his stillness to drink from a bottle of water. Arms folded, head slightly turned, his eyes impassively tracked the passing landscape through the camper van windows.

Both of her passengers unnerved Mattie. She hadn't been naive enough to expect a relaxing journey, but trying to keep both of them happy was proving an extra burden. After unsuccessfully trying to engage Gil in conversation (while holding back the crushing tide of Reenie's verbal flow) for the first few hours of their journey, she gave up and retreated into the familiar rumble of Rusty's engine. Putting on the radio only served to set Reenie off on a tirade against 'dreadful things that pass as music nowadays'; switching to a CD of 1950s hits she had brought from her shop prompted rolled eyes from Gil in the rear-view mirror and even more dubious reminiscences from Reenie.

Catching sight of her reflection, Mattie finally understood the strange, glazed expression she'd seen on her teachers during school trips. She felt as if she was holding back two powerful forces of nature while still having to concentrate on driving. As an exercise in multitasking it was nothing short of epic – and thoroughly exhausting. Her level of respect rose considerably for her sister, who had regularly spent summer holidays corralling two warring children during long drives to France. How did anyone do this and remain sane?

Eventually, Mattie resorted to James Taylor's *October Road* album because it was *her* favourite. If anyone challenged her, she decided, she would claim driver's prerogative. Thankfully, nobody did, Reenie nodding appreciatively until she started to snooze and Gil visibly relaxing as soon as the old lady was asleep. Congratulating herself on having successfully navigated the first hurdle of the road trip, Mattie settled into her seat and let the soothing music carry her along.

They made a stop at Tibshelf services on the M1 for supplies and coffee. Mattie welcomed the break to stretch out the knots from her shoulders as Gil headed to the motorway service station's coffee shop to order. Meanwhile, Reenie disappeared for 'a breath of fresh air' which, judging by the smell attached to her clothes when she joined them later, also contained large amounts of nicotine.

'So how're you liking it so far, sunshine?' Reenie grinned up at Gil, who was drinking a huge black coffee with surprising speed.

'It's the adventure of a lifetime,' he replied flatly.

'Well, if you think *this* is exciting, wait till you hear about my many, *many* years on the cruise ships . . .'

'It's good to have you with us,' Mattie's interruption was firm. It was fine for Reenie to have her joke, but not if it jeopardised Gil's involvement in the reunion. '*Both* of you.'

'Yes, it is. Forgive me, Gil. Your grandad would have been very proud of you, doing this trip and arranging the gig. He would've liked that.'

Gil looked up from his coffee cup, and for a moment a glimmer of respect passed between Mattie's fellow travellers. 'Thanks.'

'Don't mention it.' The slightest wink from Reenie made Mattie brace herself. 'Although you'll likely be joining the old fella soon, if you carry on drinking coffee like that. My second husband necked his smokey Joe all day, every day, and he was dead by the age of forty-five.'

'Is this what it's going to be like for the whole trip?' Gil addressed his question to Mattie with a smile, as though she was in charge of the elderly lady. Like *that* was even possible . . .

'*You* wanted to come,' Reenie was unrepentant. 'This is the deal, sonny.'

Fearing the trip was already descending into bedlam before it had properly begun, Mattie put down her coffee mug. 'No, Reenie, the *deal* is that the concert won't happen without Gil. It's great that he's with us. So show him some respect. And Gil, a thousand miles is going to feel very long and tiresome very quickly if you don't join in. I am not prepared to chauffeur World War Three in my van. Understood?'

'Your van's more likely to *be* Armageddon than carry it,' Reenie muttered, as Gil laughed.

It wasn't an ideal subject to bond over, but Mattie concluded it was better they find common ground mocking her camper van than be at odds with one another for the entire journey.

She left the pair of them milling around WHSmith and headed back outside, giving Rusty a sympathetic pat when she reached his parking space. 'Don't listen to them,' she whispered. 'You're a superhero in my eyes.' Taking the opportunity of five minutes to herself, she brought out Grandpa Joe's diary from its safe place in her bag and turned to the next entry.

Saturday, 21 January 1956

Made my first visit to a London nightclub with Bill tonight. Mother would be horrified. Great night, music from the best bands and plenty of pretty girls happy to dance. I think I might be made for the London life after all . . .

   Chaps at the office are good sports. I've taken to joining them after work for a pint at the Duke of Northumberland pub just around the corner from the office. Last week I met Len, a lad my age, originally from Leeds. We've become really quite good friends. I like him. We disagree on football but he laughs at my jokes – a good sign! Len reckons the best place to dance is the Palm Grove in Soho, but getting in can be tricky. His sister works there sometimes as a dancer, apparently, so hoping she'll stump us tickets sometime soon. Would be good to see it. Tommy Steele and the Steelmen are playing next Saturday night. Fingers crossed!

Mattie smiled at young Joe's enthusiasm. She remembered her grandfather being horrified at Tommy Steele becoming a song-and-dance entertainer, refusing to watch *Finian's Rainbow* at Christmas even though it was Grandma's favourite musical film. 'He was a rock 'n' roller,' he'd protest, changing the channel in disgust. 'I don't want to see him prancing about as a leprechaun.'

It amused Mattie and Jack that Grandpa could so easily forgive Elvis for *Blue Hawaii* and Cliff for *Summer Holiday*, but couldn't get over Tommy Steele with a dodgy 'Oirish' accent in *Finian's Rainbow*. But Grandpa Joe was often like that: a walking contradiction when it suited him.

Seeing Gil and Reenie weaving through the parked cars towards her, Mattie quickly pocketed the diary. It felt good to keep it as her secret. Driving back on the motorway in a decidedly calmer atmosphere than before, she smiled as the carriageway opened up before her. It was as if tiny fragments of Grandpa Joe were beginning to return to her with his new words, painstakingly restoring the picture she'd felt she'd lost since their falling-out.

The landscape on either side of the motorway began to rise up in moorland and hills, vast, open swathes of empty beauty with a faint glimmer of light from far-distant towns huddling in the steep valleys between. Here the man-made motorway seemed at odds with the wildness of nature, but they were forced to co-exist. Mattie stole a glance in the rear-view mirror and saw that Gil, like Reenie in the front passenger seat beside her, was dozing. He looked at peace, his jacket rolled into a makeshift pillow and wedged between his head and the side window, arms folded comfortably across his chest.

It appeared that even in sleep, Gil and Reenie were diametrically opposed. If Gil was calm, Reenie was anything but. There weren't many times Mattie was grateful for the volume of Rusty's engine, but this was an exception to the rule, as Reenie's loud snores rumbled on. Now Reenie's insistence on booking a room for each of them at every stop on the tour made sense. Mattie had fought this initially, arguing that it was too expensive and that she and Reenie could share a room, but Reenie would not be swayed.

'I'm paying, so what I say goes,' she'd said. 'I haven't shared a room on tour since my earliest days with Ted Farnsworth and I don't intend to start now.'

In the camper van, Reenie sniggered in her sleep and

chuntered incoherently. The enormous bag of pills Gaynor had supplied for the next ten days rested in the footwell beside her feet, rattling and bumping as Rusty changed lanes. A blue road sign confirmed it was fifty-five miles to Alnwick. Mattie wriggled her shoulders as she held on to the steering wheel, trying in vain to release the tension there. They had made good time despite Gaynor's warnings of Reenie's need for frequent breaks, and she felt as if a large tick had been placed beside the first leg of the journey.

Tomorrow they would meet Tommy Mullins in person. He'd sounded such a cheeky character from Reenie's stories that Mattie was looking forward to it immensely. Besides, she wanted to thank him for keeping in touch with The Silver Five – without the updated list of addresses he'd sent in Reenie's Christmas cards every year, this trip wouldn't have been possible.

Pulling into the car park of the hotel at the end of her first day's driving felt like crossing the finish line at Le Mans. Not only had Rusty made it without so much as a grumble, Mattie had survived the Silver–Kendrick Roadshow and they were all still talking. After the dodgy start that morning, this was definitely cause for celebration.

'Good driving,' Gil said, patting Mattie's shoulder as he offered Reenie his arm to walk inside.

'Um, thanks,' Mattie replied, feeling as if she'd been congratulated by an elderly relative. Was random shoulder-patting in fashion in London?

Bags safely delivered to bedrooms and Reenie settled in front of an early-evening quiz show with a cup of tea in hers, Mattie and Gil headed back down the corridor towards their own rooms.

'There's a pub over the road,' Gil said. 'Fancy seeing if they do food?'

'Good idea. I could do with a shower and a bit of down-time first, if you don't mind?' The thought of relaxing for a while in a blissfully quiet room was what had sustained Mattie during the last hour of their journey, and she wasn't ready to relinquish that just because she was hungry.

'No problem. I'll ask at the desk if they can book us a table. Say, eight p.m.?'

'Great.' They had reached Mattie's room, but Gil didn't look as if he was ready to leave yet. 'Er – this is me.'

'Yes. Sorry. I just wanted to know whether you think this trip will be a success?'

Was he implying it wouldn't be? 'Of course. I wouldn't have left my business and driven all this way if I didn't.'

'Right. There's just a lot riding on this gig. So, what time are we meeting Mr Mullins tomorrow?'

'In the morning.' Mattie remembered Reenie's enigmatic answer to the same question earlier: 'We're *musicians*. Any time before midday is an early start for us. We'll be there and off to the next stop before you know it. Plenty of time.'

'She *has* arranged a meeting tomorrow, hasn't she?' Gil asked with a smile, but Mattie could see genuine concern behind it.

'Yes. Of course. She said it was all sorted.'

'Right. But you don't actually have a time written down?'

'No.'

'Nowhere on the schedule?'

'Tomorrow's just allocated for the meeting. Then we're on the road again.'

'Right. But nothing more – *specific*?'

Mattie stared at him. 'Um, no.'

The possibility of an early roadblock settled on both of them as they stood between their rooms in the boutique hotel's hallway.

'I suppose we'll just have to take her word for it?'

'Yes. It'll all work out, Gil.'

It was only when she was watching television in her hotel room later that evening after dinner that Mattie realised Reenie had only ever talked about the details of the first meeting – and even those had been sketchy. She picked up her watch from the bedside table, considering a walk down the corridor to Reenie's room, but saw it was almost midnight. Whatever Reenie said about still being a party animal, Mattie was pretty sure her friend would have tucked herself into bed hours ago.

It will be okay, she repeated in her mind, the sudden flutter of nerves in her stomach daring to disagree. *Everything is going to be okay.*

Chapter Sixteen

'A Rockin' Good Way'
– Brook Benton &
Dinah Washington

♪

The house was a large, bay-windowed semi-detached home with an extension where a garage would once have stood. In the new canopy across the entrance and ground-floor windows, smart halogen inset spotlights cast triangles of light on pristine York stone paving and gravel glistening from the recent rain shower.

'Always the showman, our Tommy. Even has to have spotlights on his front porch,' Reenie chuckled.

Mattie smiled at her. 'Right, then. Are you ready, Miss Silver?'

Reenie blew out a levelling breath, and grinned back. 'As I'll ever be.'

Standing on the doorstep as Gil rang the bell, Mattie found herself surprisingly nervous. From the moment

Tommy Mullins answered the door, their mission was officially under way. While Reenie had assured her over and over that she and Tommy remained friends – and the apology would be a mere formality – Mattie understood the gravity of what they were doing. Tommy might have stayed in touch with Reenie for sixty years, but agreeing to perform with her again was a world away from a polite Christmas letter once a year. She glanced at Reenie – but if the old lady felt the same, it was well hidden beneath her proud stance and eager smile.

The door was opened by a younger man than they'd all expected, and it was clear from his clouded expression that he didn't recognise Reenie.

'Can I help you?'

'Hello, love. We're looking for Tommy. Is he in?'

Mattie saw the rise of Gil's eyebrows, and looked quickly back at the bearded forty-something standing in the open doorway.

'Dad? He's down at Barter Books.'

'Is he? Good.' The briefest hint of colour washed under Reenie's powdered foundation. 'Do you know when he'll be back?'

'Not till later tonight. He has a little gig there – sorry, do I know you?'

Gil was bristling beside Mattie like a building storm cloud threatening rain.

'Reenie Silver, love. From your pa's old band.'

The man's eyes widened. 'No way! Dad'll be chuffed you came for his gig.'

'His gig?' Gil repeated, but Reenie shifted position, bodily blocking him.

'Yes. Of course. That's right. I don't suppose you could point us in the right direction, eh?'

'She *never arranged to meet him*,' Gil growled, as soon as they were on the road heading into Alnwick.

'Oh *shush*,' Reenie countered. 'He has a gig. What better providence, eh? Another sign we're meant to be doing this.'

'Forget *signs*. What about actual, hard facts?'

'Okay, enough now,' Mattie rushed, fearful that a high noon standoff was about to ensue. 'We know where he is, and his son thinks he'll be happy to see us. Let's just – focus on that, yes?'

Reenie and Gil harrumphed their acceptance like a pair of grumpy teenagers. Mattie took a breath and focused on the directions Gavin Mullins had sketched out for them on the back of one of his father's gig flyers. Maybe her companions' differences would be ironed out as they got to know one another. If not, it was going to be a *very long* ten days . . .

Barter Books was situated in an old railway station and was the kind of bookshop you could lose yourself in. As soon as they entered, Mattie wanted to wander around its gorgeously stacked shelves, inhaling the scent of old books. Grandpa Joe used to say bookshops contained a special kind of magic – one that made it impossible to resist wandering in and taking your time. 'A good book-shop calls you in and won't let you leave in a hurry,' he'd say, weaving Mattie and Joanna around the bookcases at Severnside Book Emporium in Ironbridge when they were little.

In the old waiting room chairs had been arranged in a little half-moon around a small stage area marked out by three grey fold-back speakers. A harassed-looking woman in her twenties was trying to unfurl a looped microphone lead, which twisted more with each attempt.

'What are you doing with that, Elsa?' a cheery voice boomed from behind a bookcase and a broad-shouldered man appeared, his luxuriant sweep of pure white hair the only indicator of his true age. He reminded Mattie of Tom Jones, with his swagger and resonant voice. But then she saw his face and recognised him from Reenie's photographs. 'The knitting group meets here *tomorrow*.'

The young woman giggled. 'I can never get these straight.'

'Typical vocalist,' Tommy Mullins jibed. 'You give them one job . . .'

Mattie turned to Reenie, standing beside her. She seemed lost in thought, all the bravado she'd shown during the journey gone. 'Reenie?'

'He's taller,' she said, her voice small and far away.

'Pardon?'

'I don't remember him being so tall . . .'

Gil exchanged glances with Mattie. 'Shall I go over?'

Reenie immediately snapped out of her daydream, shouldering past him. 'Not likely. This is *my* gig, kiddo.' Striding down the makeshift aisle in the centre of the chairs, she pushed her shoulders back, her voice loud and commanding.

166

'Better make sure there's some reverb on that mic, girl. Tommy likes a bit of echo.'

Elsa and Tommy looked up, the older man slowly shaking his head.

'*Bloody hell*. In she walks . . .'

Reenie stopped a few paces from him, her broad smile confident, arms spreading wide like a star welcoming her adoring public. 'You know me, Tom. Always one for the grand entrance.'

'Aye. And the speedy exit an' all.'

Mattie saw Reenie's shoulders stiffen. 'That too, kid.'

'What are you doing here?'

'Coming to see your gig, aren't I?'

'Give over, Reenie Silver.' The pair observed one another, and Mattie wondered what they were thinking. Almost a lifetime had passed since their last meeting – what had changed, and what hadn't?

'Believe what you like, love,' Reenie shrugged. 'So, do I get a hug or not?'

Tommy chuckled and stepped over the fold-back speakers towards her. In his hearty embrace Reenie almost disappeared, a brief exchange of words muffled as she spoke against his chest. Mattie found herself smiling as she watched.

Tommy had been the first member of The Silver Five Reenie had told her about in the early days of their friendship. Whenever she mentioned him her eyes twinkled, hinting at the mischief they got up to: 'I think we drove Rico mad. We were forever being told off for playing pranks and giggling when we should've been serious. I

167

reckon we were as bad as each other. One time in Aldershot we upset the stage manager so much he nearly kicked the whole band out. I can still hear him now: "This is a place for serious *artistes*, not a bunch of kids!" But that's what we were really, wasn't it? Tommy was the kid brother I never had. I loved him for that . . .'

'I'm made up you're here,' Tommy grinned broadly over Reenie's shoulder at Mattie and Gil. 'Are these your kids?'

'Not likely! Tommy, I'd like you to meet my friend Mattie Bell. And this is Gil Kendrick – Jake's grandson.'

'I can see it!' Tommy surveyed Gil with a wide stare as he shook his hand. 'It's a pleasure, sir. Your grandfather was a great man.'

'Thank you.'

'Take a seat, all of you. There's a good café in the building. Why don't I pop there and get us all some coffee?'

'I'll help,' Mattie said, seeing her chance. She needed to know what lay ahead, as Reenie's prediction of this meeting had proved worryingly rose-tinted and it was blatantly obvious Tommy hadn't known they were coming.

'Lovely.' Tommy smiled as she joined him. 'I'll just grab my wallet from the car. Walk with me?'

Outside the rain had stopped at last, brave shafts of sunlight breaking through the heavy grey. The air smelled fresh, and Mattie felt a shiver pass along her skin.

'She's on form,' Tommy said, pocketing his wallet from the glove compartment of a smart-looking estate car. 'Girl's got balls rocking up here, I'll give her that.'

Mattie gave an apologetic smile. 'She seemed to think it would be easy.'

'Aye, I'll bet she did. But that's our Reenie for you. Truth is, I'm glad to see her. But don't you tell her that yet. Best to let her sweat a little, right?'

Given the sudden nature of their arrival, Mattie could hardly protest. 'Fair enough.'

Walking back to the station buffet, they passed a stack of old railway sleepers, the ruts and marks of ages past smoothed and polished. Mattie thought of Tommy, Reenie and the others – could time heal the deep rifts between them?

Once inside the small station café, Tommy turned to her. 'So, what does Reenie Silver want – really?'

'To apologise, mainly.'

Tommy observed her with an amused smile. 'Mainly?'

Mattie hesitated – should she let Reenie present the gig proposal? But if Tommy was more difficult than Reenie had anticipated, how likely was the tour to succeed with others who had more of a grudge against her?

'We want to reunite The Silver Five.'

'You're joking.'

'No. We're proposing to put on the gig that didn't happen in 1956, on the sixtieth anniversary. Reenie wanted to do more than apologise to you all, and this was her idea.'

'Well, I never. Good job I'm not a betting man: I'd never have guessed that in a million.'

'So, what do you think?'

'Me? I think it's barmy, love.'

'Oh.'

'And it's Reenie all over. Daft bat.'

They walked back in heavy silence, Mattie's nerves on edge. Before they entered the old waiting room, she held back.

'Tommy?'

'Yes, pet?'

'Be straight with me: what are our chances of making this happen?'

'Honestly? I've no idea. Reenie caused a lot of upset, for some of us a great deal more than others. But I'll tell you what I do know: it *won't* happen if she just strolls up with no warning. Not with Chuck, and definitely not with June. That's the kind of attitude that'll blow it out of the water before it's even launched.'

'So what should we do?'

Tommy shrugged. 'Let's get these back and have a proper talk, okay?'

'Here he is! My favourite Geordie crooner!' Reenie pushed herself to her feet, raising her cane in greeting. 'Now have *we* got an offer for *you* . . .'

The old man held up his hand. 'You can stop right there, Reen. Your wee girl here's told me all about it.'

Reenie's scarlet lips pulled into a pout aimed squarely at Mattie for stealing her thunder. 'Charming.'

'Now, let *me* tell you what's going to happen. First off, you're going to shut up, Reenie Silver, and listen to me. Now, I love you, but you hurt me. And you hurt our friends. And I think you need to understand that. So I'm going to tell you all about it. Then you can apologise. And *then* I'm going to tell you how I can rescue your daft plan.'

Chapter Seventeen

'(Sh-Boom) Life Could Be a Dream' – The Chords

♪

By the time they arrived back at the hotel, Mattie was exhausted. Tommy certainly hadn't given Reenie an easy time, and Mattie and Gil had watched in stunned silence as he had told her exactly how The Silver Five had crumbled in the wake of her departure. The picture Tommy painted wasn't pretty.

'We'd all been so excited about that gig. You remember the hours we chatted about it beforehand, don't you? Or maybe you don't. Maybe all you were thinking of was yourself.'

'No, it wasn't like that.'

'Wasn't it? Then why never speak to June again, or Alys? Why refuse every invitation I ever sent you to meet up? I know Chuck saw you later – and that was another mess muggins here had to sort. But if you were happy with your decision, why shut us all out afterwards? I think you were embarrassed. I think you knew you'd made a mistake. But you were too proud to own up to it. Pride's always been your problem, girl.'

'I do regret it. That's why I want to get us together now.'

'And you think they'll listen?'

Reenie had swallowed hard, and Mattie had found herself clenching her fists in her lap to resist going to her friend's aid. 'I – I don't know . . .'

'We didn't just split up that night. We *imploded*. It was just so sad. And Rico dropped us like a bunch of hot rocks. So much for a supportive manager.'

'I thought he would look after you all. I really did.'

'Then you're dafter than I thought. You were destined for a glittering career, Reen. What use did he have for us?'

'He promised he would . . .'

'Rico's promises weren't worth the paper they were written on. Like our contract that vanished because you weren't part of the group. Did you know that? The small print said Rico was only responsible for us as a five-piece. You leaving negated the whole thing.'

'I didn't know that.'

Tommy had rubbed his eyes as if the memory exhausted him. 'But that aside, what hurt most was that you lied – to *me*. You *promised* me Rico was just an associate. And you want to know the worst of it? I *knew* you were lying. We all did. I was as hurt as they were, but I stuck up for you. I took your side, the night of that concert, when June and Alys and Chuck were screaming blue murder about you. I told them I believed you, even though I knew you'd lied.'

The colour had drained from Reenie's face. 'Oh, kid, I never knew. What can I say?'

Tommy had shaken his head. Without his smile he looked ten years older, the dark lines around his eyes and across his brow deeper. 'There's nothing to say, love. It's over, done with. Why do you think I've kept in touch all these years, hmm? Why I've tried every Christmas for fifty-nine years to get you to join us for our get-togethers? Because deep down I believed you were a good person, with a good heart. The business turns your head, we all know that. But I knew, beneath it all, you were still Irene Silverman from Woodbine Street, Liverpool. The girl I met backstage at the Ted Farnsworth gig who helped me tie my necktie. The girl who gave me a slug of good-luck brandy from that daft hip flask you nicked from a lorry driver hitch-hiking to London. She's more money now – and fancier glad-rags – but I still see her, sitting here.'

'Oh Tommy . . .' Reenie had looked up at Tommy, tears running down her cheeks, leaving dark trails in the powder. 'Oh, love . . . I'm so very sorry.'

As they watched Reenie walking slowly to the hotel bar, Gil whispered to Mattie, 'That was *brutal*. Is every meeting on this trip going to be like that?'

'I hope not,' she replied, willing the sinking feeling to leave her.

At dinner, all traces of Reenie's discomfort over the meeting with Tommy were gone. She was on top form, her stories of gigs gone by flowing as freely as the wine.

'. . . this stage manager in Rotherham kept giving baby Alys the eye and trying to get her on her own. Dirty beggar! Mind you, back then many of them were. Thought us girls were fair game. He told her she was needed in the back for a costume check, thinking the rest of us hadn't heard him. So we all pretended to go out, only we switched places backstage. When old Wandering Fingers snuck into mine and Alys's dressing room he found Tommy and Chuck waiting for him, dressed in our costumes! We never worked at that theatre again and Rico was furious, but none of us minded. Pass us that bottle of white, Gil, there's a love.'

Gil folded his arms. 'I think you've had enough for tonight.'

'Oh, you do, do you? Well, I've had a bit of a day, sunshine, so hand over the vino . . .'

'Maybe we should all have a coffee?' Mattie suggested, relieved that Gil had broached the subject she'd wanted to mention for the last hour, but not wanting another standoff between her companions. 'It's getting late. Early start tomorrow.'

'*Pfft*, lightweights, the pair of you! We're *celebrating*. One singer signed up, three to go.'

'All the same . . .'

Reenie glared at Mattie like a recently grounded teen. 'You two are no fun. I'll see you in the morning.' She wiped her hands on a napkin and left the table.

'That's us told,' Gil grinned.

'You did the right thing. I saw the bag of medication she had to bring with her. It was scary.'

'I hope I can put them away as well as that when I'm eighty-four.'

They laughed, Mattie finally allowing herself to relax a little. Today had been an emotional marathon she hadn't trained for, and she felt exhausted. At least, with Reenie gone, she and Gil were finally able to talk alone. As they chatted, Mattie understood what her sister referred to as 'the blessed post-bedtime glow' she looked forward to every evening after Ethan and Ava had gone to sleep. It felt as if she and Gil could talk like adults without Reenie's interruptions – and before she knew it almost an hour had passed.

'I think Tommy might just have saved us today.'

'I reckon so. What was Reenie thinking, not checking ahead?'

Mattie stretched out a little in her chair. 'I suppose she assumed it would be easier that way. I think Tommy shocked that out of her, though.'

'He's a good bloke. I feel a lot happier knowing he's phoned ahead of us.' He finished the last of his wine. 'So, how are you doing?'

The question seemed to come from nowhere, and Mattie found herself smiling at him. 'I'm good, thanks. Tired now, but glad we've made a start.'

'You're good with her. She doesn't strike me as the easiest person to be with.'

'She's lovely. You two just haven't clicked yet. But you will. I think she's amazing. I've never met anyone like her. Her self-assurance is off the scale and she refuses to let anyone or anything slow her down. That's inspirational.

And I'm so proud of her for doing this. It can't be easy, facing up to mistakes you made over half a lifetime ago.'

Gil considered this for a while, and Mattie was struck by the change in him since Reenie's departure from the table. Gone was the professional coolness, in its place a warmth she hadn't seen before. Even his posture seemed different, more relaxed and open. She liked this version of him. 'Maybe we should get together like this every night of the tour,' he said, as if the suggestion had been carefully carved from the amiable silence. 'Have some time to go over everything, without Miss Silver's intervention.

'I'd like that.'

'Good.' He flushed a little, and checked his watch. 'It's getting late. I should probably let you get some sleep.'

'Probably.' Rising from the table with him, Mattie smiled back, surprised to feel a little disappointment. She reached for her room key card, and noticed another one half-hidden by Reenie's discarded linen napkin. 'Oh, hang on: Reenie isn't going to get far without this, is she?'

'Crazy woman. We'd better head her off at the pass.'

They hurried back to the hotel rooms in the far end of the building. With any luck, Mattie thought, Reenie's troublesome hip and the effects of alcohol would have slowed her progress and they might catch her before she reached her room.

The corridor on the second floor was empty, but when they arrived at Reenie's room they could hear muted music coming from inside. Of course Reenie wouldn't have let a lost key stop her doing what she wanted!

'Better just check she's okay,' Mattie smiled, knocking on the door.

The door opened, and a startled-looking Eastern European woman peered out at her. 'Good evening,' she rushed, her pale face reddening. 'Turn-down service. Two minutes, please?'

'No problem. I've come to see Miss Silver.'

The woman's expression clouded. 'Guest is not here. Just me.'

'Oh . . .' Had Reenie gone back to the bar to find her key, or to reception for a new one? 'Thank you.'

The door closed, and Mattie turned to Gil. 'We need to find her.'

'Where could she be?' he demanded, hurrying down the hotel corridor in her wake.

'I don't know.'

'Where would an eighty-four-year-old woman go at this time of night? It's an hour since we last saw her. Where is she?'

'I *said* I don't know,' Mattie replied, wishing she'd gone to find Reenie by herself. But she was worried. Reenie had seemed so bullish at dinner, so full of confidence in their onward progress. She should have been tucked up in bed, or at least lounging in self-congratulatory splendour.

At the hotel reception, Mattie rang the bell. A young woman appeared.

'Can I help?'

Mattie checked the receptionist's name badge. 'Gemma, hi. Yes, I hope so. Miss Silver – the old lady in our party – have you seen her leave the hotel this evening?'

Gemma frowned. 'I don't think so.'

Panic building in her throat, Mattie forced herself to breathe. 'Okay. Is there anywhere she could possibly be in the hotel?'

'The spa closed an hour ago. Is she not in the bar?'

'No, we've just come from there. She doesn't have her room key.'

'Wait a minute, how long is it since you last saw her?'

'About an hour?'

Gemma's face lit up. 'I was on my break then. Let me just get my colleague.' She disappeared into the small office behind the reception desk and returned a moment later with a lanky young man. 'Sam was on then. Did you see Miss Silver leave?'

He nodded. 'She asked about nightlife in Alnwick. I suggested The Briar Rose over the road.'

'A lot of our guests go over there on a Wednesday evening,' Gemma explained, rolling her eyes. 'Karaoke.'

Mattie and Gil looked at each other. 'Karaoke!'

They left the bemused receptionists, and ran out of the hotel.

'Do you think she's in there?' Gil asked, as they waited for a gap in the traffic.

'If she isn't, then we really do have a problem.'

'She shouldn't be left alone. The woman is a liability.'

'Gil, that's hardly fair. I think Reenie's more than capable of looking after herself. Stop panicking.'

'I'm *not* panicking.'

'Well, you're doing a rubbish job of being calm.'

They fell into a disgruntled silence as they crossed the

road and headed up the path of the country pub. As soon as they reached the front door, they knew exactly where Reenie was.

Muted but unmistakable, the booming tones of an accomplished singer echoed down the slate-floored hallway to the pub lounge, although Mattie couldn't quite marry Reenie's voice with her chosen song.

'Is that – "Teenage Dirtbag"?' Gil asked, stopping as Mattie pulled open the door.

Inside the low-beamed pub, a stunned audience of drinkers was watching a spry pensioner stalking the stage, her sequinned cardigan drooping from one shoulder, cocktail glass sloshing as she gave what could only be described as a *hearty* performance of Wheatus's seminal hit. Mattie ignored the vision on the stage and nodded at a shocked barman.

'How long has she been singing for?'

'Feels like *hours*. Started with "New York, New York", moved on to "Ring of Fire", and then she hit the Nineties classics hard. I don't think I've ever heard Feeder or Reef sung lounge-style before.'

Reenie's vocal gymnastics would have made Dame Shirley Bassey envious, each phrase lustily delivered. Mattie wondered just how much of the performance was fuelled by a lifetime's experience, and how much by alcohol. Whatever the motivator, she had to act quickly.

'Right, as soon as the song ends, turn the PA off,' she instructed the barman, who seemed grateful for the intervention. 'We'll get her down from the stage.'

'*We?*' Gil hissed.

179

'I can manage.' Mattie opened the door and wrapped her arm around Reenie. 'See you in the morning.'

'Nighty-night, sonny,' Reenie called out, waving a hand vaguely in his direction. 'Ah, *Gilbert*. Lovely, handsome Gilbert . . .'

'It's just Gil,' he muttered, walking away.

Relieved he had gone, Mattie helped Reenie over to her bed, kneeling down to take off her shoes and pull the sequinned cardigan from her thin arms. Reenie had fallen silent, sullenly compliant as an overtired child being coaxed into bed.

It was only when she lay down that she spoke again. 'That was a bit of fun, eh, kid? You stick with your Granny Reenie for a grand night out!'

'You can't do this, Reenie,' Mattie said, suddenly realising how like her mother she sounded. She remembered how she and Joanna had been told off as kids for wandering off at a visiting fair, her mother's initial relief turning into a torrent of frustration. Mattie shook the memory away – an argument would help nobody tonight. 'I'm not telling you what to do. I wouldn't dream of it. But you have to look after yourself. Drinking a lot when you're taking as many pills as you are isn't a good idea.'

Reenie sniggered drunkenly into the duvet tucked up to her chin. 'Aww. Were you worried about me?'

'Of course I was worried! I thought you'd done a moonlight flit.'

The mischief vanished from Reenie's eyes. 'You and the rest of the world.'

As Mattie straightened to leave, Reenie reached out and

181

Tommy now, and Gil and I are here for you too. I'd say we have a fighting chance.'

'And if I can't bring the others?'

Mattie hoped her smile concealed her own nerves. 'You're Reenie Silver. You deserve that stage, no matter who else is on it.'

Reenie planted a kiss on Mattie's hand with trembling lips. 'You're a good girl. Thank you.'

'My pleasure. Now, make sure you drink this bottle of water before you go to sleep, okay? It'll help fend off the hangover.'

'Yes, *Mum*.'

Mattie shook her head, loving the old lady despite her sarcasm. ''Night, Reenie.'

'G'night, kid.'

In the bland anonymity of the corridor outside, the full weight of it all fell on Mattie. More than weary, she felt dog-tired, the emotional and physical exertions of the day sapping every last scrap of energy from her body. All she wanted now was to collapse into bed and sleep. Her room on the floor below suddenly seemed miles away. With a sigh, she began to walk.

At least the events of the evening made sense now. Reenie wasn't trying to cause trouble; she was trying to *escape* from it. Alcohol and music, the ultimate hiding places for a lifelong performer. It proved two things: the road trip was likely to be harder work than they had anticipated, and, most surprisingly, Reenie's confidence had shakier foundations than Mattie had realised. They would have to keep a careful eye on her from now on.

'How is she?'

Startled, Mattie looked up to see a figure walking towards her. 'Gil! You nearly gave me heart failure!'

'Sorry.'

'I thought you'd gone to bed.'

'I had. Well, I tried to. I just wanted to check how Reenie was.' He looked a little ruffled, she thought as he approached, as if he had been lying down in his clothes.

'She'll be fine – apart from a humdinger of a hangover in the morning. Today shook her a little, that's all.'

'Okay.' Gil fell into slow step beside her. 'But is that really all that's going on?'

'What do you mean?'

'She's pulled some fast ones on us since this tour began. Not actually telling anyone she was going to show up, for example.'

'That was a mistake. But now Tommy's helping us, I think we'll be all right.'

Gil held open the door to the stairwell. 'I hope so. We can't afford any more episodes like tonight.'

Mattie felt her shoulders bristle as she walked past him. *You didn't see how scared she was*, she wanted to say. *Have you any idea what this trip means to her?* 'We won't have any more.'

'We'd better not. I've put my neck on the line for this gig. Promotion, press stuff, not to mention the cost of set dressing and bringing in a swing band. My brother thinks

I'm nuts. If it doesn't make money, the club could be in real trouble.'

At the bottom of the stairs, Mattie snapped. Had Gil even heard anything she'd said? 'And that's what matters, is it? Your club making money?'

Gil stared at her as if he'd been slapped. 'No – that's not what I meant . . .'

But Mattie had heard enough. She didn't need to stand and justify Reenie to anyone, least of all him. 'Look, Reenie will be okay. The tour is still on. Your precious investment is safe.'

'Hey – I . . .'

'I'm sorry, Gil. I'm tired and I really want to go to bed.'

'Of course. Forgive me.' He ducked his head and let her walk on. 'Mattie?'

She paused in the doorway. 'Yes?'

'Just tell me one thing. What's in this for you?'

'I want to help Reenie.' It was the truth, but it felt like it hid a mountain of other reasons.

'Why?'

Would he even understand if she tried to explain? For a moment, she was tempted to share it all. But weariness won. 'It's too late now. Can I tell you later?'

'Sure. Um, goodnight. Sleep well.'

London, 22 March 1956

I am in trouble with Uncle Charles. He found out about my visiting the Palm Grove with Len when I should have been studying. Called me into his office

185

*this morning and laid down the law. No dancing, no
music and no girls until my first set of exams are done.*

*He hasn't told Mother or Father. For this I have to
be grateful. But months living here with no light
relief will be hell. Besides, the club is filled with
pretty girls. I've never known what to say to ladies
before, but London makes me feel bold enough to
try. As I said to Len at the weekend, I only have a
year here, so I intend to make the most of it.*

*Lying low for the time being. But I will return to
the Palm Grove – soon . . .*

Mattie lay back against the pillows, looking across the
pages of Grandpa Joe's diary to the orange glow of the
streetlights outside that flooded her darkened room. Joe
had been careful to leave this incident out of his reminiscences of his London year. She knew he had practically
idolised his uncle, seeing him as more of a father than his
own, who had been famously distant from his children.
Uncle Charles had the exotic, privileged life Grandpa Joe
had dreamed of as a young man, and while he'd never
matched Charles's success in business, he attributed much
of his success in life to things his uncle had taught him.

But he hadn't just visited the Palm Grove a few times,
like he'd always told Mattie. What else had he hidden
from her? Smiling to herself, she closed the diary and
dropped it on top of her holdall, already packed for the
morning's departure. Today had been a day of revelations:
what would the next two days in Cambridge bring?

Chapter Eighteen

'C'mon Everybody'
– Eddie Cochran

♪

The next morning was bright and clear, with a distinct chill in the air. Rusty's heaters took a while to be coaxed into life, meaning that his passengers spent the first part of the journey wrapped up in extra layers, their breath fogging up the windows obscuring the view. It was only when they had been travelling for an hour that Mattie realised the dark blue chunky knit blanket Reenie had tucked over her knees was the throw from her hotel bedroom in Alnwick.

'Reenie, did you . . . ?'

'It's so cosy,' she protested. 'Much better than my one at Beauvale.'

Mattie saw Gil's grin reflected in the rear-view mirror, but turned her attention to the elderly cat-burglar in her passenger seat. 'You can't just nick stuff!'

'Let's call it Alnwick's contribution to our ground-breaking road trip. Look, I'll thank them in me speech at the gig, if it'll make you feel better. Things are meant to be nicked from hotel rooms, Mattie.'

'No, they're not.'

'Hotels expect it. I've all sorts of mementoes from me time on the road. I once swiped a spoon from the Ritz. I've a whisky glass from the Hôtel Bristol, Paris and a very swanky pair of slippers from the Hôtel Cap in Antibes, when I was in Cannes in '64. And I've the loveliest robe from the Regent Beverly Wilshire in Hollywood. And now a lovely comfy blanket from the Rose Grove Hotel, Alnwick.'

'Reenie, this tour is meant to focus on you putting right past wrongs, not creating new ones.'

'Oh, give it a *rest*, kid! I've a hangover the size of a mammoth and I'm too old to worry about a bit of dodgy pilfering. Tell you what I'll do. I'll leave all my ill-gotten hotel gains to you in my will, so you can take them all back to where they belong for me. How's that, hmm? You could do with a bit of an adventure. Live a little.'

A snort of laughter from the back seat made Reenie smile.

'You see? Even his nibs back there agrees with me.'

'Let's just say I'm not surprised you have a criminal past,' Gil said. It was a relief to hear him joining in the joke. Mattie wondered if he was still smarting from what she'd said to him yesterday. He had avoided her gaze this morning at breakfast, but at least he was making conversation. It was a start.

The journey passed in companionable chatter, Reenie

treating them to more stories of her long and illustrious career. With the exception of her hangover, she appeared unscathed by the events of last night, and Mattie wondered how much of it she remembered. When Gil decided to ask about her unorthodox song choices at the karaoke, she hesitated before answering.

'It was the Nineties set, wasn't it?' She rolled her eyes heavenwards. 'Always bad when I resort to that for my party piece.'

'How do you even know those songs?'

Reenie groaned. 'When I came back from America it was my manager's clever idea for relaunching my career. Do an album of pop covers, he said, something they won't be expecting. Well, it had worked for Tom Jones and Lulu, hadn't it? Honestly, kids, worst decision I ever made. We spent four months holed up in a drab little studio in Camberwell doing these covers and then the record company refused to release it. Last thing I ever did for them. Still loved the songs, though. I think I have the tapes somewhere, if you ever fancy a listen.'

'I doubt they could beat the live version,' Gil said. 'Sorry, Reenie.'

'Cheeky git.' Reenie folded her arms, but her smile betrayed her.

They arrived in Cambridge four and a half hours later, booking into their new hotel just before three p.m. With Gil heading off to catch up on work calls and Reenie retiring to her room for an afternoon nap, Mattie took the opportunity for some time on her own. Travelling was fun, but everything about it was loud and intrusive: the burr of tyres on tarmac, Rusty's repertoire of clanks, rattles and bumps, the chatter when her travelling companions were awake and their collected snores when they weren't. Being alone in the fresh air with her own thoughts and the gentle hum of Cambridge streets was Mattie's idea of heaven.

The hotel was on the outer edge of the city on a major road, so it would be easy to find her way back. Thrilled to be exploring a new place, Mattie let herself wander through the streets with no particular plan. She found interesting alleys, tiny artisan craft and food shops and spent a happy hour riffling through vintage copies of the *Lady* and *Good Housekeeping* in an old bookshop. Heading to an independent café across the road to read her purchases over coffee, she noticed a tiny vintage goods shop next door. She couldn't resist peeking inside, imagining Joanna's amusement as she did so.

'*Most people would get as far away from work as possible when they have time off. Not you. You're obsessed.*'

'*I probably am. I love what I do.*'

She smiled as the familiar aroma of the shop met her. The smell of mothballs and memories, as Laurie had once described it. And she was right. Being surrounded by old garments, hats and bags made her feel as if she were travelling back in time, a thousand stories to discover packed into the overstuffed rails and crates.

As she browsed, her thoughts drifted to the night before. It had been so strange to see Reenie and Gil in a different light: Reenie so scared and suddenly doubtful of her own ability, and Gil the hard-nosed businessman who cared more about the gig than any of the performers.

190

Wait. That's not fair, is it?

Had she been too hard on him last night? What if he had been scared, too? The thought sat uneasily on Mattie's shoulders. Despite his jokes with Reenie on the journey down, he hadn't looked her in the eye when he'd said he wanted to catch up on work. Her hand rested on the green velvet of a 1930s evening coat and she remembered their discussion about the stage curtains at Kendrick's. He'd been so animated when he talked about preserving his grandfather's club. If he cared half as much about his business as Mattie did for hers, why wouldn't he be worried?

Chastened by the realisation, she turned to leave the shop when a flash of red from a high shelf caught her eye. It was perfect – a peace offering in faded red felt with a long black tassel.

She was halfway back to the hotel when a familiar voice called her name. Turning back, she saw Gil jogging towards her.

'I'm glad I caught you,' he said, a slight pinkness to his cheeks from running. 'I was just going to get a coffee. Would you like one?'

Mattie's fingers closed around the string handles of the bag from the vintage shop. 'Love to.'

They walked a little way until they found a café overlooking a beautiful leafy park. The late-afternoon sun had broken free of the bank of cloud that had hung over the city since they arrived, bringing groups of students out to gather in the dappled sunlight beneath ancient lime and oak trees. Mattie found a table in the single bay window while Gil ordered coffee. He returned with a handful of cutlery and a bright yellow rubber duck.

'Our order number. Cute, huh?'

'Maybe you should get some for Kendrick's.'

'I think Colm would definitely kick me out if I suggested that.' He rubbed his thumb along his jaw and the direct stare Mattie had first seen at the club was back. 'Hey, about last night . . .'

'Gil, you don't have to . . .'

'No, I do, Mattie. I was out of order. I do care about Reenie, but she gave me a shock last night. I've never seen her out of control before.'

'Me either.'

'I'll admit I was worried. But the way you were with her last night, getting her to leave that pub and come with us – you were great. And I should have supported you.'

'You did. There's no way I could've got her back to the hotel on my own.'

A small smile played on Gil's lips. 'She's surprisingly strong for a little old lady. You know what I mean, though. I'm sorry.'

'I was rude to you last night. I was tired and scared but that doesn't excuse how I spoke to you. So,' she took the vintage shop bag from the chair beside her and handed it to Gil, 'this is to say sorry.'

He frowned as he peered inside, then burst out laughing as he pulled out the red felt fez. 'Oh *wow* – where did you find this?'

'A vintage clothes shop – yes, I know, busman's holiday

and all that. I thought it could help with your Tommy Cooper routines.'

'I've wanted one of these for years.' He smiled, tipped the fez onto his head at an angle and gave a deep chuckle like his idol. 'You want a bit of Tommy? "Now here's a little trick I'd like to show you now which I picked up. I don't know who dropped it . . ."'

At dinner that evening, Mattie noticed Reenie watching her and Gil as they relayed the events of the afternoon.

'. . . And then half the customers in the café started laughing. Honestly, Reenie, it was hilarious.'

'I wasn't really expecting an audience.'

'Don't give me that. You loved every minute of it.'

Gil shrugged. 'Maybe we all have a bit of a performer in us, eh, Ms Silver?'

'You should mind yourself, Gil. That bug's addictive when it bites.' She raised an eyebrow at Mattie. 'Maybe our Mr Kendrick is a bit of a dark horse. You should watch him, kid.'

Chapter Nineteen

'Mean Mama Blues'
– Ronnie Ray

♪

'Wouldn't it have made more sense to start in Cambridge and then head north for the eastern leg of the trip?' Gil asked next morning, as they set off for the meeting Reenie seemed to have been dreading the most.

Reenie grimaced in the front seat. 'It would if I was good friends with June Knight. I needed a friendly face first.'

'You and June didn't get on?'

'Not really. It's what happens when you get thrown together in a band. Rico knew June from way back. She was singing with the first dance band he managed, and he'd always promised her he'd keep her in mind when he started putting projects together. Trouble was, then he met me and changed his mind. June thought I'd muscled in on her starring role.'

'And had you?'

'*Gil . . .*'

'No, it's a fair question, Mattie. Maybe I did, son. I was seventeen years old and thought everything was fair in business. Rico didn't let on he knew her until we'd recorded our first song. I just figured she was a backing singer. I didn't know she'd been his first protégé. By the time I'd clocked what was happening it was too late to change anything. And I wasn't about to let her have my place in the group. We were called The Silver Five, not The Knight Five. That's just the way it was.'

The tall copper beech trees at the end of June Knight's drive seemed to part like stage curtains as they approached her house. It was a beautiful Edwardian villa in pale stone, rising from the perfect stripes of a pristine, carefully clipped lawn. Reenie fell silent, her crestfallen expression revealing that her less-than-magnanimous hopes for June's residence had been dashed against the smooth limestone masonry.

When Rusty was parked, Mattie clambered out, shaking the creases from her clothes and stretching before heading for the front door. Gil was about to ring the bell when he looked over his shoulder.

'Hang on, where's the star of our show?'

Mattie looked back to see Reenie still seated in the camper van. She was staring straight ahead, her only movement a rhythmic wringing of her hands. Mattie hurried back across the drive.

'Reenie? Are you ready?'

Reenie looked *petrified* – the fear Mattie had seen after the karaoke incident in Alnwick back again. Her bullishness gone, she was just a frail old lady in a car seat too high for her spindly legs to reach the camper van floor.

'Reenie?'

'Just – just give me a minute, will you? I need to . . .' Her sentence drifted off into the warm early autumn breeze.

'Absolutely. Take all the time you need.' Mattie resisted the urge to look at her watch, her insides turning themselves in knots. 'But I think June's ready to see you.'

'I'll bet she is. Probably got an army in there, baying for my blood.'

'She wants to see you. Tommy said so.'

'Oh sure, to rub my nose in it after all these years. Nothing would give her more satisfaction than seein' me come *grovelling*.' She looked up at Mattie, revealing red-rimmed eyes that hadn't seen much sleep. 'She *hates* me. Always has. Why did I agree to this?'

Mattie ducked her head into the camper van, lowering her voice so that Gil couldn't hear. 'Because it matters. Because you've planned so much and come all this way – and to back out now would be worse than going in there. You can do this. You're "Reenie bleedin' Silver"! There's nothing you can't do.'

'She won't be happy until she's made me beg. She's going to sit there like the bleedin' Queen Bee and watch me sweat it out. I tell you, kid, June Knight keeps grudges longer than anyone else on earth. She's waited sixty years to have the last word. *That's* why she wants to see me.'

Mattie's heart went out to her. Addressing Reenie as if reassuring a terrified child, Mattie touched her arm. 'I think I know what's going on here. You're scared—'

'I am not!'

'I think you are. But you're going to be okay, I promise. This is what you wanted to do. It was *your* decision to come here – so that gives you control in this situation. Yes, she might say things you don't want to hear, but I think underneath it all she wants this as much as you. Think of the gig that's waiting for you: wouldn't it be better if all of The Silver Five were there? One last gig to show the world what it once had?'

Reenie shook her head. 'You make it sound so easy. Well, it's not. June and me – we have more history than you know. There are things we said to each other we can never take back.'

'Then move forwards. You *can* do something about the future.'

'Is she coming or not?'

Mattie closed her eyes. *Shut up, Gil!* She raised her hand and hoped it would be enough. 'Shall we go in?'

'Right.' Reenie picked up her handbag from the seat beside her, pulled out a lacy handkerchief and dabbed her nose. 'If this backfires, I'm blaming you.'

In that moment, Reenie Silver was triumphantly back.

She left the camper van and walked slowly across the gravel drive in front of June Knight's house, head held high, handbag swinging like a mace readying for battle. She slowed as she drew level with Gil, jabbing a finger into his ribs.

'Call yourself a club owner, sunshine? You *wait* until the *star* is ready. Everyone knows that. Your grandad lived by it. Ring the bell, Matilda.'

197

They were met by a good-looking man Mattie guessed to be in his late forties. His welcome was like a blast of warm air, almost knocking them off the York stone doorstep. 'Hello! Lovely to see you. You found us okay? Good, good. Sorry, I'm Hugo Benecourt. Mother is itching to meet you all. She's in the conservatory and we have tea waiting. Please, come in, come in!'

Mattie glanced at Reenie, who pulled a face. 'Hugo? She called her kid *Hugo*? Well, I'm not surprised. I heard her second husband was a lord, or something.'

'Let's just – play nicely,' Mattie replied, wincing a little. How many things could she say like her mother today?

Joanna had been highly amused by Mattie's transformation in Reenie's presence. 'You're just being protective,' she'd said last night when Mattie called her. 'And by the sound of it, she's eighty-four going on sixteen. I don't know how you're handling her.'

'She's just scared. Only for Reenie being frightened comes out as laying siege to local karaoke nights and ribbing Gil.'

'How is the man himself?'

Mattie considered the question now as she followed Gil's tall frame into a stunning octagonal conservatory overlooking an expanse of perfectly cut lawns framed by blood-red maple trees and elegant weeping willows. She'd had a glimpse of a different man in the Cambridge café yesterday and she was still piecing together a clear picture of who he really was.

The link with her life back home boosted Mattie's spirits. She had been excited to set off on the trip with

Reenie, but her new-found sense of family in her rented house was a pull on her heart she hadn't expected. How were Ethan and Ava coping with being away from home and away from their father? Were they missing their aunt?

'You worry too much,' her sister had scolded gently, but there was warmth in her laughter that meant the world to Mattie. 'The kids are okay. We're working through the yucky stuff when it happens and enjoying the bits where we feel more like normal. They love the house – and Ava's taken to reading in that old wicker armchair in your room. She calls it her "happy chair". We're getting there, M. And we love you.' Joanna had then assured her that all at Bell Be-Bop was running smoothly and that Jack had managed to pop by most days. Mattie wasn't concerned about the shop, but it all helped to hear of life continuing in her absence when so much of this road trip felt likely to change at any moment.

Gil turned back. 'Have you seen her? I can't believe she's older than Reenie.' He gave a surreptitious nod towards the French doors.

There was June Knight, reclined at an elegant angle across a velvet chaise. She could have sashayed straight out of the pages of *Vogue*, a star in her twilight years blessed with phenomenal bone structure and dewy-fresh skin. Swathed in a camel-coloured pashmina over a crisp white shirt, three-quarter-length white denim crops and dainty cream ballerina pumps, her hair, once honey-blonde, now fell around her shoulders in elegant, pure white waves. Simple pearl earrings and a double string of pearls around her neck all contrived to give her the appearance of a mythical mermaid, beautifully beached on a bed of mink-hued velvet.

'Bleedin' Queen Bee,' Reenie muttered as Mattie nudged her elbow.

'So, where is she?' June asked, her voice a lilting song of benevolence.

Reenie stepped forward, professional smile on full brilliant show, holding out both arms. 'June Knight, as I live and breathe!'

They didn't move towards one another, but maintained the poses of welcome as if waiting for the gathered onlookers to slowly push them together into an embrace.

'Can it *really* have been sixty years?' June asked.

'Neither of us looks old enough,' Reenie replied, adopting a theatrical accent somewhere between Celia Johnson and Cilla Black.

'You'll forgive me, darling Reenie, for not getting up? I had an operation on my knee four weeks ago and I've been given strict instructions not to make any *unnecessary* movements.' Her dark eyes dipped on the word, as if dismissing Reenie.

Mattie saw Reenie's shoulders tense.

'It's so wonderful to see you back together,' she rushed, nodding too enthusiastically at Hugo, who followed suit. The air in the conservatory seemed to crackle as everyone watched the two former friends.

While their smiles were steady, Mattie was suddenly aware of her nerves standing to attention. She looked over at Gil, who was a short distance away, his arms folded.

It's going to be okay, she told herself. *They're getting on well. You're just being paranoid.*

'June, I understand. At your age you really should be *taking it easy.*'

June smiled again, the muscles in her cheeks flexing. 'Oh, I know. But the work keeps coming in, so what am I to do? I never expected to be popular in my later years. Gracious me, where are my manners? Sit, please, all of you. Hugo, darling, ask Consuela to bring in the tea.' She blushed a little. 'I know it's dreadfully decadent, but I wouldn't swap my *housekeeper* for anything. Consuela is an angel. So wonderful to be in my own home, at my age. Anyway, enough about me. How is life in sheltered accommodation, Reenie, dear?'

Gil gave a loud cough and looked out at the garden.

'Exclusive retirement village,' Reenie corrected. 'And they are so kind to give me a darling cottage of my own, when I am one of their *major shareholders*. The house in LA and my Cheshire mansion are bringing in an absolute fortune in rent – not that I need any more money.'

'Tea, everyone!' Hugo was ushering in a tiny, nervous-looking woman carrying a tray stacked with so many things Mattie could barely see her face. 'Consuela makes the best tea in the whole of Cambridgeshire.' He winced as June cleared her throat. 'Or, quite possibly, England.'

In the middle of the forced politeness, Grandpa Joe popped into Mattie's mind. She remembered him laughing about the previous incumbents of St Lawrence's vicarage, long before Rev. Phil and his family arrived. Reverend Enoch Williams was, according to Grandpa Joe, 'a

201

whirlwind in the pulpit and a woodlouse in his home', on account of his fearsome wife, Margaret. She insisted everyone in the parish call her by her family's pet name of Min-Min, but was anything but as cuddly as the name suggested.

'Have you ever seen anyone scared into having fun?' he used to say, the familiar crinkles appearing in his face as he grinned. Grandpa Joe had a face that seemed to lift several inches when he smiled. Grandma, when she was alive, often said he was the only man she'd ever met who could 'smile from the back of his neck'. 'You should have seen poor Enoch at afternoon tea. I swear he arranged the petits fours into HELP ME messages on the plates as he smiled frantically at everyone.'

Did the June Knight of The Silver Five bear any resemblance to the feisty lady now engaged in covert battle with Reenie? What would Grandpa Joe have made of the unfolding scene? Mattie looked across to Gil, who now hid his obvious amusement behind a cup of Consuela's finest. Her grandfather would most likely have been sitting with Gil, the pair of them stifling laughter.

Mattie pulled herself up at the unexpectedly warm image. Why did she think of *that*, now? It was obvious that lack of sleep was getting to her. She would turn in early tonight, she decided, to avoid any more confusion . . .

'Do we all have tea? Good.' June turned towards Reenie and asked the question everyone had been waiting for. 'Now, Reenie, was there something you wanted to say?'

'You have a *beautiful* home,' Reenie purred. Mattie couldn't see her face from where she sat, but she knew exactly what expression the old lady was wearing by the fleeting disappearance of June's smile. If she was going to go down, she clearly intended to delay the moment as long as possible.

'Well, that's *kind* of you to say. It's just my little abode. Six bedrooms – all en-suite – are more than enough for me. But I digress. Tommy said—'

'Ah, Tommy. Y'know, he was always sweet on me. When we saw him this week he was just as flirty as ever. He spoke very warmly of you.'

'We were always close. We've remained so ever since . . . well, I think you know from *when*.'

'Rico loved him, of course.'

That shot hit its target as June stiffened. 'Poor Rico. So much talent. Such a shame, to lose it all and then be branded a criminal.'

'He made a few errors of judgement, that's all,' Reenie snapped, momentarily abandoning her composure.

'He made more than he was ever *prosecuted* for,' June fired back. 'You were one of the lucky ones. No surprise that you got off scot-free.'

'You think?'

'You hung on to him long enough after you abandoned us. I wonder, did the fraud squad ever look into *your* accounts?'

'What is that supposed to mean?'

Missile landed, June relaxed back into her velvet throne, a steely nerve revealed. 'Let's not go over old ground, shall we, dear?'

Reenie sat bolt upright on the edge of her seat – and

suddenly all Mattie could hear was alarm bells going off in her head. 'No, *let's*. We all know what this is about. You think you should have been lead singer.'

'There's no *think* about it: I know I should have been. Everyone tells me "Violetta" was our best song. The song *I* sang lead on. If there's one question I've been asked the most at my public appearances it's "Why weren't you the lead?" Perhaps it was best we did end the group. Eventually we would have lost fans because Alys and I would never have had the chance to shine. And look at that little girl from Caerphilly now! A national treasure both sides of the border! And I have it on good authority that the Yanks love her, too. But of course, you'll know that. Tell me, whatever happened to your Vegas shows?'

'I left on a high. Left them wanting more, as any true star should.'

'That's not what I heard. But then, American divorces and bankruptcy can be so costly.'

'Mum – your heart . . .' Hugo began, but was hushed by a glare from his mother. 'Miss Silver, I think it would be best if you told us why you wanted to visit now . . .'

'I didn't sabotage the group and neither did Rico!' Reenie growled. 'Face it, June, we were over and heading down the hill long before the Palm Grove gig.'

'You decided! *You*, who slept your way into Rico's good books . . .'

'How *dare* you!'

Mattie was on her feet and between the two snarling ladies, her earlier sense of danger confirmed. 'Reenie, Ms Knight, please . . .'

'Slept your way in and *stole my place*!'

'Ohhh, so *there* it is! What took you so long to admit it, June? Too busy working on your second-rate vocals instead?'

June was struggling to her feet, pashmina flicking furiously around her shoulders. 'At least I'll be known for my voice, not my ability to drop my knickers when I want something! You're a flake and a hussy, Reenie Silver. Always were, always will be!'

They squared up to one another, Reenie all in black and June in camel and white, like gunslingers at high noon.

'Enough! Ladies, please, this isn't getting us anywhere.'

June stood her ground. 'I'm saying what we all thought, Miss Bell! *All* of us, including Tommy. For years we met up and we cursed you, Reenie! Tommy and Alys and Chuck and me. We met in hotels around the country and we talked for hours about what you did. And you not coming? It was a *gift*! Because, finally, we could all say what we really felt. You haven't come here to apologise. You've come to fool us all into one last opportunity to feel good about yourself.'

Reenie grabbed her handbag – and, for a horrible moment, Mattie thought she might take a swing at her former bandmate. Instead she turned on her heel and began to leave. 'This was a mistake. We're *done* here.'

'Oh, that's right,' June shrieked in her wake, 'walk away! Just like you always do! Can't drop your knickers to win this one, can you, Miss Silver? Because *nobody cares* what you do anymore!'

'You can forget the chance *I* was offering *you*, you

washed-up, has-been also-ran! Forget it! I'll do the gig myself.' Reenie was out of the door before anyone could stop her.

Mattie looked at Hugo, who had paled to match the magnolia paint on the conservatory's window frames. 'I'll bring her back. Just give me a moment . . .'

'Get out! All of you!' June tottered back, sitting heavily on the chaise. 'Hugo! *Tell* them.'

'It's best you leave,' Hugo said, apology filling his puppy-dog eyes. 'I'll see you out . . .'

Mattie felt she was walking through a precariously constructed house of cards, now collapsing in her wake as the party left the house. Reenie didn't even stop to say goodbye to June's son, stomping woodenly across the drive towards Mattie's camper van. Gil turned to offer Hugo a helpless shrug and handshake before following the old lady, a gesture Mattie found some comfort in. But without June and Reenie's reconciliation, The Silver Five's reunion would be incomplete. And if the remaining members felt the same as she did, what hope was there?

'I really am sorry,' Hugo said, placing both hands over Mattie's. 'I truly thought she would welcome Reenie. You'll probably not believe this, but she talks about The Silver Five all the time. The places they played, the stories from the dressing rooms and being on the road. And the other members – *all* of them. I felt sure she would accept Miss Silver's apology and all would be well.'

'Not that we ever got to the apology,' Mattie replied. 'I thought Reenie could do it, too. But maybe some things are just impossible to forgive after sixty years. Will your mum be okay?'

Hugo rolled his eyes and Mattie wondered just how easy it was for him to live with a woman so used to getting her own way. 'She'll survive. My mother isn't the easiest to live with. And when she sets her mind, she's pretty much immovable.' He lowered his voice. 'This house *isn't* hers, you know. It's mine. My wife and I moved her here after she broke her hip last year. She refused to go into sheltered accommodation, so this was the only option. My family are away this weekend, otherwise you would have had children, dogs and nannies bouncing around the place. And Consuela is mother's carer, not her housekeeper. I'm sorry we weren't straight with you. Sometimes it's easier, in the long term, to give in to their whims.'

Looking at Reenie now, stabbing the expensive driveway with her cane and demanding to be let into Rusty, Mattie was filled with sympathy for June's long-suffering son. But her heart was heavy, the prospect of an un-reunited group meaning only one thing for her: that she had failed to keep her graveside promise to Grandpa Joe.

She had to try to wrestle this back from the gaping jaws of defeat. 'Is there any chance – any hope at all – that your mum might change her mind?'

Hugo's instinctive nervous laugh made Mattie's hopes crumble. 'Sorry,' he said, clamping a hand to his mouth. 'It's just – well, you *saw* how she was . . .'

'It's such a shame, that's all.' Mattie wasn't really speaking to Hugo now, the huge weight of disappointment

207

causing words to flood out of her. 'It would have been a wonderful thing to show the world, you know? That even after sixty years of misunderstanding and hurt, problems can be solved and people can be forgiven. There's just too much grudge-keeping in this world and I'm sick of it. It's why I've always loved the 1950s – it always seems like such a hopeful time. Although the more I learn about The Silver Five, the more I'm thinking I was completely naive to believe that.'

'That's the way Mother talks about that time. Despite everything that happened in '56. If it helps, I think the years she spent with The Silver Five were some of the happiest of her life.'

Mattie smiled at June's son. They had a lot in common, both trying to move forward with headstrong elderly ladies determined to push in the opposite direction. At least she only had to live with Reenie for the next week or so: Hugo was stuck with his mother for the rest of her life. 'Thanks – for agreeing to see us. I imagine you had more than a small part to play in it.'

Her guess was confirmed as Hugo's neck reddened. 'More than you know. Tommy and I spoke about it for a long time before I dared inform my mother. I accepted on her behalf. Only told her last night that you'd be visiting, actually. And I think I will be held accountable for that for some years to come. I'm sorry we didn't succeed.'

That was it, wasn't it? The final word: the meeting between Reenie and June hadn't succeeded. There were to be no eleventh-hour changes of heart, no sudden races to bring about the reconciliation that on paper had seemed so achievable. Mattie could see Gil doing his best to talk to Reenie, but her expression said it all: *We're done here. Get me back on the bus and let's go.*

Mattie handed Hugo a business card. 'My mobile number is on there, if you ever need it.'

'Thanks. Safe journey.'

'Finally!' Reenie wrestled open the passenger door when Mattie unlocked it, batting away her attempts to help as she struggled inside. 'I was beginning to think you'd pulled.'

'No, as a matter of fact. I was trying to save the gig. Not that you care about that.'

'I told you she'd be difficult. But did you listen to me? Oh no. *You* said she was ready to talk. Like hell she was! Sitting there like the Aga Khan, looking down on me because she thinks she's oh-so far superior – and did either of you stick up for Reenie Silver? Did you heck!'

'That's not fair, Reenie,' Gil said. 'From where I was sitting you were as ready for a fight as she was.'

'Shut up, Kendrick, what do you know?'

'I think I know a wind-up merchant when I see one. I take after my grandfather in that respect.'

'Listen, kid, if you knew what I know about your grandad you wouldn't be plaguing me. Matilda! Turn this rust-bucket around and get us out of here, will you?'

Mattie had heard enough. Gil was right: Reenie was far from the innocent party in the fiasco they'd just endured. And how dare she try to call the shots now?

'I don't think so.' Even as she spoke the words, Mattie was shocked at how easily they had left her mouth.

Reenie glared over at her. 'Excuse me?'

209

'I will drive us back to the hotel when I am ready. What were you playing at in there? You said you were serious about apologising to June. About persuading her to perform at the reunion gig.'

'I was! But you saw her – she wasn't about to listen to a bleedin' word I said. So I wasn't going to grovel.'

'Rubbish, Reenie. You went in there to goad her into a fight so you didn't have to say sorry!'

'Maybe this would be better back at the hotel?'

Mattie ignored Gil's quiet suggestion. Reenie needed to know the damage she'd done. 'No. I want to say this now, while I'm angry enough not to care what *she* thinks,' Mattie replied, her knuckles turning white as she gripped Rusty's steering wheel. 'You just ruined *everything* in there, Reenie, do you understand? Everything we've worked so hard to achieve; the reason we're all on this tour; the gig; the next seven days of our lives – it all means nothing because you didn't have the nerve to be the bigger person in that room.'

Reenie's brow shrouded her eyes, her voice like distant rolling thunder. '*Drive* the *van*, Mattie Bell. You don't know the water that's passed under the bridge between her and me. I doubt you'd understand even if you did. Now this is *my* tour, *my* gig, and *I* say we're leaving.'

The only time Mattie had experienced such dizzying anger before was during the final argument with her grandfather. Shamed by its memory – and fighting the urge to push Reenie out of her seat and drive away – Mattie started the engine. She told herself she could work out how to argue the case with Reenie on the journey back.

But in truth all she wanted to do was run to her room and escape the old lady and Gil. She couldn't fight back; instead she jammed her foot flat to the floor and Rusty veered forwards, sending showers of York stone gravel clattering across the drive as they sped away.

How *dare* Reenie behave so badly and then try to blame her for it?

'So, now that charade is over, who fancies a takeaway tonight?' Reenie asked, her brightness scarily cold as Mattie fumed in the driver's seat. 'Been years since I ordered pizza. Might as well make hay while the cat's away – or whatever that saying is.'

Don't talk to me, Mattie glowered. *Don't speak to me; don't try to chivvy me into a banal conversation to absolve your conscience.*

She needed to think. Was it worth continuing, if this was Reenie's idea of making amends? They should give up the idea as a bad one and head home. Then Reenie Silver could go back to her captive audience at Beauvale and Mattie could return to the task of rebuilding her life. They would never have to meet again and she could forget she'd ever put her faith in a former music star from Liverpool.

A few times she thought she felt Gil's gaze on her, but when she checked the mirror his eyes were trained away from hers to the wide, flat Cambridgeshire fields lining each side of the dual carriageway.

It didn't matter what anyone thought. Right now, all Mattie was concerned with was salvaging what hope she could from this disastrous trip. It had to be found somewhere, some kind of lesson learned to act as penance to Grandpa Joe.

Later, after a long walk by herself and a hot bath, she considered the pieces of the past few days and tried to think rationally. She had to step back from the anger that had been her undoing in the past.

If I let Reenie win, I'm right back to that moment I walked out on Grandpa Joe, she thought. How was that helpful to anyone? She'd accused Reenie of not taking the higher ground with June. If she remained angry and let all their plans fail, how was she any better?

It was time to take a long, hard look at Mattie Bell – and dare to be different.

Chapter Twenty

'I Wonder Why'
– Dion & the Belmonts

♪

Sunday, 15 April 1956

Len introduced me to his sister last night at the Palm Grove. One thing's for certain, they don't make girls like that in Shropshire! Una is one in a million. Tall, leggy, raven-haired – she's like Cyd Charisse in Singin' in the Rain. *I kept forgetting to breathe last night, which could be why my chest is sore today. Didn't sleep much either. Uncle Charles pulled me up over it this morning. He put it down to studying too late. Oh, if only! My studies are falling behind – and it can only get worse the more I think about Una. Can't remember lying awake thinking about a girl like that for years. She has summer-blue eyes that catch your attention and won't let go.*

Look at me, talking flowery like a jazz poet! Next

thing I'll be buying a beret and quoting Proust. Let's just say that looking at Len, you'd never believe his sister could look anything like that. He made it pretty clear she was off limits. But the way she spoke to me last night, I think she might have something to say about that.

Meeting them both at the PG tonight. I shouldn't because I've an exam in the morning. But I know enough to pass and I don't intend to miss one minute of fun . . .

Well, *that* was a surprise. In all the years Mattie had heard Grandpa Joe's stories of his London 'bachelor year', he had never mentioned either Len or Una. It seemed, from what she was reading in the green leather 1956 diary, that most of the details of his year in London had been omitted. He'd mentioned he'd visited the Palm Grove, but the story had always been that a friend of his was a regular at the club and it was this friend who had bought tickets for The Silver Five's concert. She had always assumed his 'friend' to be Bill Godfrey, the evacuee who had first fired up Joe Bell's dreams of visiting London and with whom he'd spent time when he arrived in the city.

She had spent the night lost in thought, trying to find anything positive she could salvage from their current predicament. It was no use: Reenie's pride and June's need for retribution had all but killed her hopes of what the reunion concert could be. The only way anything would change would be if either of them changed their minds

214

– and having seen them in full combat mode today, Mattie knew this was the unlikeliest outcome of all.

Before she knew it, she was taken back to another sleepless night, after a row that had broken her heart and shattered her world. For months she'd hoped against hope that Grandpa Joe would change his mind – because that was the only way the situation could ever be resolved. He'd held all the cards and was refusing to deal them, leaving Mattie helpless and at his mercy.

The ultimatum had come out of nowhere, after an innocuous family dinner, when the Bell clan were settled with coffee in the farmhouse's large sitting room. A bland TV drama had been playing to itself in the corner of the room while the usual family banter passed between the three generations. Joanna was refereeing a game of hide-and-seek with her children and Jack; Mattie's mum was swapping age-old anecdotes with Uncle Reuben about growing up in Kings Sunbury, while Mattie's father and Uncle Seth exchanged opinions on the latest Formula 1 team news. Mattie was sitting cross-legged on the floor fussing over Grandpa Joe's ageing Labrador, Bertie, while she listened to his stories of early married life with Grandma.

'We had nothing, of course. Couples rarely did in those days. But we made do. Decorated the house around us, buying furniture when money allowed and accepting kind donations from friends when we couldn't. Not like today, where young people have houses all set up like show homes before they walk down the aisle. I tell you what, I'll bet your grandma and I appreciated our home more than anyone today.'

215

'I bet you did. As for me, I'll be busy filling my home with old furniture and things that were made before I was born.'

It was nothing, a throwaway comment on a well-fed Saturday afternoon, but apparently it was the last straw for her grandfather.

'I won't have it, Matilda.'

His voice had been so sharp, so utterly out of character, that every member of the Bell family had turned as one to look at him.

Mattie had laughed, thinking he was setting the room up for one of his jokes. But Grandpa Joe's smile had gone, replaced with pure, unfettered fury.

'You think Asher can give you what you need. But he can't. No granddaughter of mine will ever be shackled to a man like that.'

'Look, I know you're not his biggest fan, but how can you say that? You don't know him . . .'

'I know enough about his sort. All flowery promises and too-sincere smiles. He'll break your heart, Matilda.'

'Come on, Gramps, lighten up,' Jack had said, but a dozen pairs of eyes had silenced him. Everyone knew what was happening. There could be no doubt. Grandpa Joe hadn't raised his voice like that for years, but now he was shouting at the young woman everyone called his favourite. Maybe someone should have intervened, but right then the Bell family could only look on in shock. Later, they would offer their sympathies in private – and Mattie knew many had tried to change Grandpa Joe's mind in the days and weeks that followed. But in that dreadful moment, Mattie was utterly alone.

It was the worst day of her life. Worse even than when she'd heard he had died – or when she'd discovered Asher with his mistress. Because, in an instant, she lost the one thing she cared about most in the world: her grandfather's love.

Last night, Mattie had been assaulted again by the injustice of that moment. She had done nothing wrong, except for believing Asher loved her as much as he claimed to. Grandpa Joe had delivered the ultimatum in front of his gathered family – and Mattie had stood up for herself as he had always urged her to. And she had learned that the advice her grandfather had given her all her life didn't apply when it was aimed back at him. The moment she'd stood up for what she wanted was also the moment Grandpa Joe stopped loving her. At least, that was how it felt.

Now, with the possibility of fulfilling her promise slipping away, Mattie felt as if she'd lost him all over again. Her plan had failed – through no fault of her own. And she could do nothing to change the situation.

She was still thinking about the diary's revelations when she arrived in the hotel's breakfast room to find Gil already there. He was hiding behind the generous pages of a broadsheet newspaper, an act heightened by the eerie silence of the breakfast room. The few other guests dotted around the room ate in silence, too. Mattie recalled the silence of the farmhouse sitting room on the day of her row with Grandpa Joe. She shivered.

'Morning,' she said, pushing the memory away.

Gil lowered the paper, and Mattie could see faint traces of blue beneath his eyes. Had he not slept well either?

'Hi. How did you sleep?'

'About as well as you, by the looks of it.'

'I couldn't settle. Watching old ladies brute it out isn't my idea of a relaxing afternoon, especially when I'm likely to lose money because of it.'

Mattie sat at the table. 'I've been trying to think of a way to change what's happened, but I'm stumped. I think Reenie blew it yesterday.'

Gil shrugged, a little more open towards her than he had been. 'I reckon you're right. Crazy old lady.'

'But we all came on this tour because we believed in her,' Mattie said. Smiling seemed to require a huge effort this morning, her face aching from the attempt. 'So what does that make us?'

'I dread to think. Coffee?'

'Yes, please. Black with one sugar.'

'Black? You're as bad as me.'

'I'm not usually. But I need to keep going today and decaf tea isn't going to help me.' She watched Gil take a stainless-steel cafetière and fill a mug for her. At least he was still here. After what had happened yesterday, she had half-expected to discover he had checked out and gone home. Mattie felt comforted by this, even if every other part of the plan was in question.

'So, any idea what we do now?'

Contingencies had occupied Mattie's thoughts since the early hours. Even now, she wasn't entirely sure what their next step should be. 'I don't think we abandon the attempt. We have Tommy and Reenie on board; Chuck and Alys may yet agree.'

'And June?'

'I think we have to accept that she won't be part of this.'

Gil blew resignedly across the top of his coffee. 'I agree. I can't say I'm thrilled about having a reduced line-up. But I think you're right.'

'I spent hours last night trying to work out if we should have done something differently.'

'We could have *not* taken Reenie with us. That would have made the meeting far more civil.' The mischief in Gil's comment made Mattie laugh despite her brooding headache.

'Yep, that might have done it.'

'Hey,' he said, reaching across the table but stopping just short of touching Mattie's hand. 'None of this is your fault.'

'Maybe it was too much to ask. Sixty-year grudges aren't likely to disappear overnight.'

'Maybe not. But you believed Reenie could do it. Personally, I think that's great – even if the rest of this trip is a disaster.'

Mattie felt like hugging him, the vote of confidence more of a boost than the very strong black coffee. 'Thank you. Whatever happens, we'll have a gig next Thursday.'

'You reckon the others will be up for it?'

'We have to hope so. Reenie said it herself: she and June were always two steps away from all-out war, even when they were supposed to be friends. Expecting anything else after sixty years of bad feeling was unrealistic. I should have understood that from the outset. Reenie had certainly given me enough clues in her stories.'

When Mattie once asked her about their song, 'Always Where You Are' – a particular favourite of her late grandma's that featured a rare duet between the two singers – Reenie had been less than complimentary about June's contribution.

'It should never have been a duet,' she'd stated as they'd walked slowly around Beauvale's well-kept grounds. 'And if I'd had my way, it would've been me singing the melody *unhindered*.'

'But it's such a lovely song about friendship,' Mattie had begun, stopping abruptly when Reenie's cheeks flushed to almost the same shade as the red dahlias in the border. 'Isn't it?'

'Shows what you and Joe Public know about the art of great lyrics, kid. Bert Friedrich, who wrote it, always intended the song to be a woman singing alone, waiting for her lover to return home. Not a cheesy "I'll plait your bunches if you plait mine" song.'

'Why was it changed? I thought you said Rico did what you asked him to in disputes.'

'Well, usually he did – I had a way of persuading him. That's how I kept the main line on "Because You Loved Me". June was still sore about losing that one when "Always Where You Are" came up. But we'd been touring and only had a few hours in the studio to cut the track, so when Miss I-Should've-Been-Lead-Singer Knight got all uppity and stormed off, he had to find a compromise. He apologised, of course. He was all, "In my eyes *you're* the star and the song would be best as yours alone, but we have the record company to think of . . . "' Reenie had rolled her eyes then, the irritation of years gone by still raw. 'That was his Get Out of Jail Free card, every single time. "We need to think of the label . . . Our promoters are placing their trust in us and we can't afford to lose it . . . Think of the *exposure*!" *Pfft*. Like he knew the foggiest thing about it!'

'So June was given half the song?'

'He thought he was being fair. *I* thought he was being an almighty pushover. He was scared of what June might do if he didn't give in to her. Every time that woman decided to make an issue of something, she implied that she could damage Rico's reputation. Nasty piece of work, June Knight. Plays the innocent "woe is me" role like a pro, but she'd stab you in the back as soon as look at yer.'

There had been arguments and resentments, stormings-out and near mutinies right across Europe as The Silver Five had toured cities still picking up the pieces after the Second World War. According to Reenie, June had threatened to go to the papers with salacious details of Reenie and Rico's affair, which at the time would have been catastrophic for the clean-cut image of the group.

'We were just never designed to get along,' Reenie had admitted another time, as they enjoyed afternoon tea in Stone Yardley on a trip out from Beauvale. 'Chalk and cheese, you could say, although to be frank we were more

221

like paraffin and a naked flame. The others, I got on with pretty well. But June was an enemy from day one . . .'

'It's going to be a hard sell without all of them,' Gil said, folding the newspaper and resting his chin on his hands. 'I won't lie. Colm's dubious we can even half-fill the place, even if we discount tickets for late sales.'

'They'll come, all right.'

Mattie and Gil turned to see a remarkably fresh-faced Reenie approaching.

'How do you know that?'

Reenie prodded Gil's foot with her cane as she sat opposite him. 'I *know*, kiddo, because *I'm* the star they'll come to see. The Silver Five was four years of a sixty-year career for me. Most people will have forgotten my humble roots. I'm Reenie Silver, doyenne of Las Vegas, occasional TV star, legendary vocalist . . .'

'Reenie, the whole point of this tour is—' Gil began, but the old lady was having none of it.

'The *whole point* of this tour, Gilbert Kendrick, is that I get the chance to say sorry to people I may have hurt in the past. Who appears with me at the gig is immaterial.'

Gil glowered. 'I beg to differ. And it's *just Gil*. Not Gilbert.'

'Oh?' Reenie shot him a smile as sweet as arsenic. 'My mistake.'

As they ate breakfast, it was clear to Mattie that Reenie was more than just resigned to her failure to apologise to June; she was actually *relieved*. Before they'd set off, Mattie could remember Reenie making a remark about June's apology being what she least wanted to do. She seemed pleased with herself this morning – or had Mattie imagined that? Could Reenie have planned to fight with June from the beginning? It would certainly mean a starry comeback gig without her biggest rival . . .

No. Reenie couldn't be that calculating, she decided. It was just her way of braving out a bad situation.

'So, we crack on to Bath and Wales, then? Forget June and go for Chuck and Alys?'

Shelving her doubts about Reenie, Mattie nodded. 'We've lost time and we need to pick up the pace. If we hit any more problems –' she was careful to avoid over-emphasising the word in case Reenie felt targeted – 'I want to make sure we have a little time in hand.'

'I spoke to Colm, and everything is going well at the club. I think I might head back a little before you two, once we've spoken to Alys,' Gil said. 'I don't want my brother to have to do it all.'

For the slightest moment, Mattie felt her spirits drop at the thought of Gil leaving. She glared at her reflection in the stainless-steel cafetière. What was wrong with her today? Watching Gil and Reenie discussing plans over the breakfast table for transforming Kendrick's back into the Palm Grove, Mattie was struck by a sudden desire to talk to Joanna. She felt certain her sister would have a rational take on it all – and right now she needed to hear a comforting voice. Too much was happening for her to make sense of everything. Joanna would know what to do next.

'I'm just going to make a call,' she said, but nobody was listening. Unnoticed, she slipped from the room and headed for the gardens at the front of the hotel, where a tiny courtyard with an Italianate fountain formed a centre-piece. She found a bench beside a gorgeous swathe of lavender spilling over onto the dark grey slate setts, and nearly dropped her phone when it rang. Could Joanna have had a moment of ESP and called her first?

She didn't recognise the number on the screen, but this was nothing new: her sister had a habit of changing phones regularly and hardly ever took her number with her.

'Hello?'

'Matilda?' The voice was vaguely familiar, but Mattie had been thrown by the unexpected call and couldn't place it.

'Yes.'

'It's Hugo Benecourt. June's son.'

If the water in the fountain had suddenly frozen at that moment, Mattie wouldn't have been surprised. It was as if her world had tipped on its axis. 'Oh. Hi.'

'I think I've managed to persuade Mother to try again,' Hugo rushed, and Mattie could picture nervous sweat beading across his cheeks as he spoke. 'She may still refuse to accept Miss Silver's apology, but she's prepared at least to meet her again.'

Mattie bit her lip to stop the squeal threatening to escape. 'That's – that's wonderful! What time do you want us to visit?'

'Not at my house. Not again. She has too much of an upper hand there. I suggest a neutral venue this time. Somewhere new to both of them.'

It was a perfect solution. The situation would never be resolved while one party felt in control. Mattie still wasn't

224

sure Reenie would even agree to try again, but this was a lifeline she could never have anticipated during the long hours of last night.

'Okay, great. Tell me where and when, and I'll get Reenie there.'

Ending the call, she saw Joanna's number still waiting on the screen. *I'll call her this evening*, she decided, hurrying back inside. Chances were she would have something else to tell her sister after the eleventh-hour meeting had happened.

Chapter Twenty-One

'Let's Try Again'
– Clyde McPhatter

♪

'I don't know why you want to see Cambridge,' Reenie scoffed as Mattie drove purposefully towards the city centre. '*You* said we were on a tight deadline. You said we had to get to Bath before nightfall. Where does sightseeing come into that plan, hmm?'

It was almost an hour since Hugo's call – and Mattie was determined to get Reenie where she needed to be as soon as she could. Glancing to the back seat, where Gil wore a plastered-on grin like a startled ventriloquist's dummy, Mattie did her best to remain calm. But inside her nerves were as jumpy as a duck's feet thrashing under the surface of the water. Reenie wasn't going to know they were on their way to meet June until they arrived and it was too late for her to refuse. It had been a split-second decision as she'd walked back into the hotel – and she was convinced it was the right one.

'I was thinking, so far all we've done is to rush from one place to the next. A couple of hours wandering around aren't going to scupper the whole trip.'

'And you've nothing to say about it, Kendrick?' Reenie twisted to stare at Gil.

'Apparently not . . . Far be it from me to argue with our driver.'

'You're both nutters this mornin'.'

Mattie found a car park just around the corner from the hotel Hugo had suggested, grateful it wasn't too busy. They climbed out, Gil offering his arm to Reenie, who simply looked up at him and laughed. They stepped out into the beautiful bright sunshine, between elegant buildings on the edges of the famous college grounds. Brave blue sky arced above them and gaggles of tourists milled around, a dozen umbrella-toting tour guides delivering the history of the city in different languages.

Passing through the quintessentially English architecture was a sublime experience, so much so that Mattie almost forgot why they had come to the centre of Cambridge instead of embarking upon the next leg of their journey. But it was time she took charge. Reenie had called the shots thus far, almost threatening the entire road trip in the process. If she was serious about keeping her promise to Grandpa Joe, Mattie had to step up.

As they neared the front of the Riverside Mews hotel, Mattie jogged over to Reenie, who was several paces ahead and scowling ferociously. 'Why don't we pop in here for coffee? I read on the internet last night that they have a beautiful roof terrace overlooking the river and several of the university colleges.'

Reenie tutted. 'Is there a bar too?'

'It's barely eleven a.m.,' Gil interjected.

'That's near enough to midday for me. I fancy a double sherry.' She jabbed a bony finger into Mattie's stomach. 'And *you're* paying.'

'Fine. Shall we?' Mattie held her nerve as they entered the building, knowing that Reenie wouldn't be making it as far as the hotel bar this morning – at least, not until a certain meeting had taken place.

She saw Hugo before Reenie did, and discreetly raised a hand to him. He nodded and addressed a tall, wingback chair directly in front of him. Reenie, oblivious to all of this, was squinting at a board in the reception area. She looked up – just as Hugo and June began to walk towards them – and her hand dropped from Mattie's arm. 'You have *got* to be kidding me . . .'

Fast on her feet, Mattie blocked Reenie's path as the elderly lady made a bid for freedom. 'No, wait. June wants to talk to you.'

'I'll bet she does. Move aside.'

'Not until you've at least heard what she has to say.'

'Absolutely not.'

'Talk to her, Reenie! This is what we came here for . . .'

'It might be what *you* came here for. *I* came for a drink.'

'Then you're going in the wrong direction. The bar's *this* way,' Mattie jabbed a thumb over her shoulder in the direction of Hugo and June.

'I don't like the clientele here. Now *shift* . . .'

'No!' Mattie could feel the eyes of startled guests in the elegant reception turning to her in shock. But she wasn't about to let Reenie throw away the opportunity that even two hours ago had seemed impossible. 'I'm sorry, but you're not skipping out on this chance. You *need* to do this. Both of you do.'

Furious now, Reenie stared her down – or rather *up*, due to the difference in their heights. 'And have all and sundry watching us?' she hissed. 'I don't bleedin' think so.'

'It doesn't have to be in front of everybody. It can be just the three of us,' Mattie answered, her mind one step ahead of her words as she tried to counter every obstacle Reenie threw in her path. Gil wouldn't like it. His express wish had been to witness every one of Reenie's apologies. Hugo wouldn't be impressed either, she guessed. But it was the only solution she could offer. 'We can go for a walk – by the river, maybe? That way nobody else has to know what's happening. Say yes. Please?'

'You make it sound like I have a choice,' Reenie grimaced, and Mattie felt her heart lift. Had she really won? 'But this is the *last time* you pull a stunt like this on me, d'you understand?'

Ten minutes later, Mattie, Reenie and June were walking along a narrow gravel path alongside the River Cam. The reception manager had directed them there, promising excellent views of the city from a secluded vantage point. He certainly hadn't exaggerated its beauty. Lush green lawns stretched elegantly to the water's edge and Cambridge's

229

historic college buildings rose up beyond, their gables and turrets reaching for the sky.

Once she was satisfied neither woman was going to attempt to push the other into the river, Mattie let Reenie and June walk a few paces ahead. She wanted to keep an eye on them in case tempers flared again, but was keen to show Reenie she wasn't interfering. The initial signs were promising, at least: ten minutes together with no repeat of yesterday's hostilities was practically cause for celebration.

In the neutral surroundings of the riverside walk, the two seemed softer, as if the gentle morning sun had warmed their skin and smoothed their edges. They kept a respectful distance from one another still, a protection mechanism designed to prevent harm. But the air between them had stilled.

Mattie chose her words carefully as she walked behind them. 'It's good that we can be here now. Without the audience.' She thought of Gil and Hugo waiting in the hotel's rooftop bar. Both had protested at Mattie's decision – the last she had seen of them was their backs as they stormed off to drown their sorrows. *Well, let them*, she thought. *This isn't about them, anyway*. For once in their lives, June and Reenie required privacy.

'Never thought we'd want a crowd to leave,' June said, casting a glance towards Reenie. Though only a small comment, it felt like a significant invitation.

'Oh, I don't know,' Reenie replied, looking out over the river, where tourists were being punted along in traditional boats. 'That mob in Warrington back in '52 could have done one as far as I was concerned.'

June chuckled. 'Oh yes. I'd forgotten that. What was the name of the club again?'

'The Warrington Waldorf! That was a bleedin' joke. No more than a working men's club with a couple of plaster pillars stuck on the front.'

'And the dressing room! It was a broom cupboard with a curtain across and a light that kept flickering.'

'We had a few of them in our time, didn't we? That pervy old letch manager who kept "popping in to fix the light bulb" didn't help either, did he?'

'Oh, now he was creepy. Didn't Rico know him from somewhere?'

'I wouldn't be surprised. Rico had friends in very strange places.'

June laughed and moved a step closer to Reenie. 'But that audience – if you can call them that – they were something else. Do you remember that chap on the front row shouting, "Sing something we can join in with! Do 'Danny Boy'!" all the way through our first three songs? You know, I'd never wanted to punch anybody before that night.'

'As I recall, Tommy did the deed for you.'

Hearing that, June stopped walking. 'Did he?'

'Oh yeah. Pretty near broke his hand, too. Rico went up like a rocket when he found out. Surely you remember? That's why we never went back to Warrington.'

'I never knew that. I thought Rico fell out with the promoter. He seemed to do that a lot in the early years.'

'He did. Liked a fight, did our old Harry Slack.'

'And to think all these years I thought Tommy was a pacifist.'

They began to walk again, both women falling silent as their steps dropped heavily on the gravel path, their walking sticks punctuating the rhythm of their feet. Mattie was tempted to say nothing, hoping one of them would take the initiative. But when the silence remained after a few minutes, she knew she had to intervene.

'It's beautiful here.'

No reply, although she saw June's shoulders drop a little.

'All the college backs look so elegant, don't you think? Funny how the sun can make everything look different. Lighter.'

'It's what I've always loved about the city,' June replied. 'Cambridge comes alive in the sunshine.'

Keen to keep the conversation going, Mattie pressed on. 'How long have you lived here?'

'Since Hugo's final year of university. I loved it so much whenever I came up from Tunbridge Wells to visit him in his university digs. And then I met Barney and moved here to be with both my boys.'

'Barney the Lord, eh?' Reenie chuckled.

'Life peer,' June corrected, and Mattie imagined she had made this clarification many times before. 'So no baronial home, no vast family fortune.'

'Did all right for himself, though.' Blushing, June looked away. 'From what Tommy mentioned, you know, over the years.'

'We were comfortable. And happy. That's all that matters in the end, isn't it?'

Reenie sniffed. 'Always pictured you marrying a duke.'

'Did you?'

'I did. I mean, you were the high-falutin' one out of us all, weren't you? Elocution lessons, ballet classes, deportment – you wouldn't have got those where I grew up. Me and Chuck called you Lady June. I figured you'd do all right for yourself.'

June gave a sad smile, and Mattie could see how much she missed her late husband. 'I met Barney at the right time. I – didn't choose well at first.'

Fifty years after her first, very unhappy marriage, the pain of it appeared as fresh as ever.

'You didn't deserve a brute like him.' Reenie suddenly reached out to rest her hand on June's arm. 'You didn't. Nobody should have to live like that. You deserved better.'

'Reenie, I—'

Right then, Mattie saw a flicker of something new in her friend. It was more than sincerity, more than sympathy: it was recognition.

'I'd say we *both* did, love.'

Startled, June turned to face Reenie. 'Did you . . . ?'

She nodded. 'Second husband. Lasted two years that were two years too long.'

June appeared on the verge of tears. 'Oh Reenie, *no*.' June clasped Reenie's hand. 'But we made it out alive, didn't we?'

'We did. Plenty of girls didn't.'

'I didn't think I would.'

'How long were you with the bastard?'

June shook her head. 'Ten years, give or take. I left

when he turned on Hugo. Went running home to Mother, who hid us with an aunt in Anglesey for a year until the divorce had been granted.'

Reenie's face was pale as she observed her friend. 'Oh, I'm so sorry, love.'

'It's water under the bridge now.'

And then, as Mattie watched, something amazing happened: Reenie Silver threw her arms around her former enemy and burst into tears. June froze, looking to Mattie for help, not knowing what to do. Eventually, she lifted a hand to Reenie's head and gave it a tentative pat.

'Whatever's the matter?'

'I'm just so sorry. I am. For what I did. For letting you down. I've been angry with you a long, long time, but we could have been friends when we both needed a friend.'

June closed her eyes. Mattie saw a single tear betray her as it fell. 'We could have. But . . .'

Reenie pulled away, her hand still gripping June's. 'What you said about Rico – you were right. I was *with* him. And I shouldn't have been. I left that night because he told me to. There were reasons I – I can't tell you, love. But I do know I was wrong to trust him.'

'Nonsense. He gave you your career.'

'At the expense of my friends.'

June let out a sigh. 'Oh, let's face it, dear, we were never friends. I hated you as much as you loathed me, and to have both of us in one group was the daftest idea Rico ever had. I was angry with you for deserting us all like you did. But I wasn't surprised. You always were about your career before your friends. I know that because I was the same. I *hated* your success after we finished. I bought five of your records and smashed them.'

'Bleedin' 'eck, girl! I'm impressed.'

'Don't be. It wasn't my finest hour. I'm sorry, too. Not that I wasn't justified in being upset. But I didn't need to carry it around with me all these years.'

Seeing a bench nearby, Reenie guided June there and the two women sat. Mattie stood a small distance away, not really knowing whether to believe what she was seeing. After their battle yesterday, she didn't fully trust the peace between them. But something seemed to have changed, their body language beginning to mirror each other rather than block.

'Come back to the Palm Grove next week?' Reenie offered. 'Do the gig with Tommy and me – and the others, if they'll have us?'

'I don't know. It's been such a long time . . .'

'As I remember, *you* were the one who wanted to play at Jake Kendrick's club. Almost a whole year you bent Rico's ear about it. "Anyone who's anyone plays that venue. We'll be stars overnight if we appear at the Palm Grove . . ." He fought with you over it, didn't he? Time and time again. Thought it wasn't as happening as the Soho coffee bars were. But heaven knows you were right.'

June sighed. 'We're not twenty years old anymore, though. Who's going to take a load of rickety old pensioners seriously?'

'It hasn't stopped the Rolling Stones.'

'Oh, Reenie . . .'

'Or Lulu. Or Tom Jones. Or Tony bleedin' Bennett! We aren't just any old bunch of duffers, Junie! We're The Silver Five. Don't tell me there isn't still a part of you hidden inside that glamorous-granny exterior that wants to get up on stage one last time.'

A tiny smile made a brave appearance on June's face. 'It would be fun to perform again. I haven't picked up a microphone since Barney died.'

'Then what's your excuse? Say yes.'

Chapter Twenty-Two

'To Be Loved'
– Jackie Wilson

♪

'We need to celebrate!' Reenie exclaimed as she, Mattie and Gil gathered back in their hotel bar later that day. 'I feel *fantastic*! I haven't felt this good in years.'

'I'm glad,' Mattie smiled, still buzzing from the extraordinary reunion she had witnessed.

'And I want to say thank you – to both of you. If you hadn't tricked me into that meeting, the gig would have been very different. So: I am taking you out on the town tonight.'

Mattie's horror mirrored Gil's as they exchanged looks. 'Reenie, I don't think . . .'

'Oh, don't worry. I won't be repeating my karaoke session, kids. I had a chat with Rachael on reception and she recommended a place not far from here. Come on, trust little old Reenie, will you?'

An hour later, in a pretty former Methodist church hall, Reenie led a very worried Mattie and Gil into another world. Before them were whooping, whirling couples dressed in

Fifties' circle-skirts and sharp suits, dancing for all they were worth to music by Eddie Cochran, Bill Haley & His Comets and Jerry Lee Lewis. It was as if Reenie had transported them back in time to the very beginning of her solo career, the excitement and energy impossible to resist.

'They call it the Shoo-wop Shindig,' Reenie called over the music. 'Most of these kids are students at the university. Rachael said it started as a dance club and then turned into a whole Fifties lifestyle thing. Who would have thought this old stuff would be back in vogue?' She beamed up at Mattie. 'Better than drunk karaoke?'

Mattie squeezed her shoulder. '*Much* better.'

'Shall we sit down?'

Slowly they made their way between the tables laid out around the edges of the room, finding space near the bar. Mattie helped Reenie to her seat and for a while the three of them watched without speaking, feet involuntarily tapping to the irresistible rock 'n' roll beats.

It was only when she took a photo on her mobile phone to send to Joanna that Mattie realised Reenie was crying. She lowered the camera and stared as Gil reached for Reenie's hand and quietly held it.

She wasn't imagining what she saw: Gil was genuinely moved watching Reenie's reaction to the spectacle. Reenie acknowledged it with a brief nod, but didn't pull her hand away. Mattie couldn't take her eyes off them. It was as surprising as it was intriguing. Could this road trip mean more to Gil than he'd said?

The song ended and the couples on the dance floor applauded as if a live band had just entertained them.

Reenie cleared her throat. 'If you're getting the beers in, Kendrick, mine's a double brandy.'

'Right. Okay. Mattie?'

'Orange juice, please. I want a clear head for driving to Bath tomorrow.' Gil nodded and headed over to the bar.

'These kids have more energy than I did,' Reenie chuckled. 'One of the reasons I became a lead singer: you leave all the jumping and twisting to the dancers behind you. I reckon Gil likes this place.'

'Me too,' Mattie said, her gaze following Gil moment-arily until she caught Reenie watching her. 'You should be very proud of what you did today. That wasn't easy.'

Reenie scratched her chin. 'Wasn't exactly my finest hour. But – I think we did a good thing there.'

'You did. You did an *amazing* thing.'

'June Knight was never going to give me an easy ride, was she?' She gave a rueful smile. 'Serves me right for making her my mortal enemy all these years.'

'And now?'

'Honestly? I don't know, kid. We'll never be bosom chums, but I think we can both be happy there's a line drawn under it.'

'Stupid Cupid' by Connie Francis began to play, and the floor filled with strutting, twirling dancers again.

'Reenie?' Mattie asked.

'Hmm?'

'Why did you leave The Silver Five?'

Reenie blinked. 'I had my reasons.'

239

'So you keep saying. But you've never told me why you left *that night*.'

'Where's my brandy? The service round here is shocking . . .' She made a hammy show of looking over her shoulder, careful to keep her gaze away from Mattie.

'Stop avoiding the question.'

'Matilda, I'm thirsty and I want a drink. I'm not avoiding anything.'

'Liar.'

Reenie looked at her then. 'I don't have to tell you anything. All you need to worry about is making this gig happen.'

It was another slammed door. The question remained stubbornly lodged between them: in all their meetings and planning for this trip, Reenie had refused to broach the subject. What could have been so terrible that she didn't want to talk about it, sixty years after the event? She certainly didn't shy away from talking about anything else, even the failure of her marriages. So what was it about *that* event, that night, that she couldn't say?

Gil returned, and Mattie let her mind wander as Reenie launched into her 'the time I met Connie Francis' story. Rico *had* to be behind what had happened. She knew from what Reenie had confessed to Tommy and now June that she'd been romantically involved with the Svengali – despite him being married to someone else at the time. Reenie had admitted during their meetings at Beauvale that she'd loved him and stayed with him for a year after the breakdown of his marriage – yet a few months after that, she had married someone else, a drummer from her backing band. Had the reality of a real relationship with Rico been a disappointment? Had it always been his plan to single Reenie out from the group? Was he possessive of her?

Save for admitting she'd been in love with him, Reenie had only talked of Rico in terms of his effect on her career: the doors he had opened, the promises he had made and (mostly) kept, and the confidence he had given her in her ability to become a star.

Had Rico known Reenie wasn't going to appear at the Palm Grove that night? Had he been waiting for her outside, leaving the rest of the group behind?

'Okay, okay, a bit of *hush*, please.' Reenie was tapping her brandy glass with her acrylic nails. 'I'd like to propose a toast.' She gave Gil a sly glance. 'To Mattie.'

Gil raised his eyebrows. 'Oh?'

'And you. But mainly this lovely girl. I wouldn't be sitting here now if she and Hugo hadn't set me and June up today. And if I'd known what was being planned, I'd've staged a sit-in in the hotel car park this morning. But our Mattie was right: it was bad air that needed clearing. So –' she raised her glass – 'thank you, Mattie. You're not always right, but this time you were.'

It was only later, when Mattie left the celebrations to go back to her room, that she understood the significance of Reenie's toast. She had stood her ground – and would have fought harder if Reenie hadn't agreed to go ahead with the meeting at Riverside Mews. And she had walked with the two former bandmates, gently leading their

241

conversation towards the reconciliation. Ultimately, it had been Reenie and June's decision to apologise and forgive: but without Mattie's determination to make it happen, it simply would not have been possible.

She had *stood her ground*. Mattie's eye fell on Grandpa Joe's diary, lying on the teak-effect bedside cabinet. What if . . . ? She winced as her stomach contracted. What if she had refused to let him disown her? What if she'd marched into his hospital room and demanded her share of his last precious days?

It was a new thought, sitting awkwardly within her as if there wasn't quite enough room to accommodate it yet. All along, she had been telling herself that Grandpa Joe had been right to doubt Asher and that she had been wrong to follow her heart. But at the time, it had been what she'd wanted more than anything: more, even, it turned out, than Grandpa Joe's love. Why hadn't he allowed her to follow her heart like he had done all his life?

She picked up the diary, opening it to the now-familiar youthful handwriting of the headstrong Joe Bell, following *his* heart in the bright lights of London.

Tuesday, 8 May 1956

Len reckons I should be apprenticed to an escapologist, not an accountant. He said he's never met anyone who can sneak out of a locked house as easily as I can. But I have my scheme now – and Uncle Charles has no idea. A chap I met playing snooker at the Duke showed me how to pick a lock.

It's surprisingly fast when you know what you're doing. So when Uncle C locks the front door at night I wait till he's gone to bed, do my little trick and walk out of the house like a lord. Who needs to shin down drainpipes when you can leave by the main entrance?

I can lock it, too, when I get back. It takes a little longer, but I'm gradually getting the hang of it. Thankfully Uncle C is a creature of habit, rising every morning at a quarter to seven. Mrs Johnson the housekeeper wakes at six, so as long as I'm back by five o'clock I'm home safe. The only time I forgot to lock the door, Uncle C assumed Mrs J had unlocked it early – and Mrs J is so old and forgetful that she assumed he must be right.

I'm tired, though. Don't think I've ever been so weary in my life. I'm at my desk by eight o'clock, remaining there with the ledgers until six in the evening. But all I can think about is the PG and who I'm going to see there. Last night it was Ted Farnsworth and his Orchestra. Cracking girl singer, too. Her voice was the kind you think you've heard somewhere else. When she started to sing the first number the crowd stopped dancing to watch. I've never seen that happen before. Una likes to dance. And Len doesn't seem to mind now if I dance with her.

I think I might be falling in love . . .

Picking locks? Defying his uncle? But what intrigued

Mattie more was the act Grandpa Joe had seen at the Palm Grove. Did Reenie know Ted Farnsworth's Orchestra had played there, months before The Silver Five were due to appear? She had never mentioned whether or not she'd kept in contact with Ted after leaving him to join The Silver Five. Did she know about her replacement who had so impressed Grandpa Joe?

Chapter Twenty-Three

'That's Amore'
– Dean Martin

♪

'Can this traffic go any slower?' Reenie slumped in the front seat. The journey from Cambridge had started well, bright and dry with easy-flowing traffic. But as they joined the M4, the vehicles around them began to bunch up, the tell-tale red of brake lights making Mattie's heart sink.

The Cambridge leg of the journey had taken considerably more time than they'd allocated and now they were chasing the clock. They were already a day late – and the road ahead suggested further delays.

'It's like having a kid in the front seat,' Gil said, adopting a whining voice. '*Are we nearly there yet?*'

'We should have brought her some colouring books,' Mattie replied, enjoying the joke. 'Or would you like to play I Spy?'

Reenie laughed. 'Fine. I'll go first. I spy, with my little eye, something beginning with *cheeky B . . .*'

Gil laughed. 'You asked for that.'

'I did.'

'What I want to know,' Gil said, tapping Reenie's shoulder, 'is if you *really* met the Beatles.'

'I did, several times. First time, at a party in Soho. Had no idea who they were, mind. They were with their weaselly little manager, and him and Rico fell out over a card game. So I ended up hunkering down with them in a corner, hiding from the fracas. Nice lads. Obviously, coming from Liverpool, we had a bit in common.'

'I don't know whether to believe you, but I like the story.'

'Well, it's a good job you do, Gil, because there are plenty more where that came from . . .'

The traffic eventually cleared and the rest of the journey passed with a surprising lack of drama – for which Mattie was extremely grateful. The last thirty-six hours had been a rollercoaster ride of celebration, disappointment and relief, and she was in no hurry to repeat it. Reenie spent most of the drive reminiscing, while in the back Gil slept.

Just before two p.m. Rusty descended a steep, curving hill to bring them into the historic city of Bath. The sun that had lurked behind a thick bank of grey cloud for most of their journey chose the best time to appear, bringing a sparkle to every building they passed.

They had booked rooms at a large pub, and as they turned into its car park Mattie heard a collective sigh of relief from her passengers. They piled out, the routine of unloading bags now feeling familiar to Mattie.

'I tell you what, why don't we all head into Bath once

we've settled in?' Gil suggested. 'It would be good to get out for a while.'

'Definitely.'

An hour later, the group reconvened in the cosy bar of the pub. Mattie felt brighter after a shower and change of clothes, the creases of the journey finally removed. Just before she'd left her room to join the others she'd transferred Grandpa Joe's silver sixpence tiepin to her new clothes, fixing it carefully to the collar of her shirt. It had certainly witnessed some amazing scenes over the last few days – and now it was about to see the lovely city of Bath, which had always been one of its former owner's favourite places.

In the courtyard by Bath Abbey in the centre of the city, they agreed to spend the next hour exploring. Reenie declared that what she most wanted was to find a comfy chair in a nearby restaurant and 'just watch the world go by'.

'What are you going to do?' Gil asked Mattie when she had gone.

'I fancy a walk around,' she said. 'I haven't been here for years and I want to stretch my legs after all the driving I've done.'

'Mind if I tag along?' His smile was warm, and the offer more than tempting.

'Not at all. Have you been here before?'

'Never. So you can show me the sights. Believe it or not, I'm excited to see the city. Reenie makes me feel like I'm the curmudgeonly old person on the team – I've been

247

suffering strange cravings for a pipe and slippers in the back of that van.'

'You are a bit of an old git, you know,' Mattie laughed, dodging his hand as he mimicked a swipe at her. 'Come on, you are! Sitting in the back seat, all grumpy.'

'Grumpy? I prefer *aloof*.'

'Nope. Definitely grumpy. You're not eloquent and Darcy-ish enough to be aloof.'

He laughed. 'Oh, charming. And there was me thinking I could bowl you over with my unattainable allure.'

Was he flirting? Heat prickled the back of her neck. 'There's a pretty square somewhere near here. I think it's this way . . .'

She caught his smile as she glanced back. 'Okay. Maybe we can find somewhere to fuel my unhealthy caffeine habit, too. It's been at least three hours since I indulged.'

Mattie's instincts proved correct, and at the top of the next street they entered a small square surrounded by restaurants and cafés. At its heart was a marketplace, the skeletal frames empty of stalls now, beside a tall elm tree whose leaves arced gracefully over the honeyed stone paving. Mattie remembered having lunch with Jack here one day, during a Bell family weekend to celebrate their grandparents' ruby wedding anniversary. It had reminded her of a Parisian square then and it did today, too, the effect enhanced by the chairs and tables set outside the cafés and restaurants. It was a pleasant afternoon with a refreshing breeze, and the sun shone through dappled cloud. It was as if the whole of Bath was taking a long, leisurely breath, and the tension of the last few days ebbed from Mattie's shoulders as she settled at a table outside a coffee house while Gil went inside to order.

She *needed* this – time out to think and absorb what had happened during the past week. Nothing had gone to plan, and yet, as she reflected now, it had all felt right. Reconciliations were never going to be as easy in reality as they had been on paper. Life wasn't quantifiable in lists and schedules. It was a huge achievement to have three of The Silver Five signed up for the concert – and significant barriers had been broken in the process. With the meeting with Chuck tomorrow already something Reenie seemed to be looking forward to, and then only one more meeting to negotiate, Mattie was optimistic about the outcome. The concert was going to be wonderful; five old friends reunited in the restored former glory of Gil's grandfather's club.

Her fingers instinctively touched the smooth, cool silver pin on her collar and she smiled. *One step closer to taking you back there, Grandpa Joe.* Remembering his diary in her bag, she reached for it. She'd intended to find a quiet place to read it this afternoon, excited by the thought of being in his favourite place with his words. She hadn't reckoned on having a companion – lovely though it was to spend time with Gil – but seeing him waiting in a considerable queue inside the coffee shop, she seized her opportunity and opened the diary.

Thursday, 21 June 1956

I kissed her.
  Nothing will ever be the same again.

Len doesn't know. He thought I'd left early, but I came back after he'd gone. Una and I met behind the PG and we couldn't keep our hands off one another. She's got me, hook, line and sinker. I'm utterly lost.

I have to see her again. Alone . . .

'What's that?'

Startled, Mattie snapped the diary shut and threw it into the bag at her feet.

'Nothing.'

Her head was spinning from what she'd just read and she didn't know what to make of it. The passion in Joe Bell's words had shocked her.

'Doesn't look like nothing to me.'

Mattie looked up at him and he instantly relented.

'I'm sorry. I wasn't sure if you wanted cake, but I brought some anyway.'

'Oh. Thanks.' She reminded herself to smile, torn between enjoying Gil's company and wanting to be alone so that she could read on. 'What do I owe you?'

'Don't be daft. My treat. It's the least I could do after you've put up with my back-seat grumpiness.'

'It's no problem, really. I'm starting to find it endearing.'

'Endearing?'

'Mm-hmm. Like Statler and Waldorf from the Muppets, commentating on everything from the theatre box.'

'So, let me get this right: I'm the equivalent of *two* grumpy old men?' The playfulness was back again, and his green eyes twinkled in the afternoon sun.

'It's a skill,' Mattie smiled into her coffee cup.

When they met Reenie again in Bath Abbey's courtyard, everyone's spirits were high. Reenie was glowing and smelled suspiciously of gin, although she swore it was the lingering odour from the restaurant she'd been sitting in. Gil began to rib her about it, their back-and-forth banter filling the air. Walking a little way behind them, Mattie considered Grandpa Joe's infatuation with Una. Had Grandma known about his affair? True, it would have been several years in the past by the time they met, but had Grandpa Joe ever told his wife about his former girlfriend?

Mattie hadn't known much about Asher's past dating history when they had been together, save for the girl he'd been seeing for a year before he'd met her. They'd had a tempestuous relationship by all accounts, culminating in an acrimonious break-up, the reasons for which he had never gone into. Now it occurred to her that he might have done to his former lover what he did to Mattie.

Reenie declared she was tired when they returned to their hotel, so Mattie arranged for her dinner to be delivered to her room.

'You should have a night off,' Reenie insisted, when Mattie protested. 'Go and enjoy yourself, love. Have a drink – better still, have a few. You need a blowout after being Sandra Dee for us all. Here –' She thrust a worryingly warm twenty-pound note pulled with panache from beneath one bra strap into Mattie's reluctant palm. 'No, now, you can't refuse an old lady her little indulgences. Call it a chauffeur's tip if you must. Enjoy yourself.'

Mattie considered waiting until Reenie had gone before

heading straight for her own room, giving in to the lure of an early night and a comfortable bed. She could have a bite to eat, watch something mindless on TV in her pyjamas and drift off to sleep, knowing that she had hours to enjoy it. After a week on the road, a part of her longed for something normal. She had long since stopped worrying about how Joanna and Laurie were coping without her at Bell Be-Bop, but she felt a little at sea without the constancy of her work routine to mark the hours of her days. Last night, when she had phoned Joanna, her sister had laughed at her.

'You're a nutcase! Honestly, Mattie, only you could spend ten days off work wishing you were back at the shop. Make the most of it. If your recent form is anything to go by, it'll be a good five years before you grant yourself any time off again.'

Was she really that bad? Running her own business inevitably meant it was on her mind constantly. She didn't switch off at five p.m. – she couldn't run a successful shop without putting in significantly more hours than she would ever claim a wage for. But having left her business for the first time, she had started to ask herself if some of that dogged commitment to the shop was a diversionary tactic. If she was consumed by work-related thoughts, there was less time to think about other things, like Grandpa Joe and Asher. In her rented home, in the few hours in her week free of work commitments, she found herself at a loss. She had become her job. It had begun as a survival tactic when the rest of her life was crumbling about her ears. But did she still need that now? Joanna and the kids were at home, filling her former empty evenings with life and laughter. Going home after work no longer scared her like it had before their arrival. So much of what she had discussed with Reenie in the weeks preceding this adventure and the days on the tour had begun to lay to rest ghosts that had haunted her since losing her grandfather. She loved her business, and it would always have to claim the lion's share of her time. But what else did she want from her life? Maybe hiding in a hotel room, however appealing, wasn't the best way to discover the answer.

I am in one of the most beautiful cities in the country, she reminded herself. *I'd be crazy not to make the most of this evening.*

'Thank you,' she said, planting a kiss on Reenie's cheek. 'Have a good night.'

'You too.' Reenie started to walk towards the stairs, turning back and miming knocking back a drink, then fake-drunk-staggering to the steps, making Mattie and Gil laugh.

'So. What *are* your plans for a wild night out?' he asked.

'Find something to eat. And a bar, apparently.'

'Sounds good to me. Want some company?'

'Oh, I . . .'

'Reenie is going to demand more than your word as proof you let your hair down,' he grinned. 'I can be your witness.'

'You'd do that – for me?'

He gave an exaggerated sigh. 'It will be a hardship, but if I *must* . . .'

'I'd like that.'

He smiled again and Mattie returned it. 'Excellent. Shall we?'

Chapter Twenty-Four
'Love Potion Number 9'
– The Clovers

♪

It was a beautiful evening to be walking out to dinner, and Mattie couldn't help remembering long holiday nights of her youth playing out under starlit West Country skies in the house her grandparents rented for family stays in Bath. Remembering one of her favourite places in the city, she led Gil down a set of steps, emerging by the distinctive crescent weir overlooked by beautiful Pulteney Bridge. As a child she'd adored the fairytale structure, modelled on Florence's famous Ponte Vecchio. The smooth, blue-green glassy waters of the River Avon made a perfect mirror of the colonnades of the building opposite before tumbling over the weir beneath in clouds of frothing white bubbles. Above the floodlit historic buildings the late September evening sky was a luminous deep dark blue, a few brave stars peeking out from the highest point of the arc.

'Wow,' Gil breathed, leaning against the railing as he drank in the view. 'This is awesome. You'd have no idea you were crossing that bridge from the roadside.'

'It's special, isn't it? That's one of the things I love about Bath, all the secrets it hides away, along alleys and down steep steps.' She giggled. 'Listen to me. I sound like a tour guide.'

'It's a pretty good tour, so far.' Gil's elbow was barely an inch from hers on the steel railing and Mattie was suddenly acutely aware of his closeness. In the light from the buildings across the river his eyes seemed darker, the contours of his face more defined. If she remained where she was too much longer, she might forget the view opposite entirely . . .

'We should find somewhere to eat,' she said, quickly. 'There's a good restaurant not far from here.'

'Great. Lead the way, Mademoiselle Tour Guide.'

The restaurant back up on Argyle Street was busy, despite it still being early. Mattie was relieved when the waiter found them a table overlooking the street. They ordered and shared a platter of bread and olives while they waited. Although their conversation moved to safer territory, Mattie found herself returning to the moment by the bridge just before. The thought caused a flutter of butterfly wings in the pit of her stomach, and she resolved to pack it away for this evening. She was determined to relax in Gil's company and enjoy the evening out.

An hour later, when dinner was over and they had settled the bill, Gil grinned at her as he shrugged on his jacket. 'Right. We'd better find a bar, hadn't we? Colonel Silver's orders!'

As they walked further into the city, Gil kept up the joke, trying to make Mattie march beside him and launching into an army-themed commentary on their evening.

'Hup, two-three-four, scouting party Private Kendrick and Corporal Bell reporting for duty, *Ma'am*!'

'Gil, stop it.'

'Can't stop, Corporal Bell. Important Silver Company orders to follow. Here you go, how about this place?'

They had stopped outside a bar near the floodlit arches of Bath Abbey. Outside, a blackboard covered in flamboyant script declared the place to be:

CLOISTERS –
HOME OF THE TWILIGHT HOUR
EVERY EVENING, 8 P.M.

'Twilight hour? What's that?' Mattie asked.

'No idea. But it happens in five minutes, so I guess we'll find out.'

They found a seat in the Gothic-themed bar, Mattie amused by the plaster gargoyles gurning at them from the ceiling. Besides that, the place was unremarkable, with the same inset spotlights, wooden booths and slate floors she had seen in countless other bars and pubs.

Until, that was, a tiny bell chimed and the house lights began to dim around them.

Suddenly tiny specks of light appeared, lining the bar and glowing from every table. Looking down, Mattie realised that plastic glow-in-the-dark stars had been scattered everywhere. She remembered them from her teenage

257

years, when she and Joanna had stuck them on their bedroom ceilings. The effect was utterly magical, as if a thousand glow-worms had laid siege to the restaurant.

Gil smiled. 'Now that's clever. I might try that back at Kendrick's.'

As they ordered drinks, Mattie decided to address Gil's joke about Reenie. 'So what you're saying is that I'm gullible.'

'Eh?'

'All that Corporal Bell and Colonel Silver stuff.'

'No, not at all. It's a joke.'

'I see it written all over your face. You think Reenie's taking advantage of me.'

'No, I don't.' Despite his denial, Gil's head bowed a little and Mattie knew she'd hit a nerve.

'Yes, you do. You think she's running me ragged. And I'll do whatever she says.'

'What? No, that's not what I—'

'I know it looks that way. And maybe you're right. I need Reenie on this trip as much as she needs me – we established that from the very beginning. She wants to make amends for the past, and I –' She stopped speaking, aware that to carry on would mean telling Gil the real reason she was part of this.

'Why did you get involved, Mattie? I know you said the club was special to your grandfather, but how did that lead you to take an OAP on a road trip?'

'Here you go. Enjoy.' The barman handed Mattie a mojito, the scent of mint and lime like a breath of fresh air in the warmth of the bar. Gil received his single malt and a jug of water, but didn't seem to notice, his full attention on her.

'I fell out with my grandpa before he died, and never had the chance to make things right. I don't expect you to understand, but this trip and the concert next week are probably the closest I can ever come to making it up to him.'

'What did you fall out over?' His eyes were intent on her, willing an answer, but it was too soon. The words she could have shared wouldn't leave her throat and she flushed in the twilight of the bar.

'It doesn't matter. The point is, I'm here because I wanted to make a difference. I realise that sounds lame.'

'No, it doesn't. A little extreme, maybe. We all have things we wish we'd done differently when we lose somebody. There are a thousand things I wish I'd spoken to my grandad about before he died, but I didn't get the opportunity. That doesn't make me want to travel across the country in ten days and organise a reunion gig for a bunch of old people I don't know.'

Mattie had to smile at the irony of his statement. 'And yet, here you are.'

Realising his mistake, he laughed. 'So I am.'

'But you're not jumping to the beat of Reenie's drum like you think *I* am.'

'That's not true . . .'

Mattie sipped her drink. 'It's okay to admit it. I'd rather you did, actually. It saves me the bother of admitting it to myself.'

'Where is this coming from?'

259

Mattie thought of what she was learning about Grandpa Joe – and her own growing suspicion that things might have ended differently if she'd only had the guts to stand up to him. 'The thing is, Gil, I'm tired of people telling me what to do. Everyone's done it, all my life. Reenie has my number on this trip; she knows what it means to me so, yes, she is able to determine what we do and where we go. I don't think she took too kindly to my tricking her into seeing June again yesterday, so she'll try to get the upper hand again. And I know I'll let her, if it means the concert happens.'

'But I don't see this as being all about her. I mean, look at what you've done. You organised this trip, put up with everything Reenie, me and everyone else has thrown at you, and we're all still here. The gig is on for next week, the club is being transformed as we speak and the tickets go on sale tomorrow. I spoke to my brother this afternoon and he said the media interest is good so far. *You* made all this happen. Trust me, you're amazing.'

His words floated in the warm bar air between them, and Mattie raised her eyes to the ornate plastered ceiling, half-expecting to see actual letters coasting on the air currents above their heads. The noise of the bar retreated a little.

'What did you say?' Her question was soft against the metallic thud of the background music.

Gil leaned a little closer. 'I said, you're amazing, Mattie Bell.'

Right then, she wanted to kiss him.

The feeling took her completely unawares, so strong it

almost knocked her off her seat. More unexpectedly, she saw her desire mirrored in his gaze as it dipped to her lips and back. He reached for her hand and the bar around her began to swim as their skin made contact.

'Gil . . .'

'Shh . . .'

They were too close now to escape the inevitable. To her surprise, Mattie felt no fear, no urge to run. It only took the smallest bow of her head for their lips to touch; by then it was too late to decide to do anything else. As they kissed, her initial shock at the contact merged into something deeper, and then she was wrapping her arms around him, jealously guarding their closeness. This is where she wanted to be; where, she now understood, she had been heading for some time. All thoughts of Asher, Grandpa Joe and the betrayal flew from her mind, and she gave in to the welcome of Gil's kiss.

A shrill wolf-whistle erupted from the bar and she felt Gil's lips smiling against hers, the warm rush of his breath against her skin from his self-conscious laugh. But their kiss remained: perfect and beautiful and completely un-expected.

When they eventually parted and Gil had raised his hand to thank their delighted audience, he took both her hands in his. 'When this is over and everything is back to normal, we need to talk. I really like you, Mattie. I want to be with you.'

She saw her smile reflected in the deep green eyes gazing at her. Breathless from his kiss, she leaned her head against his shoulder and shivered a little as his arm slipped around her. Could this really be happening?

'I know this is out of the blue,' he continued, his thumb tracing small, gentle circles on the top of her shoulder. 'And I know it's completely the wrong time and you're still getting over everything with the last bloke, but . . .'

Instantly, the romantic atmosphere disappeared. Mattie sat up, shrugging free of his arm. 'Wait a minute. How do you know about that?'

'Reenie told me.'

'Reenie? When?'

He gave a sheepish smile. 'We've been talking – about you – for a while.'

'What?' She struggled to make sense of what she was hearing. Since when were they close enough to discuss personal matters? And what did Reenie think she was doing telling Gil about Asher and her break-up, anyway? Mattie had told her about it in confidence – or so she'd thought.

'Don't be embarrassed. Reenie asked me straight out how I felt about you.'

'And you told her? Just like that?'

'It surprised me, too. She has a way of getting information out of you. I asked her about you and I guess she put two and two together. There wasn't any point trying to deny it.'

This road trip was certainly not short of curveballs. 'What else did she tell you?'

'Nothing else, I promise. I know about your grandfather, but you told me that.'

'What exactly did Reenie say about me?'

'Does it matter?'

Mattie folded her arms, the chill of the bar suddenly seeping into her skin. 'Yes, I think it does.'

He gave a sigh. 'She said you were engaged to an idiot who couldn't see what a gem he had. She said if she'd been on the scene when it happened, she would have gone round his house and torn him a new—'

'Okay, okay, I get the picture.' Mattie's smile wouldn't stay hidden. 'That's quite sweet, actually.'

'She cares about you. And yes, she can be possibly the most annoying person on the planet, but she knows who she likes, and right now you're at the top of the list. She has a good heart and she cares about you. I'm starting to think the only reason she agreed to reunite The Silver Five was because you asked her to do it.'

'Really?'

'Yes. I can see how much she respects you. And I like you too, so it seems Reenie and me agree on one thing.'

The rest of the evening passed in a blur of laughter and stolen kisses beneath the benevolent gaze of Bath's ancient buildings. Mattie put aside her irritation with Reenie for the time being, letting herself be swept along by the newness of it all. It had been years since she'd kissed somebody for the first time – and, compared with her first contact with Asher, being with Gil felt more grown-up somehow. But the combination of quiet confidence and electrifying touch was more powerful than anything she'd experienced. His hand fitted hers in a way no other had done before. Most surprisingly, she sensed this was as

263

much on her terms as it was his. She let herself relax into it, enjoying the discovery of how she fitted within Gil's embrace, how his lips moved across hers. Everything felt new and wonderful – and for once she didn't care what might happen next, or what might wait in store for them down the line. Tonight was theirs – and nothing could steal it from them.

When Mattie returned to her room she was still smiling. It had certainly been a night of surprises. She reached into her jacket pocket to retrieve her room key, but found something else besides: a small star, its glow diminished but still there. Gil must have slipped it into her pocket.

Smiling, she placed it on her bedside table, where its soft glow fell upon Grandpa Joe's diary. She was struck by a sudden need to see how his feelings for Una would play out. Her life had inexplicably moved in parallel with his: would it remain so?

Tuesday, 10 July 1956

I don't know what to do. Una says she wants to spend the night with me.

I hadn't thought this far ahead when we began and I didn't expect her to be so forward. I know girls are more so in London than back at home, and I consider myself a man of the world now I'm here. But still. All of the fellas at work think I'm like them, bedding anything that passes my way. But I never expected to feel this way for a girl I have no confirmed plans for a future with. We are not

engaged and there is no understanding between us.
When I have thought of sex, I've pictured a wedding
night. It's what I was brought up to think of and I
don't know if I'm ready to let that go.

But it's Una Myers. And it would be the easiest
thing in the world to say yes to her.

I want to be with her, to feel the fullness of her
against me, all barriers gone, all caution thrown to
the wind. I think she knows it, too, and it's
tormenting me.

Why am I so prudish? Why can't I be a man and
do as I wish? I'm driving myself to distraction over it
when it should be the most natural decision in the
world. Una thinks it endearing of me. But she keeps
asking – and now I'm scared she'll stop and walk
away. I have to decide soon or I could lose her . . .

Chapter Twenty-Five

'Johnny B. Goode'
– Chuck Berry

♪

Mattie awoke to birdsong and the hum of the hotel guests making their way to breakfast. The sun streamed in through her window and she snuggled down beneath the lavender-scented bed sheets as memories of last night came flooding back. Snoozing the alarm clock on her phone for another ten blissful minutes, she pictured herself back in Gil Kendrick's arms.

She was still smiling when she arrived in the hotel restaurant to meet the others. Reenie was engrossed in a dog-eared copy of *Hello!* magazine. Gil looked up and grinned, instantly allaying Mattie's concern that this morning's first meeting after last night might be awkward.

'How did you sleep?'

Reenie's head shot up, her sparkling grey eyes missing nothing. 'And why would you care about that, Gil Kendrick?'

'Just asking.' He shrugged, but his smile betrayed him. 'Oh-*ho*, what have we here?'

'Nothing, Reenie.' Mattie raised a hand to her forehead, hoping to distract Reenie's interest with a faked hangover. 'And could you keep it down a little, please? Turns out your advice to me last night had a sting in its tail.'

'Hung over, are we? *Good*. About time you lived a little, kid. Pull up a pew and I'll get them to bring you a pot of extra-strong medicine. Vince!'

The waiter at the far end of the restaurant turned. 'Yes, Reenie?'

'Pot of your most potent smokey Joe, if you please.'

'*Vince?*' Mattie asked, taking her seat and reaching for a slice of toast. 'How do you know his name?'

'He brought me my dinner last night. Turns out he's a fan of the Beatles like you, Gil. Well, I told him about that night in India I shared with John, George and the Maharishi. Spiritual enlightenment and a damn fine bottle of cognac. Anyway, now Vince is my new best friend.' She leaned forward, her finger to her coral-painted lips. 'So it's extra sausages all the way for us this morning – if you can stomach them.'

Leaving the leafy grounds of their hotel, Rusty carried the reconciliation road-trippers out through the heart of the historic city. It was as if the houses, trees and people they passed all shared the feeling of optimism within the camper van. Today was a good day, Mattie thought. She could feel Gil's gaze on her as she drove, a delicious secret only she and he shared. With so much of her privacy compromised by the practicalities of travelling at close quarters with other people, it was wonderful to be able to hide something. Gil had caught her hand as they'd walked from the hotel and raised it to his warm lips for a kiss while Reenie went on ahead, oblivious to what was happening. Mattie didn't know how long their stolen kisses would go unnoticed, but for now Reenie seemed none the wiser.

Reenie, meanwhile, had been noticeably happier this morning at breakfast, her tales of the mischief she and Johnny 'Chuck' Powell had unleashed on their bandmates making Mattie and Gil laugh. In marked contrast to how she'd talked about June, it was clear how close she and Chuck had been; closer, it seemed, than she was with Tommy in the beginning.

'We once sewed Rico's sheets to his mattress in a motel near Rome,' she said now, her eyes following the buildings as they drove through a particularly pretty part of the city. 'About two-thirds of the way down from the bed-head to the footboard. We had old woollen blankets back then, with cotton sheets underneath. Chuck had this old darning needle – heaven only knows where he got that from – and thread the same grey as the blanket. He sewed great big tacking stitches across from one side to the other. So when Rico tried to get into bed, he couldn't work out why his feet couldn't reach the end of it! He'd had a few, too, so he thought his body had grown and his legs had shrunk. Chuck was a demon for that sort of thing. He was forever hiding alarm clocks under your bed and setting them for three in the morning, scaring the living daylights out of you.'

'How come you didn't keep in touch with him?' Mattie had asked. If they had been as close as she was making out, surely that was a friendship that could stand the test of time?

Reenie gave a sigh. 'Just *stuff*, you know. Things got in the way, bad decisions were made, all of that. I am looking forward to seeing him again. We had good times, him and me.'

'Maybe you can pick up where you left off?'

'I'd like that. Not sure if he'd say the same, of course! He always talked about living here, you know.' Reenie pressed her nose to the passenger-window glass, peering up at the elegant town houses sailing by. 'Thought himself a bit of a Mr Darcy, he did. Me and Alys used to rib him mercilessly because he read Jane Austen. I mean, what twenty-two-year-old chap does that? It'll suit him now, though. Tommy says he's quite the country squire.' Her mockery of Tommy's Northumberland accent was pin-sharp and made Mattie and Gil laugh.

'So, were you closest to Chuck when you were in the group?' Mattie asked, navigating a mini-roundabout that challenged Rusty's squeaking suspension.

Reenie's smile tightened a little. Were nerves finally setting in after her confident start this morning? 'We got on well.'

Chuck's home was in Widcombe, not far from the centre of Bath. In the morning sunshine the sandstone glowed a beautiful honey-gold, both welcoming to the eye and striking against the deep blue sky dotted with candyfloss wisps of white.

'Is it his house?' Gil asked from the back seat.

'His eldest daughter's, according to Tommy,' Mattie replied.

'Gorgeous,' Gil said.

Mattie felt herself blush, thinking the comment might not have only been about the pretty suburb they were driving through.

Ten minutes later, Reenie and Gil stood beside Mattie as she rang the brass doorbell.

'Are you ready?' she asked Reenie.

'Been waiting for this for years, kid.'

The large black door opened slightly, yanked to a sudden halt by its brass chain.

'Yes?'

Mattie couldn't see the face of the voice's owner, but the tone of it caused her nerves to tip. Did they have the right house?

'Hi. We're here to visit Chuck – um – Johnny Powell? Tommy Mullins called a couple of days ago. I'm Matilda Bell, and this is Reenie Silver . . .'

Abruptly, the chain was released and the door whisked open to reveal a woman in her late forties who looked as if she had been crying. 'You *came*,' she stated, her red-rimmed blue eyes widening to a blank stare.

'Who is it?' came a voice from inside.

The woman at the door opened her mouth to speak, but then clamped a pale hand to it. Behind her another face appeared, rounder and younger, wearing the same haunted expression.

Mattie took a step back, the horrible prospect of not

270

only turning up at the wrong house but also intruding on what was clearly a crisis slowly sinking in. 'Oh gosh, I'm so sorry . . .' she said, mentally calculating how quickly she could shift two people and herself from these poor women's doorstep.

The younger woman moved gently towards them. 'No, Miss Bell, Miss Silver, *we're* so sorry. I'm afraid he's – not here. You'd better come in.'

Chapter Twenty-Six

'Seven Lonely Days'
– Georgia Gibbs

♪

Jack had said it was a miracle that all five members of The Silver Five had survived into their eighties. His words came back to Mattie now as she sat with the others, stunned by the news. They had missed Chuck. By a day and a half.

If only we'd been on time . . . If only Reenie and June hadn't taken so long to talk . . . If only traffic hadn't delayed us . . .

It was Mattie's job to stick to the schedule, her responsibility to get Reenie to each member of The Silver Five at the right time. How could she not blame herself that delays had cost Reenie the chance to say sorry to a friend she had loved – and missed – for years?

Sitting in the house where, just two days before, Chuck had been present was a strangely hollow experience. It was as if his spirit still pottered around them through the high-ceilinged rooms, making himself tea in the large green and cream kitchen with its slate floor and black marble worktops and sitting at the piano in the room where everyone now sat quietly.

Mattie hadn't felt this with Grandpa Joe; not being in his life at the end had meant not having to join with the family in a similar situation at the Bell farmhouse during the first few hours of loss. She had heard from Joanna that he had passed away, but by that point she'd run into Asher's arms for comfort. By the time Asher's affair had been exposed, the family were already busy with the tasks of preparing for a funeral and a house sale.

But the palpable sense of loss here, as tactile as the brocade fabric sofas on which they sat in stunned silence, was as personal as if Mattie had lost her own grandfather all over again. Gil looked utterly mortified, staring at the red Moroccan rug beneath his feet, and Mattie felt her heart sink every time she met the gaze of one of Chuck's family and had to offer a sad smile in return. She had hated such smiles from family and friends when they'd heard of her loss; smiles that always came across as insincere and pitying, regardless of the giver's intentions.

Reenie was white-faced and unnaturally quiet in their midst. She suddenly looked like a little, lost old lady again – small, vulnerable and bemused by a world she now didn't recognise.

'It was so fast,' Chuck's daughter Sheena was saying. 'We went to A & E because he said his stomach was so bad. I honestly thought they'd give him some laxatives, maybe keep him in overnight at worst, but then send him home. Dad's always been so healthy – always *was* . . .'

273

A young, pretty girl Mattie guessed to be in her mid-teens hurried across the room from her seat by the piano to embrace her mother. The room sank into suffocating silence once more.

Mattie looked at Gil for support. He gave a small cough. 'So – um – was this piano his?'

Chuck's granddaughter gave a sad smile that broke Mattie's heart all over again. She recognised the haunted look the young girl wore because she had seen it in her own mirror. 'He played every day. Sometimes for hours at a time.'

Chuck's piano must have always been a large, looming presence in the room, but was now made more so by the vases of pure white lilies placed carefully around it on the parquet floor. Tiny white tea lights in simple glass votives burned alongside them. It had become a shrine. Would it ever be played again, Mattie wondered? And what did you do with a piano when its owner passed away? Would its removal take away the heart of the room in which it had lived for years? The instrument was beautiful: anyone could appreciate the craftsmanship, the polished walnut gleaming as if it had been carved from a slice of mottled amber. Its body was half-shrouded in a bottle-green velvet cloth, and at its base were wheels and foot pedals made of shiny brass. It was old, but very much cared for. Mattie caught Chuck's daughters and his granddaughter casting glances at it, as if he was likely to appear at the piano stool, ready to entertain them again.

'Six in the morning,' Eleanor, Chuck's youngest daughter, rushed. It was a sound halfway between a laugh and a sob, a bittersweet noise that Mattie knew only too well. 'Most expensive alarm clock in the neighbourhood. Dad liked to be up early and wanted everyone else to be up, too. Most mornings it was Fats Domino or Neil Sedaka. On the days when his pain was bad he'd wake us up with Chopin's Nocturnes or Debussy's "Clair de Lune".' She shook her head. 'Mornings have been too quiet since we lost him.'

'Did he ever play our songs?'

Everyone turned to see Reenie staring at Chuck's oldest daughter.

'He did,' Sheena smiled. 'When he knew you were coming, we heard little else. He was determined to serenade you with a medley when you arrived . . .'

'If we'd been here when we said we would . . .' Reenie's voice trailed away and her eyes welled as the awful truth hit home.

'Oh, Ms Silver, you couldn't have known. None of us did. It's been such a shock. We still don't really know what happened. The coroner hasn't got back to us yet, but . . . I'm just so sorry he didn't get to see you. I can't tell you what it's meant to him to know you were coming. He was like a teenager jumping around the place, and all the old stories came out again. He hadn't told them for years, you know, but this week it's been all we've heard. The last thing he said . . .' Her voice cracked and her sister caught her hand. 'Before we left him to speak to the doctor, the very last thing he said was, "They'd better not keep me in here. I've a date with Reenie Silver and sixty years' worth of stories to share."'

Reenie gave a loud sob, and buried her face in her

handkerchief. Mattie leaned across to touch her arm, but Reenie batted her hand away. 'I'm okay. It's just I – I can't believe we missed him.'

Mattie closed her eyes. All the hours they had wasted, delayed by stubbornness and traffic jams – when time was slipping away like shoreline sand pulled by receding waves. It could have been so different. It *should* have been how they'd planned this meeting: full of fun and laughter, and past hurts being healed.

'When is the concert going to be?' Eleanor asked, pulling Mattie back into the room.

Gil looked up. 'This Thursday night. At least –' he turned to Mattie – 'if it's still possible?'

What could she say to that? The plan had been for all five members to perform. Wouldn't it be disrespectful to his memory to go ahead without him?

'There'll be no gig.' Reenie's voice spoke sharply into the room. 'Not now. There can't be.'

Gil shot to the end of his seat. 'Reenie, I understand how you must be feeling, but—'

'But *nothing*, Kendrick! The deal was all of us or none of us. That's what we said when June agreed to join us. I won't get on that stage – or *any* stage, for that matter – without Chuck Powell.'

Mattie looked on helplessly as Gil began to argue with Reenie. Chuck's daughters were insisting that they wanted the concert to proceed, too. But Reenie would hear none of it, her replies rising in both volume and pitch.

'I won't do it, so stop asking! Chuck *was* The Silver Five. He kept us together during that first year, when the rest of us would just as easily have jacked the whole thing in and gone our separate ways. In the end, we stayed for Chuck, for his sake. That's why –' Her eyes grew wide, and she suddenly turned to Sheena and Eleanor. 'Oh, *girls*, I feel awful that I never said sorry to him! All those years, *wasted*. I loved him, you know, like a brother. More than a brother, most of the time. He was always the peacemaker for us. Always putting the group first and his feelings last. We owed our success to him, not to Rico or the music business. *Chuck* was the glue that stuck us together through the tough times. Without him, there'd've been no hit records, no tours, nothing. We'd've ripped each other to shreds long before we ever recorded a single if he hadn't stepped in.'

'He loved you, Reenie,' Sheena replied sadly. 'I hope you know that. He loved you more than you could ever return.'

Chastened, Reenie bowed her head. 'He told you.'

Mattie stared at Reenie. What did Sheena know that she didn't?

'Of course he told us, love. He wouldn't have been Dad if he hadn't been completely honest. You know what he was like. Wore his heart like cufflinks, he used to say. He loved you. Even when you turned him down. *Even* when you left the group and ended his career. And even later when—'

'Stop! Please, just – *stop*.' Reenie gave a heavy sigh, a hand against her brow.

'What happened later, Reenie?' Mattie couldn't hold the question back. She had to know. Until now, Reenie had insisted she and Chuck had been close friends, but there had always been an unspoken omission Mattie couldn't decipher.

'Ah, it's been too long. Too much else crowded in.'

'He never blamed you.'

'Don't say that . . .'

'He didn't, Reenie. Even when he flew back from seeing you and was in bits for months. He always said it had been your decision, and he had to honour it.'

'Decision to do what?' It was one thing to upset a friend, but quite another to break a heart – several times over, if what Chuck's daughters were hinting at was true.

Reenie's lilac-rinsed curls were shaking furiously now. '*Not here*. Not now he's . . .'

'He loved you, that's the truth,' Eleanor stated, her smile conspicuous by its absence. 'I can't say I liked it, but there it is. When Mum died, you were all he could talk about. I think Mum knew you were The One That Got Away. That's why he flew to America to be with you.'

'I couldn't say yes,' Reenie replied, her voice thick. 'I wanted to, but—'

'But you had someone else.'

'No. I lied.'

The room seemed to repeat her confession as if it didn't believe it. Chuck's daughters shared a glance. 'Lied about what?'

'I had nobody! I was alone, dumped and practically bankrupt after that snake divorced me. I was a *mess*. Your dad was a good man. A wonderful man. It would have been so easy to let him take the brunt of all my crap. I mean, that's what he offered. And anyone else would have snapped his hand off. But I couldn't. Not after what I'd done. I'd lied to him before that, you see. I told him I was falling in love in '56, just before the group split, and when he assumed I meant with him, I let him think it. I'm not proud of that. But I couldn't let anyone know I was with Rico. It would've ended everything.' Reenie's shoulders seemed heavy with it all. She slumped into the armchair and rubbed her eyes, streaks of brown mascara staining her cheeks. 'So when your dad came out to see me in Florida in '89, and asked me straight out to marry him, I couldn't accept. Lord knows he deserved better than me and my baggage.'

'So you said you were seeing someone.' Sheena was grave-faced.

'I was going to tell him all of this today. I wish I could have.'

Mattie didn't know what to think. She had arrived here with the team bursting with hope for the rest of the tour, but now – well, now what? They had made such great strides forward two days ago with June, but how could they compete with death? Reenie appeared to be devastated by the news, for once deserting her natural inclination to bring every conversation back to herself. She was adamant the concert could not go ahead without Chuck – and even though both of his daughters urged her to reconsider, she wouldn't listen.

'I'm truly sorry for your loss,' she said as she struggled to stand. 'Mattie, fetch my coat. It's time we left these good people to their mournin'.'

'*Talk to her*,' Gil hissed by Mattie's ear.

'I don't think she'll listen,' she whispered back, desperately trying to summon a reason to keep Reenie in the room.

Reenie was halfway to the door when a single piano

279

note stopped her in her tracks. The note played again, summoning the attention of everyone in the room. Mattie turned to see Chuck's teenage granddaughter sitting at his piano, one slender hand resting on its keys.

'Thalia – not now,' Sheena warned, but a slow progression of notes silenced her.

Each note from the walnut grand seemed to infuse the room with light and love as Thalia Powell-Cutler played her grandfather's beloved piano. Her mother broke down as her aunt comforted her. Mattie gazed, dumbfounded, and Gil, who minutes before had looked ready to punch something, now appeared to be holding his breath.

And then, Thalia began to sing.

Instantly, Mattie recognised the words from Grandpa Joe's favourite song, played so many times through her childhood and in the church when Grandpa Joe had been brought home for the last time. But the melody was unlike anything Mattie had ever heard. It was a simple arrangement of voice and piano, but every note seemed suspended in the air above the room. 'Because You Loved Me' was transformed from a 1950s love song to a heartfelt modern ballad of love and loss, Thalia's fragile, haunting voice forging a bittersweet edge to the well-loved song:

Because you loved me
All my crazy dreams
Find their feathered wings and fly
I am free, love
Because you loved me . . .

Nobody moved. It was impossible to stop looking at this diminutive singer with her china-doll complexion and long dark hair. Even when she reached the final line and repeated it for the last time, nobody said a word. The ultimate note reverberated from within the body of the piano, gradually ebbing away as her startled audience took in what they had just witnessed.

Slowly, Thalia looked up, tears spilling free as she did so. 'Let me do it. Let me be there for Gramps. Because I wasn't there when . . .' Her words were stolen as she broke down.

Mattie's heart went out to Thalia. The concert would be a tribute to Chuck as much as it had been designed to restore something to Grandpa Joe – and, she suspected, Gil's grandfather Jacob. She almost said yes. But then she remembered Reenie. Turning to look towards the open doorway, she saw the singer was no longer on her way out. Instead she looked into the room, her face ashen, focusing on Thalia and the piano Chuck would never play again.

This isn't my decision. Only one person can make that choice.

'Reenie, what do you think?' Mattie's question was as soft as she could make it.

'I think you've got a gorgeous voice, kid,' Reenie replied, never taking her eyes away from Thalia. 'And you play like a dream.'

Thalia wiped her eyes with the sleeve of the long black jumper she wore. 'So?'

'I don't know. It's all such a shock. I need a moment to think . . .'

281

She wobbled a little. Gil sprang to his feet and caught her elbow, helping the startled pensioner to a nearby chair.

'You're an incredible performer,' he said to Thalia. 'The group would be crazy not to let you join them. Come on, Reenie. What do you say?'

'Please, Ms Silver. I know every one of his songs – we used to play them together. I think I could play them in my sleep . . .'

Considering the dark smudges beneath the teenager's eyes, Mattie wondered if she'd slept at all in recent days.

'Dad was so excited to play at your club, Mr Kendrick,' Eleanor said. 'He bent everybody's ear about it around here. Even the postie and the young lad who delivers the free papers. Thalia would be a wonderful addition to your concert. And she could accompany the group, too. You've heard how well she plays.'

'It's your decision, Reenie,' Mattie reminded her, aware that her friend was facing questions from all sides. 'But consider this: could you forgive yourself if you had this chance to make Chuck proud and you missed it?'

Reenie blinked back at her. '*No.*'

Mattie's stomach churned. Was this really it? Were all the wonderful things achieved in the last week destined to come to nothing?

'But—' Thalia's protest was halted by Reenie's raised hand.

'I said, *no*, I *couldn't* forgive myself. Chuck wanted this gig to happen. So it'll damn well happen.'

Chapter Twenty-Seven

'Dream Lover'
– Bobby Darin

♪

Saturday, 21 July 1956

The Silver Five are coming to the Palm Grove in September!

I have wanted to see them perform since I heard their song 'Because You Loved Me' at Len's house. I've bought four of their records since and while I have nothing to play them on, several of the clerks at work have gramophones. Since I passed the last exam, Uncle C seems to be slackening his rules about my evening jaunts, so I'm often out at a pal's house after work to listen to music. He doesn't know about the PG, of course. I know he wouldn't approve. He thinks I stopped going there when he forbade me back in March.

Una says she'll wait for me. I don't know how

long for. I know the decision won't go away, but today I'm just going to be happy that I have tickets to see my favourite group and a beautiful girl to accompany me . . .

Reading this gave Mattie a strange sense of completion. Joe Bell couldn't have known when he wrote those words that it would be two generations before The Silver Five took to the stage at the Palm Grove. What would he have thought – then or now – of the efforts his future grand-daughter was making in his name?

After the turmoil of the day, Mattie had escaped to her room for a few hours. She felt as if she needed oxygen; as if she had been holding her breath for the entire day. Between the horribly sad news of Chuck Powell's passing, the very real possibility that the concert had been grounded once and for all, Thalia's sudden emergence as Chuck's worthy heir and the constant question beneath it all of what might be happening with Gil, Mattie had lost track completely of what she should think or feel. She needed to be able to set off for Wales in the morning with at least a basic sense of control, and for that she needed space she couldn't find when cooped up in a camper van with two other people.

Gil had tried to persuade her to spend time with him – and, for a moment, she had been tempted. But so much had happened today and she needed time to think. She'd promised to see him after dinner, which was booked for seven-thirty p.m., leaving her with two hours now for a bath and a nap.

So, Joe Bell had planned to see The Silver Five with Una? In the years he had talked about missing the concert, he had never mentioned that anyone else was going with him. There must have been a reason he didn't mention Una or her brother, Mattie supposed. But why had he missed a gig he was so obviously looking forward to?

He'd always maintained he'd abandoned the concert because a friend needed him. Had that been Una, or Len? Had Uncle Charles found out where he was going and put a stop to his Palm Grove jaunts? Certainly Grandpa Joe was a proud man, so the humiliation of his uncle's intervention would probably have continued to annoy him even decades after the event. That much Mattie could still be certain of. But with everything she now knew, she found it hard to trust any of his recollections of that night. What had really happened? Would his diary reveal the secret?

Mattie groaned and put the book on the bedside table. She'd had enough revelations for one day. The answer – if it was contained within the green leather-bound pages – could wait one more day to be discovered. Closing her aching eyes, she let the unfamiliar contours of the hotel bed pull her gently into a deep sleep.

When she awoke with a jump, daylight was pooling into her room from the still-open curtains. Confused, she found her watch and squinted at the face.

No, it couldn't be, could it?

An insistent growl from her stomach corroborated the watch's story and she sat up, punch-drunk from nearly fourteen hours of sleep. Clambering out of bed and padding across the thick carpet to fetch the kettle, she noticed a small rectangle of paper by the bottom of the door. When she picked it up she saw her name, unfolding the paper to read the note within:

Hey you
Missed you this evening.
Just know that I'm thinking of you and I can't wait to see you in the morning.
Sweet dreams, Mattie Bell.
Gil x

Mattie smiled. The note was undeniably sweet. Gil *was* sweet, she was discovering. Reenie had once used the word to describe Jacob Kendrick, and Mattie half-wondered what Reenie really made of his grandson. Was it the similarity to Jacob that sometimes irritated her when she was around Gil, or was it the difference in his character that marked him out? Mattie wanted to ask her – but to do so before she and Gil were ready to tell everyone might be a mistake.

She was considering this later, on her way to the hotel's breakfast room, when a noise almost scared her witless.

'*Psst!* Mattie!'

She turned to see Gil, half-hidden behind a large potted palm in an archway near the reception area. 'You crazy man, you almost gave me a heart attack! What are you doing?'

He grabbed her hand and pulled her out of sight of the communal sitting area. 'I wanted to do this before we have to face Reenie.' Before she could reply she was in his arms, giggling as he kissed her.

When he let go, she reached out to steady herself against the wall, trying to reclaim her breath from her amusement and his kiss. 'Someone might have seen us,' she said.

'And what if they had? It's our business. And a *wonderful* business it is . . .' He reached for her again.

'Gil, stop it!'

'I missed you last night.'

'I know. I got your note, thanks.'

'So, now you're well rested . . .'

'You are impossible! Put me *down* . . .' She cast her eye over her shoulder in case anyone was nearby.

'It's okay, I've sworn this pot plant to secrecy.' Looking down, Gil's smile broadened. 'Which, according to its *laminated name badge*, is "Horatio". Who does that? Who names their plants? Man, some things about this hotel are *odd*.'

'The delights of being on the road.'

'Only one delight I'm interested in . . .' His lips made a bid for her neck, and it took all of Mattie's resolve to push him back.

'We can't. Reenie could be here any minute.'

'Fine, have it your way.' He raised his hands as if Mattie had suddenly become an exposed live wire. 'But you aren't telling me you'd rather hang out with a hell-raising OAP than be with me, are you? Because I find that hard to believe.'

'Sad though it may be, yes. For now, anyway. Don't groan like that, Gil. Time isn't on our side and we have to get to Wales as soon as we can.' *And I need to concentrate*, she added in her head. The unexpected turn of events

287

yesterday, and Gil's obvious intention to pursue whatever was happening between them, was making her dizzy. She had to maintain her focus on the road trip she'd invested so much time and energy in. Whatever else might be happening could wait – she hoped – until later. It was too new for her to be able to work out whether it was real or not. She wanted to enjoy it, not analyse too much, but she felt cautious after what had happened with Asher. For that she needed a clear head and, however difficult it might be to resist the lure of giving in to the heady pull of chemistry, she had to be responsible.

Gil feigned offence, but his smile told her she was forgiven. 'I get it. This isn't going to go away, I promise. I wasn't expecting to find you; there's no way I'm letting you go.'

Mattie was still buzzing when she reached the table, where Reenie was holding court as usual, joking loudly with neighbouring diners, her trademark high spirits firmly back in place. Mattie suspected the professional smile was there for a reason, but it was good to see her sassiness back.

'Ah, here she is, the filthy little stop-out,' she grinned. 'I do hope you were up to no good last night, Mattie Bell. It'll restore my faith in humanity.'

'It's all true,' she grinned, happy to play along. 'So much so that we have to leave today whether we like it or not. Bath won't have me back for a while.'

'Drummed out of town? That's my girl! So, when do we leave?'

'As soon as everyone is ready. It isn't a long drive today,

but I think the sooner we get to Wales the better.' She caught Gil's smile out of the corner of her eye, and fought the urge to giggle. Maybe when they arrived at their accommodation she and Gil could spend some time alone. *That* possibility would keep her warm all the way to the Brecon Beacons.

As Rusty carried them through stunning countryside in early-afternoon sunshine, Mattie could feel Reenie's eyes steady on her. She chanced a look to her left and instantly saw suspicion staring back.

'Everything okay?'

'Peachy, kid. Just peachy.'

'We should be able to find somewhere to stop soon, if you need a break?'

'Oh, don't you worry about my bladder, Mattie Bell. From the look of you, you have more important things to concern yourself with.'

'Such as?' Mattie could hardly believe she was egging her friend on: even a week ago, she wouldn't have dared court controversy over her own life.

'I dunno. You tell me.'

'Just focusing on the driving. Like you told me.'

'Bollocks you are,' Reenie grinned. 'But you'll keep, girl.'

Mattie didn't dare look in the rear-view mirror in case Reenie saw it, but she knew Gil had heard their conversation by the way he shifted position in the back seat.

Half an hour out of Bath, the heavens opened. Within another hour, iron-grey clouds shrouded the road in gloom as the rain turned to hail. The noise on Rusty's roof was deafening, drowning out the engine noise and conversation.

Ahead of them, a row of cones across the road confirmed its closure, the first yellow diversion sign peering out through the rain. Tuning the radio to a local news station, Mattie's worst fears were confirmed: the road she'd planned to take was impassable due to floods, and was unlikely to reopen for several days.

With a sigh of resignation, Mattie followed the diversion.

Another crushingly slow hour later, the suggested route was fast becoming a road to nowhere. Thick forest on either side of the dual carriageway stole what little light the storm hadn't already blocked, cloaking the road in impenetrable shadows. Mattie could feel the ache growing across her shoulders and neck, and realised she was gripping Rusty's steering wheel.

Gil and Reenie's conversation had long since waned, leaving the occupants of the camper van sitting in uneasy silence. Only the thunderous pelting of rain on the windscreen and protesting squeak of Rusty's failing windscreen wipers filled the space where chatter had been.

'It's a filthy day,' Reenie said finally, peering out of Rusty's steamed-up windows. 'I'll be glad to get to my bed later.'

'Me too.' Mattie tried to release the tension in her neck. 'I can't believe anyone thought this was a suitable diversion.'

'It could be a while till we get there. Why don't we try to find somewhere nearby to eat and have a break?' Gil suggested.

Frustrated by their slow progress, Mattie was keen to press on, but the mention of food changed her mind.

Twenty dragging minutes later, the welcoming beacon of a roadside pub burned into view.

It was a blessed relief to enter the warm and cosy interior of the pub. In the corner a roaring fire blazed, dried hops were strung over rafters and generous tweed armchairs nestled around tables, while soothing music played. Despite her concerns about their spiralling schedule, Mattie was glad of the sanctuary.

She joined Gil at the bar while Reenie commandeered a table.

'How's the shoulder?' he asked.

'Still a bit stiff. It's times like these I long for power steering.'

'I don't know how you can drive that thing. Especially in this weather. Although I'm impressed it hasn't broken up from sheer effort. Do you think it'll survive the entire journey?'

'Of course,' Mattie replied, as the words of her long-suffering mechanic Steve rang in her ears: *I've done all I can to get this thing roadworthy. But I can't work miracles. If you push this van beyond what it can do, it'll fail . . .*

'I see Reenie's made herself at home already,' Gil smiled, nodding over towards the singer. She was deep in conversation with a young couple at the next table. 'More souls to add to her people collection. How does she do that? Just walk up to complete strangers and start a conversation?'

'She loves meeting people. She said years of meeting adoring fans means she can chat to anyone. But I think she likes the interaction. She always commands an audience at Beauvale.'

'I'll bet.'

'Actually, I think she gets lonely. It can't be easy, going from being the toast of the town to a little old lady in a retirement village.'

The gruff-looking barman took their food order and started to prepare their drinks. Mattie was aware of Gil looking at her. 'Is that part of the reason you agreed to this?'

'Maybe. I think Reenie's great. Infuriating, too, and more than a handful to look after, but she has a good heart. My grandfather used to say that the best people hid gold hearts beneath their skin. "The kind of gold that shines out, no matter how they try to conceal it".' She thought of young Joe Bell, travelling to the big city with a million dreams in his pockets, drawn into the Soho club scene by a sense of loyalty to Una. Had he considered himself as one of the golden-heart bearers?

'Do you miss him?'

'More than I can say. Even though at the end we weren't speaking.' She shrugged off his concern, not wanting to explain further. 'Easy to be wise after the event.'

'My grandad is the reason I run the club,' Gil said, suddenly. 'My brother Colm thinks I'm insane.'

'Why?'

'We're losing money. Every week we get offers from developers wanting to buy us out. Colm thinks we've run Kendrick's for long enough and should take the money. But I just can't bear the thought of someone tearing the place down and building faceless apartments nobody can afford. Grandad was proud of that club. He worked hard to make it a success. To accept defeat now would be like betraying his memory.'

'But I thought you agreed to the gig because of the money?'

'I did. Because we need it to stay afloat. I called Colm this afternoon. Tickets are almost sold out. We haven't had a full house for seven years. That's why I asked to come with you. I have to make sure this gig happens.'

Mattie followed him to their table, her thoughts a blur.

There had been a moment, back when they'd first met in the club, when she'd thought she caught a glimpse of sadness in Gil's soft green eyes. She'd dismissed it then, but now she wondered: had she misjudged his motives all along?

'Ah, kids, let me introduce you to my new friends,' Reenie announced as Mattie and Gil sat down. The young couple had moved from their table to join Reenie. 'This is Kelvin and Pru. They've had a bit of an ordeal, by all accounts.'

The young man gave a shy smile. His companion hid behind a veil of vivid auburn hair. Everything about her was a closed fortress: arms folded into a shield across her body, legs crossed, hair falling onto her knee. The only indication she gave that she was involved in the conversation was a definite nod of her head. They seemed the opposite of each other – him open and her shut off – but had a closeness that seemed at odds with this. There was plenty of room on the bench seat even with five bodies, but the pair huddled together, knees and elbows touching, like the rows of paper cut-out dolls Mattie and Joanna used to make as children.

'Tell them what happened. You won't believe it.'

'We hitched a lift with this bloke from Bristol. He said he'd take us back home to London, but then he wanted money. So we had to get out . . .'

'Drove off with their stuff,' Reenie pouted, angry on the couple's behalf. 'Money and all. Isn't that so, Kelvin?'

Kelvin nodded. 'I had a tenner in my back pocket and my iPhone in my hand. But everything else was in my bag.'

'So the poor kids had to walk here. In *this* weather!'

'He took your bags?'

The auburn curtain parted to reveal a pale face. 'We left them,' Pru said. 'We jumped out at the traffic lights on the motorway island and he drove off with our stuff.'

'That's miles back!' Mattie recalled the journey from the closed motorway junction along the darkened A-road. It had taken them well over an hour – how long must it have taken Kelvin and Pru, walking through driving rain? 'Is there anyone we can call for you? At least let us buy you something to eat.'

'My shout,' Gil said, jumping up. 'Anything you like.'

'We'll take you home,' Reenie said.

And suddenly, Reenie Silver was centre-stage. Four pairs of eyes stared at her; two with shocked delight; two with utter horror.

'Reenie,' Mattie hissed, 'what are you doing?'

'I'm offering these poor young things a bit of a hand.'

'A *bit of a hand* is lending them money to catch a train, not bringing them with us.'

'We're going that way, aren't we?'

'Not until Thursday. And we have to get over to Crickhowell and back first.'

Reenie raised an indignant chin. 'Then the kids get a bit of a holiday into the bargain.'

'This is insane! We don't have time for this. We're late as it is, and the detour tonight won't have helped.'

'Exactly!' The old lady snapped her fingers. 'So we don't have time to drop them off at a train station, like you say. This is the most *time-efficient* option.'

'You are unbelievable.'

'I'm not leaving them.'

'Reenie – do you want this gig to happen? Because if you do, we have to leave soon. *Without* extra passengers.'

Reenie's pale grey eyes darkened. 'I *said* they're coming with us. Now I don't care if you like it or not. The fact is, I'm paying for this trip. I am more than happy to give them a room for the night. All you have to do is *drive*.'

Mattie felt sick, as if the slate floor of the pub had begun to buckle beneath her. Reenie's directness stung, blindsiding her. She took a step back, hurt and resentment like she'd felt after Grandpa Joe's ultimatum burning in her stomach. 'Fine,' she stated. 'Have it your way. If we miss the gig, it will be down to *you*.'

She didn't wait to see the effect of her insinuation, turning her back on Reenie to march outside. As the driving rain pelted her head, she heard footsteps behind her.

'Mattie. Slow down.'

'The woman is *impossible*! Did you see what she just did?'

'She was out of order, sure. But it looks as if we've been overruled.'

'*We*, Gil? I wasn't aware you'd expressed an opinion.'

'Mattie, come on. You have a hard enough time controlling Reenie. She's hardly likely to listen to me.'

'Great. Well, thanks for your support.'

'Look, I know I'm the last person to support Reenie, but don't be too hard on her tonight.'

'Excuse me? Did you hear what she just said?'

'Mattie, she just lost somebody. Someone she'd expected to see. All of her apologies mean nothing because Chuck's not here to hear them. That's got to hurt. Time ran out for them. Maybe she sees this as a way of making amends in his absence.'

Like I'm doing for Grandpa Joe, Mattie thought. All she'd seen was the insult. Could there have been more to Grandpa Joe's offence, too? She felt weary, as if the raindrops were lead weights falling on her shoulders. 'I just want to get to Crickhowell. We've a long way to go, and it's getting late.'

Gil reached out and touched her arm – a small but deliberate act of solidarity – and Mattie no longer felt alone.

'I've never been to Wales before,' Kelvin said as they drove across the Severn Bridge. Lights across the Severn Estuary shone in the dark waters on either side of them, and the young man appeared intent on capturing every moment on his phone camera. Beside him, Pru sat in stoic silence. Mattie couldn't work out whether she was asleep or just hiding behind the protective shield of red hair. They were certainly a contrast. Kelvin chattered incessantly, Pru brooded. Her trust in him was clear to see, but Mattie wondered how much of it was ever verbalised. They didn't seem to be a couple, but the way Kelvin looked at his friend betrayed feelings he obviously assumed were hidden.

'You been to Wales before, eh, Kendrick?' Reenie asked over her shoulder.

'My uncle used to live in Harlech,' he replied. 'That kept us London kids in exciting holidays for a few years. Between that and my dad's side of the family in Cork, we had quite a broad Celtic experience.'

'You'd need it, livin' in the Big Smoke,' Reenie said. 'My third husband was Welsh, actually.'

'Now, this I *have* to hear.'

'Well, hear it you shall, Gil. I was down in the South of France holidaying with a few friends, when darling Tom Jones turned up with this chap. Friend of his, very Welsh, built like Superman's better-looking brother. I'd just finished my second divorce and was feeling a bit sorry for myself, you know? My friends egged me on, and TJ was all, "You're all work and no play, woman. Have a bit of fun!" Well, when the great Voice from the Valleys tells you to have fun, you do as you're told. It was only meant to be a fling, but Davey followed me back home and after a while I didn't bother telling him to leave.'

'How long were you married for?'

'Oh, it was eighteen months or so. Turned out he was

a bit too fond of el vino and none too happy when I asked him to choose between the bottle and me. Anyway, he went back to the Land of his Fathers and as far as I know he's still there.'

Mattie listened with passive frustration. She was still smarting at the way the old lady had spoken to her earlier. It was as if battle lines had been drawn where before no conflict existed. Reenie sat beside her in the front seat, nodding as Kelvin launched into another long-winded conversation. Did she know how her words had hit Mattie? Did she even care?

Gil was doing his best to pour oil on troubled waters, his too-bright replies to Kelvin edged with nervous laughter. Maybe he was right: perhaps Reenie saw the young people as a way of finding redemption in the wake of Chuck's death. Mattie resolved to talk to her about it in the morning. Nobody needed an atmosphere for the final meeting of the trip.

They arrived at the beautiful old stone hotel on the edge of Crickhowell just before four p.m., the stormy day brightening around them. Gil had called ahead during the journey and, though no more rooms were available, he had managed to arrange for fold-out beds to be added to his room and Mattie's room for Kelvin and Pru respectively. Now, he helped Reenie inside to check in. As Pru followed them, Kelvin offered to help Mattie with the luggage.

'I'm sorry we crashed your trip,' he rushed, reaching into the back of Rusty to pull out Gil's holdall. 'But I appreciate this so much. I'd given up hope of us getting back.'

'Don't you have family you could have called?'

Kelvin's pale skin turned a startling pink. 'They don't know I'm here. My mum thinks I'm on a climbing weekend in the Lakes.'

'And Pru's family?'

He let out a sigh. 'They're the reason she ran in the first place. She's always fought with her mum as long as I've known her, but six months ago they had a huge row. I mean, *epic*. I've never heard Pru so angry as she was the night she called me. She was already in Manchester by then, kipping on a friend's floor. I thought she'd be okay, you know, stay there until the dust settled and then come home. But she didn't.'

'You stayed in touch?'

He nodded. 'She's my best friend. I couldn't let her do that alone. She kept telling me she was all right – she'd got a job at a café and was sorting out proper accommodation. But then on Friday she called me and said it had all been a lie. She'd been chucked out of her mate's place, her money was running out and she was scared. Terrified. The guy she'd started seeing had turned nasty – she wouldn't give me details, but I guessed the rest. She said she was going to try hitching a lift to the Lakes. There was no way I was letting her do that. So I got a lift to Manchester with my uni mate and went to get her. Here, let me get that.'

Mattie handed him her rucksack and locked the camper van. 'So why hitch-hike home? It's so dangerous.'

'I know. We were idiots. I just thought I could protect her . . . Honestly, I can't thank you enough for helping us.'

Mattie chided herself for feeling aggrieved. 'You're welcome. Where do you need dropping off?'

'I'll call Mum tomorrow and tell her what's really happening. She'll rip a strip off me, but I know she'll come and get us. If you could get us to Beaconsfield services on the M40, that would be great.'

Once they had left bags in their rooms, Reenie announced she was taking Pru and Kelvin for afternoon tea.

'We have lots to discuss,' she called as they headed for the restaurant. 'And cultural experiences to catch up on. Can you believe these kids have never tried clotted cream or Welsh cakes? What kind of a life is *that*?'

Mattie and Gil were left side by side in the hotel foyer.

'I guess that just leaves us, then. You weren't planning on another epic snooze, were you?'

'No, I think I'm sorted in the sleeping department, thanks. Come on. Let's get away for a while.'

They left the hotel and walked on recently rained-on roads and pavements towards the pretty market town of Crickhowell. The air felt fresh from the earlier shower, the smell of flowers from hanging baskets and wet earth mingling with wood smoke from the chimneys of grey slate cottages. Mattie had always loved this about Wales: the way the countryside seemed renewed after rain. Despite it being a weekday and children being back at school, the town was filled with visitors drawn to its charms on the edge of the Brecon Beacons. Gil suggested they find somewhere for coffee, but Mattie refused.

'We've been stuck inside rooms, hotels and camper vans for days now,' she argued. 'We're in a beautiful place neither of us has visited before. And you *really* don't need any more caffeine today. Let's just walk?'

'I might not be very nice without caffeine,' Gil warned. 'I might be terrible company.'

Mattie grinned back, enjoying the game. 'I'll take my chances.'

'Well, *okay*, don't say I didn't warn you.' He caught her hand, his fingers lazily curling around hers. 'Um, is this all right?'

Gil Kendrick was a man of many surprises. His vulnerability was unexpected and utterly charming, and even now, as he laughed at his own question, Mattie felt drawn to him. This side of him wasn't something the others would ever see, of that Mattie was certain. It was as if she saw an undiscovered path snaking up around a mountain that only she could take.

'Yes. Thanks for asking.'

'I'm sorry. It's been a while since I last did this. Running the club means I haven't had much time for dating. I'm not sure I can remember what to do.'

'You're doing fine so far.'

'Oh well, that's comforting to know.' He took a deep breath and smiled. 'It's gorgeous here, isn't it? My brother always raves about this part of the world. He comes here with his mountain-biking buddies. I think they stay in Abergavenny. He lives for his weekends away. If it wasn't for the club I think he'd be out of London like a shot.'

'Has he always been into that kind of thing?'

'Colm? No. Bit of a midlife crisis, only he had it ten years early. I was always the active one growing up. You know, it's weird: we've totally changed places in the last few years.'

'Is he older than you?'

'Same age.'

Mattie looked at him. 'You're twins?'

'Non-identical. It confuses people all the time. When you meet him you probably won't believe me, but it's true. He's older than me by four minutes. That buys him no superiority rights in our family, though. He's far more laid-back than me, maybe because he'd already won the "older brother" prize, so he didn't need to do anything else. I, on the other hand, have spent a lifetime feeling I have something to prove.'

'In my family being the oldest sibling wins you the dubious privilege of sorting out everyone else's problems. My sister Joanna takes it all in her stride, but I grew up being glad it wasn't my job.'

'Do you get on?'

'Oh yes. We love each other to bits. I'm sharing my house with her and my niece and nephew at the moment, which is lovely. She's managing my shop while I'm here, actually.'

They had reached a footpath that led down to the riverbank and ducked beneath low-hanging elder trees to follow it.

'Hmm, Colm's holding the fort for me right now, which makes me keen to get home tomorrow.' His eyes grew wide and he stopped walking to face her. 'Not that I'm – I mean, I'm not in a hurry to leave *this* – us – whatever it is that's happening here.'

Mattie laughed. 'It's okay. I'm missing my life, too. Being on the road has been fun, but I want to get back to normality.' Whatever *that* is, she thought. Because, after this adventure, anything felt possible . . ..

'Mmm, your own bed,' Gil said, as if describing the most desirable luxury. 'Your own blend of coffee. With more than a thimbleful of milk to make it with.'

'Ooh, decent teabags,' Mattie agreed, loving the joke as her fingers rested comfortably between Gil's. 'And beds that feel like only *you've* slept in them recently.'

'Yeah, and pillows that don't either swallow your head or crack your skull. It's all very well wrapping a bit of cardboard around the pillows that boast about you having a "choice". If it's uncomfortable versus violent that isn't much of a choice.'

'You know, I didn't realise about the cardboard thing the first night in Alnwick,' Mattie admitted, remembering her consternation at her pillows feeling strange for the first couple of hours of trying to sleep on them.

'You never did? That's hilarious.'

'I know. The things you learn on the road, huh?'

'Now you sound like a true professional. Reenie would be proud.' Gil's hand wrapped around Mattie's with a gentle squeeze. 'I really don't want to leave you tomorrow. Can't we just carry on walking? See where we end up?'

This was feeling dangerously like Mattie could fall too far at any minute. Wanting to protect herself, she forced a giggle. 'Nice try. You have a concert to prepare for. What time's your train?'

'Four-thirty from Abergavenny. Reckon we'll be done with Alys Davis by then?'

'Our appointment is at ten a.m., so I should hope so.

303

Reenie is obviously jealous of her but she talks about Alys very warmly. I think it'll be straightforward – if Miss Silver behaves.'

'She's *so* jealous of Alys, isn't she?' Gil smirked, a little unkindly.

'She is.' Mattie didn't want to think of the road trip now, but a subtle glance at her watch confirmed it was time to return to the others. 'Talking of which . . .'

'No, don't say it.'

'Gil, we have to.'

'Don't say it! Not yet!' He gathered Mattie into his arms and began to kiss her. 'Say we were unavoidably detained . . .'

Mattie giggled, wanting more than anything to hide away in this beautiful place with him. 'Who by? That lone angler over there? He doesn't look the type.'

'Say we got lost. Walking up a mountain. And they had to send out a search party. Which took *hours*. And the only way we could keep warm was to share our body heat . . .'

'You're dreadful!' Mattie struggled out of his embrace. 'Come on, we need to go.'

'Five more minutes,' he pleaded.

And this time, it was Mattie who kissed him first.

Chapter Twenty-Eight

'Shake, Rattle and Roll'
– Bill Haley & His Comets

♪

'How are you feeling about tomorrow, Reen?' Kelvin asked between mouthfuls of bread and butter, as the team ate dinner together that evening.

'To be honest, I'll be glad when we're done and heading down to London. I mean, it's been fun, but I am *done* with apologising. Looking forward to seeing little Alys, of course, even if she is the Queen of Wales these days.'

'Were you friends when you were in The Silver Five?'

'Oh, yes. Idolised me, she did. We were her first professional job, you know. Practically picked her up at King's Cross station and shoved her straight on the stage. Gorgeous voice, but it took a bit of coaxing out of her. I've always felt the worst about lying to her when I went off. We talked about everything back in those days, and she felt like my little sister. They were all my family, like it or not, for nigh on five years. I mean, I saw them more often than me own flesh and blood, livin' in each other's pockets all the time. Alys and me would sit up in our digs long after the others had crashed, talkin' about our dreams. She just wanted to sing, bless her. It was never about the stardom for her. I liked that – envied it, too. And now she's the biggest bleedin' star of all of us! I should have done that. Held everything lightly. My problem was that my ambition was bigger than anything else in my life.' She pulled a face. 'Bleedin' hell, listen to me jabbering on! I need more wine. Mattie, Gil, help an old biddy over to the bar, would you?'

It was a strange request, not least because Reenie had been more than capable of visiting the bar earlier. But the intent in her smile made Mattie and Gil do as she had asked. They made slow progress to the bar, and when they were almost there Reenie unlinked her arm from Mattie's and turned back to make sure Kelvin and Pru were out of earshot.

'It does my heart good to see what's happening with the two of you. Now, don't try denying it. You're a proper pair of lovebirds. I know I've only known you a short time, Mattie – and Gil, even less – but you both mean a lot to me. I hope you know that.'

'Of course we do.'

She gave a contented sigh and patted Mattie's cheek. 'You're a good girl. I'm sorry I dropped those two on you. But I hope you understand why?'

Mattie glanced at Gil. 'I'm starting to.'

'You're smashing, the pair of you,' Reenie said, her voice suddenly cracking. 'Would you take a walk with me?'

306

'Now? But what about . . . ?' Gil looked over towards Kelvin and Pru.

'They'll manage without us for five minutes.' Reenie held out her hand and Gil took it. 'Come on.'

The sound of the river met the crunch of gravel as they walked out to a small garden in the hotel grounds. Mattie was aware of a stillness that had settled over Reenie. She stopped beside a slate bench and leaned on her walking cane, inhaling the sweet country air.

'This place is beautiful, isn't it? No wonder Alys wanted to live here.' She smiled. 'And now here I am with my two new favourite people. I know I've not been the easiest passenger, but we've had fun, haven't we? And tomorrow we make our final visit and then the show . . . I wasn't sure we'd pull it off, but here we are. That's why I want to say this now, before the final push. Before it all gets too busy to talk. Sit down, will you?'

'I couldn't sit while you're standing. Please—'

Reenie rolled her eyes. 'Gil Kendrick, just do as you're told for once in your life! This won't take long, and I'm not a complete invalid.'

Amused, Mattie and Gil sat together.

'Thank you. Now, I hope you know I've come to see you as surrogate grandkids – don't giggle, Mattie! I'm serious. We started out as friends, but now you're family, as far as I'm concerned.' Her smile had gone, grey eyes earnest in her pale face. 'You need to understand that.'

It was a lovely gesture, but Mattie sensed more waited in the wings behind it.

'And because I think of you like that, I want to tell you everything.'

Mattie's senses stood to attention. Could this be the last piece in the puzzle of what had happened at the Palm Grove? 'Everything?'

Reenie's jaw tightened. 'I want to explain what happened that night. Why I left. I've never told anybody else, because . . . well, I didn't trust anyone enough to understand. But I think you two understand me.'

Now Gil was listening too, his expression steady. 'What happened, Reenie?'

'I didn't leave because I had a glittering career waiting for me. It came later, of course, but that's not the reason I skipped the gig. And I didn't let your grandad down, Gil. It was *his* idea.'

'I don't follow.'

'Jake was the only one who knew the truth. He was a friend to me when nobody else was. And he kept my secret for the rest of his life.'

Mattie could feel Gil beginning to tense beside her. 'What secret? I thought Rico arranged it so you could leave the band.'

'And why would I skip out on the biggest gig of my life? Think about it: even if my new contract was waiting backstage for me, why lose the chance to make a name for myself one last time as lead singer of The Silver Five?'

'But that was Rico's plan . . .'

'No, love. That's what I told everyone else. Better for them to think me a selfish cow than risk Rico learning the truth.'

308

Mattie couldn't take it in. Rico knew the truth, didn't he? That he'd secretly brokered a solo contract with the record company, and was already planning Reenie's first tour? It was what Reenie had insisted since they'd begun discussing the road trip – and what she'd repeated several times during the last week and a half. 'I don't understand . . .'

Reenie's body sagged as if the sheer effort of carrying her secret had finally proved too much. 'I didn't run away *with* Rico that night, Mattie. I was running away *from* him.'

In a moment of stunned silence, her words arranged and rearranged themselves in Mattie's mind and still made no sense. 'Why?'

'Because I was scared. And – *pregnant*.'

The bombshell shattered the peace of the garden, blowing apart everything Mattie had assumed about the events of that night. She had pictured Reenie as a head-strong, ambitious performer, making a mistake she would only later regret. The folly of youth, giving no thought to the consequences of her actions until it was too late.

'Whose baby was it?' Gil's question had an edge of ice that tipped Mattie's nerves.

'That's the worst of it, Gil. I knew who the father was. But the father wanted it dead.'

'But you said my grandfather knew. Are you saying . . . ?'

'Gil—'

'No, Mattie. She said Grandad knew about it. I want to know what she means by that.'

'Did he? Did Jacob know?' Mattie asked.

'Who do you think opened the back door to let me go that night? Who paid for my cab fare out of town? Jake was the only one I knew would help me.'

'Why would he do that? I didn't even know you were that close to him.'

'Because he thought the baby was *his*! He thought he was saving his kid.'

The last of Reenie's words came out as a sob, echoing around the drystone walls of the garden. The wind momentarily stolen from his sails, Gil could only stare dumbfounded back at her.

'Oh, Reenie . . .' Mattie's heart ached for her friend. How could she have kept this hidden for so many years?

'You see? This was why I almost didn't tell you. No good comes of knowing the truth. I thought you of all people would understand that, love.'

'But I'm here because I *want* to know the truth. However hurtful it is.'

'Even with your cheating chap? Wouldn't life have been better if you'd been none the wiser? If you'd had your lovely house and your dream wedding, and just been happy?'

Mattie shook her head. 'No. Because it wouldn't have been real. And I would have found out, years down the line. The truth always comes out, Reenie. It always does.'

'Why did Grandad think it was his baby?' Gil's question was a quiet demand. Mattie could feel pain etched into the surface of every word.

'Love, you don't want to know . . .'

'I *said*, why?'

Reenie let out a sigh that seemed to carry the weight of years. 'I found out I was carrying it in Edinburgh, just before we came back to London for the gig. Doctor reckoned I was three months gone. Forgive me, Gil, but I knew it was Rico's. I was young and I was an idiot. I didn't think of the consequences of anything, just followed my stupid heart. It wasn't the first time it had happened to Rico: he'd got a young band singer knocked up about a year before he met me. He was married then, too. He said he'd sent her away to friends in the West Country who would raise the kid as their own. But my mate Ruby knew different. She told me he'd forced the girl to get rid of it. Down some horrible, seedy back alley somewhere. She died. She was twenty-four. Same age as me. Well, I didn't want a kid, but I sure as hell didn't want the alternative. So I lied.'

She looked up at Gil, as if willing him to understand. But Gil couldn't raise his eyes to look at her. Mattie could feel shock and pain almost radiating out of his body, but she was powerless to reach it. This was far beyond the borders of their fledgling relationship; and if she intervened to stop the discussion now, Reenie might never reveal the full truth.

'What was the lie?' she asked, breath tight in her throat, already suspecting the answer.

'I'd met Jake Kendrick six months before and, oh, he was a smashing bloke. Funny, kind, handsome as all get-out. He was everything Rico wasn't. I used to visit him at the club, after closing time. Just for drinks and a natter. That's all it started as. But we got really close, and then just before I left to do the month of gigs in Scotland, we spent the night together. Gil, I need you to know that it wasn't just a fling for me. I really liked him. I thought when I got back from the tour we'd have a chance. But then on the train up, Rico told me your grandad was engaged. He'd never told me that. It broke my heart.'

'You're lying. He wouldn't have cheated on my grandmother. She was his world . . .'

'That's as maybe, but I wasn't the one who started it, son. I'm sorry to tell you, because I know you idolise him. But he never said he had anyone. I thought he was free. If I'd known, it would never have happened. I didn't want to be someone's bit on the side anymore. It was no way to live. I was sick of it with Rico.'

'So you went for revenge on him by lying about your baby?'

Reenie reddened, jabbing her stick at Gil. 'Don't you dare suggest that! I didn't know I was already pregnant when I slept with him. I'd been feeling poorly for a while, but I put it down to working too much. I fainted during rehearsal in Edinburgh, and the stage manager called a doctor. That was when I found out. I knew I was too far gone for it to have been Jake's. I wished with all me heart it had been. But I was terrified of Rico finding out. So I chose what I thought was the best of a bad deal. I told Jake the baby was his. He was a good man and I knew he'd look after me. I wasn't wrong, either. He was wonderful. Promised me and the kid would be looked after. And I believed him. What other choice did I have?'

'So why did he let you leave the Palm Grove that night?'

'Someone told Rico, two days before the Palm Grove gig. He was *livid*. Blamed me for wrecking my career. And then he said he knew a bloke in Soho who could "help me out". He was going to take me there that night, after the gig . . .' She shuffled backwards, dropping heavily onto the low stone wall that circled the garden, hugging her arms to her body.

'Oh Reenie, *no* . . .' Mattie went to help her, but Reenie held up a hand to stop her.

'Don't, love. I'm all right. You wanted to know the truth. So let me say it.' Confident that Mattie wasn't coming any closer, she continued. 'I was sick with worry and I didn't know what to do. Jake saw it, and I had to tell him. So we made a plan: I'd do the sound-check with the group, then wait for Rico to go for his drink, like he always did before a gig. He'd go up to the manager's office of the clubs we played in with a bottle of whisky and share a dram or two before the doors opened. His 'little extravagance', he called it, to keep the promoters sweet. He was known in London for it, and the club owners loved him for bringing the best single malts.

'Jake settled him in his office, and then left one of his associates to keep Rico busy while he helped me out of the back door. He'd arranged a cab outside and a room in a boarding house in Brighton for me to stay in until I could figure out what to do next. I couldn't tell the others because one of them might have let something slip to Rico – and then we'd have been done for. I knew full well what I was giving up: all my dreams, everything I'd worked for.

313

But I couldn't let him take my baby. Gil, Jacob did the right thing. He looked after me so well. You should be proud of him.'

Gil's frame was cast into silhouette as a security light snapped on behind him. 'Don't tell me how to feel about my own grandfather! So when did he find out the baby wasn't his?'

Reenie hung her head. 'He never found out.'

'What are you saying? Did he assume he had another child living somewhere?'

Mattie could suddenly see where Reenie's story might be heading, turning to warn him. 'Maybe we should leave this here for now? It's getting cold, and we're all tired . . .'

'She's asking me to believe that my grandfather, who adored his wife and loved his family, knew he had another child from an affair. That isn't somewhere you can leave a conversation!'

'Mattie, let him be.'

'You don't have to tell us any more,' Mattie urged, seeing evidence of her pain before any words.

'I do, love. Not for his sake, but for mine. I lost the baby, Gil. Two months later. The woman who ran the boarding house was like a mother to me that night. She took my little one away and she looked after me for two weeks, day in, day out. Even slept in my room, in case I needed comforting in the night. News got back to Jake, and it broke his heart. Because he thought *his* baby had died. Without that, there was no obligation to have me. I wouldn't hear of it. He'd done enough, more than enough. I would've stayed friends if I could, but I knew it was

314

over. He couldn't look at me without seeing the kid he could've had. And he *did* love your grandma, Gil. He was so upset that he'd cheated on her. I'm guessing he took that secret with him to wherever he is now.'

Mattie closed her eyes, the horror of what had happened finally sinking in. 'That's so awful. For all of you.'

'Why should I believe you, Reenie? My grandfather was a good man. He loved his family.'

Mattie turned to Gil, shocked by the venom in his question.

'Kid, it's the truth. He was a wonderful man. I'm sorry I hurt him. I'd do anything to take it back.'

'I can't listen to this.'

Mattie reached for him. 'Gil, calm down.'

'No, I won't! She lied to my grandad. What makes you think she's telling the truth now? All right, Reenie, answer me this: if Rico was such a monster, how come barely a year later he was masterminding your solo career, eh? If you hated him that much, why did he stay on as your manager for the next ten years?'

'Because I had to support myself.'

'I suppose with no baby to hold you back you could do what you liked, couldn't you?'

'That's *enough*, Gil!'

'One question, Reenie: did you ever love my grandfather? Or was he just someone you used to cover up your grubby mistake?'

'Gil! You're talking about a child here.'

'A child Jake thought was his – a child he secretly grieved over for the rest of his life. You condemned him to carry that pain and never be able to tell anyone about it. How could you hurt him like that?'

'Reenie had that hurt, too . . .'

'But he didn't need to, don't you get that? She lied to him.'

'Jake was good to me. I *did* love him, whatever you think. And I didn't have any choice.'

'You could have gone home.'

'Could I? Single and pregnant, with hardly any money to my name? And how would I have got home? You have to believe me, kid, there was no other way. I was scared and alone and couldn't think straight. If I'd gone to that back-street abortion doctor, I would have died. Your grandfather was an angel of mercy . . .'

'Who you repaid with lies,' Gil stormed. 'I can't listen to this anymore.'

'Gil – wait. Let's talk.'

'You've made your position crystal-clear, Mattie. We have nothing more to say.'

'We have another meeting tomorrow,' Mattie stated, her hackles rising. 'A meeting *you* insisted on being a part of. I know this has been a shock. I understand you're hurt. And I am the last person to tell you what you should believe. But I know what we all set out to achieve, and we are *so close* to seeing it happen.'

'It doesn't mean anything now, though, does it? We're celebrating a sixty-year lie.'

'No. We're putting the past to rest. And honouring what Jacob Kendrick did.'

His laugh was bitter, mocking her. 'I don't think so.'

He began to leave the garden, but Mattie ran after him.

'Gil. *Gil!* What does that mean? What about the gig . . . ?'

She hated herself for mentioning it, but they had come so far, invested too much to fall at the final hurdle. Instantly, it was as if she was transported back to the hotel in Alnwick, after rescuing Reenie – but this time the roles were reversed, and she had become the mercenary one.

It was as if her question sickened him; she wished she couldn't see the disappointment in his eyes. 'Oh, it will go ahead. We don't have a choice. But then this is done. *Over*.'

As he walked away, Mattie knew he wasn't just referring to his association with Reenie.

'Kid – I . . .'

Mattie shivered. 'Forget it, Reenie. I'm glad you told me.'

'But I didn't think he'd go off like that.'

Neither did I, Mattie thought, tears building behind her eyes. *It turns out I didn't know Gil Kendrick at all.* 'It's cold out here. Let's get you back inside.'

Mattie was numb when she returned to her room, too angry to cry, too hurt to think. How had a moment where she'd felt closer than ever to Reenie and Gil turned into such a scene of devastation?

Of course, Gil had a right to be upset. Reenie's confession, meant as a sign of her trust in him, had led to the unexpected dethroning of his beloved grandfather. While Mattie could see Jacob Kendrick's actions as a mark of a good man, Gil could only see the betrayal of his memory. But this whole journey had been about redemption – about

317

not letting past mistakes change the future. How had he so easily abandoned that?

She hadn't been wrong to take Reenie's side. What had happened to the young singer had been terrifying and, ultimately, terribly sad. And despite everything that had happened this evening, Mattie was touched that Reenie had chosen to break her vow of silence for *her*. It felt like the most precious gift.

'Is everything okay?'

Mattie had completely forgotten she had a roommate for the night, and almost jumped out of her skin. 'Pru! I didn't see you.'

Pru's auburn head emerged from a tangle of clothes on the other single bed. 'Sorry. I've learned not to take up a lot of space.' A hint of a smile was gone as soon as Mattie saw it. She sat up, pushing a length of hair from her eyes with a self-conscious flick of her hand. 'I heard shouting.'

Mattie sank onto her bed. 'I'm not surprised.'

'Is Gil all right? He sounded upset.'

'He is.'

'Does this happen a lot with you guys?'

Her question was so innocent that Mattie almost laughed. 'Not usually. I'm putting the kettle on. Fancy a tea or coffee?'

Pru nodded, pulling her black hoodie on. 'Tea. Please.'

Mattie had been dreading the prospect of a night spent with this young girl who had barely spoken ten words to her, but now she found herself glad of the teen's company. She wouldn't have wanted to be alone with her muddled thoughts tonight.

318

As she made tea, Pru observed her from the other side of the room like a pale hawk. She hid striking features behind her hair, high cheekbones and large blue eyes, bee-sting lips and a perfect freckle on one cheek that an eighteenth-century lady would have been proud of. Mattie wondered if Pru would ever find confidence in her appearance. She hoped she would.

'Fighting sucks,' Pru said, accepting the mug of tea from Mattie. 'I should know. My mum could bicker for Britain.'

'Is that why you left?' Mattie asked, immediately thinking better of it.

A sound almost like a laugh came from the young woman. 'Kelvin told you. I knew he would. It's okay, I don't mind. He *rescued* me, after all.'

'And brought you here. With a bunch of crazy people in a camper van.'

Pru nodded. 'Who else would have done that for me, hmm?'

'I'm sorry. You shouldn't be in the middle of this.'

'I'm used to it. And trust me, compared to my family you lot are a bunch of *amateurs*. I didn't leave home because of Mum. I left because of her creepy fella. Skulking around, making suggestive remarks when he thought Mum wasn't listening. He tried it on with my best friend and when I ratted him to Mum she wouldn't believe me. The guy's a total loser. Skanks money and fags off her, goes off for days on end without telling her where he is and still expects her to welcome him back.'

'It's hard when your mum doesn't listen to you,' Mattie said, the sting of her own mother's reaction in the wake of Grandpa Joe's death still smarting, even though both of them had since made progress to heal their relationship. 'You deserve to be heard. But maybe, if you keep talking long enough, the message will get through?'

'Maybe.' Long fingers wrapped around the mug. 'So, what happened downstairs?'

'Gil and Reenie had a row. A bad one. It's too complicated to explain why.'

'And you took sides?'

Mattie blinked. 'How did you know that?'

'Lucky guess.'

'Oh.'

'He seemed like a nice bloke, for what it's worth. But even nice blokes can be thick sometimes. Reenie's great, too. And you.' She ducked her head into the black hood, hiding her embarrassment as she drank.

'Thanks. Do you have everything you need? Toiletries and things, I mean?'

'I borrowed your shower gel. Hope you don't mind.'

'Not at all. Anything else?'

'I'm good. So, are you okay? With the row and everything?'

Mattie was touched by Pru's concern, but the answer to that question evaded her. She wouldn't know how she really felt until it was all over. Gil was going home after the meeting with Alys tomorrow, and then all efforts would be ploughed into making the concert happen. After that . . . she wasn't sure.

Chapter Twenty-Nine

'Someone Loves You, Joe'
– The Lana Sisters

♪

In the early hours of the morning, Mattie checked Pru was asleep and reached for Grandpa Joe's diary. She needed to feel close to him again, her heart still reeling from the row with Gil. The meeting with Alys Davis was hours away, with a long drive after that, and she knew she should be sleeping – but her mind was too awake. The gig was getting closer and she still didn't know why Joe Bell had missed the original date. The small plastic star Gil had given her fell out onto the bed sheets, its glow long gone. The sight was impossibly sad. Tossing it to the floor, she turned her burning eyes to the diary page:

Sunday, 9 September 1956

I've made a decision. I'm going to ask Una to marry me.

In all my life I will never find another woman like her. But I can't be with her in the way we both want without knowing we are fully committed. I might be old-fashioned in a town where everyone else seems to be hopping in and out of bed with each other, but that is how it is. I want to cherish her, to treat her as a rare gem, not a commodity. For me, this means marriage. I can't imagine living without her in my arms.

I confided in Len. He's sworn to keep it secret. I needed to know what their father's reaction might be to my request, but Len said he died some years back. So, in lieu of a father to ask permission, I asked Len. I think he was quite touched! I told him I intend to look after his sister and that I've been saving my wages for some months now and I am pleased with how much I've been able to put by. I want to ensure security for us for at least the first six months – and I want Una to have a beautiful ring. She deserves the best. Uncle C has offered me a better position within his company and it comes with more money, so I can at least offer her a decent living. What she earns as a dancer isn't much, but together we may be able to afford a modest home. Mother and Father will be shocked, I dare say. But when they meet Una, I'm confident they will love her as much as I do. I have never been more certain of anything. I love her and she loves me. What more reason do we need?

I'm meeting her after the last number on Friday night at the PG. I've told her it's important. I think she knows what I'm going to ask . . .

Mattie stared at Joe's words, letting them percolate through her tired mind. People married younger in the fifties, she understood that, but this decision seemed out of character, even for the brave young man emerging from the diary pages. He was in love and rebellious, but choosing to spend the rest of his life with Una was a big step. She had to know Una's answer. She turned to the next entry, revealing the truth:

Friday, 14 September 1956

Tonight I asked Una Myers to be my wife. And she said no.
  I can't write any more. There is nothing to say.

Sixty years and a lifetime away from the event, Joe Bell's pain was tangible. Mattie's hand flew to her mouth as the starkness of Grandpa Joe's words struck her a body blow. Why did it matter now that he'd been turned down? If Una had accepted, Mattie wouldn't even exist today – yet there was something in her grandfather's distress that reached forward through the years to touch her heart.

Unsettled, she got out of bed and paced into the bathroom, her thoughts returning to Gil. She had to find a way to get through the next few days. She didn't want to have to go through the final Silver Five reconciliation today with the effects of their row hanging over them. That would be unbearable.

In the silence of her hotel room, she made a decision: she was going to talk to him.

By seven-thirty she could wait no longer, even though she still wasn't sure what she would say to him. If she wanted to be able to get through the next couple of days, she needed to call a truce.

Slipping out of her room, she hurried down the corridor to his room. Would he be sleeping? Or had the events of last night kept him awake, too? Steeling herself, she knocked . . .

. . . but the door swung open, daylight from the already-opened curtains revealing a stripped bed with an industrial vacuum cleaner leaning against its base.

'Hello?' she called, her heart in her throat. 'Gil?'

A tiny lady with a hesitant smile appeared in the doorway to the room's en-suite bathroom. 'Good morning. Can I help you?'

'I'm looking for my friends who were staying in this room. Have you seen them?'

'The younger man went to breakfast at six-thirty.'

'And the other?' Mattie asked, already fearing the answer.

'Oh, he left. Early.'

'Do you know what time?'

The woman shrugged. 'I just came in when the young man left. That's all I know, sorry.'

He'd gone? Without trying to talk to her? And what did this mean for the concert? With a ball of dread forming in her stomach, Mattie hurried down to the reception desk, almost sending the brass bell skidding across its polished wood as she hit it.

'Can I help – er – madam?' the receptionist asked,

scurrying out of the room behind and peering at Mattie as if he wasn't sure she was safe or sane.

'One of the guests in Room 12 – Gil Kendrick – could you tell me if he checked out this morning?'

'Is Mr Kendrick a friend?'

That was a question Mattie couldn't answer in all honesty. 'He's a member of my party,' she opted for. 'And was due to stay one more night.'

The receptionist's frown relaxed. 'Ah, right. Let me just check for you . . .' He tapped on a keyboard and squinted at a computer screen embedded in the reception desk. 'Here we are. Mr Kendrick left just after six this morning. My colleague called a taxi for him and I believe he was heading for Abergavenny station. Oh, hang on . . .' He turned to a bank of boxes behind the desk and took a folded sheet of notepaper from one of them. 'Are you Miss Bell, Room 8?'

'Yes.'

'Mr Kendrick left this for you.'

Mattie accepted it, the sight of her name in Gil's handwriting making everything else fade into the background. At least this was something . . .

'Anything else I can help with?'

Distracted, she sent a vague smile in his direction. 'No, um . . . thank you.'

She wandered from the desk and pushed open the large oak and glass door into the cool, fresh dampness of the morning outside. The sound of rushing water and breeze in the tall trees surrounding the hotel filled her ears, and she moved towards the small garden, the River Usk visible now where last night it had been hidden. A group of picnic tables had been arranged beside the drystone wall and she chose the one furthest away from the hotel entrance to sit, hardly noticing when the early-morning dew soaked into her jeans.

She unfolded the note.

> *Mattie*
> *The gig's still on. But I can't do another day on the tour.*
> *I hope you understand why.*
> *Gil*

That was it? No mention of the argument? It all felt too clinical, too final. There was no emotion in the note. Everything he had said to Mattie before last night – the warm words and tender kisses that had promised so much – was gone. Mattie stared down at the fast-flowing water beside the garden, her thoughts as difficult to pinpoint as the swirling eddies of the Usk.

So, that's the end of it.

She hated herself for feeling so betrayed; and more, for letting herself fall so quickly for someone she barely knew. In that respect, she and Joe Bell had much in common. Touching the cold, dew-damp wood of the picnic table, she filled her lungs with Brecon air and banished every thought of Gil Kendrick from her mind. She had work to do, a concert to prepare for; and that was all.

Chapter Thirty

'Won't You Come Along with Me?' – Nat Couty & the Braves

♪

'I still can't believe he just *left*.'

'I suppose he had his reasons.'

'He's an idiot. *There's* a reason.'

'Pru! You didn't see how upset he was last night.'

'And *you* didn't see how upset *she* was, Kel.'

Mattie kept her eyes on the road as the not-so-whispered row in the back seat raged on. Kelvin and Pru had received the news of Gil's departure with shock. But with each only knowing their half of the story with what they'd witnessed last night, who could blame them? Gil's letter had been passed around the breakfast table like a vital scrap of evidence in a manhunt, but returned to Mattie like a cryptic crossword puzzle nobody could solve. She checked the satnav, seeing the chequered flag of their destination approaching, and cut across the debate.

'Looks like we're here.'

'Wow!' Kelvin exclaimed, scrabbling for his iPhone as the camper van pulled up at a set of enormous steel and iron gates. 'I've got to get a photo of this.'

Pru grabbed his arm. 'Careful. You don't want to upset her. She's probably got Rottweilers on the other side of those gates. And armed guards.'

'Baby Alys never needed security when she was in the group,' Reenie scoffed, craning her neck to look up at the gates. 'We're less than ten miles from Abergavenny. Who's going to try breaking in here, eh? Sheep? Posh ramblers?'

Mattie stared up at the metal fortifications. They wouldn't have looked out of place in front of a Hollywood mansion, or perhaps a military compound in the Middle East, but here on the outskirts of a pretty village on the edge of the Brecon Beacons National Park, they were incongruously large and obtrusive. 'She's famous now, though. People in the public eye have to be more careful about security these days, don't they?'

Reenie glared at her. '*I'm* famous, kid. *I'm* in the public eye. But you don't see me sticking bulletproof glass in my cottage windows or hiring Arnold Swarfega to be my bodyguard, do you?'

Kelvin sniggered in the back seat.

'It's *Schwarzenegger*, Reenie. And Alys might have very good reasons for wanting to feel safe in her home.'

'I'll bet. Probably keeping the taxman out,' Reenie

muttered darkly. 'You don't get that rich doing a parochial chat show and the odd Eisteddfod, trust me.'

'Let's just get in and do what we have to, okay?' Mattie wound down the driver's window and pressed a sleek grey button by the side of the gates. After a few seconds, the small speaker crackled into life.

'Yes?'

'Oh, hi. Matilda Bell and Reenie Silver to see Miss Davis, please.'

There was the sound of rustling paper and a mumbling Mattie couldn't make out, then the officious voice returned. 'You're early.' It was more of an accusation than a compliment. 'You'll have to wait on the drive inside the gates until Miss Davis is ready to see you.' The speaker snapped off, and a loud click indicated the gates were opening.

'. . . Wait on the drive? My *arse*,' Reenie scoffed, jamming her arms across her ample chest. '*Nobody* tells Reenie Silver to wait on a bleedin' drive!'

Mattie parked the camper van and turned to her friend. 'Right, listen to me. I know it's been a long journey to get here, and I understand the row with Gil last night hasn't helped your mood. But this is our last stop, Reenie. Our *last stop*. Once this meeting is over we're back down to London for the concert tomorrow, and then it'll all be over. We have everyone who is able to join us signed up to this gig so far. And whatever you think of Alys, we have to make this work. For your sake, for the group – and for Chuck. You said you were doing this for him now, remember? Well, nothing's changed. So let's just meet Alys, ask her to join us and then we can make the rest happen. Agreed?'

Reenie hunched in her seat like a pouting eighty-four-year-old toddler. '*Fine*. But don't ask me to bust a gut to be her friend, all right?'

'I wouldn't dream of it,' Mattie replied. Everything hurt this morning, from her neck where she'd failed to find a position she could sleep in last night to her heart, which Gil had so easily stamped upon. Reenie might wish for an end to the reconciliation road trip, but she couldn't want it more than Mattie did today.

I've been away from home for too long, she concluded, struck by a sudden need to be back in her shop with Joanna and Laurie, sorting out new purchases for Percy to make for his new home and finding vintage pieces for online customers around the world. She would call her sister and Laurie when she returned to the hotel that evening, she decided. After so long away – more days now than she had ever been absent from her business before – her shop and the life she'd managed to rebuild beyond it seemed almost dreamlike, as if she couldn't be altogether sure any of it had existed at all. The sooner she could return to her own life, the better.

'Oh, here we go,' Kelvin said. 'Looks like she's bringing us in.'

Pru lifted her head and followed his pointing finger. Mattie followed suit and saw a figure approaching across the expansive driveway.

'She has *staff*?' Pru was incredulous. 'Is she some kind of celebrity?'

Reenie snorted. 'Maybe in *Wales*. Not in the rest of the world.'

'She's been voted National Treasure in Wales for the last ten years in a row,' Kelvin informed them, scrolling through text on his phone screen. He looked up. 'Wikipedia says so.'

'Wikipedia? *Pfft*. She could have written it herself, then.'

Mattie ignored Reenie and opened the driver's door as a harassed-looking young man in jeans and a black shirt neared Rusty. 'Good morning.'

'Hey,' he panted, a smile passing at breakneck speed across his face. 'Sorry to keep you waiting, but Miss Davis was unavoidably delayed. If you'd like to follow me, I'll show you into the residence. I've arranged for tea, hope that's okay?' He looked a little shocked when Pru and Kelvin emerged from the back of the camper van. 'Oh, is it *all* of you?'

'We don't mind waiting here,' Pru whispered to Mattie.

'No need. You're both welcome to join us. I'm Teifi Miller, by the way. Miss Davis's PA.'

'Matilda Bell – Mattie – we spoke on the phone, I think? And this is Reenie Silver.'

On cue, Reenie emerged, like a diva at her eighth curtain call, from the other side of the camper van. She held out her hand as if bestowing a blessing on the young man.

'*Hello*, Mr Miller.'

'It's an honour, Ms Silver. I'm a huge fan of your work. Your Vegas album was my favourite record in my dad's collection when I was a boy.'

Thrilled, Reenie feigned a self-conscious laugh. 'What

a sweet boy you are. Remind me to sign you something before I go. Little memento, you know.'

'That would be fantastic. Well, if you'll all follow me . . .'

The house Teifi ushered them into was by far the grandest they'd visited on their journey. The road-trip team filed behind Alys's PA into a wide hall rising through two storeys, with beautiful stained-glass windows on both levels bringing patches of sunlight in dappled shades of red, blue, green and gold. The carpet on which they walked was thick and luxurious, the drapes at the windows and across doors an expensive silk brocade.

A grand staircase rose from the centre of the hall and split midway to head to the east and west wings of the house. 'It's a bleedin' *palace*,' Reenie muttered. 'Good on her.'

Teifi's mobile buzzed angrily in his hand. 'Ah, Miss Davis is ready. Would you all like to follow me into the sitting room, please?'

Calling it a sitting room was a little like calling the Millennium Stadium a school playing field. Three sets of sofas, armchairs and occasional tables were laid out in the long, spacious room, the walls and soft furnishings in shades of yellow, old gold and white. It gave the impression that the sun had been locked in the room, causing everything to glow. Two pure white and peach-patched long-haired Chihuahua dogs were snoozing in matching wicker baskets at either side of a grandly carved marble fireplace, apparently unaffected by the sudden intrusion of four strangers into their home.

'Don't mind the dogs,' Teifi said. 'Mork and Orson are about as vicious as a pair of slippers. They won't even notice you're here. Make yourselves at home, and I'll have the tea brought in.' He scurried out, and Mattie wondered if he was ever able to simply walk from one place to another, or if everything had to be done at a canter.

'Our little Baby Alys a lady of the manor,' Reenie said, running a wistful hand across a gold velvet cushion. 'Lucky girl.'

Mattie glanced at Reenie to check how she was. While she had been full of jibes and jokes this morning, now it was as if someone had reached inside her and dimmed the switch of her personality. Leaving Pru petting the sleepy dogs by the fireplace and Kelvin taking surreptitious photos on his phone, Mattie sat gently beside Reenie.

'Hey. How are you doing?'

'Don't worry about me. It's just this place. It's a little overwhelming.'

'It's bound to be. Alys has worked hard for her money, and good for her for wanting to show it off.'

'It's amazing. It's just more than I expected . . .'

Mattie laid her hand over Reenie's on the white brocade sofa seat. 'Let's face it, very little of what we planned for this trip has turned out the way we thought it would. But it's been fun because of that, don't you think? Mostly fun.'

'I'll go with *mostly*. But I'll tell you somethin' for nothin', Mattie, I'm glad this is the last one. I don't think my heart could stand any more shocks this week.'

'So you finally came back, then?'

Mattie turned with the others to see a small lady dressed in a long, fitted burgundy dress with a deep green pashmina draped artfully around her neck. She had her arm linked through the good-looking PA's, and seemed to float rather than walk into her impressive sitting room. Mattie would have recognised her anywhere, her face a regular feature of the banks of magazines lining Kings Sunbury's newsagents. Her fame had spread far beyond her native Wales, boosted most recently by a raft of prime-time television appearances.

Reenie stood, doing her best to hide the walking cane behind one leg as she found her feet. 'I thought it was about time I looked in on you.'

Alys greeted Reenie with a kiss on the cheek, then ditched any semblance of decorum and gathered her startled former colleague into a huge bear hug. 'It's great to have you here, Reen! Even if it has taken you sixty years to do it. How the devil are you? You're looking amazing – as ever. Still breaking hearts across the western hemisphere, I'll bet!'

Reenie grinned. 'You don't scrub up too badly for an old chook yourself.'

'I know! Who'd've thought it? Us glamour pusses, a couple of doddery old eighty-somethings – and still causing trouble. Now sit yourself down and let's chat. What are you drinking? *Tea*? Bloody hell, Teifi's got no idea how stars behave. I'm having to teach him everything from scratch. Listen, I've some divine cognac from my last trip to Paris. Care for a glass, lovely? Of course you would! I remember, back in the day, you sneaking that old hip flask of yours into our dressing room when Rico wasn't looking. Cherry B and burn-your-throat-Bourbon, wasn't it?'

Reenie smirked. 'Whatever I could swipe from the bar, usually. It was never the good stuff.'

'Too right! Mind you, remember that fit barman at the club we played near Düsseldorf back in '53? I seem to remember you sourcing a rather fine malt whisky from the chap. Heaven only knows what you had to trade to get that.'

Reenie's chuckle was filthy and guttural. 'That secret'll go to my grave.' She watched her friend as she sailed over to a globe-shaped drinks cabinet and poured brandy from an expensive-looking carafe into two cut-crystal glasses. 'You've done all right for yourself, haven't you, kid?'

'Can't complain. Telly work helps now, and once you're on the circuit here it runs itself. I have a good agent, mind. Sacked off the old geezer ten years ago, took up with a young ankle-biter and haven't looked back since. Gets me in on everything, she does. Oh, how rude of me. I completely forgot to say hello to your pals.'

Reenie gave a weak smile. 'Prudence, Kelvin – and this is the famous Mattie Bell, who is the real reason I'm here.'

Alys nodded at them all and smiled. 'Then thank you, Mattie. I didn't think I'd see this lady again until both of us got to Glory.'

To see the woman Reenie had always referred to as 'Baby Alys' as a confident, brash and, it had to be said, slightly inebriated eighty-one-year-old was a sight to behold, and despite Reenie's obvious jealousy, Mattie could see a deep fondness in the old singer's eyes for her former friend. She'd told tales of their questionable exploits at gigs across the country and further afield, Reenie's version of events painting herself as the ringleader and Alys as her wide-eyed, innocent partner in crime. Meeting Alys now, however, Mattie suspected she'd had more input than Reenie had admitted. Now that she had seen Reenie with all of her surviving former colleagues, it was clear to see where everyone had stood in the group: Tommy was the optimist, always hoping for the next big break, and the oil on troubled waters when fights occurred; June, the talented but prickly diva; Alys, the young star in the making, looking to Reenie for inspiration. Mattie could imagine them as young people – younger than she was today – embarking on a bright future, with the world seemingly falling at their feet. Had they all believed Rico when he'd promised them stardom and all the trimmings that came with it?

After almost an hour of swapping stories from their years in The Silver Five, Reenie's face grew serious. She reached out to pat Alys's knee. 'Now, love. It's time for me to say what I came here to tell you.'

Alys put down her glass, and clasped Reenie's hands between hers. 'There's no need.'

'There is. I should have said something years ago, but I was a coward. Easier to move forward feeling like a star than look back to see the dirt you left behind. For what it's worth, I'm sorry. I'm sorry I left the way I did. More than anything, I'm sorry I didn't say something before I skipped out on *you*. We chatted about most things, you and I, but I couldn't tell you what was happening that time. That was a big mistake, love, I realise that now. You used to say I was like a big sister to you and – well – you deserved better than I gave.'

Alys observed Reenie for an uncomfortable minute, then, without warning, threw back her head and laughed. 'And that's what you came here to say? Oh, sweetheart, I don't blame you for that! I'd be mad to. You leaving gave me the push I needed.'

'Come again?'

'Well, before that night, I never thought I had it in me to really sing, you know. Not solo. I used to watch you and June up there, giving it welly, and just thought, "I can never be like them!" I assumed I'd always sing backing for stars like you two. Nice Welsh girls from Caerphilly don't always push themselves forward – at least, they didn't in my day. My mother had kittens hearing I was singing in a club with a bar. If she'd known what else I was getting up to, she'd've had a coronary on the spot! Another brandy for anyone? Plenty here.'

Mattie, Kelvin and Pru mumbled their refusals but Reenie held out her glass, an odd look in her eyes.

'There you go! Lovely.'

'I don't get this: when I left, your career was pretty much over. June said as much when I saw her a couple of days ago. And Tommy.'

'You'd think so, but it wasn't for me.'

'But you'd had your heart set on that gig. It was all you talked about, you and June, for months. I did you out of your first booking at the Palm Grove.'

'Second.'

'Sorry?'

Alys smiled. 'My second gig at the club. Oh, Reenie, didn't you know? I played Jake Kendrick's club months before The Silver Five were supposed to.'

Reenie's eyes narrowed as she knocked back half the brandy in her glass. 'When? And how?'

'With Ted. On the sly, mind, but it was the first time I'd tried performing without you all. And to my surprise, I found I was pretty good at it.'

'Ted? *My* Ted?'

'Depends. How many Teds do you have?'

'Ted Farnsworth. The bandleader I started out with.'

Alys clapped her hands. 'The very same!'

And then Mattie remembered. The singer with the Ted Farnsworth Orchestra that had made Grandpa Joe, his friends and most of the audience stop what they were doing, compelled to listen to the 'cracking girl singer'. It hadn't been just any singer drafted in to replace Reenie: it had been her very own bandmate, the girl she'd considered to be a protégé.

'I think my grandfather saw you perform that night,' she said, as Alys turned towards her. 'He said everyone in the club stopped to listen to you.'

'He said that?' The glamorous lady's eyes misted over. 'Aw. A moment like that, it changes you. It makes you believe you can be as big as you dream. I watched that crowd falling silent and just listening to me – and that was when I knew, as soon as I could leave the group and strike out on my own, I had to do it.'

'Alys Davis, you sly old mare! When were you going to tell the rest of us? Did Rico know?'

'Heavens, no! I wasn't that daft, even at twenty-one years old. And as for the rest of you, I knew we wouldn't be together indefinitely. We were all pulling in different directions: it was only a matter of time. So when you did your moonlight flit, I knew that was my chance to move on, too. You did me a favour, *cariad*.'

Reenie shook her head. 'No, no I didn't! You could've had international fame instead of being a local celebrity. If the group had survived we could've been bigger than bleedin' Cliff Richard – playing arenas and singing when it rains at Wimbledon . . .'

'Better to be a raging swan in a tiny pond than a little duck paddling in the sea,' Alys intoned, cackling with laughter. 'I found my niche early on. I wasn't likely to pass up that opportunity. I'm the *Gloria Hunniford of the Valleys*, don't you know? *The Darling of the Brecons*, the – oh, what is it they called me last year at the Green Man Festival? Oh yes, *the Powys Goddess of Gold*! I owe the chap at the *Daily Mail* a few quid for that one, I reckon. Point is, Reenie, without you doing a bunk and leaving us all flailing about, my career would've been dead and done years ago. Instead, I have everything I wanted and more. Nice house, recognition, regular work and a rather fit boyfriend . . .' She leered over at Teifi, who sent a dazzling smile back before leaving the room.

Reenie looked as if she'd opened a ring box and found a slug. '*That?* You expect me to believe you're shagging that young bloke? Pull the other one, it's got bells on!'

'He's only a few years younger,' Alys purred.

'He's young enough to be your grandson, you dirty old woman!'

'*He* keeps *me* young, in more ways than one.' She roared with laughter. 'Your face! Don't look so surprised. The nights get long and lonely out here in the Welsh wastelands. What else are we supposed to do?'

Reenie rolled her eyes. 'Trust you, Alys Davis. Trust you to be the dark horse out of all of us.' She shook her head, but a grudging respect took the place of her disappointment. 'Will you come and do the gig, love? As an *old hand* at Palm Grove performances?'

Alys threw her arm around Reenie's shoulders and refilled her brandy glass. 'Oh, Reenie Silver, I wouldn't miss it for the world!'

Chapter Thirty-One

'Hey You!' – Tommy Steele and the Steelmen

♪

That night, Mattie declined Reenie's enthusiastic invitation to 'a celebratory dinner', choosing instead to order food to her room. Pru had offered to take Gil's vacant bed, for which Mattie was grateful and Kelvin visibly over the moon. 'No funny business,' she'd assured Mattie quietly. 'I just figured you might need some space.'

With Gil gone and Mattie determined to press on regardless, she wanted to rest as much as her aching body would allow tonight and catch up with events at home, before the journey back to London tomorrow and the gig that would follow. Knowing she was almost at the end of her adventure made her long to be back in Kings Sunbury, living a life she recognised. It would be a long time before she went away again, she promised herself, climbing into bed and reaching for her phone.

The sound of Laurie's crazy Labrador barking when

the call was answered made her want to laugh and cry simultaneously. 'I *said*, get down! Take my advice, Mattie: don't ever get a dog if you want a quiet life. So how are you after your epic trip?'

'Good. Tired. I just want to do the concert and come home. How's everything at Bell Be-Bop?'

'Bop-tastic as usual.' It was an old joke, so overused it was practically fraying at the seams. 'No, but seriously, your sister is a *dream*. Better than you. I'm kidding! I'm not, actually. She's amazing. You won't recognise the place when you get back. Organised like you wouldn't believe. I swear we'll never find anything again, but it looks pretty.'

'And you? Everything okay?'

'Aw, thanks for asking. I'm dating Percy.'

Mattie sniggered, but the extended silence this was met with indicated Laurie wasn't pulling her leg. 'No! When did this happen?'

'Just after you left, actually. I didn't say anything before because I didn't want to jinx it. You know how I've rushed into stuff in the past. I know the age gap is – well – *huge*, but he's wonderful, M! I can't tell you the laughs we've had. So much in common, too. Apart from him being hospital-admission-level allergic to dogs, which was a bit of an issue. But we're working on that.' She paused, and Mattie pictured her assistant chewing the end of the biro that was always by her phone. 'I really like him.'

Nothing could surprise Mattie today, not after all the recent shocks she'd encountered. 'I'm thrilled for you both. I want to hear all about it.'

*

Picking over the enormous Caesar salad that room service had delivered almost an hour earlier, Mattie scrolled through the available TV channels, settled on a rerun of *George Clarke's Amazing Spaces* and opened the next page of Grandpa Joe's diary. The revelation of his proposal – and Una's refusal to marry him – had played on her mind all day, and she was keen to find out what had happened next.

Sunday, 23 September 1956

I should have slept with her. Maybe if I had she would still be mine. Then I wouldn't have made an almighty fool of myself trying to propose, and she wouldn't have taken offence thinking I was calling her a scarlet woman. She called me a stupid country boy and is refusing to see me.

I can't eat or sleep. Uncle C has called out the doctor, thinking I'm ill. But there's nothing he could give me for a broken heart. He suggested bed rest, so Mrs J is force-feeding me tea and bread. I have no desire to tell them what has happened, or to admit I've been lying to them, so I'm playing the invalid. I feel so awful about everything, but what can I do?

Mattie stared at the considerable portion of chicken and salad she had yet to tackle. Loss of appetite was another thing she had in common with Joe Bell. She pushed her plate aside, not wanting to consider that Gil might have affected her as much as Una had Grandpa Joe. It wouldn't help to think like that – not when tomorrow she would have to face him again. Closing the diary, she shut her eyes and let the sleep that had been so absent last night finally claim her.

An atmosphere of calm descended inside Rusty on the journey back across the border towards London. The M4 was mercifully free-flowing, and Mattie put the cares of the recent past to rest as she let the radio and the rise and fall of her passengers' conversation soothe her. The satnav screen marked off each mile driven closer to their destination and the further they travelled, the more Mattie realised she was on the cusp of achieving her dream. Her silver sixpence tiepin caught the sunlight where it was pinned to the folds of her deep burgundy scarf, occasionally throwing a small, oval circle up onto the grey fabric of the camper van's ceiling, dancing across its surface. It was almost as if Grandpa Joe was playing a game with her, catching sunbeams with a magnifying glass and projecting them onto a wall for her to catch. Was he watching them heading to the club where he and Una had first laid eyes on one another?

A snort of laughter from Reenie suddenly summoned Mattie from her thoughts, and she glanced down at the speedometer. *Wait – 40 mph?* How had she been driving so slowly? A look at her watch and a quick mental calculation confirmed her fears: time was not on their side.

Kelvin and Pru were due to be dropped at Beaconsfield services on the M40, and Mattie knew Reenie would need a comfort break before the last push into London. The rest of The Silver Five were arriving at Kendrick's around four-thirty for a five p.m. sound-check, and if the traffic was bad on the last section they would be cutting it fine.

Instinctively, Mattie pressed her foot on the accelerator, watching the speedometer needle shakily respond . . .

45 . . . 50 . . . 55 . . .

Steady 56 mph maximum all the way, Steve the mechanic's voice warned from her mind. *If you push the van it won't cope . . .*

60 . . . 65 . . . 70 . . .

The satnav beeped to warn her of mobile cameras, and she pulled back only slightly. She needed to push it if they were to have any hope of getting there in time. Willing all her strength into Rusty's creakily objecting frame, she pressed on.

Precious minutes began to shave off the satnav's estimated arrival time and soon it became an addictive game, Mattie congratulating herself for each sixty seconds taken off the small white box on the screen. She *was* going to get them all to the service station in plenty of time and deliver Reenie to the restored Palm Grove in a manner befitting a star of her calibre. It was all part of Mattie's determination to make the plan work, to see it through to the final, triumphant event. No matter what Gil or anyone else thought.

When the service station appeared ahead, Mattie felt as if the road was applauding her, the pronounced *bump-bump* of Rusty's wheels over the worn tarmac noticeably louder as she slowed to pull into the car park. They had arrived with more than enough time to spare, and she was relishing the prospect of a small rest before the final leg of the journey.

As the rest of the team headed into the services, Mattie patted Rusty's bonnet. 'Well done, old friend. Just the last bit to get us to the gig, and then we can go home.'

Confident all was well, she joined Pru and Kelvin, hurrying over to the entrance to the ladies' loo when she saw Reenie emerging.

'How are you doing?'

'Oh, I'll be fine after I've had coffee,' she said.

'What time is your mum picking you up?' Mattie asked Kelvin.

'Three,' he said. 'Which gives us time to call Pru's Mum.'

Pru let out a long groan, but brightened a little when Kelvin hesitantly took her hand.

Mattie and Reenie exchanged glances.

'We talked it over last night,' Pru said. 'We talked about a lot of things, actually. Kel's right. I need to talk to Mum again, give her the chance to listen. I'm still reserving the right to walk out for good if things don't improve, though. And I'm not moving back yet.'

'Mum says Pru can have the spare room at ours.'

Reenie smiled. 'She sounds a good sort, your mum. And *yours* might be trickier, Pru, but it's worth trying.'

'I know.' Pru smiled at Kelvin, and Mattie wondered what else they might have discussed. Certainly the pair had been noticeably closer since leaving the hotel in Crickhowell that morning. 'Thanks again, Mattie, Reenie, for having us on board. When things settle down, Kel and I will come up to see you.'

'You make sure you do,' Reenie beamed, wagging a grandmotherly finger at them. 'I'll be wanting to hear all your news.'

'I'm sorry we'll be missing the gig. But it's bound to be epic,' Kelvin grinned. 'By the way, have you seen the Kendrick's website today?'

'No. Should I have?'

'Here . . .' He found the page on his phone and passed it across the table.

On the News section a new entry gave details of the reunion gig, a large red SOLD OUT banner spread across the top.

The Silver Five, who were top of the hit parade for four years in the early 1950s, are re-forming after sixty years for a final, once-in-a-lifetime concert this week at Kendrick's. And in their honour, the club is being transformed back to its former glory as the famous Palm Grove. Owners Colm and Gil Kendrick have masterminded the transformation – watch the video below to see it taking shape . . .

Below the article a time-lapse video played, revealing the changes in the club that had been taking place while Mattie, Reenie and Gil had been away. In speeded-up motion dustsheets were laid out, tables and chairs replaced, screens painted the original colours of the Palm Grove erected in front of the black walls and an enormous chandelier brought in and hung over the re-laid dance floor. Towards the end, Mattie peered closer to see if she could catch sight of Gil, but he was nowhere to be seen. When it ended, she turned to Reenie.

'It's going to look amazing. And great news about the ticket sales.'

'*Final, once-in-a-lifetime concert*,' Reenie mumbled, her hand gripping the edge of the table like a claw. 'Final.'

In the middle of the packed café, Reenie Silver began to cry. Huge tears rolled from her eyes, splashing over the wood veneer of the table, her loud sobs rising above the white noise of the service station. Kelvin and Pru looked on in alarm, and complete strangers stopped to stare at the old lady breaking her heart at the next table.

Shocked, Mattie reached for her hand. 'Reenie? What's the matter?'

'This is it, isn't it? My final gig.'

'The last one with The Silver Five.'

Reenie's lilac curls shook in angry defiance. '*My* last gig. After tonight it's over, Mattie, don't you see? Everything's done. I'll be forgotten. No more Reenie Silver, world-famous singer. Just Irene Silverman with a dodgy old hip and a bagload of medication. Nobody will need me anymore. You'll drop me back at Beauvale tomorrow and forget all about me.'

Where was this coming from? 'Of course I won't. We're friends, Reenie.'

'You think that now, but ask yourself, what use will I be to you once this gig is done? Once you've made it up to your grandpa? You've heard all my tales, kid. You *know* my story. What else can I give you?'

'*You*, you daft old lady! This might have started because of Grandpa Joe, but he isn't the reason I'm still here. You're one of a kind. Spending this time with you has

been precious to me. And I wouldn't change it for anything.'
Even Gil, she added silently.

'Really?'

'Yes, really.'

'Even the karaoke?'

Mattie grinned. 'Even that.'

Reenie looked up at her. 'You're one in a million, Mattie Bell. My career might come to an end tonight, but it's good to have you.'

'I don't believe you're finished,' Mattie said, her voice gentle. 'And even if this is the last big gig, why not make it one last hurrah? Tonight, at the Palm Grove. You've made this happen, remember? You've brought Tommy, June and Alys back together and healed a rift that's lasted for almost sixty years. That's incredible. *You're* incredible.'

Reenie sniffed. 'You're not so bad yourself. Kids, we should probably be going. Come and see us off?'

Relieved that their new friend had regained her composure, Pru and Kelvin readily agreed. The four remaining road-trip members made steady progress across the wide car park towards Rusty.

'It's been fun,' Pru said, bumping her arm slightly against Mattie's. 'Thanks for the chat the other night. For listening, too. And sorry about – you know – *thick* blokes.'

'Don't mention it. I hope your mum listens to you.'

'Keep talking at her, eh?'

'It's worth a shot. At least you'll be able to say you tried.'

'Now I want to hear that you're both safe home, right?' Reenie said, patting Kelvin's arm as he led her between the rows of parked cars. 'You have my number. And I shall expect a visit *soon*.'

By the side of the camper van they said goodbye, Kelvin kissing Reenie and Pru surprising Mattie by giving her a hearty hug.

'I'll miss those kids,' Reenie said, when she and Mattie were buckled in. 'Good hearts, both of them. So, Miss Bell, are we ready for the final leg?'

Mattie took a deep breath. 'I think we are.' She reached over . . . and the key seemed to stick in Rusty's ignition. Keeping her smile steady, she tried again. 'Come on, dude,' she urged. 'Don't be awkward.'

'Talking to your car. It's one thing I'll never understand about you.'

'Sometimes it helps.'

The key finally shifted and Rusty let out a metallic, gut-wrenching sigh – then, nothing. Mattie tried again with the same result, a puff of acrid black smoke rising from the exhaust.

'No-no-no, don't do this,' Mattie growled at her beloved van, frantically trying to coax the engine into life. 'Don't you dare do this to me. Not now . . .'

'Very funny, kid. Now let's get going.'

'He won't start.'

'Sorry?'

Mattie turned to Reenie. 'I can't start the van.'

'Of course you can. Just try again.'

'I *am* trying. Look – nothing's happening.'

'So, what are you saying? Can you get it working again?'

Panic squeezed Mattie's voice. This couldn't be happening.

Not now! Not when they were so close to completing their journey . . . 'I'm not sure.'

'You are *joking*.'

'I'm not.'

Reenie threw up her hands. 'Oh, well this is *magnificent*, isn't it? We're supposed to be sound-checking in two hours – how are we meant to get there if your camper van won't take us?'

'I don't know! This isn't my fault.' Mattie had to think, and the current rapidly chilling climate in Rusty's heart didn't help her.

'I don't see anyone else here with the keys. Maybe if we'd had *reliable* transport in the first place, we wouldn't be in this mess.'

'He has been reliable – until now.'

'*It* is a *vehicle*, Mattie Bell, not a bleedin' relative! Call the breakdown people; say you have funds to cover repairs on the spot if they get someone here smartish. I'll foot the bill.'

Mattie stared at her. 'I can't ask you to do that.'

'And how else are we going to make this bleedin' concert, hmm? *Exactly*. Make the call.'

Mattie was still shaking as she left Rusty and walked a little way away with her phone. Heart heavy, she found the breakdown service number and called. It seemed like almost sixty years until her call was fished out of hold-muzak hell, and she allowed herself to breathe as a breakdown service call-centre worker took her details and passed her on to a local garage.

'Old girl let you down, has she?' the too-happy mechanic

on the end of the line asked. 'I'll get one of the lads out to you as soon as I can.'

'That's brilliant, thank you. We really need to be getting back on the road as soon as possible today.'

'Today?' Never had one word been imbued with such incredulity.

'Yes. I'm sorry, I thought I'd explained: we've broken down on our way to a very important event tonight and we have to be in London by four-thirty p.m. at the latest.'

The ominous sound of someone shuffling paper came from the other end of the call. Mattie's heart began to head towards the tarmac.

'I'm sorry. We'd have to bring the van in. I have three tow trucks and they're all out on jobs. It will be at least an hour till we get to you, and then I'll need to take a look at her here.'

'What are you saying?'

The mechanic gave a heavy sigh and Mattie wondered how many callers he'd had to deliver bad news to today. 'Look, you have my sympathy,' he said, the kindness in his tone giving her no comfort at all. 'But between you and me, the chances of fixing a vintage camper van and getting it back on the road today are pretty much non-existent. My brother has a '67 VW Splitty, and when it broke down last time he was off the road for a month. I mean, parts are hard to come by – as you'll know. It might be worth finding another mode of transport. Could you call a taxi from where you are?'

A taxi from Beaconsfield services on the M40 to central London? How much would that cost? She couldn't ask

Reenie to pay for that as well – especially not after the row they'd just had.

'So, what am I supposed to do?'

'Hang tight. We'll bring the van in as soon as we can. I'll call you when someone's on the way out to you.'

Ending the call, Mattie cried out in frustration, a disgruntled seagull leaving a half-eaten box of French fries in disgust as she did so. She turned slowly to face Reenie's smugness – but the old lady wasn't in the passenger seat. The door stood wide open, as if she'd been kidnapped while Mattie's back was turned.

'Reenie?'

She walked to the camper van, ducking her head inside to see if Reenie might be hiding in the back. But there was no sign of her: her handbag had gone from the foot-well by her seat, and only a diminishing cloud of perfume remained as evidence she had been there at all. Then an awful possibility dawned on her: had Reenie Silver done another bunk, on the eve of her chance to make up for the last one?

The full horror was just beginning to sink in when she saw Pru and Kelvin walking towards her.

'Is everything okay? We noticed you hadn't gone.'

'Rusty – my van won't start. I've called a garage, but it could be an hour until they can send someone to pick him up. By then it'll be too late. And now Reenie – have you seen her?'

'We thought she was still with you,' Pru said, looking over at the open passenger door. 'Oh . . .'

'We could wait until the tow truck arrives, if you can

353

find another way to the gig,' Kelvin offered. 'Mum won't be here for ages, and I'm sure she'd hang on if they were longer than that.'

'No, I couldn't ask you to do that. Thanks anyway, Kelvin.'

'But Reenie has to be at the sound-check. It's the only rehearsal they'll all get before the gig,' Kelvin argued. 'And you can't have driven all that way just to miss it. Give me the keys, and see if you can get a taxi or something.'

Mattie looked at Rusty – poor, exhausted Rusty who had valiantly carried them nearly one thousand miles in the last eleven days. She felt as if she was abandoning him, but Kelvin was right. Reenie couldn't miss the sound-check; it wasn't as if the group could just wing it, sixty years after their last rehearsal. Reluctantly, she handed over the keys.

'Okay. Tell the garage I'll settle the bill tomorrow. Thank you.'

'So, where is Reenie?' Kelvin asked.

'I don't know. She could have gone back inside, I suppose . . .' A deep sense of dread had taken residence in Mattie's gut, and was spreading. What if Reenie had gone for good? There was a very real chance that the concert Mattie had worked so hard to put on would simply repeat history, sixty years on: an incomplete Silver Five, reeling in the wake of their lead singer's departure.

Where *was* she?

'Want us to go and look for her?' Kelvin asked.

Mattie willed herself not to cry in front of them. 'Yes. Do that. Call me if you find her.'

They hurried back inside, leaving Mattie with nobody but her broken van. The cars that had been parked on either side when they'd arrived had gone one by one, making Rusty a sad, lonely island in a sea of cracked tarmac. She leaned against his faded red side and forced herself to consider the worst.

If Reenie has gone . . .

If she'd run away at the eleventh hour, the gig would still go ahead. It had to. Because it was no longer just about Reenie. Or Mattie. Or Grandpa Joe. It was about Tommy Mullins making it back to the stage he'd abandoned when his beloved group imploded. About June Knight who, despite her age and medical problems, maybe should always have been the lead singer as she was promised, because she could sing Reenie off the stage and had waited so long for her chance to shine. It was about Thalia Powell-Cutler, seventeen years old, with her whole life – and no doubt countless stages – sparkling ahead, dedicating her first public performance to her inspirational grandfather, Chuck. And it was about Alys Davis fulfilling a sixty-year-old wish to perform a return concert at the club where she'd first forged her own dream of stardom.

Instinctively, Mattie raised a hand to Grandpa Joe's tiepin. A plan had been forming in her mind that still wasn't complete, but when it was, this would be an integral part of it.

What if this entire journey hadn't been about Reenie Silver at all?

If Reenie isn't here, the concert goes ahead. I'll make certain it does.

355

Grandpa Joe wouldn't have been deterred by a last-minute spanner in the works. The thought hit her without warning. But what she'd known of her grandfather during his life, and what she was learning about the young Joe Bell and his willingness to bypass authority, friendships and even his own common sense to get what he wanted, told her as much. What would he think of her now, of what she was willing to do if Reenie didn't come back?

She checked her phone to see if a text had arrived from the breakdown service. Nothing. In her car-park isolation, she was at a loss to know what to do. Until Pru and Kelvin came back – or Reenie resurfaced – there wasn't much else she could do. She slid open Rusty's side door and sat on the metal step inside. It was as if all the constant momentum of the road trip had suddenly been culled; like a switch had been flicked accidentally, and she was in limbo until someone noticed their mistake.

There was no sign of anyone approaching this far corner of the vast car park. A few intrepid birds twittered hesitantly from the surrounding trees as if not really sure they belonged here. Overhead, the distant droning of an aeroplane engine arced across the sky. In the place of her anger, a cool resolve now rested. Whatever Reenie Silver decided to do, Mattie could make this work.

Then a sound caught her ear, a low, growling hum that seemed out of place in the large car park. Mattie looked around her, but could see nothing that could be making it. Beyond the constant hum of the motorway in the distance the noise began to rise: an undulating, metallic roar like a swarm of enormous, angry bees. It seemed to come from the ground itself, the boom of an earthquake without the movement.

Mattie could see Pru and Kelvin approaching. She raised a hand, but it was left hanging in mid-air as they suddenly halted, staring back in the direction from which they had come as if seeing an alien invasion approaching. Mattie stood up and began to walk towards them, but stopped in her tracks, too, hardly believing her eyes . . .

Chapter Thirty-Two

'You Can't Catch Me'
– Chuck Berry

♪

From around the side of the main service station building, a bank of revving motorcycles appeared: an imposing black convoy, snaking its way around the parked cars, riding seven abreast, each rider clad in black leather emblazoned with silver designs. As it came towards Mattie she instinctively hurried back to Rusty, slamming his door shut as if it might protect the old camper van from the approaching horde.

It was an impressive sight and an awesome sound as the motorbikes – fifty at least – fanned out across the empty parking spaces in formation, pulling up just a few feet away. Up close, she could see that most of the riders had long, well-cared-for beards of varying hues, and none of them seemed a day under fifty years old. They didn't smile as they stared at her. What did they want? Had she unwittingly chosen the middle of their unofficial meeting ground to park?

She was about to say something when a familiar face grinned at her around the broad shoulders of the lead biker.

'Stuff the garage, kid. I got us a better ride into town!'

Mattie had thought she'd seen it all on this journey, but Reenie Silver had floored her again. The sight of an eighty-four-year-old lady clinging to the ample, leather-clad frame of a Hells Angel, an open-face black helmet balanced on her lilac curls, was the most extraordinary thing she had ever witnessed.

'Reenie, what on earth are you doing?'

'Well, you didn't seem to have many ideas about getting us to this gig and, let's face it, that van of yours won't be going anywhere in a hurry. So I went looking for alternatives. This is Keith. I met him in the queue for the disabled loo.'

'Dodgy knee,' Keith said, his cheeriness a surprise given his scary appearance. 'Came off me bike at Canvey last spring, knocked it right out of place. Hasn't been the same since.'

Mattie could barely find words. Had she fallen asleep in Rusty and entered the weirdest dream of her life? 'Oh – um – sorry to hear that.'

'Nah, s'fine. Still get to ride out with the lads of a weekend, you know. Won't be doing the TT any time soon, o'course.'

'Aren't they smashin'? We got talking and the boys offered to give us a ride into town. They reckon they can bring our stuff, too.'

'Yeah, luggage ain't a problem,' another, equally friendly

biker offered. 'Sid, Reg and Creasie have good, roomy panniers.'

'Creasie?' Mattie repeated, realising too late that she'd said it aloud.

'Lost over two stone this year on that 5:2 diet thing. So his leathers are a bit baggy now, like his skin.' Keith grinned back at a svelte-looking biker who gave a cheery wave. 'Used to be Fatso – but we couldn't keep calling him that for obvious reasons.'

'Ah, I see. Um, Reenie, could I have a word?'

'We don't have time for *words*, Mattie! We have to get to the sound-check and it's gettin' late. They have extra helmets. Hop on, kid!'

'But the van – and the breakdown people . . .'

'We'll wait for them,' Kelvin said, as Pru nodded.

'See?' Reenie grinned. 'It's all sorted. Now stop fretting and choose a chauffeur!'

It occurred to Mattie, as she clung for dear life to the portly hulk of Sid, Keith's right-hand man in the bikers' Chapter ('We've ditched the Hells Angels thing. Not good PR nowadays. We prefer "the Braintree Banshees" now'), that nobody at home was *ever* going to believe this story.

'Lovely day for it,' Sid yelled over the throaty roar of his Harley-Davidson.

'Yes,' she shouted back, not really sure what else to say. Insulting her last chance to make it to Kendrick's would not be advisable. Thankfully, the biker chattered on.

'My missus loves the Smoke. *Loves* it. Shopping. Theatre. Wine bars. The lot. You been there much yourself?'

'Not really.'

'You take my advice: stick to the museums. You can shop anywhere, but you don't see the Elgin Marbles or a Van Gogh every day, do you?'

Mattie's brain hurt. It was too much to take in: from the row with Gil to the journey almost back to London followed by Rusty's breakdown, to her fight with Reenie, and now this unscheduled, ridiculously impressive convoy bringing them to the final event of their extraordinary adventure. Too busy being swept along by the flood of highs and lows, she'd hardly had time to catch her breath. But at last she could see an end to it all. Ahead of her lay the culmination of her dream: the group reunited, history altered, peace restored.

Except with Gil. And the mystery surrounding Joe Bell's absence from the concert he'd set his heart on attending. These two things remained stubbornly unresolved. At least Mattie had Grandpa Joe's diary, where some of the answers might be found. As for Gil – that was a problem she might never find the solution to.

She was dreading seeing him, still angry about how he'd spoken to Reenie and lumped Mattie into his anger. What would she say to him? If she weren't so concerned with hanging onto her motorcycle escort driver at that moment, Mattie would have kicked herself. She'd believed Gil was a good man and had dared to trust him – but the tirade he'd launched at Reenie challenged everything she'd been so certain of. Heart hurting, she told herself that the water streaming from her eyes was just the cold breeze from the city as Sid and the Braintree Banshees drove magnificently into town.

The convoy arrived outside Kendrick's with fifteen minutes to spare, and Mattie and Reenie climbed gratefully down from their rides. Handing her helmet back to Sid, Mattie turned to Keith, who was grinning with all the triumph of a Viking return.

'Thank you. The gig wouldn't have been possible without your help. Do you and the boys want to come tonight? It's going to be wonderful.'

'Nah, we'll take a rain-check if you don't mind,' he replied. 'It's been a pleasure but we should be headin' off. My missus will go certifiable if I ain't back in time for dinner. And it ain't really my style of music – no offence, Reenie, love.'

'None taken, Keith. But if you easy riders are ever up Shropshire way, you come and see me, yeah? I'd love to see the faces of the Beauvale lot if fifty of you fellas rocked up.'

'We'll do that. Ladies, it's been fun.' He revved his engine and every Braintree Banshee followed suit. 'Banshees! We ride!'

Mattie and Reenie waved like rescued damsels wishing farewell to their knights until the motorbikes rounded the corner from the club and the square fell back into London hum.

'I'm sorry, kid,' Reenie said quietly.

'What for?'

'For shouting at you. And being rude about your camper van.'

Mattie gave out a long breath. 'We've both said stuff we shouldn't have.'

'No, listen to me. You gave up a lot to get us here. I appreciate it. All of it. Even that grandson of Jake's. He's hurt, but he's harmless. Poor lad just found out the chap he'd idolised all his life was flesh and blood, like everyone else. That's hard; I get it. You know it better than anyone, too. Time gives you a strange perspective, Mattie. And the more of it you have, the more the truth moves from black and white to a shade of grey. I'm not proud of every choice I've made, but they were *my* choices. I'm a survivor – and in the end, isn't that what everyone wants to say?'

That was what Mattie wanted – she understood it now. She had survived Asher's betrayal and Grandpa Joe's decision. She was still standing, when either blow could have ripped the ground from beneath her feet. And Gil? Well, she was wounded by his words but she'd survive that, too. After tonight's concert her life stretched out before her, an uncharted road she no longer feared. 'Is that why you went back to Rico? To survive?'

Reenie looked up at her. 'Yeah. I had to shove everything to the back of me mind and focus on the road ahead. It was the only way to move forwards. In the end, you see, Rico could get me where I wanted to go. And I slipped back into old ways with him for a while because – well – it was just easier. Once I'd established myself I broke things off, romantically speakin'. But by then we'd been through it all, he was older and maybe a little wiser, so he stayed as my manager for ten years. And then I finally got shot of him when I met young Bill O'Shea in Vegas.

Billy worked for me until last year, when he passed on. His son represents me now, as a favour to his dad, I think.' She gazed up at the former Palm Grove and gave a sad smile. 'Sixty years ago, I arrived here knowing I was goin' to lose four friends overnight.'

Mattie smiled. 'We should go in. They'll be waiting for us.'

Reenie linked her arm through Mattie's. 'Here's hoping, eh?'

Chapter Thirty-Three

'I Was the One'
– Elvis Presley

♪

'Miss Bell, Ms Silver, a pleasure to see you again!' Derry met Mattie and Reenie just inside the door, his hair Brylcreemed at an odd angle. 'Forgive the barnet. I've been trying to perfect a quiff and I'm failing miserably.'

'Give me that comb, young man. I'll show you how it's done,' Reenie said. 'Bend down a bit . . . More than that, love! Right . . .' She set to work, pulling and working the bar manager's hair until it glistened in a quiff any Teddy Boy would have been proud of. 'There.'

Derry ducked down to see his reflection in the glass covering a display board in the club's foyer. 'That's the business! Thank you, ma'am.' He planted a kiss on Reenie's cheek. 'You should see the old place. Gil and Colm have totally transformed it. Let me take you through.'

Mattie looked at Reenie, butterflies suddenly dancing in her stomach. 'Ready?'

'Ready. Let's go.'

Derry pushed open the double doors. 'Allow me to present – the Palm Grove, circa 1956!'

All the breath in Mattie's body left her as she gazed at the scene. Beside her, Reenie swore loudly.

It was *beautiful*. Where dark walls and floors had been, swathes of cream satin and warm wood were now in place. Tables had been placed in a wide arc around the curved dance floor and stage, each one covered with a long white cloth that reached to the floor. Each table had six gold chairs around it, cream satin bows tied to the back. Crystal candelabras formed centrepieces with tall white candles, and more candles in glass hurricane lanterns edged the dance floor and stage. When these were lit it would flood the space with warm, dancing light. High above the centre of the room, three huge shimmering crystal chandeliers were suspended from the lighting gantry, sending a shower of tiny rainbow flecks floating across the floor and tables below.

A swing band was setting up beside the stage, their gold and cream music-stand pennants decorated with two letters: *P* and *G* – the ampersand between them topped with a stylised cluster of leaves to resemble a palm tree. Meanwhile, a group of dancers rehearsed jive routines on the newly laid dance-floor squares.

But it was the stage that really caught Mattie's attention – and summoned tears to her eyes. The old red velvet curtains she had admired so much on their first visit had been edged with two new horizontal lines of shimmering gold.

'It's just like I remember,' Reenie breathed. When Mattie hugged her, she gave out a loud sob. 'The kid did good.'

On cue, Gil walked into the centre of the remarkable scene. He was dressed all in black, like a young Johnny Cash: black jeans with a black open-necked shirt rolled to the elbows. He carried a clipboard, which drew Mattie's attention to his hands – immediately making her regret looking, as memories she wanted to forget suddenly returned. Beside Gil was another man, of identical height but with cropped auburn hair and a more athletic frame. He was smiling where Gil frowned, a perfect yin-yang of Kendrick brothers.

'Who's that?' Reenie asked.

'That must be Colm, Gil's brother. They're twins.'

'Get away! They're about as similar as me and that baby grand piano over there.'

'It's true, apparently.'

'If I were you, kid, I'd take everythin' that lad told you with an almighty pinch of salt.'

The piano began to play the opening bars of 'Because You Loved Me', and a small group of people moved slowly across the floor towards it. Mattie watched Alys, June and Tommy take each other's hands and share excited hugs and kisses, as Thalia smiled from beside the piano.

'There they are, Reenie,' Mattie said. 'Back together, just like we planned.'

'They look happy.' Reenie's smile had gone as she leaned heavily on her walking cane. 'I shouldn't spoil it.'

'You won't. Go and join them.'

'The thing is, Matilda, they were always goin' to be better off without me. I was never comfortable being part of a team. They all were. I often think I did them a favour, skippin' out on them.'

'But you had your reasons. If they knew why you'd had to leave . . .'

'No, love. They don't need to know that. Not now.'

Gently, Mattie took Reenie's hand. 'You listen to me, lady. That group aren't called The Knight Five, or The Davis Five, or The Powell-and-Mullins Five. They can't be The Silver Five without you. They never could be. You've brought them back here for a reason. You're the returning star, not the forgotten fifth member. Go. They're waiting for you.'

With one last look at Mattie, Reenie Silver walked down the steps and across the dance floor. As she neared the others they turned, throwing their arms open wide as if welcoming home a long-lost sister.

Mattie watched from a distance as The Silver Five became one hugging, weeping entity, the wrongs of years gone by finally forgotten, permanently put aside. She saw smiles breaking out across the group, followed by laughter and loud recollections of their past experiences. And at that moment, she no longer saw four pensioners by the ebony-black baby grand, but five young people, the world at their feet, looking to their bright future with eager eyes. Sixty years ago today they had gathered here like this, preparing for the culmination of their career to date. But one of them had hidden a dark secret behind her excited smile; a devastating device set to detonate just before The Silver Five were due to take the stage.

It didn't matter now. The Silver Five were back where

they belonged – and Mattie had fulfilled her promise to Grandpa Joe. But what of Joe Bell, whose plans had taken him from his beloved club on the night he'd anticipated the most?

Mattie had to know the truth.

As the group began to run through their songs with Thalia at the piano and the swing band's leader standing beside her, Mattie found a seat at one of the booths, now covered with gold lamé cushions. She took Grandpa Joe's diary from the zipped front pocket of her bag, opening it to the page where she'd placed the fraying spring-green ribbon marker last night.

Tuesday, 25 September 1956

THERE IS HOPE!

Len visited today. He's angry I lied to him, of course, but he understands why. Una told him everything – it seems she is as confused as I am. But she still loves me!

The problem is their stepfather. He wants Una to marry a man of means. There is a son of a director at his company he's marked out for her, but Una says she won't have him. He's unlikely to be impressed by me, or my uncle's business.

Una wants to see me. If I can convince Uncle C to let me visit Len, there's a chance I'll be able to see her. I will need to act out the fastest recovery, but I'm determined to do it. Knowing Una still wants me is enough of an incentive to succeed . . .

Thrilled for Joe Bell – even though the woman he'd loved in 1956 wasn't the grandmother she'd adored – Mattie turned the page and read on:

Thursday, 27 September 1956

She has accepted me! Una will be my wife!

And we have a plan. As neither her father nor my family are likely to consent to our marriage, we are going to elope. I never thought I'd consider something so daring, but for her I would go to the ends of the earth. We can work everything out once we're man and wife. But it has to happen soon.

Una has accepted a dancing job at the Garrick Theatre in a musical that will run for six months initially, and maybe even transfer to Broadway in New York. Until I can support us both, her wage is vital to our survival. Rehearsals begin on 4 October. If we don't act now, it may be a year or more before she's free. I am not prepared to wait that long.

We have tickets for the night train to Gretna Green on Saturday. I will meet her at Waterloo station when she finishes her last shift at the PG. It means I will miss The Silver Five – and here I must admit to a great deal of sadness. I'm consoling myself with the certain knowledge that they are headed for great things and are bound to appear at the PG again. Jacob Kendrick, the owner, likes to keep popular acts. But I can't let the opportunity to be with my Una pass by.

I'm taking my silver sixpence tiepin to give to her on our wedding night. It isn't much of a gift, but she has always admired it. I hope it will be the first pretty thing of many I can give her during our life together.

I'm telling my uncle that I've been invited to Brighton for the weekend by one of the lads from work. He will be suspicious if he sees me taking my best suit, so Len has arranged to collect my suitcase after work tonight. As far as Uncle C is concerned, Len is borrowing my case for a trip of his own to see his maiden aunt in York. I've put the money from under my mattress in the case for safekeeping and I'm going to meet him and Una at the station.

I don't know what will happen when Una and I return as man and wife, but I'm prepared to face all of it, knowing the woman I love is beside me. Once we're married, they will have to accept us.

I'm terrified, but I'm on fire. I couldn't stop this if I tried. All I can think of is that in three days' time I will be lying with my new wife across the border in our honeymoon hotel. This is all that matters to me now . . .

So *that* was where Joe Bell had been, sixty years ago! Running from everything that might have prevented him from being with the woman he loved. It was wildly romantic and unbelievably foolhardy, but Mattie loved him for following his heart. She wished that in later life he might have afforded her the same opportunity. But this couldn't be the end of the story. Hardly wanting to look, she turned the page.

Saturday, 29 September 1956

I waited for over two hours. But she never came.

It was the worst thing to read, but a part of Mattie wasn't surprised. Una had seemed too good to be true, and now it had been proved she was. The money in the suitcase given to her brother, who had seemingly accepted their relationship after being so violently opposed to it in the beginning – it was all too convenient, too obviously a ruse.

Mattie's heart broke for her grandfather, the image of the young man waiting in vain at the station for the dream he'd invested everything in – and risked his livelihood for. How had he come to the conclusion that Una wasn't turning up that night? Had he denied it until the train had gone, the station cleared of passengers? Had a kind porter seen his distress and suggested he leave? And how must it have felt, sneaking back into his uncle's house, explaining his sudden return from his supposed trip to Brighton? The answer came in two lines scrawled in heavy script on the next page.

Sunday, 30 September 1956

I have confessed all to Uncle C. Tomorrow, I leave London for good.

'You must be Mattie.'

Still reeling from Joe Bell's jilting, Mattie looked up to meet the smiling green eyes of Gil's brother. 'Yes, I am. Hello.'

'We meet at last,' Colm grinned, shaking Mattie's hand as she stood. 'Don't get up on my account. After your epic adventure, I imagine you could do with a rest. Can I get you a pot of tea or something?'

'Tea would be great,' Mattie smiled back. Gil had been right about his brother, at least: aside from the green eyes and identical height, the two could not have been more different.

'Cool. I'll get Derry to put the kettle on. So, what d'you reckon?' His hand made a broad sweep of the club.

'It's amazing. I can't believe you pulled this together in such a short time.'

'Me either, but it was Gil who arranged most of it. I tried to send him over to say hi to you, but he's being a complete foreman this afternoon. He's obsessed with getting every detail right.'

Too busy to face me, Mattie thought, her heart sinking. 'Well, it's paying off. The gig is going to be amazing.'

'Personally, I think he's pulled a blinder,' Colm said, with a wink that threw Mattie for a second. Did he mean the gig, or something else? 'I'll get that tea. Sit down, relax. You've done it, Mattie.'

Mattie settled back, but her spirit was uneasy. She'd wanted to see how she felt when she saw Gil again; but now it was obvious he wanted nothing to do with her. Heart heavy, she watched the activity in the club, the set dressers putting final touches, lighting technicians running through their changes and sound engineers testing microphones. *I've done this*, she thought, remembering back to when the idea for the reunion had first struck her. There had been many times she'd doubted the likelihood of success. Yet here she was, watching last-minute preparations for an event that was about to rewrite history. *I did it: I made it happen.*

And then The Silver Five began to sing. Gathered around the baby grand piano, their voices rose from gentle beginnings – at first in unison and then, as the chorus swelled, splitting into perfect three-part harmonies. Mattie sat forward to watch them, the sound so familiar from her childhood listening to Grandpa Joe's records filling the room. The notes may have been a little hesitant and delivered with more *vibrato* than the original performance, but the sound of The Silver Five was there in an instant, strong and joyful as it summoned the attention of everyone. Mattie could see Reenie, Alys, June and Tommy exchanging surprised smiles as they sang.

Reenie took the main line, and watched as her bandmates leaned over to touch her hands. Mattie marvelled at how pure Reenie's voice still was, how well it fitted with her bandmates' tones. She heard exactly why Reenie Silver had found stardom, why Rico had foreseen and masterminded her career and why she'd rightfully earned her reputation as one of the most enduring artists in the music industry. Her voice soared above the others – and even in rehearsal, without microphones or amplification, the quality of her sound was unquestionable. She was a *star*; from her confident ad-libs that peppered the melody with sparkle, to the way her voice seemed to fill the room as if it were ten times the size. This was what she had lived her entire life for, what she had sacrificed so much to be able to do. Husbands and lovers had been and gone, her only chance at motherhood had broken her heart with its passing – but the music had remained, a rock in the turbulence of Reenie Silver's world. And even now, officially retired and unlikely to perform in public again, she was proving to the world how much poorer it would have been without her incredible talent.

Mattie let her tears flow as she watched her friend doing what she had been created to do. She may well have been the most difficult, unfathomably cantankerous and opinionated person Mattie had ever had to deal with. But Mattie loved her – from her highly dubious showbiz recollections to her absolute refusal to accept she was an old lady.

If I'm half the woman Reenie is when I'm her age, I'll have lived a great life, she thought as the song ended. She and the other people preparing the room stood and applauded the surprised and delighted Silver Five.

'That was only the rehearsal,' Reenie yelled into the auditorium. 'Just you wait till you hear the real thing!'

The reunited members of The Silver Five were still smiling and hugging when Mattie joined them.

'You were amazing! Just like your records. Congratulations, everyone.'

'Thank you, pet. It's good to be rubbing shoulders with these beautiful songbirds again,' Tommy grinned. 'We scrub up okay for a bunch of old-timers, don't we?'

'And young Thalia here did her grandad proud,' Reenie added, pinching the young performer's cheek. '*You* are a star in the making, kid. When this is all done, me and you are going to talk turkey, okay? I have some contacts still in this industry and me name counts for something.'

Thalia looked as if she'd been crying, tell-tale salt streaks staining her pale cheeks. Her smile was sad when it reached Mattie. For her to be able to perform with the level of poise and sophistication she'd just shown, less than a week after losing her grandfather, was an astounding achievement. Even though Mattie had been at odds with Grandpa Joe when he'd died, the days immediately following his death had been so hard that simply breathing in and out had required a huge effort.

'Just to be able to do it for him . . . It means the world.'

June turned to Mattie. 'So how long do we have until curtain up?'

'About two hours, I think.'

'Let's check the schedule,' Alys said, holding a sheet of paper at arm's length and squinting at it. 'Can't read the damn thing, mind.'

'The show starts at eight o'clock. The swing band are doing a set for the first forty minutes,' Thalia read. 'Then there'll be a small interval till nine, and we're up after that.' She smiled shyly at Chuck's former colleagues. 'I've just been through the music with Chas, the swing band's leader, for the six songs we're singing, and the swing band is going to play behind us. We'll have headset microphones so we don't have to worry about holding them.'

'Ooh, like Madonna!' Alys grinned. 'Always wanted to

do a bit of naughty-grindy dancing in a pointy-boob corset, me.'

'Don't you try any bumping and grinding, sweetheart,' June kept a perfectly straight face as she wagged a finger at her friend. 'You'll put your hip out again.'

'Time to rest a bit until showtime, then,' Reenie said, beaming up at the others. 'Dunno about you lot, but I could murder a little tipple or two.'

'Someone keep an eye on her,' Tommy joked, putting his arm around Reenie. 'Only we got this far last time, remember, and then she high-tailed it.'

Mattie smiled at Reenie, who grinned and shook her head. 'Oi, Tommy Mullins, you may be an old codger but you're still young enough to go across my knee.'

Tommy clasped his hands together and looked to heaven. 'I live in hope, Reenie, I live in hope!'

Reenie made her way over to Mattie. 'This is what it was like with us, most of the time. When we weren't threatening to murder each other, that is.' Her smile ebbed a little. 'Listen, Mattie, there's something I've been meaning to tell you . . .'

'Miss Silver?'

Mattie and Reenie turned to see two ladies beside them. They each held an armful of records, and were gazing at Reenie as if seeing the Queen.

'Yes?'

'So sorry to interrupt, but we wanted to catch you before you had to get ready for the concert. I'm Aline and this is my daughter, Clare. We're *huge* fans. I can't tell you how thrilled we are to see you perform tonight. I wonder, would you mind signing these?'

Remembering Reenie's fears from earlier, Mattie smiled and moved a respectful distance away. Right now, Reenie was a star and her adoring fans needed her.

Ten minutes later, Colm arrived with what looked like the clipboard his brother had been nursing all afternoon. If he had that, where was Gil?

'Ladies – and *gentleman* – your stylists are waiting for you in your dressing rooms. If you'd like to follow me?'

This brought amused murmurs from the gathered group.

'A stylist?' June repeated. 'My word, the closest we all got to a stylist last time we were here was some girl in the chorus who had heated rollers!'

'Cathy and her team are excellent,' Colm continued, leading The Silver Five to the area behind the stage. 'She's brought a whole rail of clothes for you all, and she'll put together a great look for the gig.'

'One shirt,' Tommy said. 'That was my wardrobe back in the day.'

Alys chuckled. 'Oh, *that shirt*. It was so crusty, I swear it gave a more animated performance than you most nights.'

'Still doing the cruise-ship circuit, last I heard,' Reenie joined in, and Mattie could see her joy at being one of the group again.

On it continued, the light-hearted mockery and sharing of memories, through costume fittings to hair and make-up. Mattie let it all sink in, thinking about how Reenie had missed all of this the first time around. Grandpa Joe, too: and that made her the saddest of all.

What would Joe have spent that afternoon doing? His case already packed and in Len's supposed safekeeping, all he had to do was enjoy his daydreams, whiling away the hours until he had to be at Waterloo. She thought of the bright hope emanating from two venues in 1956 London: both parties preparing for events they believed would change their lives. And both would, but not in the way they'd planned.

They were sitting in the largest dressing room, The Silver Five looking wonderful in black and silver outfits as they warmed their voices with a mixture of vocal exercises and a bottle of best-quality Bourbon 'for old times' sake', when a knock sounded at the door – and Gil Kendrick walked in.

His eyes met Mattie's as soon as he entered the room, quickly drifting away again as he addressed his special guests. 'How are we all doing?'

'We're ready to go. And the place looks better than it did when your grandpa was in charge.' Tommy rose to shake Gil's hand.

Mattie had never wanted to disappear into thin air as much as she did at that moment. Gil had resolutely avoided her since she'd arrived – and even now, in the enclosed space of the dressing room, he might have been a thousand miles away from her for all the interest he displayed. She hadn't expected a warm welcome, but she'd hoped at least for some professional courtesy. Determined not to let him see her hurt, she took a schedule from one of the dressing tables and busied herself with reading it. She would *not* give him the satisfaction of seeing she cared.

'. . . By the way, your families have arrived and, if I remember rightly, Jacob had a tradition of allowing visitors backstage for his headline acts before the show. Shall I send them in?'

His suggestion was met with loud murmurs of approval and, smiling, he opened the door fully, beckoning out to the corridor. Mattie, her head kept resolutely low, thought Gil looked over at her momentarily before stepping out of the room, but before she could make sure, the room was filled with a rush of excited, chatting bodies and he was gone.

She recognised Thalia's family, who were noticeably quieter than the other visitors, fiercely proud of their girl but no doubt battling the bittersweet reality of being there without Chuck. Teifi fussed around Alys, who threw back her head and laughed loudly, clearly adoring every minute of his attentions. June's son Hugo and his wife were admiring her transformation by the stylists, while Tommy's daughter and grandson presented him with a flask of tea 'in case you're thirsty'. He quickly pushed his empty Bourbon glass behind Alys's make-up bag without them noticing.

Mattie looked over to Reenie, but her chair was empty. She remembered what she'd said about visiting hours at Beauvale; how she watched every week as her neighbours received family and friends, quietly envious of the riches they didn't know they possessed. Had this sudden flood of familial admirers been too much for her? Quietly slipping out into the corridor, she looked left and right to see where Reenie had gone.

'Hi, Mattie.'

She closed her eyes and reluctantly turned to face Gil. 'Hello.'

'So, it's happening, then?'

'I said it would.'

Gil abandoned his attempt to smile. 'Listen, I—'

'It's going to be a wonderful concert,' Mattie rushed, wishing she could leave. 'The club looks great. A sell-out, I hear?'

'Yes. I want to . . .'

Behind him, Mattie spotted the familiar shape of her friend shuffling down the corridor towards the stage door. There was so much she'd wanted to say to Gil – not least to demand a reason why he'd left the hotel in Crickhowell a day early – but she was struck by a sudden sense of déjà vu as she realised Reenie was retracing her steps from the original gig. The steps that Gil's grandfather had taken alongside her, thinking he was speeding their unborn child's escape from imminent danger. Was Reenie leaving again?

'I have to go,' she said, pushing past him and racing down the corridor. Behind her she could hear Gil calling her name, but she couldn't turn back. If Reenie was running away, she had to stop her.

There was a loud slam ahead as the stage door swung shut behind the elderly singer and Mattie skidded to a halt, her hands grappling with the entry bar as she scrabbled to push it open. Outside, the street was a dark silhouette against a bright blue evening sky, the golden light of the setting sun gilding the end of the alley. And there, in the natural spotlight, stood Reenie Silver, her shoulders rising and falling as she caught her breath.

Mattie hurried towards her, praying that a cab wouldn't arrive and take her away from the club for good. With enormous relief, she reached out to touch her shoulder – then froze as she realised Reenie wasn't alone.

Four strangers were gathered to her left, nodding as she spoke to them. Were they fans? Groupies from her long and illustrious career? On closer inspection, only one of them appeared old enough to be a contemporary of Reenie's, the other three consisting of a woman Mattie guessed to be in her early sixties, a younger man of about forty and a girl who looked no older than Pru or Kelvin.

Reenie stopped talking and turned around, her smile vanishing when she saw Mattie. 'Oh, I didn't see you there, Mattie. I was just catching up with – in fact, I'll be back in the club in five minutes, so why don't you—'

'Mattie?' the eldest lady repeated – and Mattie saw Reenie slump. '*The* Mattie Bell? Oh, this is wonderful!' She stepped forward and planted two kisses on Mattie's cheeks. 'Thank you. From the bottom of our hearts. Truly. You have no idea how Mum's enjoyed your visits, and *this* – well, it's just fantastic.'

Mattie stared at Reenie, who appeared to be trying to hide behind a road bollard. '*Mum?*'

'And Granny and *Great*-Gran,' the man smiled. 'Not to mention soon-to-be Great-Great Nan.'

'Reenie?' Mattie asked, the sudden realisation of who

the group were dawning with sickening clarity. 'This is your *family*?'

Reenie looked small in the middle of them. 'I tried to tell you . . .'

The family who she'd sworn didn't exist looked at Mattie and grinned as one.

'We don't get to see Mum as much as we'd like,' Reenie's surprise daughter explained. 'We do a lot of travelling with my husband's job, and we've just spent four months in Dubai. So when she told us you were visiting – and what you were planning with this concert – well, we were all over the moon.'

'Just how many of your family are there?' Mattie folded her arms as Reenie stared at the pavement.

'I tried to say . . .'

'Only the four of us are here tonight, but there are more who couldn't come. So, I'm Delora, Reenie's daughter, then there's my sister Deanna who lives in Toronto and my brother Derek, who works with my husband in his construction business out in the UAE. This handsome chap is my son Nick, and this is his youngest daughter, Lucy. His eldest daughter Frankie is expecting Mum's great-great-grandson any day now, so she couldn't come. But we want you to know, Mum considers you a granddaughter. And after seeing what you've done for her tonight, we'd like to welcome you into our family, too.'

Mattie was overwhelmed by this sudden introduction to Reenie's very large family. 'That's kind of you, but—'

'Talking of which, not long till the show starts.' Delora kissed Reenie and drew her into a huge hug. 'We'd better get in and find our seats. Break a leg, Mum. You're going to be wonderful!'

As they left, Mattie rounded on her charge. '*You said* you didn't have any family . . .'

'Yes, I know.'

'It was all, "I never got the chance to have kids of my own, love." That was why I started visiting you in the first place – why I didn't stop you picking up Kelvin and Pru . . .'

'I never meant to lie to you, kid.'

'But you did! Worse still, you got Gaynor to lie, too. You could have made her lose her job by covering for you being on this road trip, do you realise? Why didn't you tell me about your kids? And grandkids? And flippin' *great*-grandkids, for heaven's sake?'

Reenie began to rally. 'And if I'd told you I had family, would you have visited me at all? Would you have done any of this?'

'I might have.'

'Only if you'd liked me enough to see beyond the link I had with your grandad. Because let's be honest here, love, you used me as much as I used you.'

Mattie had heard enough. 'Have you ever told me the truth, about any of this? I stuck up for you when Gil was accusing you of lying – I might have lost someone I was beginning to really care about because I took your side. Do you even get that? Not that I suppose it matters to you. You got what you wanted. You can clear your conscience and have a final, glittering farewell in the glare of publicity we've all kindly created for you. You know what? I fulfilled my end of the bargain. You can take it from here. I don't even want to be here now.'

'And how do I get home, eh? You brought me here.'

'You can hitch a lift with your family, seeing as they're here. I am *done*, Reenie. It's finally over.'

She turned to leave, but Reenie followed her. 'I wanted to tell you, kid. I meant to tell you the first time you came. But then I started looking forward to your visits and – I don't know, the time to say something passed.'

Mattie stopped walking. 'Is that what you tried to tell me earlier?'

Reenie nodded. 'Yes, love. And I felt awful that I didn't . . .'

'Because you knew you were going to be found out.'

'No! Maybe . . . But I didn't lie about all of it, Mattie.' The old lady's sudden grip on her arm was strong, desperate. 'I *didn't lie* about this place. About the baby. Not even my family knows that, kid. They think Rico persuaded me to leave The Silver Five and go solo. That's what I've always told them. What I've told everybody until this week. They don't know about Jake Kendrick and they don't know I was almost a mother, seven years before I gave birth to Delora. I didn't lie about those things. I *chose* to tell you them.'

Unsure of what to believe, Mattie took a long, hard look at Reenie Silver. 'Then why me? Why agree to have me visit you – to all the rest of it – when your kids and grandchildren could have done it for you?'

'Because I *like you*, Mattie Bell! *Really* like you. And I loved that you wanted to hear my daft old stories and gave me the time of day. I love my family and they love me, but after a while you just become the dotty old grandma, blathering away in a corner at Christmas about the life you had before any of them were born. They care, but they don't *care* like you did.' She batted a tear from her eye. 'I'm sorry I didn't tell you. Although *technically* I didn't lie about not having visitors lately: it's a bit of a trek from Dubai to Beauvale every Sunday morning to visit. But I should've told you the truth. And I didn't. And I'm sorry.'

It was too much to take in, after so many half-truths, rumours and unreliable stories. Mattie wrestled her arm free and moved a few steps away from Reenie, thoroughly confused.

'Why should I believe you?'

In the fading evening light Reenie was a little old lady again, almost shrinking before Mattie's eyes. 'Oh, I don't know. I guess it's your call, kid. *I* probably wouldn't believe me if I was in your shoes. But for what it's worth, it's true. You made me feel like a star again. I told you my stories and you lapped them up: I'm not ashamed to admit I may have embellished a few here and there for your benefit.' She gave a hollow laugh, looking up at the darkening sky. 'Never thought I'd be begging somebody to listen to me. How the mighty have fallen, eh?'

Mattie kicked a discarded plastic bottle at her feet. Should she believe the old lady or just call it a night before the concert happened? 'You're still a star. A sold-out venue tells you that.'

'Want to know why I changed my mind? When I'd said I wouldn't do the reunion you'd planned?'

'Hit me with it.' One more dubious story couldn't make things worse . . .

'Because I'd just had a visit from my financial advisor. She suggested I tie up all my affairs immediately, and I quote, "because at your age and with your health problems, you probably don't have another ten years to do everything".'

Forgetting her irritation, Mattie stared at her. 'That's awful! You'll outlive everyone. A born survivor, that's what you said, right?'

'You and I know that, Matilda, but she just tripped out her offensive little phrase, like I was meant to thank her for it. Well, I sacked her on the spot, of course. Didn't want her getting her grubbies on a penny more of my money, cheeky mare! But what she said wouldn't leave me. And I thought, that's what people think of me now, isn't it? Some washed-up has-been, crumbling to bits in a care home. But *you* never considered my age when you suggested this crazy idea. It was all about getting everyone back together. *You* believed in me. You thought I was up to it. And so I thought to myself, I'll bleedin' show *Felicity Gordon-Smythe, Financial Advisor* what I can do. So I said yes. And look what happened, Mattie Bell.'

'Okay, fine. But I have one question.'

'Name it.'

'You don't have any more earth-shattering revelations up your sleeve, do you? Because honestly, Reenie, I don't think I can handle any more.'

'I once left me knickers in Frankie Laine's dressing

387

room . . .' she grinned up at Mattie as she took her arm. 'Nah, you probably don't want to know the rest of that story. No more revelations. Not that I can think of, at any rate. Shall we go to this bleedin' gig, then, or what?'

Mattie smiled back. 'I'm not letting you miss it, Miss Silver!'

Chapter Thirty-Four

'Little Things Mean a Lot'
– Kitty Kallen

♪

The sound of the swing band swelled into the club, and Mattie watched The Silver Five fall silent as they stood in the wings. When one of the lights dancing across the stage illuminated them momentarily, she noticed they were holding hands. Tommy pulled a crumpled handkerchief from his trouser pocket and dabbed at his nose, while Alys rested her head on Reenie's shoulder. June had her arm around Thalia's waist, comforting the poor girl, who looked likely to throw up from nerves. Here stood The Silver Five, after so many years apart, awaiting their cue to take the stage.

It was almost as if the anticipation of the audience was sweeping onstage, an unseen energy that willed and pulled the stars they had come to see back to their rightful place. Mattie had never performed, but she remembered Jack describing the atmosphere between audience and stage as a 'riptide', pulling you forwards and making you giddy, drawing out your best and rushing their appreciation back like a swell. It was electrifying and terrifying all at once, and Mattie understood how it had intoxicated each singer in the group, making it the only thing they could imagine doing – and setting the course for their lives.

She wasn't performing tonight, but she felt as nervous as if she were. At least she looked the part now, having changed into a Fifties-style black evening dress she had packed for the trip, her hair swirled up in a French pleat and a pair of low black kitten heels in place of the boots she'd practically lived in for the last fortnight.

'Five minutes,' the stage manager informed them, handing out headset microphones and helping the singers to fix them in place.

Mattie gave the group a thumbs-up. 'I'll head out front. Break a leg, everyone!'

Reenie caught her hand. 'This is it, kid. And it's you we owe it to.' Quite without warning, she threw her arms around Mattie and the others joined her, until, giggling like teenagers, they released her.

As she hurried backstage towards the corridor that led to the bar, Mattie saw Gil. He was standing in the darkness, his face lit by a sliver of blue light coming through a gap in the curtains. He didn't smile, but his gaze was directed straight at her. Tired and shaking with the emotion of the night, Mattie walked on. Whatever had happened between them was over: all that mattered now was the culmination of her promise to Reenie and Grandpa Joe.

Emerging into the restored heart of the Palm Grove,

Mattie was dazzled by what seemed to be a thousand lights burning brightly. Above the chandeliers a star curtain had been draped: myriad tiny stars shimmering high above the audience. Now she understood why Joe Bell had adored this place so much; and why he'd found his heart amongst its twinkling lights. *It would be easy to fall in love here*, she thought, her heart aching with the irony. She had come so close to falling for its owner; now she was here, she knew any chance of that had gone. Gil wasn't interested, and she didn't want to be with someone who could so easily let her down. Grandpa Joe had never returned here after Una left him. Now it occurred to Mattie that she would soon leave it behind her, just as he'd done. Maybe the Palm Grove was a breaker of hearts as well as the maker of passions. How many dreams had been tested here? And how many had been dashed?

She didn't want to think of it anymore. Tonight belonged to the group of reconciled friends now being introduced to rapturous applause.

Gil held the microphone in the centre of the stage. Safe in her seat at the back of the club, Mattie forced herself to look at him. His smile towards the group seemed warm and genuine – a world away from the rage he'd displayed towards Reenie in Wales – and the coolness of his expression backstage. Mattie was certain she saw Reenie sneak a playful dig into his ribs as The Silver Five took to the stage. Perhaps he had apologised this afternoon. Or maybe she was simply having the last word. That was a right Reenie Silver guarded most jealously of all.

'Excuse me, is this seat taken?' asked a gruff voice,

dragging her attention from the stage. Mattie turned – almost shrieking when she saw Joanna and Jack grinning beside her.

'Oh wow! What are you doing here?'

'We couldn't miss your finest hour,' Jack said, planting a kiss on her head and flopping into the next seat. 'This is unbelievable!'

'Where are the kids, J-J?'

Joanna took the seat opposite. 'Granny's looking after them at the house – I hope that's okay?'

'Yes, of course,' Mattie replied, the thought of her mother babysitting in her home strangely amusing. 'I do hope Mum knows what she's let herself in for.'

'Don't worry. We're driving back straight after the gig so we can rescue her. You did it, M! How do you feel?'

'It's – a lot to take in. And a lot's happened. It might take me a while to answer that.'

Joanna laughed. 'Take all the time you need. Now *enjoy* this, Mattie. You deserve it.'

'. . . Ladies and gentlemen, would you join with me to welcome – The Silver Five!' Gil left the stage, and the house lights began to dim until a single spotlight remained on the group. Thalia nodded a count and began to play. Mattie felt the audience around her lean forward instinctively, awaiting the first notes sung by their idols, the beginning of a landmark concert few fans had thought possible. The thrill when Reenie sang the opening bars of their 1955 song 'Sweet Little Heart of Mine' was practically tangible. From then on, the crowd hung on every note, every harmony and each new arrangement Thalia played, applause beginning before each song had ended. Tommy, Alys, June and Reenie beamed through each number, as if utterly stunned by the reaction of the crowd.

Mattie realised she was touching the silver sixpence tiepin she'd pinned to her simple black evening dress. Now she understood why Grandpa Joe had cherished it: not only because it had been a present from a school friend, but also because it served as a constant reminder of the folly of his youth. A wedding gift that never was, it would warn him never to let himself be fooled again. Mattie had loved it all her life, but now she could see it for what it was – a warning passed down through the years.

But she hadn't needed him to save her from all the mistakes she could have made. How else was she supposed to learn from her life? By his insistence that she follow his lead, he had denied her the chance of growing, of chasing her heart, of staying true to herself. In the dazzling, dancing lights of the club he had once loved, the tiepin on her dress became something different. It wasn't a gift. It was a curse.

If Joe Bell had never met Una here, if he'd remained the idealistic, heart-driven dreamer so in love with London and the Palm Grove, perhaps his life would have been different. Mattie wanted to remember him as the young man he had once been, before heartbreak made him cautious and determined to prevent anyone else from making the mistakes he'd made. Looking back towards the stage, she knew what she had to do.

The swell of applause that greeted each song was

becoming stronger as the audience willed The Silver Five to perform their biggest hit. Charting in almost every decade since its number one placing in July 1954, their signature tune had been covered by everyone from Elvis Presley, the Supremes, Aretha Franklin and Tony Bennett, to Rod Stewart, Diana Ross and most recently, Michael Bublé. It would live on as future generations discovered it, and while the song's original singers might be forgotten, a rare agreement between the songwriter Sid Matheson and the young band back when they recorded it ensured their legacy would remain.

'Sid was a big fan of ours and he always said he'd written the song just for us,' Reenie had told her during the long drive from Cambridge to Bath. 'When we recorded it in January 1954 he was so thrilled that he instructed the music publishers to add our names. I don't know if he ever thought it would be a hit, but when it was he said the credit should remain. One-fifth of twenty-five per cent doesn't seem like much, but when your song's been recorded as many times as ours has, it adds up. It's been a good boost to our incomes for years. So I suppose even when we stopped talkin', that song kept us together.'

'Because You Loved Me' had been Grandpa Joe's favourite, perhaps because it reminded him of a time in his life when he'd been free to dream, before reality stole the ground from beneath him. Now, as Thalia's heartfelt version introduced the song to the rapt audience, Mattie closed her eyes and let the melody wash over her . . .

Because you loved me
I can face today
Chase my blues away and smile
It's because of you
That happiness is mine

Because you loved me
All my crazy dreams
Find their feathered wings and fly
I am free, love
Because you loved me

Tommy, June and Alys began to bring their harmonies and the band kicked into life, bringing 'Because You Loved Me' to a lively swing tempo, taking the arrangement back in time and every person in the club to the edge of their seats. The Silver Five sang it as if welcoming back an old friend, and Mattie imagined the spirit of Johnny 'Chuck' Powell standing tall behind his granddaughter playing the piano so beautifully, tears streaming from her eyes.

Because you loved me
All the world is mine, darling
And in time we'll see
Joy forever
Because you loved me

The final bars sounded – and the whole room erupted into an ovation that swept every person to their feet. At its centre The Silver Five stood, dumbstruck, their hands clasped to their hearts, finally receiving the adulation they'd dreamed the Palm Grove audience would give.

It seemed an eternity before the applause subsided, the house lights rising a little to allow the ecstatic group to take their final bow. Their families rushed forward, greeting their loved ones with loud congratulations – and Mattie saw Reenie Silver in the arms of her family, finally allowing her tears to fall.

Unnoticed, Mattie slipped between the gathered well-wishers and hurried up the steps onto the stage. Out of sight of the crowd, she ducked down in the wings and pulled up a section of the restored red velvet stage curtains. The final act of her graveside promise was now upon her, and she had never been more certain of anything than she was of this. Reaching up to the strap of her dress, she unpinned Grandpa Joe's silver sixpence on its candy-cane-twisted stem and tucked it carefully into the wide fold of the curtain hem, just below where it could be seen.

'I'm leaving you here, Joe Bell,' she whispered. 'Where you should have been, sixty years ago, instead of having your heart broken by someone who didn't deserve you. I love you, Grandpa Joe. But it's my turn to live now.' She lifted the curtain hem to her lips and kissed it, then quickly left the stage.

Chapter Thirty-Five

'It Doesn't Matter Anymore'
– Buddy Holly & the Crickets

♪

'Reenie! You did it!' Reenie's tear-stained face beamed as Mattie pushed through the crowd by the stage.

'*We* did it, kid. And this must be your family. About time I met them.'

Joanna and Jack stepped forward to greet Reenie. 'It's a pleasure to meet you, Ms Silver. Mattie's told us so much about you.'

'I'll bet she has. Lovely you could make it.'

'Family is important at times like these,' Mattie said, casting a wry grin at her friend.

'It is indeed. Any news on the van, love?'

Mattie's heart deflated a little. She'd received a text message from Kelvin after the concert:

Rusty at garage. Not a big problem but won't be fixed till the morning. Sorry. K ☹

It was hard to bring her mind back to practical concerns

after the emotion of the night, but Mattie did her best to think of solutions. 'I suppose Reenie and I could call the garage tomorrow and see if we can pick Rusty up from them.'

'I have a better idea, love. Leave it with me. I'll get my daughter on the case – she's a whizz at this sort of thing. She can arrange our transport home tomorrow and get the garage to send the rust-bucket back, too.'

Mattie wasn't listening, her brain jammed with logistical considerations. 'We need to think about how we'll get from the hotel to the garage. It could be quite a trek across town tomorrow.' She wished now she had chosen accommodation nearer the club for tonight. When she and Reenie had booked the last night's stay, they had assumed they would be able to drive in and out of Soho in Rusty, and needed to be somewhere close to the motorway for the drive home.

'That crappy Premier Lodge in Chiswick? No, I cancelled that, love.'

What was it Reenie had said about revelations she'd forgotten? Mattie turned to her. 'What? When?'

'Yesterday. Made other arrangements.'

'How, exactly?'

Reenie gave Mattie a look like a teenager pitying her parents for trying to be cool. 'I know the interweb, love. How do you think I keep tabs on my intellectual property, hmm? I've one of those iPad thingies in my handbag. It's all arranged.'

'Reenie, where are we staying tonight?'

'Only the best place in town!' Reenie spread her arms

wide like a ringmaster introducing a show. 'Tonight, my good friend, we are living it up at the Ritz!'

'Oh wow – Mattie, what a lovely surprise!' Joanna exclaimed. 'I feel better leaving you here now.'

'But—'

'Enjoy every minute,' Jack said, kissing Mattie. 'We have to get going. Ms Silver, thank you.'

'Safe journey,' Reenie grinned.

Stunned, Mattie accepted their hugs and watched them leave before turning back to her friend. 'Reenie, do you know how much it costs to stay there?'

'Of course. Look, we've slummed it enough. I am a star – as are you. More than that, you're my *family* now. As much as that lot over there are. Besides, if I can't treat you for all the support you've given me, it's a poor show. And anyway, where else are you going to kip tonight?'

Put that way, Mattie had little choice. She'd had enough fighting to last her a long time, and Reenie was so pleased with herself for surprising them all.

Leaving a delighted Reenie to be welcomed by her real family, Mattie headed for the dressing rooms to collect their bags. Backstage, the air was still and cooler than the main club, as if only the ghost of the performance remained. She caught sight of herself in the make-up mirror, her face illuminated by the old-fashioned light bulbs surrounding the frame. She looked tired, but there was something new in her expression: peace. She had done everything she'd set out to do, brought Grandpa Joe to the concert he'd regretted missing sixty years before and put her own feelings about what had happened between them to rest at last.

Reenie was waiting for her when she arrived back in the club. Most of the audience had gone, the few remaining family members standing at a respectful distance while The Silver Five gathered in the middle of the dance floor to say goodbye.

'Thank you, Mattie,' Tommy said, holding out his hand to her and pulling Mattie into their circle. 'On behalf of us all, thank you. You believed in us, not just as members of The Silver Five, but also as people willing to give our long-lost sister a second chance. Without you, this couldn't have happened. And it's been wonderful.'

'Oh, leave it out, Tommy,' Reenie scoffed. 'You planning on running for Lord Mayor with that speech?'

Alys, June and Thalia laughed as Tommy feigned offence.

'Thank *you*,' Mattie replied. 'For all agreeing to take part tonight. Everyone loved you. I reckon you could go far.'

As a group, they embraced, five weary performers and an exhausted concert organiser celebrating their triumph together. Then, one by one, the group dispersed to their families and friends, until only Reenie and Mattie remained in the centre of the empty club.

'Are you off?' Colm and Derry were walking towards them, looking as tired as Mattie felt.

'We are, lads,' Reenie grinned. 'Colm, your grandad would have been mighty proud of you and Gil tonight. Thanks for taking a chance on us old biddies.'

'My pleasure, Miss Silver,' Colm smiled, kissing Reenie's

hand. 'Any time you fancy a repeat performance, just give me a shout.'

'I might take up stand-up comedy and storm your open mic night,' she chuckled. 'Never too late for a career change, I reckon.'

Colm looked over his shoulder towards the bar. 'I should find Gil before you go. He'll want to see you.'

Reenie shot a look at Mattie and quickly shook her head. 'It's late, kid. He has my number. I'm sure we'll chat soon.'

'Well, if you're sure?' He seemed to direct his question to Mattie.

'Come on, lady. The Ritz awaits!' Reenie led the way out of the club. At the doorway, Mattie paused, taking one last look at the club she felt she knew so well through Grandpa Joe's diary. This was how she would always remember it: the decadent nightclub in all its splendour. With a final nod towards the stage, she hurried outside.

They were walking away from Kendrick's when Reenie stopped and turned back. Mattie turned too, and saw Gil. He was standing on the pavement outside the club, hands shoved into his pockets, watching them.

'Listen, you go ahead. They're expecting you at the hotel. I just need to do one more thing before I join you. Go, go, it's fine!' Patting Mattie's arm, Reenie began to walk away, calling, 'Oi! Kendrick! I want a word with you . . .'

'. . . And here's your room, Miss Bell.' The white-gloved porter opened the door – and Mattie almost passed out.

It was the most sumptuous room she'd ever seen, let alone stayed in – decorated in opulent Louis XVI style, with an ornate fireplace at one end and a huge, expensively dressed bed at the other. Every piece of furniture and light fitting had been decorated in gold leaf, and elegant swags of thick brocade fabric surrounded the full-length windows.

It took Mattie the best part of an hour to feel at ease in the room, half-expecting someone to burst in and evict her at any moment. But once she had found the minibar and changed into more comfortable clothes, she began to relax. One thing still intrigued her: what had happened after Grandpa Joe had been jilted?

Settled against the luxurious pillows on her bed, she retrieved Grandpa Joe's diary and found the next entry.

Tuesday, 9 October 1956

Father has news from London. It's shattered any hope I have left. I have been an utter fool.

Una and Len Myers are not brother and sister. They are man and wife. And they do not exist. Their real names are Jack and Isobel Lacey. And I am not their first victim. According to the police, Scotland Yard is pursuing them for charges of multiple fraud.

I thought Una loved me. I believed her with all my heart and trusted her with everything I had. Instead of making me the happiest man alive, she has taken me for a fool and destroyed my life. Uncle Charles was remarkably fair about it all, but I couldn't stay in his employment knowing I'd lied to him. I've lost

all the money I'd saved for my London year, together
with everything I've saved while working. Most of all,
I've lost faith in my own convictions. I'm going to
work on the farm with Father until I can decide what
best to do.

And the worst of it is that every day I wonder
how Una is. Where she is. What she truly thinks of
me. Did she ever feel anything for me? And what of
Len? What kind of husband allows his wife to be
unfaithful in the hope of material gain? I have lost a
friend, the love of my life and all my money.

Never again will I let my head be turned by my
heart. I will not allow this to happen again in my
lifetime. My heart will not survive another such
beating . . .

Suddenly, it all made sense: Grandpa Joe's transformation from devil-may-care adventurer to moralistic pillar
of the community. It wasn't a progression into maturity;
it was a shield to keep his heart safe. Mattie knew that
her grandmother had become the real love of Joe Bell's
life and his absolute soul mate, but she could see now
that he had chosen to pursue security and the fiercely loyal
love of a woman who wouldn't let him down. Una Myers
– or Isobel Lacey, as she was revealed to be – had shown
Grandpa Joe the dangers of following his heart. Hurt and
humiliated, he had changed his worldview overnight to
ensure his heart was never broken again. No wonder the
young man writing his diary in 1956 had been worlds
away from the man Mattie had known and loved. He *was*

as far removed from that person as it had been possible to be.

He was a good man and had gone on to build a great life for himself, growing a family who'd rightly loved and admired him – and still did. He'd established a dynasty that led to a granddaughter who would do anything for him – or so he'd thought. When he'd seen how completely in love Mattie had been with Asher, no wonder alarm bells had begun to ring! Mattie knew how she'd been when she and Asher got together. It had felt like the beginning of something that couldn't end. And while she could see now she'd been wrong to trust him, back then it had been more natural than breathing itself to believe that Asher was the man she would grow old with.

Grandpa Joe had long said that Mattie reminded him of himself as a young man. She used to brush it off, but now she could see how much that must have scared him as well as made him proud. It must have served as a warning to him. But had his resulting actions come from a desire to protect Mattie, or out of fear for himself? Did he look at his granddaughter and see a chance to absolve himself for entrusting his heart to a woman who lied to him?

Confused and battered from the journey she'd taken to this evening, Mattie needed answers. There was only one person she could speak to. Finding Joanna's number in her phone, she called her sister.

'Hey you. We're almost home. How's the Ritz?'

'Opulent. But I feel weird being here, especially after ten days on the road.'

'I'll bet. Make sure you enjoy it, though.'

'I will. I just –' Tears filled Mattie's eyes as emotion jammed at the back of her throat. 'I think I know why Grandpa Joe stopped talking to me.'

She could hear the steady flow of her sister's breath quickening down the line as she relayed the tale from Joe Bell's diary, and a definite sniff as she delivered the dramatic revelation of Una Myers' true identity.

'Oh M,' Joanna breathed, her voice shaky and small. 'That explains so much.'

'I know I should feel peaceful after finally finding the answer he promised me, J-J, but the worst thing is, I don't. I feel angry with him. He decided I was exactly the same as he had been, and he reacted accordingly. He made me feel like it was my failing for not instantly agreeing with his decision. But it was my decision to make: *my* mistake to trust Asher. He had no right to demand to call the shots in my life like he did. I don't know if that's fair of me to say so but for months now I've been trying to put right a wrong I thought I'd inflicted on him, when he should have been the one making amends. Does that sound terrible? Because even if it is, it's how I feel. And I think I've finally come to the point where I've accepted this was *never* my problem.'

Her sister made a sound somewhere between a sob and a whimper, and Mattie realised Joanna was crying too. 'My darling, you're right. You're so right. I should have said something before but I – oh Mattie, I'm so, so sorry.'

Mattie stared at her reflection in the hotel room window, the lights of London painting her confusion in soft shades of orange, blue and white. 'Why should you be sorry? It wasn't your fault he . . . Hang on, are you telling me you *knew*?'

'No, not about the woman in London. But I knew what he was like when he decided something was right. And I should have spoken up then, but everything with Fred had become so very difficult and I – I'm ashamed to say it, Mattie – I wasn't strong enough to tell you.'

'Tell me what?'

'That you weren't the first person in our family to receive an ultimatum.'

Her words seemed to reverberate around the room, even though they came from one hundred and forty miles north of where Mattie stood. She couldn't reply, her open-mouthed glass doppelgänger staring goldfish-like back at her.

'He wasn't right about Fred being the only man for me. That's what he said. Only my ultimatum wasn't delivered in front of the family, so I had no witnesses. He'd obviously refined his approach when it was your turn. For me, it was given in private, with a strict instruction not to tell anybody else. At least you stood up to him. I didn't. And I can't help thinking my life would have been happier if I'd been more like you.'

Slowly, the terrible truth dawned. 'He made you choose, too?'

'Yes, he did. I wanted to travel, see the world a bit before I settled down. Fred wanted a home, a wife and kids immediately after we left university. Grandpa Joe made it clear what my priorities should be. And I was too scared to stand up to him.'

'Oh J-J, I didn't know . . .'

'Nobody in the family does. Not even Mum. In a funny way, I don't blame him. He was mistaken, but he stuck to what he believed. I blame myself for being so easily swayed. Don't get me wrong – in most respects Grandpa Joe was a wonderful, kind, funny, infuriating man and I will miss him every day of my life. But he wasn't a plaster saint. He got things wrong.'

'I think I understand that now. He just couldn't let go of his own regret and assumed we were all the same as him. He was wrong – and now I wonder if he'd worked that out when he told Phil to give me his diaries. Maybe this was the only way he could say it.'

'Maybe it was.'

'I just wish I'd known about you and Fred. I could have done something.'

'Would you listen to yourself? We are not your responsibility to put right, Mattie, any more than Grandpa Joe was. You have done so much to help me turn my life around. You made me believe in myself again.'

Tired and bewildered by the turn of events, Mattie sank into a luxuriously upholstered armchair by the window. 'How did I do that?'

'You let me look after Bell Be-Bop. You've opened your home to the kids and me. And you let me share the journey you've been on. Every night we've chatted over the past ten days I've heard the change happening in you. You've started to find what you want for yourself. And you've given me the space to discover what I want for *me*. You haven't just changed your life, Mattie Bell; you've changed ours, too.'

'Wow. I don't know what to say, Jo.'

'Don't say anything. You're incredible, little sister. Now, what happened with Gil after Jack and I left?'

Mattie closed her eyes. 'Nothing. Whatever happened on the trip was a fluke, I think. He just blanked me tonight. To be honest, I'd hoped him seeing Reenie and the band sing again might bring him back to wherever he was in his head when we got together. But – I'm not going to pursue it. I want to get back home, you know? Back to my life. And make it what I want it to be. It'll be good to be able to do that without asking for anyone else's input. I've learned that much from Grandpa Joe. I suppose I have him to thank for it, in a strange way.'

'No. This is all *you*, M. All of it. Don't ever feel guilty for being right. It was your decision to choose Asher, your right to make the mistake. And it was a mistake only because *he* stuffed up, so there's no need to blame yourself for that, either. Listen, if Gil can't see what an amazing, courageous woman you are then screw him, quite frankly.'

Mattie laughed at her sister's uncharacteristic bluntness – and all at once the tension and stress from the night dissipated. 'I'll call you tomorrow evening, okay? And promise me, Jo, if you need me you'll say so? I don't want us to have any secrets from now on.'

'Deal. Now, get some sleep in that ridiculously over-priced room you're in. And order room service with champagne – that's what I'd do. It's about time you celebrated everything you've achieved tonight. I love you, baby sis.'

'Love you, too. G'night.'

Alone in her luxurious room, Mattie considered everything she now knew. Joe Bell's mistake and the changes it had wrought in Grandpa Joe; Joanna's secret pain; and the row that had stolen her own final precious weeks with her grandfather. Not everything had been resolved – some things had been gained, and some lost. Despite it all, she was proud of herself. Nobody could take that away from her. Just as Reenie had reclaimed her place tonight in the group she'd abandoned, Mattie felt as if she had finally made peace with her past.

Like her, Grandpa Joe had made mistakes he couldn't change. He would continue to do so for the rest of his life, as Mattie no doubt would, too. Because, when all was said and done, that *was* life: a constant carousel of triumph and defeat, of if-onlys and bright possibilities. What made the difference between a life shackled by regret and a life given wings to soar over it was whether you let the past affect your future. Mattie wanted to fly. And it felt like the greatest achievement.

Chapter Thirty-Six

'Whatever Will Be, Will Be (Que Sera, Sera)' – Doris Day

♪

Next morning, after an impossibly sumptuous breakfast, Reenie and Mattie stood in the grand foyer of the Ritz, their bags packed.

'So, this is it,' Reenie said, her smile edged with sadness. 'The end of our incredible journey.'

'Looks like it.' Mattie hugged her. 'Thank you. It's been – eventful.'

'Excuse me, Miss Silver?' A liveried concierge was approaching them.

Reenie turned like a dame of the realm. 'Yes?'

'Your car is here, madam. Can I take your luggage?'

'Certainly, *Michael*,' she replied, winking at Mattie.

Mattie had to stifle her amusement as the concierge

solemnly carried her battered old gym holdall outside. 'Poor bloke.'

'I wonder how much it would be to get *him* to drive us,' Reenie grinned, paying far too much attention to the departing man's figure. 'I've always nicked things from hotels but I reckon there's still room in my cottage for a concierge.'

Leaving the hotel, they emerged onto damp Piccadilly, where a gleaming Aston Martin with darkened windows and leather seats was parked. A smart-suited chauffeur stood smiling by the open rear passenger door.

'What's this?' Mattie asked, hardly believing her eyes.

'This is a *car*, Mattie,' Reenie answered, a wicked glint in her eyes. 'Have you not seen one before?'

'Very funny. Is this for us? Really?'

'If anyone deserves to ride home in style, it's *you*, Mattie Bell. I think you've done enough driving. Marcel here is going to drive us home, aren't you, love?'

The chauffeur nodded.

'See? Lovely. You can forget your old draughty camper van. *This* is the way to travel!'

The journey home felt as if they were travelling on air, the suspension of the Aston Martin soothing every bump that Rusty would have registered. Mattie's thoughts were a million places and nowhere at all, ten days of triumphs, tribulations and turbulence combining to make her feel as if she'd endured the longest out-of-body experience. She wasn't sure how much it had altered her: when she returned to her own life in a few hours' time, would it still fit? Fundamentally, she felt changed: what mattered now was how she moved forward. What did she want from her life? She didn't know exactly, other than she had a burning determination to make her own decisions in future. She had relationships to heal – starting with her mum – and plans to make, to find a home that fit her instead of a house she didn't quite fit into.

'Not long till you're shot of me for good,' Reenie said, staring out of the passenger window.

'Don't think you're getting rid of me that easily,' Mattie replied.

'Glutton for punishment, are we?'

'Something like that. Besides, you said last night I was your family. I'm planning on keeping you sweet till you leave me a fortune in your will.'

Reenie chuckled. 'Touché, kid. Great comeback. Obviously you've spent too long with me.' She reached across the expensive leather seat and rested her hand on Mattie's, the paper-thin skin and swollen finger joints her only concession to old age. 'You'd better keep visiting me. With contraband.'

Mattie grinned. 'Just you try and stop me.'

The heavy rain eased as Marcel turned the car into Beauvale's wide driveway. Reenie peered up at the building.

'Not exactly the Ritz, but it'll do.'

A grim-faced Dr William Lancaster strode out from the entrance, Gaynor Fairchild hurrying beside him.

'Oh, dear.'

'Time to face the music, kid,' Reenie said, as Marcel

parked and walked around the car to open her door. 'After everything I've done lately, this'll be a piggin' walk in the park. Ah, *Billy*, how on earth are you?'

'Relieved to have you back,' Dr Lancaster replied. 'And trying to work out how one of my residents – who has one of the most complex health requirements in the entire village – managed to headline a club in Soho last night. Care to enlighten me?'

'Look, Bill, what can I tell you? A star's first responsibility is to her fans. Now I could've stayed here and denied them the chance to see their idol, or I could have valiantly battled to their side, putting aside all thought of my own wellbeing. They wanted to see Reenie Silver, Bill, and who am I to deny them?'

Mattie could see the battle in the Beauvale director's eyes as he fought his admiration for Reenie.

'This can't happen again. You understand that? And Miss Bell, I trust you'll help Gaynor and me to ensure Reenie *rests* from now on?'

Mattie hid her smile. 'Of course,' she replied, knowing full well that trying to stop Reenie doing what she wanted was like commanding the tide not to rise.

'I want to do a full check on you once you're settled back in your apartment.' Dr Lancaster turned and marched back inside.

'Are you in trouble with old Billy-boy?' Reenie asked Gaynor.

'I was. But then I made him dinner and, funnily enough, I was able to take his mind off the situation.'

'Gaynor Fairchild, you little minx!'

'You taught me well, Reenie. I'm still in the doghouse, but at least I have my job. Thanks for taking care of her, Matilda. I was chuffed to bits to see the concert preparations on the club website. I'll see you later, Reenie?'

'That you will.' When they were alone, she took Mattie's hands in hers. 'Now, do you fancy coming in for a cup of tea to wait until your van gets here?'

'It's coming back today?'

'The garage rang me before breakfast. All fixed and good as – well, not new, but probably better than it was.'

Mattie laughed. 'Reenie Silver, you are a constant surprise.'

'So are you, girl. Time you started believing it, too. In fact, watch out world when that happens. Oh, hang on, what's this?'

Mattie turned as a familiar sound reverberated along the country lane beside the retirement village's premises. Around the hedge that shielded the car park from the road, Rusty emerged, his every rust-spot, dent and scratch making Mattie's heart skip. She'd feared the worst yesterday and was prepared to accept that her camper van had made its last journey. But here he was, as loud, cranky and ungainly as ever. It was good to know, after all the ups and downs of the last ten days, that some things would never change.

Reenie squeezed her hand. 'By the way, love, you know I said there'd be no more revelations on this trip?'

Mattie laughed. 'You mean besides booking us into the Ritz and bringing us home in an Aston Martin?'

'Mm-hmm. Well, there's one more I need to hit you with . . .'

414

She nodded in the direction of Rusty, now parked at the other end of the car park. Mattie looked over as the driver's door opened – and everything went quiet.

Gil Kendrick climbed out of the camper van and stood by the open door. He held up his hands but didn't approach, as if uncertain whether he was allowed to or not.

'What's he doing here?'

'You two need to talk. It wasn't going to happen last night, but now it can. Don't lose a chance to be happy because of me, Mattie. I loved you for sticking up for me, but I had no right to ask you to do that. Oh, don't stand there like a prize onion, kid! Go and talk to the fella. If you want him to leave, fine. I'm sure Marcel here will give him a lift home. But *you* have to ask him to go. I'm going in for a brew. The Three Furies will be itching to hear my news. Marcel, love, you come with me. We're not needed here now.' As she let Mattie's hands go, she winked. 'Be happy, Mattie Bell – whatever that is for you.'

Mattie didn't move at first. She wanted to grab her keys and drive away, but to do that would mean approaching Gil and getting past him. What was Reenie thinking? Surely they'd said all they needed to say last night?

'I didn't know . . .' she began, hating the hesitation in her voice.

'Reenie's idea.'

'Obviously. Look, thanks for driving my van back, but I have to get home.'

'Let me drive you there.'

'No. Thanks anyway.'

Gil took a few steps across the gravel drive, each one

seeming to boom around the retirement buildings. 'I was wrong, okay?'

'About what? Reenie? Leaving the hotel without talking to me? Blanking me last night?'

'I didn't blank you last night – what did you expect me to do? We had a concert to put on. We were run off our feet . . .'

'You could have said *why*.'

'You know why.'

Mattie groaned. 'No, Gil, I don't. One minute you were supporting the gig and part of the team, and the next you just ran away. What was I supposed to think?'

'I was angry.'

'I know you were. So was I. You didn't wait to find out what I thought. You just left. How am I supposed to answer that?'

'I thought Reenie was lying. I'm still not sure she isn't. But she cares about you and – so do I.'

I can't listen to this now. What does it even mean? 'All my life, I've had people try to tell me how to think, how to feel, what's best for me. And when I don't do what they say, it feels like I'm the one at fault. I believe Reenie's story. She had no need to make it up – not when the story she'd told everyone about Rico poaching her from the group to be a solo star painted her in a far more favourable light. You were upset about Jacob's part in it – and trust me, I understand that – but you dismissed me because I chose to believe Reenie. And then you just became like every other person who has claimed to know my own mind better than me. Even Reenie – she meant well getting

416

you to come today, but it's just someone else's idea of what I want.'

Gil frowned. 'So what *do* you want, Mattie? No, come on, I'm asking.'

Mattie willed the heavens to open so she could make her escape. Why was Gil staring at her like that? Like he was willing the answer she hadn't been able to avoid for days to come out?

'I want to be happy. Being me. I want to make my own decisions, stumble over whatever obstacles life throws at me, and make my own mistakes. And more than anything, I don't want to worry constantly about what anyone else thinks. Including you.' Her voice dropped to little more than a whisper. 'Especially you.'

He began to walk towards her. She didn't step back. 'I had no right to make you feel like that. I'm sorry.'

'Forget it. It's done.'

'I don't think I can. And I don't think it is. Do you?'

Mattie thought of Grandpa Joe, then; of the dreamer he had once been. And how he had resolutely packed that person away when he'd returned to Shropshire, broken and ashamed. She had two options: let the past define who she was now, or take the risk that her heart might be vulnerable in the future. When she thought of it like that, there was only one real choice.

Whatever happens, it's my decision to make.

'It isn't over,' she said.

And as she pulled him into her arms and kissed him, she finally understood what Reenie Silver had told her during one of their earliest meetings: 'If I'd waited around

417

for everyone to be happy with me, I'd still be waiting now. You'll *always* know what you want. It might be hidden deep beneath great stacks of worry, or other people's rubbish, but if you dig down enough, it'll be there. The question is, are you willing to search for it, no matter what?'

Anything could happen in the future. But Mattie wasn't scared. *I'm ready*, she decided, as their kiss deepened. *I'm going to follow my heart . . .*

Chapter Thirty-Seven

'You Send Me'
– Sam Cooke

♪

'Ray Charles?'

'One barmy night in . . .' Reenie caught Mattie's smile. 'No, I didn't. Only in my dreams.'

'Lonnie Donegan?'

'Met him. Loved him. Didn't shag him.'

'Marty Wilde?'

'Ah, Marty. Little terror, he was.'

'Buddy Holly?'

'Adored him. Never met the poor lad, though.'

Mattie watched the Beauvale residents milling around the garden with their visitors. The December afternoon had brought everyone out wrapped in so many layers against the wintry chill that it appeared the garden was being laid siege to by an army of Arctic Weebles. 'Okay, did you ever meet Adam Faith?'

'I did.'

'And?'

'Not telling. Next!'

Mattie still didn't know how truthful Reenie's tales were. Maybe she never would. The stories were fantastic either way – and better still because Mattie suspected they were now all for her benefit.

'Burt Bacharach.'

'Do me a favour.'

'He wrote amazing songs.'

'That's as maybe, but he didn't float my boat. His face was too big.'

Mattie giggled. 'Johnny Cash.'

'Now you're talking! Never met him, wish I had. Sex in a Stetson, that one.'

'Ugh. Thanks for that.'

'What? You don't stop lusting when your faculties get dodgy, you know. Let a girl dream, eh?'

'Dream on, then. Um . . . Bee Gees?'

'Too many teeth.'

Gil grinned as he stopped beside Reenie. 'The Pogues.'

'Not enough teeth.'

'Harsh.'

'Get away with you, Kendrick. You don't appreciate my stories anyway.'

'Fine. I know when I'm not wanted,' he smiled, kissing Mattie and heading into the frosty garden, where Gaynor and the catering manager were serving mulled wine and mince pies to the residents and their families.

'He's all right, your chap. For a southerner. I'd prefer his brother, given the choice, though.'

'Colm's happily married, so mitts off.'

'Shame. Ask me another.'

'Um . . . Vince Eager?'

'*Eager* in every sense. Met him when I was playing the circuit on my own. Next?'

'Cliff Richard?'

'No fear. His Shadows were far more interesting, mind.'

'You're too picky, that's your problem.'

'And you're too pushy nowadays. Honestly, Mattie, you do one little tour and you think you're bleedin' Cameron Mackintosh.'

'So, tell me about Elvis. In Vegas.'

'Can't.'

'Why not?'

'I promised him, didn't I? It would break poor Priscilla's heart if she knew.'

Mattie smiled into her plastic cup of mulled wine. 'Right.'

'But it was special. I'll tell you that much.'

'Okay.'

'Skin so soft it took your breath away.'

Mattie stopped smiling and gawped at her. 'Really?'

'I'm not sayin'.'

'But you just—'

'Pass us those violet crèmes, now. You're hogging them.'

Mattie caught Gil's eye and turned to her friend. She hadn't been sure when to broach the subject they'd come to present to her, but now seemed as good a time as any. 'Reenie?'

'Mm-hmm?'

'How would you feel about another gig?'

'Another one? Does Gaynor know about this?'

'Not yet. It's just an idea.'

Reenie pulled up the cowl neck of her diamante-strewn navy blue knitted shawl. 'Where?'

'Remember the time-lapse video on the Kendrick's website? It was made by Colm's friend, a documentary filmmaker. He filmed the gig and loves your story. He's interested in making a short documentary on the reunion, adding some extra pieces to camera with us all. BBC Films liked his pitch, and they want to launch it with The Silver Five performing . . .'

'A launch, you say? Would there be a press conference, too? I've always fancied doing one of them. In a posh hotel, preferably.'

'I'm not sure. Maybe.'

'Sounds fun. Gaynor will probably have to take up pole-dancing classes for Bill Lancaster to keep him sweet, but I imagine she won't mind. I can persuade the others to come, no problem. Since the Palm Grove gig, Tommy's been insufferable with round-robin emails. So where's the gig? London again?'

Mattie smiled. 'In Cannes. At the film festival. Next May.'

The violet crème stopped midway to Reenie's lips. 'Now you're having me on.'

'What do you think?'

'I think you're bleedin' nuts, Mattie Bell. What do you want to hang around with a bunch of geriatric has-beens for?'

Mattie leaned over and pulled the shawl up closer around Reenie, as if tucking in a small child at bedtime. 'Because they're the most wonderful people I've ever met. And the world needs to remember them.'

'Oh – *love* . . .' Reenie clutched Mattie's hand, pale grey eyes wide as she held her gaze. For a few moments she was silent, as if trying to construct a worthy response. And then the Reenie Silver that Mattie loved made a magnificent, glittering return to Beauvale's wintry garden. 'So, Mattie Bell, what are we waiting for?'

THE END . . . ?

Acknowledgements

♪

When my first book was published, I was stunned that anyone other than my family wanted to read my stories. Eight books later, I'm still amazed.

First – and always first – thank you to *you*, dear Reader, for picking up this book. I wrote it for you xx

Huge thanks to my amazing agent Hannah Ferguson for her unwavering faith in me and her excitement about everything I write. It means more than I can say. Much love to my editor, Caroline Hogg, and the wonderful team at Pan Macmillan, in particular Claire Gatzen, Fraser Crichton, Camilla Rockwood, Amber Burlinson, Alex Saunders, Francesca Pearce, Wayne Brookes and Jeremy Trevathan.

Lots of love to my incredible writer friends, who are my biggest cheerleaders, vital support network and source of incredible inspiration: Julie Cohen, Rowan Coleman, Kate Harrison, Tamsyn Murray, Cally Taylor, A. G. Smith, Kim Curran, Rachael Lucas, Cathy Bramley and Kat Black.

Big love to the Dreamers for your advice and support. Sincere thanks to Lesley Snowdon (www.vivacity-health.co.uk) for wise words and support. Big love to my church family at Springs Church, Gornal.

Once again, I asked the gorgeous lovelies on Twitter, Facebook and via my newsletter to suggest things to include in this story. I even sneaked some of them in! Take a bow, beauties!

Reenie's karaoke songs were chosen by @kezzacahill and @AllyyyVixoxo. Cambridge was suggested by @bookish_yogi. Llangynidr is included for my sister Bev, brother-in-law Ro and nieces Freya and Anya. Aline Sommerville and Clare appear as Reenie Silver's fans. Gemma Harris @gemmiejewel appears as the receptionist at the Alnwick hotel. @MrDerryDude appears as Derry, bar manager at Kendrick's. And Charlene Wedgner @hellosweety26 appears as Charlene, the Beauvale nurse.

This book couldn't have happened without the support of my wonderful families. Being a full-time mum and full-time writer can be tough, but Mum, Dad, Mom and Popsy have helped so very much. Thank you!

Finally, all my love to my amazing husband Bob and stunningly fab Flo. I love you to the moon and back, and twice around the stars xx

This is a book about second chances and the power of forgiveness, for hoping for better and for never being defined by the past. I hope it inspires you to believe for the best.

Miranda xx

♪

*Read on for exclusive material
from Miranda Dickinson . . .*

Reenie's Cocktail - The Blood and Sands

♪

Miguel, the head bartender at The Sands Hotel, Las Vegas, invented this cocktail for Reenie during her five-week residency there in 1971. It's a riff on the classic 1920s cocktail, Blood and Sand, named after the Rudolph Valentino movie. This version blends Reenie's favourite cherry brandy with fresh orange juice and ruby-coloured Italian vermouth. But instead of the classic Scotch, Miguel used smoky, intense mezcal, the agave-based spirit from south of the Mexican border. The red-gold colour matches her jewellery and her lipstick. Like Reenie, the drink is potent stuff: sweet, smoky, fruity and not for the faint of heart!

Ingredients:
1 shot mezcal (or Scotch for traditionalists)
1 shot freshly squeezed orange juice
1 shot sweet (red) vermouth

1 shot cherry brandy (e.g. Cherry Heering)
Garnish: orange wheel, maraschino cherry, sprinkle of edible gold dust

Method:

Chill a martini or wine glass by adding a couple of fresh ice cubes to the empty glass (discard before pouring the drink). Add your ingredients to a cocktail shaker or large lidded jar. Add plenty of ice, close and shake for 10 seconds, then strain into the chilled glass. Garnish with the orange wheel, cherry and a sprinkle of gold dust. Serve with smoked nuts and a huge shot of sassiness . . .

Recipe by **Kate Harrison,**
author and huge cocktail fan
@katewritesbooks
www.kate-harrison.com

Author Q&A

♪

I asked my lovely readers what they wanted to know about this book and my previous novels. Here are the questions they gave me and my answers. Enjoy!

1. Which character is most like you?
(Lara Fletcher @LaraMitch)
That's a tough one to answer because I think most of my characters have aspects of me. I suppose Rosie in *Fairytale of New York* is the most like me because the first character you write tends to be the closest to you. Romily and her band in *It Started With a Kiss* were very much based on me and my musician friends – their wedding gig stories are inspired by actual concerts we played! In *Searching for a Silver Lining* I think Mattie's sense of humour and delight in other people's stories probably come from me. But I also hope to be as ballsy as Reenie when I'm eighty-four!

2. Which character did you have the most fun creating in all your books?

(Sharon @ShazsBookBlog shazsbookblog.blogspot.co.uk)

They are all fun in their own ways, but I have to say I've had an absolute blast creating Reenie Silver. I wasn't expecting her at all but as soon as she arrived on the page she was so much fun to write. I loved creating the relationship between her and Mattie, too, which I think is the central focus of *Searching for a Silver Lining* – how each one needs the other to forgive the past and believe in better for the future.

3. Which of the books you've written is your favourite? And why?

(Vicki Bowles @Vikbat rockchickblog.wordpress.com)

That's like asking a mum to choose between her children! I love them all because they've kind of documented my life for the past eight years. I know exactly where I was and what was happening when I wrote each one. *Fairytale of New York* will always be special because it's my first book. *Welcome to My World* was set in the town I grew up in, so is very close to my heart. *It Started With a Kiss* is special because my best friends (as The Pinstripes) and lovely in-laws (as Uncle Dudley and Auntie Mags) are in it. *When I Fall in Love* was written as I was preparing for my wedding to lovely Bob, so it represents the love and trepidation I felt on the verge of making a commitment for life. *Take a Look at Me Now* was our honeymoon and falling head over heels in love with San Francisco, *I'll Take New York* was going back to my first character crew and imagining new stories, and *A Parcel for Anna Browne* was the first book written with my gorgeous girl Flo. I love *Searching for a Silver Lining* because I've wanted to write a story with a road trip and 1950s storyline for a long time – and because it looks to the future as well as the past!

4. Who influences your writing most? Who are your writing heroes?
(Kate @murronsmama thequietknitter.blogspot.co.uk)
The people I meet and the stories I hear inspire me more than anything else. A lovely part of being a writer is that people want to share their stories with you. I'm a bit of a magpie for shiny bits of information, so when I write it's a little like weaving all of the things I hear and see into a story. My writing heroes are people who refuse to be boxed and who write what they love – Sarah Addison Allen, Sir Terry Pratchett, Neil Gaiman, Cecelia Ahern, Ian Rankin, Ann Cleeves and Simon Toyne are my go-to writers when I want to be inspired.

5. Have you found writing harder since having the distraction of mummyhood and having an adorable little person living with you?
(Natalie @Flutterbybat myflutterbybooks.blogspot.co.uk)
Good question! Yes, I have. Being a full-time writer and a full-time mum is exhausting – not least because my brain never switches off. And time to write has become a luxury rather than the norm. Book deadlines and two-year-olds aren't particularly compatible! What I do like about my

new life, though, is having time to *think*. So I'm learning to make use of any scrap of time I can to immerse my mind in the stories I'm writing. I keep a stack of Post-It notes with me and jot ideas down as they arrive. I'm becoming much more of a plotter, too, which helps me stay on track with my writing. I naturally write better in the evenings and always have, so this has stood me in good stead for writing after Flo has gone to bed! Also I have to say that our families have been incredible in helping look after Flo when I've had a deadline looming. I appreciate their support so much.

6. Are there any of your characters you're desperate to revisit to discover what happened to them since we last saw them?
(Catriona Merryweather @shoefiend1984
fabulousbookfiend.blogspot.co.uk)
I always said I would never go back to any of my characters, feeling very strongly that I'd interfered in their lives enough. But then I wrote *I'll Take New York*, which was a lot of fun, and a Christmas special novella on my blog, which featured characters from all my books, so now I'm not sure . . . I did always wonder what happened to Elsie, Woody and their unorthodox choir The Sundaes from *When I Fall in Love*, but I wouldn't go back to them unless there was a strong enough story to tell. So for now I'll say I won't write another sequel, but in the future, who knows? ☺

7. What three pieces of advice would you give to aspiring writers?
(*@AnnetteHannah sincerelybookangels.blogspot.co.uk*)

1. Write – as much as you can, as often as you can.
2. Cultivate your love of writing – keep reminding yourself *why* you wanted to write in the first place by writing stories you love. That passion will carry you through the hard bits, blocks, setbacks and general slog of writing a novel.
3. Write like you've made it already – believe in yourself, share your writing with others, ignore doomsayers and never give up on your dream.

8. If you could live inside a book for a day, which story would you choose and which character would you be?
(*Amanda Moran @onemorepage www.onemorepage.co.uk*)
Oh wow – so many possibilities! I would probably go for *The Sugar Queen* by Sarah Addison Allen and I would be Chloe Finley, who is followed around by books that magically appear whenever she needs them. I adore Sarah Addison Allen's book worlds – so inventive, adventurous and sparkling – so to spend a day in my favourite one would be heaven!

If you have a question you would like to ask me, email **mirandawurdy@gmail.com**, comment on my Facebook page (**MirandaDickinsonAuthor**) or tweet me **@wurdsmyth**. I'll answer your questions in my regular vlogs – subscribe to my channel at **www.youtube.com/mirandawurdy** to see them all x

Searching For a Silver Lining Playlist

♪

I created two playlists that I listened to while writing this book. The first – of songs released and recorded in the 1950s and early 1960s – can be found in all the chapter headings. The second, of more modern songs, is below. Enjoy!

1. 'Does Not Bear Repeating' – **The Weepies** (*Sirens*)
2. 'Love Life' – **Natalie Taylor** (Single)
3. 'Ordinary World' – **Duran Duran** (*Duran Duran – The Wedding Album*)
4. 'Wild Horses' – **Charlotte Martin** (*On Your Shore*)
5. 'Changes' – **Sarah McLachlan** (*Laws of Illusion*)
6. 'Keep It There' – **The Weepies** (*Happiness*)
7. 'If Wishes Were Horses' – **Kris Drever** (*If Wishes Were Horses*)
8. 'Grace' – **Will Young** (*Let It Go*)

9. 'A Sky Full of Stars' – **Coldplay** (*Ghost Stories*)
10. 'The Star That Guides You Home' – **Emma Stevens** (*Waves* – Deluxe)
11. 'I Was Gone' – **Finnegan Bell** (*I Was Gone*)
12. 'In Love' – **Miranda Dickinson** (*January Nova* – EP)
13. 'Place From Where I Fell' – **Elenowen** (*For the Taking*)
14. 'Together' – **Brandon & Leah** (*Together* – EP)
15. 'Life Keeps Moving On' – **Ben Rector** (*The Walking in Between*)

Bibliography

♪

While researching background for The Silver Five, Reenie Silver and Joe Bell's diary entries, the following books and resources were invaluable:

The History of British Rock 'n' Roll: The Forgotten Years 1956–1962 by Robin Bell (Robin Bell, 2014)

Picture Post on Liverpool by Colin Wilkinson (The Bluecoat Press, 2011)

Ministry of Rock website – www.ministryofrock.co.uk

extracts reading groups
competitions books new
discounts extracts
extracts
competitions discounts
books
new
events extracts events
events books
extracts
books
new titles reading groups
interviews events
extracts extracts
discounts new books
new books events interviews books extracts
events new events new books
discounts extracts discounts
www.panmacmillan.com
extracts events reading groups
competitions books extracts new books